SPIDER-MAN

REVENGE OF THE SINISTER SIX

SPIDER-MAN®

REVENGE OF THE SINISTER SIX

ADAM-TROY CASTRO

INTERIOR ILLUSTRATIONS BY

MIKE ZECK

bp books inc
New York

Special thanks to Mike Thomas and Mike Stewart

SPIDER-MAN: REVENGE OF THE SINISTER SIX

A BP Books, Inc. Book
An ibooks, inc. Book

PRINTING HISTORY
BP Books, Inc. hardcover edition / June 2001

All rights reserved.
Copyright © 2001 Marvel Characters, Inc.
Editor: Dwight Jon Zimmerman.
Cover art by Mike Zeck and Phil Zimmelman
Cover design by Mike Rivilis

The BP Books World Wide Website is
http://www.ibooksinc.com

ISBN 0-7434-3466-8

PRINTED IN THE UNITED STATES OF AMERICA

10 9 8 7 6 5 4 3 2 1

FEB 2 1 2002

To Keith DeCandido, for being the sheet of protective plastic draping the watermelon-spattered front row of the literary Gallagher Concert that the writing of this novel has been; it may have been an awful lot of juice, and it's too bad things got so sticky, but viva la ridiculous metaphors, especially where life's sledgehammers are concerned; if you know what I mean.

Thanks also to Pete Rawlik, George Peterson, Judi Goodman, Meir Pann, Tom Cool, Dave Lowrey, and the other assorted past and present members of the SFSFS writing workshop.

AUTHOR'S NOTE

The lag between the writing of this novel, and its publication, has led to tremendous differences between the status of Peter Parker's life as depicted in this novel, and the current state of affairs as it appears in the regularly-published comic books.

Therefore, those of you who like to keep track of continuity should keep in mind that this book, and its upcoming sequel, both take place in the short period between the death of Peter's clone Ben Reilly, and Norman Osborne's villainous take-over of the *Daily Bugle*. During this point in Marvel history, Peter's Aunt May was still believed dead. Billy Walters and Peter Parker were edging toward friendship. Mary Jane Watson-Parker was an only sporadically-employed model and actress best known for her parts in soap operas and B-Movies. Spider-Man may have been distrusted by the authorities, but he still enjoyed something close to public acceptance on his better days. He was a reserve member of the super hero team known as the Avengers. So was his past (and, alas for those who believe in super-villain rehabilitation, future) enemy, the Sandman. The relations between Dr. Octopus and the rest of the Sinister Six were strained, but not yet the open vendetta they would someday become. Alert readers will no doubt notice other telltales, which may have changed drastically in the issues that followed. Who knows? By the time this advisory is printed, they might even have changed back.

Either way, I hope you enjoy this look into the not-so-distant past.

Adam-Troy Castro

PROLOGUE

In the fires of war-torn Europe, in a world under assault by tyrants, he had emerged from nowhere to symbolize the terror of the times.

Nobody had ever seen his real face. Nobody had ever heard his real name. Nobody knew anything about him except that he advised conquerors, commanded armies, and embodied the chaos a few charismatic madmen had set loose upon the world.

And they knew one other thing: that he could not be killed. In the course of his mad crusade, he was shot, blown up, thrown off bridges, buried beneath cave-ins, trapped in crashing airplanes and in exploding dirigibles . . . and yet he kept coming back, his perversely triumphant laughter a mockery of everything that had ever been noble about the human race. He wore a death's-head, stained scarlet as if it had been drenched in blood . . . and when he finally disappeared, after the Allied victories in Europe and the Pacific, the world finally dared to hope that it would not see his like again.

For years, that hope had seemed justified.

But that hope had been false.

The man who wore the mantle of the Red Skull sat behind a mahogany desk in the back room of a warehouse in Tangiers. The warehouse was a nondescript white building on the outside, a luxuriously appointed office on the inside. The floor was polished marble, the tapestries rich velvet, the framed painting on one wall a Rembrandt missing since the war. The chamber was pleasantly appointed in the manner of the region, its alcoves punctuated with potted palms and doorways curtained off with beads; it seemed more appropriate as the headquarters of a wealthy rug merchant than that of a notorious monster whose name could still inflict nightmares.

It was necessary, though. As the war that had spawned the Red Skull had proven, even the greatest terror requires a certain degree of . . . bureaucracy. Paperwork. Employee relations. That sort of thing. It may not have been as exhilarating as battle, but wars are won by more than battle.

The Skull was deeply involved in a telephone conversation with one of his lieutenants, involving a discipline problem at one of his desert bases, when two of his other associates entered. It was the young American couple. Estranged from their government, and desperate for cash, they had been here several times in the past several weeks, selling assorted classified information at exorbitant prices. They were charming and attractive people, when they wanted to be; but they were also cynical, ruthless, and sociopathic, not to mention downright nasty to each other, which made them the kind of associates the Skull most appreciated. The Skull, who did not feel affection for many people, had come to look forward to their visits; he had always been unfailingly pleasant to them, paying them promptly and in cash, and never failing to compliment the woman on her beauty. The Skull, who was genuinely happy to see them, smiled as they were ushered into his presence. He gestured toward a pair of plush chairs, showed them the phone so they'd know he'd be a few minutes yet, and nodded pleasantly as they sat.

Today, as they awaited his pleasure, shooting daggers at each other with their eyes, the Red Skull regarded the pair as if seeing them for the first time. The man was a blandly handsome, athletic ex-soldier in his early thirties, notable for a certain boyishness that made him look younger—and therefore less formidable—than he really was. He had a strong jawline, and intense brown eyes that precisely matched the color of his close-cropped brown hair: features that made him likeable when he wanted to express warmth but could also be frightening and full of gravity when circumstances required him to be cold. They'd been cold a lot, lately: the look of a man who'd become embittered and disillusioned and interested only in the bottom line. The Red Skull had known him only a short time before judging him the most effective kind of monster: the kind almost impossible to recognize as a monster.

The wife was a soft-faced, black-haired woman whose fresh, country-mouse features should not have been able to convey the cruel, uncaring greed of the person the Red Skull had known these past four weeks. Conventionally pretty, she usually smiled only to express satisfaction in cruelties successfully inflicted—but the Skull had seen her wear warmth and innocence equally well. The rest of the time, she was openly contemptuous of her husband, frankly disinterested in anything but money, and capable of tolerating even the most brutal atrocities as long as they provided her with a momentary advantage. From the nasty looks she gave her husband today, they must have had one of their frequent fights—a common-enough occurrence in marriages that seemed to be cemented more by mutual hatred than mutual affection. The Red Skull felt a certain degree of admiration for such unions; he was himself a man incapable of love, who understood no other kind of alliance.

He kept them waiting ten minutes while he barked Arabic into his desk phone, nodding again as another associate entered the room. This one was a tall, gray-haired figure in his seventies who despite the heat wore both an elegantly tailored black suit and a long white raincoat loosely draped around his shoulders. It was the affectation of a man obsessed with his self-image who thought he looked more fashionable that way. The Red Skull privately considered the look ludicrous, but the old man had his own uses.

The American grew grim, even impatient. His shrew of a wife looked bored. The old man in the raincoat chain-smoked gauloises and stared at them, his expression as blank as that of any corpse. They were clearly taking each other's measures—a more than natural act for people who could be ordered to kill at any time.

The kind of people the Red Skull appreciated.

His previous business concluded, the Red Skull hung up the phone, and allowed the mockery of a warm smile to spread over his ghoulish, rubbery features. "My apologies," he said, as he removed a French cigarette from the dispenser on his desk and fitted it into his obsidian cigarette holder. "The major problem with being the hand's-on leader of an organization as far-reaching as mine. There are always annoying details to iron out for those employees whose work is not quite, shall we say . . . up to expectations."

The American grinned nastily. "You never struck me as an understanding boss."

"Oh, I'm not. Trust me, I'm not. Indeed, this little labor problem will probably result in a number of summary executions." The Red Skull lit his cigarette and blew out a plume of smoke, aware as always that his death's-head features rendered the effect positively demonic. "But it is a pleasure seeing you again, Richard. And you, Mary. You have become almost family to me, these past few weeks."

The Americans nodded, their eyes showing no real warmth.

The Red Skull's gaze flickered toward the man in the raincoat. "I would like you both to meet my oldest and most loyal employee. His name is Karl, but his professional name—one I am pleased to note I personally provided for him—is The Finisher."

The man in the raincoat nodded almost imperceptibly.

"An assassin?" the American said.

"A . . . facilitator, you might say. Assassination has long been within his many duties. Why? Are you surprised?"

The American shrugged. "He seems a bit . . . old and feeble for the work."

The Finisher pursed his lips unpleasantly at that.

The Red Skull chuckled at the blood successfully drawn. "He probably would be, if martial artistry were among his required skills. No, his gifts lie in organization—in planning. In the setting of traps. And he has proven quite useful to me many times in the past."

"I have killed countless men," the Finisher intoned, in what was clearly a challenge to the American. "Can you say the same?"

"Try me," the American said.

Another moment and the Finisher might have taken him up on it.

But the Red Skull waved away the incipient hostilities

with his hand. "Please. We are allies here. Indeed, I called you here today for a specific assignment. Are you interested?"

"As long as the price is right," Mary said.

Her husband flinched unpleasantly at the sound of her voice. We're discussing business, darling. Will you please shut your pretty mouth long enough for the man to tell us what he has in mind?"

"No, I will not," she said stridently. She turned to the Skull, her eyes afire with low mercenary cunning. "I have to take charge of such things, because my husband has never shown a head for it. Don't worry. We can do anything you want us to do—and we'll do it gladly. But it has to pay. We have expenses. We need cash—and lots of it."

"You will have it," the Red Skull said, with a mildness that belied his fearsome reputation. "I promise you, I have every intention of making sure you both get what's coming to you. You need not agree unless you're pleased with the terms. But the nature of your task—"

"Go ahead," the woman said. "As long as you know that I'm the one making the final decision here."

Growling in a manner that perfectly captured his growing disgust with his wife, the American stood up and turned his back on her, facing the Red Skull again. Ignoring his anger, the woman glanced at the Finisher, whose eyes had tracked her husband across the room; her own eyes narrowed suspiciously, and she took on the look of a cat about to hiss.

The Red Skull turned his attention to the husband. "It is a small task. A minor one, for fair recompense. However, it is one that, if performed without flaw, might well lead to more lucrative opportunities for you both. Thanks to my sponsors across the globe, I pay my mercenaries generously."

"If it will establish our credentials," the American said, "my wife and I agree to it."

"Commendable," said the Skull. "So willing to cooperate." The Red Skull drummed his gloved fingertips upon the desk, gathered his thoughts, and said, "It is a courier assignment. I have some very important papers for you to deliver. They must be brought to a certain location in Prague. The delivery will be . . . opposed, but the papers must not fall into American hands. Is that clear?"

"You can count on me, Skull."

"Yes," the Red Skull said, his smile growing, "I am sure I can." He reached into his desk and pulled out a business-sized envelope sealed with wax. "The letter inside is encrypted, of course. You are not to open it for any reason. The Finisher, here, will drive you to the airport and provide you with your destination and your contacts."

"You haven't mentioned payment," the woman said.

"Mary," the American said between clenched teeth, "shut up!"

That actually elicited a chuckle from the butcher behind the desk. "No, no . . . she has a legitimate point. You will find a hundred thousand in laundered American dollars in a secure briefcase in the rear of your plane." He gave the letter to the American, who took it, bowed, slightly, and visibly burning with pretended irritation at his wife, turned away to follow Mary and the Finisher out the door.

They had almost, but not quite, made their getaway before the Red Skull called after them. "Remember! This mission is highly critical!"

"I'll make sure it gets done," the woman said.

"I know my job!" the American muttered, not bothering to look at her.

"Of course!" the Red Skull said, with a gaiety that would have surprised most of his victims. "Of *course* you do!"

It was a small plane: single engine, two-seater, built for utility rather than speed, maneuverability, or comfort. The two people aboard could feel every alteration in the air currents right through the soles of their shoes. That wasn't the problem; they'd both flown this model many times before, sometimes in the line of duty, and sometimes just for fun. If there was any unspoken fear between them, any uncertainty of living to see their next sunset, it had nothing to do with the plane. It had to do with what they'd just left behind on the ground—and what they'd be able to reclaim when they touched ground again.

Even so, the pilot, Richard Parker, sighed with unexpected relief as he banked to head into the desert. "Almost there," he said.

In another context, it might have seemed a silly comment. After all, they'd just taken off, and their rendezvous—(not the one on their official flight plan)—was still two hours away. How could they be almost there when their flight had only started?

But his wife Mary, who occupied the passenger seat, understood his sentiments perfectly. He was not just talking about the flight, but about the longer journey that had consumed their every waking moment for the past four weeks: a journey that had led them across three continents, to the side of a monster. She showed her husband a pale smile. "Almost."

"We'll be home soon."

"I know."

They were two people who could not have been more alive. They were young, and healthy, and desperately in love with each other, and living a life filled with the glory and adventure that most of their contemporaries grasped only in dreams. They were doing something vitally important that they both believed in with all their hearts, and they had something to return home to, when this temporary little nightmare was done.

Richard said: "You have the feeling I do? Of needing a nice long bath?"

Mary shuddered, thinking back to the people they'd both been dealing with for the past four weeks. "They were pretty awful, weren't they?"

"Yeah . . . well . . . so were we, this time."

It was a reference to the personalities they'd adopted, over this past month: personalities that better suited a couple supposedly willing to betray their country for money. They'd both acted pretty contemptible. "Don't remind me," she said. "I'm still counting up all the things you said that made me want to slap you."

"Coming from the conniving dragon lady I've had to live with this past month, that's high praise." He shook his head with genuine admiration. "You have a knack for evil, honey. I was almost afraid of turning my back on you."

"Well," she said, "maybe next time you do, you'll be in for a surprise."

He raised an eyebrow. "I'll take you up on that."

"Mmm-hmmm." But though she wanted to continue flirting, the words died in her throat. She couldn't now. Not while she felt so unclean.

She knew she shouldn't. It had been duty: nothing more. And they'd soon be able to put it behind them. As she glanced out the window, staring not at the ground but at the bright, cloudless sky, she took comfort in the awareness that this same sky also sheltered Cairo, and their next stop London, and their next stop Washington, and their next stop after that—where they planned to stay a while—Forest Hills, Queens.

Her features softened even more when she thought of that last place. She'd left something very precious behind in that place. She knew she wouldn't feel right until she was back there.

Why had this particular assignment taken so much out of her? This wasn't the first time her profession had required her to pretend to be somebody else; more than once she'd had to be people she wouldn't have liked. But this time she had trouble dealing with the person she'd been pretending to be. Maybe because this time, she and her husband had been using their own names. They hadn't altered their looks, or used fake identities, or assumed backgrounds at all different from their own—all elements capable of providing a little emotional distance from the unsavory natures of the characters they were sometimes obliged to play. This time, for reasons that had seemed to make some sense at the time, they'd remained Richard and Mary Parker, albeit a sick, funhouse-mirror version of themselves, not only willing but anxious to sell out to the highest bidder. They'd pretended to be unhappily married, and staying together only out of mutual hunger for the payday that their intelligence connections could buy. Remaining herself, and simultaneously becoming a woman she would have crossed the street to avoid, had bothered her a lot more than she'd expected. Especially since her own transformation had been mirrored by the acts and words and carefully sculpted cruelties of her husband.

Yes. That was part of what was bothering her.

But part of it was also the nature of this particular mission: finding, and gaining the trust of, one of the worst monsters who had ever lived. Sitting in the same room with him. Sharing a drink with him. Even joking with him. Pretending that the very sight of him didn't make her sick to her stomach.

She took comfort in the knowledge that Richard was making an unauthorized course correction that would take them, not on the first leg of a journey to Prague, but toward a pre-arranged offshore rendezvous that would provide them transportation toward their planned debriefing in Cairo. They were still carrying coded information and a hundred thousand in laundered cash. But their true cargo was themselves. Their intelligence would enable Interpol, backed by United Nations peacekeeping forces, to smash the Skull and his organization forever.

Richard said: "You know, I thought he would look silly."

She turned away from the window. "You did?"

"Uh huh. Oh, I know he's a monster and a maniac and a mass-murderer . . . but somehow, without realizing it, I always imagined that my biggest problem when we finally found him would be managing to keep a straight face. I pictured a rubber novelty mask, pulled down over his head, being able to see his real eyes and real lips through the slits. But . . . that's not the way it is when you meet him, is it? That mask of his really works. It really is like being in a room with the face of death." He grimaced. "Maybe the good guys ought to wear masks more often."

"Or maybe not."

Richard didn't immediately get the irony. "It's not a bad idea, if you think about it. An all-concealing mask like that, on somebody who wants to scare the bad guys instead of the good. Maybe—"

She rested her hand on his arm. "Or maybe not. Maybe there have been enough masks. At least for us there have."

He glanced down at her hand, and then at her face. And then this time he got it. He saw where her heart was, and joined her in casting his thoughts to a poor child waiting in that small house in Forest Hills, and he swallowed heavily as all his enthusiasm was suddenly replaced by longing and shame. His expression softened. "I thought you enjoyed the work."

"I did. For a long time. But not any more."

"You want to quit?"

"I think we both should," she said. "And you know why."

It took him a second to understand what she meant.

Then his eyes searched hers. "We'll make it up to him. You know we will."

"Yes. And I also know we've both said that before. It's the kind of promise that keeps getting postponed, for years on end until it's far too late. The kind that robs children of their childhoods and parents of the chance to see their kids grow up. I think we're fooling ourselves. I think that if we're ever going to make it up to him, I think it's high time we both got started."

For almost a full minute, the only sound in the tiny cockpit was engine noise.

And then Richard shook his head ruefully. "You know, every once in a while, you remind me why I love you."

"Is that a yes?"

"It's a 'yes.' You're absolutely right. We owe it to him. And to each other. We can tender our resignations right after debriefing."

Mary could scarcely believe she'd persuaded him without an argument. "And you're sure? Really?"

"Hey. After setting up the Red Skull, where can we possibly go but down?"

Against her will, she felt her vision start to go blurry. It

14

was stupid to cry, of course; tough undercover agents just don't do that sort of thing. Not even with happiness welling up from someplace deep inside, and burdens long shouldered about to be exchanged for a new and idyllic life.

That's when they both found out that the Skull's parting words to them had not been faith in their loyalty, but a deadly, knowing sarcasm.

The engine noise changed character, from a steady, comforting roar, to an angry protesting wail. The cockpit shuddered, the wheel jerked in Richard's hands, and the steady vibration beneath their feet became the insistent jerking of a vehicle abruptly determined to shake itself to pieces. The noise was deafening. Richard had to scream, to make himself heard, "The controls! They've seized up! They're not responding at all!"

"It's the Skull's doing!" she shouted back. "He's learned the truth about us!"

"But the money! The hundred thousand! Why would he—" Realization hit, and his face was stricken. "My God! He's setting us up as real traitors! He wants the home office to think we really sold out to him! He's—"

The aircraft lurched, and the windshield filled with a view of the ground far below. Almost no sky was visible. Mary's body jerked painfully against her seat restraint. Something in the cargo hold smashed against the fuselage, the cabin filled with roaring wind, and the air around them was suddenly alive with fluttering hundred-dollar bills, flying all around them like a perfect visual accompaniment to the hornet noise of the sabotaged engine. She saw her pocketbook sail past, trailing its contents like confetti. She smelled smoke. She knew without looking that if she unbuckled herself and survived the uncontrollable turbulence long enough to get to the parachutes, they would be totally useless:

slashed, or in shreds, or replaced with boobytrapped replicas. She screamed: "Can you regain control? Can you land?"

"It's going to be close! But if I can only level out—"

Richard Parker performed magic with that plummeting airplane. He showed courage and resourcefulness that would have had most professional pilots shaking their heads in admiration. He imposed his will on the locked controls, exerting what influence he could, refusing to go gently into that good night.

He came tragically close to managing it. The plane did start to level off. Had the Parkers been cruising at another five hundred feet, he would have managed a bumpy but passable landing, reducing the incident to just another anecdote about the kind of cliffhanging hair's-breadth escape that came so frequently in the lives of top undercover agents like Richard and Mary Parker.

Alas. They weren't flying at another five hundred feet.

They were both killed on impact.

The crash destroyed so much. Their lives. The future they might have known. And for a time, even their good name. The small fragments of planted evidence that survived the fire was enough to brand them both as traitors to their country, until the day many years later when their grown-up son, Peter, by then the super hero known as Spider-Man, traveled to Tangiers and discovered the evidence that cleared their names.

For many more years, Peter would consider this a happy ending, of sorts.

And then . . .

Peter was having an unusually normal evening, for once—a rarity for him, since the radioactive spider bite that had turned much of his life into a series of battles with megalomaniacal super-villains. It was winter, but the particularly bitter cold of the last few days had lightened a little, just enough to set the stage for storms yet to come; tired from days of chasing a particularly violent perpetrator all over New York City, he had returned to his clapboard house in Forest Hills, eaten dinner with his wife, Mary Jane, and fallen asleep at 8 PM cuddling with her over sitcoms.

A normal, quiet evening.

A little bit after 9, he saw Mary Jane come down the stairs with something under her arm. It took him a second to recognize it as a photo album and several seconds more to connect that with some long-lost photographs of his parents she had found inside an old dresser a week earlier. The album itself was new; Mary Jane must have purchased it just for the shots in question. A sheepish grin spread across his face. "Oh boy. Would you believe I actually forgot all about those?"

Her green eyes twinkled. "I don't blame you, Tiger. The last few days, you had a lot on your mind." She kissed him as she gave him the album. "Go ahead, take a look. I'll put on a coffee for my favorite caffeine fiend."

"Hey, I'm not a caffeine fiend!"

"Are you kidding? You're an absolute addict. It's probably what gives you the ability to climb walls."

"Naah. I got Jonah for that."

The reference to his newspaper-publisher boss, who was not, to put it mildly, the most congenial employer in the world, made her smile again as she toodled off to put on the coffee.

He set the album down on the coffee table and sat down on the couch to examine it. As he turned the pages, appreci-ating once again just how beautiful his mother had been, and how much he looked like his father, he was grateful to see that Mary Jane had even organized the snaps into something approaching chronological order. They were mostly pictures of his mother and father in some vaguely European city, but there were also pictures set in Washington, D.C., and others posing them alongside Peter's also deceased Uncle Ben and Aunt May. His eyes misted as he gazed through these little windows into his lost past. His parents had died so early in his life, and had been gone so frequently before their untimely deaths, that he barely remembered them, but what he did remember he missed. So he lingered especially long on the close-ups, measuring the paradoxically familiar nature of those close-ups against the scanty store of memories they had provided him.

It was sad, but nothing more than that. His Uncle Ben and Aunt May had done a fine job raising him. They had been his real parents, in every important way. He had never had a problem finding enough room in his heart to also love the memory of the biological parents who had been taken from him so soon. He had never been able to find it in himself to resent his Mom and Dad for letting their responsibilities get in the way of their parental duties. As Spider-Man, he had already learned the heavy price paid by those forced to shoulder such greater responsibilities. He knew his parents had loved him; he knew that they had made sure he was loved. And he knew that that was more than what many people had.

Peter Parker, who had not made his peace with many things in his life, had made his peace with that.

But all of a sudden, now, looking at their photographs, he felt that peace shattered. The world turned upside down. He sat bolt upright, his heart pounding like a jackhammer in his chest. After three attempts at speech, he croaked: "M-mary Jane! Mary Jane!"

She poked her head out of the kitchen. "What?"

"These pictures—I can't believe it—!"

She raced over. "What? WHAT?"

He rotated the album and tapped three pictures appearing on opposite pages. One was a picture of his mother pregnant in some rain-clouded European city; one was a picture of both his parents beaming as they posed beside a baby stroller; one was of his radiant mother posing before a picket fence with a round-faced infant in her arms. Peter had seen all of these shots just the other night, when he made his first cursory scan of the collection, but he hadn't looked closely enough to notice what now seemed obvious.

"I don't see anything unusual," Mary Jane said.

"Look at the dates," he said, in a voice that sounded very lost and very far away.

Mary Jane examined the developing dates stamped on the white borders of each photograph. Her puzzlement gave way to a frown, and then to shock. "Peter, the pictures of your Mom pregnant are dated almost two years before you were born. And the one of her holding the baby . . ." She looked at him. "That baby's wearing pink. That's—"

"A girl," Peter said. His voice broke. "My sister. Nobody ever mentioned it, but I have a sister." He looked at Mary Jane; she was easily as stunned as he was. The next obvious questions occurred to both of them, but Peter was the one who asked them out loud: "But where is she? What happened to her? Is she even still alive?"

The questions hung in the air between them.

They both knew that, Peter being the man he was, he would not rest until they were answered.

CHAPTER ONE

Manhattan is a city of secrets. Pick any house and you can find a murder, a theft, a lie, a miracle, an obsession, a love story, a hidden resentment—or a gathering of monsters.

The five men in the townhouse were monsters.

They did not think of themselves as monsters. They were, like many monsters, the stars of their own personal movies; they lived their lives and committed their crimes and fought their wars and experienced absolutely no difficulty justifying everything they chose to do. They had power; they used it; they wanted something, they took it; they hated something, they destroyed it. To their minds, this was as elementary as arithmetic, as basic as the alphabet, and as beyond debate as gravity. But they were monsters all the same. For even one of them to be free was an obscenity. For all five to be at large at the same time—warm, comfortable, and free to come and go as they wished—was a threat to everything that lived.

Because they had this in common, and because they possessed a certain easy familiarity with one another—mostly expressed in shop-talk, wry remarks, and solicitousness of one another's feelings—it would have been easy to mistake them as friends. But they were not friends. They were not the kind of men who made friends. They may have affected an easy cordiality, and they may have been respectful of each other's needs, but that was just one of the prices of partnership—a requirement that made working together not only desirable but possible. Beyond that, they all knew that while circumstances required working together now, a momentary change of fortune could easily place them at each other's throats at any moment. Until then, it was wise to remain separate nations, existing in uneasy truce, shunning open warfare only because of the benefits to be found in mutual association.

It helped, of course, that this was one of the most luxurious headquarters they had ever shared. It was an exceedingly comfortable townhouse: airy, well-lit, with enough bedrooms to accommodate twice as many guests. There was a well-stocked library, with both popular and scholarly reading; a huge kitchen excellently stocked with the basics and with prepared gourmet meals; a collection of fine wines; a huge fireplace with enough chopped wood to keep it burning for a month; a stereo and a projection TV. It was a fine place to wait . . . if only for a little while. But the confinement had begun to pall for all of them.

The one named Quentin Beck sat on the couch, scowling at the TV. He scowled, in part, because it was the expression he wore most of the time—it was the look the muscles of his face assumed at rest, and the look that best summarized his opinion of the world. When he smiled, which wasn't often, nobody considered it an improvement. An athletically-built man in his late forties, Beck had black eyes that constantly burned his resentment over past injustices. He occupied the couch about as comfortably as a jaguar about to pounce.

Even pointing the remote control, he had the look of a swordsman presenting his rapier. When the static overwhelming the TV picture decided to stay right where it was, he openly snarled. "Some safehouse!" he growled, glaring at the others. "They couldn't even get the cable to work!"

The stooped old man by the canary cage grunted. "I had no problem last night." His name was Adrian Toomes, and he bore the various insults of old age like a gnarled old tree far too rigid to fall. He had ragged yellowing teeth, a long pointed nose, and a leathery old scalp flecked with liver spots. Today he was dressed in a ratty green sweater, gray old-man pants, and a tweed jacket, all of which looked like they'd been salvaged from a clothing donation bin. Anybody who saw him for the first time would have thought him feeble, expecting the first strong wind to blow him over. It was an impression Toomes cultivated. A very wrong impression. He said: "Watched *The Birdman of Alcatraz*. Perfect reception. Whatever's wrong now is new."

The TV screen showed only a blizzard of static. Beck grunted again. "Remind me to kill everybody at the cable company." (As always, when he said such things, he was serious. He'd indulged such vendettas before—most recently, against old associates, less than a week ago.) "I ought to go right now, in fact. I can probably be back before our mysterious patron decides to show up."

Max Dillon, who had claimed the easy chair, chuckled grimly. "You want some help, Beck? I'm up for it. I'm more stir-crazy here than I was in prison." He was significantly younger than the other two; a crewcut man of average height and average build whose lean face would have been completely forgettable if not for the chain-lightning that seemed to flash behind his dark, hate-filled eyes. Even that might have been easy to ignore were it not for his unique method of fidgeting: namely, by maintaining an arc of jagged, buzzing electricity from one index finger to the other. The fingers themselves were invisible in the glow. "Maybe we can go down to Times Square. Lots of lights in Times Square. Lots of things to do—"

Toomes cackled. "Things to blow up, you mean."

"Same difference," Dillon said, shooting off an especially strong spark just for emphasis.

At which point the snow on the screen intensified, and Quentin Beck exploded in realization, "For God's sake, Max, do you know why I can't get a TV picture? I'll tell you why! Because you're doing that thing with your hands! You're the one making the static!"

Dillon was abashed. "Sorry, Beck." He made a gesture, and the lightning sucked back into his fingertips. As soon as it did, the picture on the screen cleared up considerably. Snow still polluted the image, but Humphrey Bogart and Ingrid Bergman were discernable, exchanging good-byes as an airplane revved up in the background.

Beck was not at all disturbed to find the movie almost over. Indeed, he was almost gleeful. "See that airplane, Max? The one with all the workmen around it? It's not real! They used a half-size model, and hired midgets as extras! Isn't that brilliant? Isn't that a monument to the power of illusion?"

Dillon grunted. "Fascinatin'. I'd rather blow up Times Square."

At which point the President of the United States came down the stairs in a velvet smoking jacket. The expression on his face was anything but presidential; it was, in fact, more demented, off-balance, and downright cruel than anything even his staunchest opponents in the opposition party would have ever expected of him. He spoke to the other men in the room in the same deep, measured voice he had used during his last State of the Union Address: "I know how you feel, my friends. We all crave some kind of decisive action; we have all had to put aside our own personal ambitions for the sake of meeting our contractual obligations. Believe me when I say that I share your pain."

Toomes had gotten the canary to perch on his finger. "It wasn't funny the first time, Smerdyakov."

The President of the United States shimmered, faded, and was replaced by a form without identity, without personality, and without character. Despite that, the change was noticeable. The new figure was Anatoly Smerdyakov, whose real face was forever hidden behind his featureless white mask; though the mask was flexible enough to allow facial expressions, it was also inherently distancing. Only his blue eyes, shining coldly through the eyeholes, testified to the maliciousness of the soul beneath. He said, "I am sorry, my old friend. In fact, I must apologize to all of you. When I gathered you together here, I did not know how long it would take our patron to finalize his arrangements."

"Yeah, well," Dillon said. "Whoever he is, you oughtta tell him we're big time. We don't sit around cooling our heels for nobody."

"You will be able to tell him yourself," Smerdyakov said. "I just got off the phone with him. He called from his limousine to say he'll be arriving within the next couple of minutes."

"Finally!" Toomes murmured, placing the canary back in its cage.

"Really," Dillon said. "It's gonna be a relief, just seeing what the guy looks like!"

They had all been waiting to meet Smerdyakov's employer for several days. Smerdyakov, the only one who even knew who he was, had gathered them together for just that purpose, a process that in three cases had required him to first liberate them from police or military custody. To make sure they stayed put, he'd even paid them each fifty thousand dollars in cash just to agree to listen to this mystery figure's proposal. They were grateful for that, of course, but they were not men with long memories in terms of debts that needed to be repaid—unless, of course, those debts involved vows of revenge, which they'd all been known to nurse for years at a time. A fifty-thousand dollar retainer did not fall into that category. It was just commerce, and at that rather petty commerce by their standards. Another couple of hours of inactivity, getting on each other's nerves, and they would have considered the retainer a fair fee for having their time wasted like this.

Beck glanced at the stairs. "Have you woken up the Doctor? He's going to want to be here for this."

"I looked in on him before I came down. He—"

A voice like Antarctica in winter finished the sentence for him. "—was not sleeping."

It was Otto Octavius coming down the stairs.

Nobody who looked at Octavius now would have suspected him of being one of the most dangerous men alive. He was a short, softly-rounded man, with a noticeable gut and shoulders that tapered to a head without much of a pause for a neck. He wore his hair in soup bowl-bangs that made it look like an alien presence on his head, and he peered at the world through coke-bottle spectacles that magnified his eyes to almost twice their actual size. His walk was especially odd for a man so physically unimpressive—it gave the impression that he was used to being much larger than he was. He seemed incomplete—and he was, because he was not used to possessing only the normal human allotment of limbs.

Smiling, he might have been a clown. Grimacing the way he was, he exuded hate at the world and everything in it.

All four of the others fell into uneasy silence as he faced them from the base of the stairs. Beck narrowed his eyes; Dillon frankly stared; Toomes grinned with absolutely no sympathy at all; Smerdyakov hid his reaction behind a freshly blanked mask.

Octavius faced them all. "I have been trying to re-establish contact with my arms."

He meant his mechanical arms, which were far more precious to him than the soft, fragile flesh-and-blood things he'd been born with.

Dillon said: "No luck, huh?"

Octavius turned toward him and sneered—a totally off-putting expression, but one which coming from him might have been sincere thanks for the sympathy. "Luck has nothing to do with it. My rapport with those arms is absolute; in the past, I've been able to control them from a hundred miles away. I should be able to reach them, but as hard as I try, I still sense . . . nothing. Either they're locked up behind state-of-the art psionic shielding . . . or they've been . . ."

And for a moment the arrogant mask slipped. Octavius couldn't bring himself to say what he was thinking. He looked down, and descended the rest of the way down the stairs.

"They're made of adamantium," Beck said. "The only truly indestructible metal in the world. Do you really believe they could have been disassembled?"

"It would not be easy. Their individual components are connected so intricately that it would take a scanning electron microscope just to locate the seams. But they are made out of moving parts, and they can be disassembled for serv-

icing, and my enemies in the law-enforcement community—
which is to say, all of them—must be profoundly motivated
to find a way to take them apart. What if the authorities
have managed it? Can you imagine how ruthlessly they'll
destroy the cybernetics inside? How distantly they'll scatter
the pieces? How impossible it would have to be, to track
down those parts and make them what they once were?"

"Maybe you can put together another set," Dillon suggested.

Octavius did not look at him. "I could. But I wouldn't be
psionically linked with them. They would not be part of me.
They would not be mine. They would be dead . . . things."

The general silence that followed this was broken only by
a soft chuckle from Toomes. Everybody looked at him, with
various degrees of disbelief; he just faced them down with a
broad, superior, unrepentant smirk. It should not have been a
surprise; Toomes was a malicious old man at the best of
times, and he'd been nursing a grudge against Octavius for a
couple of years now. Stemming from a certain occasion
where the not-quite-Good Doctor had been less than forthcoming with his partners in crime, it was not quite the murderous vendetta that Toomes had sworn that day . . . but it
was still grim satisfaction at seeing the supremely arrogant
Octavius get taken down a peg.

A complete Octavius would have torn the townhouse
down all around them in his determination to make Toomes
pay for the casual insult.

Toomes might have wreaked as much damage just fighting back.

But this Octavius was not complete.

He just glared.

It was Smerdyakov who attempted to break the tension.
"Come, my friends. We are all professionals here. We know

where we stand with each other . . . and where we don't. We should remain civil, so we can hear our benefactor's proposal. I promise you, it will be worth everybody's time."

Octavius continued glaring at Toomes. "Do you think I am helpless without my arms? I am still the world's leading authority on radiation. You do not know how much I could do if I—"

The doorbell rang.

Smerdyakov said: "Hold that thought." He transformed again, this time into an actor currently in a TV sitcom about a pompous butler, just to go to the door. He did not actually open the door until he peered through the peephole and confirmed that the people outside did not include the NYPD, the FBI, the Avengers, or anybody else in the superheroic or law-enforcement communities. Then he said, "It's them," and let the newcomers in.

There were two of them.

The first was one of those rare old men who retain both impressive height and perfect posture while the rest of their contemporaries seem to shrivel like salted slugs; though he walked with a cane, it was clearly an affectation of his advanced years and not an emblem of physical weakness. He wore a hat and an unbuttoned camelhair coat over an elegant black suit that fit him far too well to be anything but tailor-made. His face, though obviously well-lined—enough to establish him as at least as old as Toomes—had aged in a manner that emphasized his aristocratic nature; between his flaring white eyebrows and his elegantly sculpted cheekbones and his aura of intense self-satisfaction, it was clearly the face of a man who had succeeded in all of his ambitions, and who had every reason to believe that the world would continue to provide. It was even still possible to think of him as handsome, and imagine how very striking he must have been as a younger man. But there was a coldness to him; the chill that followed him as he marched through the door had nothing to do with the January temperatures outside.

Dillon murmured, "My God. It's Boris Karloff."

Beck whispered back, "The actor? He's been dead for years!"

"I know! But this guy looks like Boris Karloff!"

The woman who entered next looked like a teenaged girl; she was thin, and round-faced, and only a hair above five feet tall, with a button nose and big brown war-orphan eyes that seemed like a catalogue of every bad thing that had ever happened to her. As she came further into the room, following the old man like a puppy afraid of being abandoned, the others perceived a face slightly older than they'd originally estimated; she was probably in her mid-to-late twenties, but still hard to consider anything but a frightened child. She wore no hat; her short brown hair, so dark it was practically black, sat slightly wind-tossed above ears and cheeks that had turned pink from the cold. The vertical white scars on both those cheeks stood out in sharp relief. She wore a plain black muffler, a zipped white jacket, and tight black pants with legwarmers and boots. Unlike the old man, she did not make eye contact with the others. She just averted her eyes and stood behind him, as if waiting for a cue.

The air surrounding Max Dillon glowed impressively before resuming its normal level of contrast as he muttered, "Uh."

The old man's eyes flickered in his direction, before looking away. "Good evening, my friends. I apologize for the long wait. As with any worthwhile venture, the details proliferated in the planning." He removed his hat—revealing a thinned but still impressive head of white hair—then took off his coat and handed both to the woman, who took them without hesitation. "Introduce us, Anatoly."

It was not spoken as a request, or even as an order, but as a command. Everybody in the room heard the subtle difference.

"With pleasure," Smerdyakov said. "The man on the couch is Quentin Beck, aka Mysterio, the master of special effects and illusion. If you recall, you personally observed his handiwork, destroying that Broadway theatre, just a few days ago."

As the old man crossed the room, stabbing the floor with his cane, he walked right past the others without acknowledging the introductions. He grunted: "I am not yet senile, my friend. I am capable of remembering recent events without your aid."

"Yes, well." Smerdyakov continued his recitation even as the old man went to the bar for a cognac. "The one in the easy chair is Max Dillon, better known as Electro, the Living Dynamo. His body can generate enough electricity to run this city—or blow it up, depending on his mood. That elderly gentleman by the birdcage is Adrian Toomes, the high-flying Vulture; with his flying suit, he's nearly a hundred times stronger than he looks. And that scowling man by the stairs is Dr. Otto Octavius, better known as the international terrorist Dr. Octopus. He's not wearing his adamantium arms right now, because he doesn't have them—a point I make only because they're very much the least dangerous thing about him. As for you, my old colleagues, I would like you to meet our patron and benefactor. He calls himself the Gentleman. And he has some things he wishes to discuss with us."

Dillon indicated the sad-faced young woman, who had just returned from hanging up the Gentleman's coat. "What about you, miss? Don't you have a name?"

Her eyes were wide and moist. She looked away hurriedly.

The Gentleman smacked his lips. "Her name is Pity. P-I-T-Y, like the emotion. She does not speak."

Dillon's expression softened as Pity, refusing to look at him, moved quickly to the canary cage. "What's her problem? Is she mute or something?"

"No. She just doesn't speak. A disciplinary measure I enacted several years ago. I assure you, any questions regarding her are best directed toward me." He rolled his cognac in his hands. "I must say, it is . . . interesting . . . to be in America, under the same roof as all of you. I have long been a sponsor of unusual talents, but over in Europe, where I now conduct the majority of my business, the costumed element has not enjoyed quite the same degree of ubiquity it has over here . . . Von Doom and assorted other anomalies excepted. I am looking forward to . . . what is that childish phrase your newspapers like to use so much?"

"When Titans Clash," Beck provided.

"Ah, yes. That. I am very much looking forward to that. Indeed, that and the profit I hope to realize will almost be worth enduring this country's graceless architecture, bankrupt culture, tasteless food, and brainless citizenry."

With the possible exception of Anatoly Smerdyakov, an expatriate Russian, the others in the room did not take this remark well. They were not patriots, of course; they did not hold their country sacred. At least one of them, Octavius, had tried on more than one occasion to overthrow it. But there was something about the Gentleman's taunting manner, that invited them to take it personally—something that enflamed their own considerable reserves of arrogance. Several of them made eye contact with one another, sharing their distaste for this strangely unpleasant man.

It was Octavius, the most arrogant of them all, who reacted first, marching to the bar and staring the Gentleman down from across a gulf of inches. "What. Do. You. Want?"

The Gentleman, uncowed, merely raised a mocking eyebrow as he swirled the cognac in his glass. "Impatience, Doctor? For the cash advances I have already paid—not to mention, for three of your number, my assistance in escaping police custody—I would have expected a trifle more humility."

Octavius drew himself to his full height, such as it was, and cried: "You won't get humility from me, old man! It's a weakness of those shackled by their limitations!"

Across the room, the canary chirped. Pity had taken it from the cage, and begun stroking it across the back. The hint of a smile tugged at the corners of her lips.

An identical infatuated smile tugged at the corner of Max Dillon's. Even Toomes, the biggest misanthrope of them all, who could see the simple joy she took in handling the bird, allowed himself a snaggle-toothed grin. Her smile was that pure, that unconscious, that completely without artifice.

The smile that spread across the Gentleman's face was a cold and loathsome thing by comparison. He raised his glass to Octavius, in a mock toast: "And if you are truly a man without limitations, then why aren't you wearing your wondrous mechanical arms? Isn't it true that the authorities confiscated them the last time one of your schemes failed? And that you remain at a loss as to how to retrieve them?"

Octavius said: "I have defeated many even greater challenges."

"And you have also been defeated by many others—chief among them the crime fighter known as Spider-Man." The

Gentleman sipped his cognac, took his time savoring the taste, and said: "Please don't misunderstand, Doctor. I do not mean any disrespect. You are, as you are no doubt about to remind me, one of the world's leading scientific minds. But all men have their limitations. And as the authorities have done an excellent job seizing and confiscating your resources, both financial and, dare I say, mechanical, your limitation right now, is poverty. You cannot afford to sneer at gainful employment—let alone the unique proposal I have called you together to hear."

Toomes rolled his eyes. "Then get on with it, already! We're listening!"

For several seconds the only sound in the room was the chirping of the canary, as Pity lovingly stroked its wings.

The Gentleman smiled to himself, then shouldered aside the fuming Octavius, and walked to the center of the room, so he could face the others more directly. Commanding their attention by sheer presence alone, he spoke so softly that they almost had to strain to hear him: "Very well. Let us put it this way. Consider what course of action you five would take without my sponsorship. Forget the details and look at the larger picture. If your past habits are any indication, you would essentially wreak havoc, and seek revenge against Spider-Man."

Beck and Toomes spoke almost simultaneously. "So?"

"So I am willing to pay you each ten million dollars in cash—half now, half on completion of our partnership—just to wreak havoc, and seek revenge against Spider-Man."

That got their attention. Beck sat up so straight he seemed about to jump off the couch. Toomes stepped closer to the Gentleman, his beady eyes narrowing in calculation. Dillon looked away from Pity for the first time since her entrance, and regarded the Gentleman with something that might have been respect. Octavius scowled with displeasure. They all glanced at Smerdyakov, who had been the Gentleman's liaison since the beginning; he was as impossible to read as always, but he nodded confirmation anyway.

Toomes regarded the Gentleman with one cocked eye. "It can't be that simple."

The Gentleman acknowledged that with a bow. "I confess it isn't. There will be a number of specific tasks I must ask you to perform along the way—but nothing beyond your shared capabilities. Beyond that, I ask only that you act according to your natures . . . to do what precisely what you would do otherwise . . . except as my subcontractors."

"And what do you get out of it?" Beck demanded.

"In part: revenge. I have my own grudge against Spider-Man, which is at least as near and dear to my heart as any of yours."

Beck asked, "Then how come we've never heard of you?"

The Gentleman raised an amused eyebrow. "Spider-Man himself hasn't heard of me. I'm not an actor. Though he doesn't know it, we have been bitter enemies for a long time. Indeed, though it is far too long a story to go into now, I daresay I have already taken more from him than the rest of you put together."

Beck glanced at Toomes, who shrugged expressively. Every answer they got from this man succeeded only in raising more questions—and they both felt the frustration of not knowing precisely which question to ask next.

It was Octavius who made that decision: "And if you're such an effective enemy of his, why do you need us?"

"Because I want to face him directly. But I do not have electrical powers," he indicated Dillon, "or skill at illusion," he indicated Beck, "or the power of flight," he indicated Toomes, "or a great scientific mind," he indicated Octavius, "or even the mastery of disguise," he indicated Smerdyakov. "The years may have been exceptionally kind to me, but I am still an old man. My only super powers, so to speak, are my wealth and my imagination. Underwriting your activities, and providing you with some badly needed sense of direction, is my way of buying a direct confrontation." The Gentleman removed a cigar from his vest pocket, and placed it unlit in his mouth. "But even that is not all of it."

"Yeah?" Dillon asked. "What else is there?"

"This: if you do agree to follow my instructions, our little enterprise will turn a profit beyond even your wildest dreams. The ten million apiece is merely payment for your labor; the actual dividends, I assure you, will be on an entirely different order of magnitude. They will be as great as anything you've ever known—literally, enough to start empires."

If nothing else the Gentleman said possessed the ring of truth, that did. Beck and Toomes glanced at each other; Dillon showed the first signs of genuine enthusiasm. But Octavius was not yet ready to give in, "If you want our cooperation, you'll have to tell us your full plan now!"

"Alas," the Gentleman said, lighting his cigar, "that is impossible."

"We're not your lackeys! We don't appreciate being kept in the dark!"

"Understood," the Gentleman puffed. "However, the plan is what I bring to this partnership. If I tell you everything now, you will doubtless kill me and proceed on your own. I promise you, further details will be forthcoming on a need-to-know basis. If you cannot abide that condition, then you may keep this townhouse and the retainers I've already paid you and go ahead with your own endeavors. As for me, I shall seek partners elsewhere. As Smerdyakov can no doubt confirm, I've already sent queries to the Zodiac and the U-

Foes. They will do, but I don't believe they've ever fought Spider-Man, so they won't bring that all-important sense of personal involvement which will make this endeavor such a pleasure for all of us."

Toomes said: "And what if your plan isn't as good as you say?"

"It is," Smerdyakov said. "At least, what I know of it. Trust me, if you don't trust him."

Dillon let loose a laugh at those words, rolling his eyes as he did.

The Gentleman's eyes flickered in his direction, showing more annoyance than gratification. Then he focused on Toomes: "I shall brief you fully at each stage of the operation. If there's any point where you don't like what you hear, or believe you have been asked to take unnecessary risks for insufficient reward, you are free to resign, keeping both the retainer and the initial five million payment. You sacrifice only the payment due on completion."

Beck said: "You sell yourself really well, mister."

The Gentleman waved away a cloud of smoke. "I have a product worth selling. I take it this means you're in?"

"I am."

"Me too," Toomes said. "Conditionally."

Dillon stole another glance at Pity. "And me."

The Gentleman nodded in approval, then turned to face Octavius. "And you, sir?"

The man known as Doctor Octopus was seething. His fists trembled at his sides like a pair of boilers ready to explode; he spoke through gritted teeth in a voice that managed to betray both defeat and arrogance at the same time. "I am not for sale! I am a leader of men!"

"I anticipated your reaction, sir, which is why I have arranged a bonus you'll value infinitely more than the cash."

The Gentleman nodded at Smerdyakov. "Anatoly, will you please retrieve the rest of the good Doctor's retainer from the trunk?"

Smerdyakov smiled. "With pleasure, sir." He winked at Octavius, twirled a set of car keys around his index finger, and disappeared out the door.

There was a moment of silence.

Followed by a communal intake of breath, as the implication hit everybody at once.

Beck stared. "You've got to be kidding me."

The Gentleman shook his head. "I do not kid."

"But his—how did you get your hands on . . ."

"My organizational skills," the Gentleman said, "are second to none. I would not gather you all together and omit such a necessary detail."

After a moment, the front door opened again. Smerdyakov entered, wheeling an oblong case on a handtruck. The case was metallic silver and embossed with a series of red serial numbers above the seal of the United States National Security Agency. Near the lock were two small lights, one red the other green. The red light glowed with a steady light. Smerdyakov rolled it into the living room, then let go of the handtruck and took a single step back.

Octavius took a single hesitant step forward. He trembled, though whether with anticipation, joy, or perverse anger, was a judgement even his long-time colleagues remained hesitant to make. He whispered: "You brought them here. My associates can force you to give them up."

"I have no intention of holding them hostage, my good Doctor. Consider them a token of my eagerness to come to terms. All I have to do is deactivate the psionic shields, and they will be yours to command again."

The Gentleman reached into his coat pocket, took out a tiny electronic remote about the size of a garage door opener, and pressed a button. The red light began to flash, then went off. The green light went on.

Almost immediately, the lid of the crate burst open. A gleaming metallic tentacle, tipped with a snapping pincer, shot out, extended to ten feet, then curled downward and braced itself against the living room floor. Three other tentacles followed, wavered like snakes tasting the air in search of prey. They each snapped their pincers several times, as if testing their reflexes. Then they, too, braced themselves against the floor, lifting up the structure that linked them together: an O-shaped metal harness, just large enough to fit around the waist of the pudgy Otto Octavius. Intricate dials on the side of the mechanism spun and whirled endlessly, testifying to the days before the laboratory explosion that had granted Octavius his uncanny psionic control of the tentacles, when he had still needed those controls to direct their movements by hand; now, summoned by thought alone, the tentacles danced gracefully across the room, positioned the central harness over the Doctor's head, then gently lowered it onto his body. There was an audible hydraulic hiss as the cushioned interior inflated to form a seal against his abdomen.

Octavius smiled.

The Gentleman puffed out another cloud of smoke. "You are quite welcome."

Hatred gleamed in the doctor's eyes. He lifted himself off the floor with his tentacles, bade them to carry him across the room, and stared down the Gentleman from across a gulf of inches. "I have no intention of thanking you, old man. You have merely returned to me something that was already mine—something you had no right to possess. You will remain alive only long enough to tell me how you managed it."

The Gentleman seemed totally unconcerned about the threat. "I think it's clear that your arms were not encased in cement and dumped in the ocean, as your friend Colonel Morgan proposed. He was, in fact, overruled by the NSA, which ordered them encased in cement and kept in a stasis vault at the bottom level of a certain underground facility the United States reserves for the relocation of its military leaders in the event of extraterrestrial invasion. Since you had no clue where they were, these measures would have been more than sufficient to keep them out of your possession indefinitely."

"Again: how did you get them?"

"Easily. I blackmailed a certain official, who has since helpfully committed suicide, into replacing them with nonfunctional duplicates before delivery to the NSA. The arms actually delivered to that facility aren't even made out of adamantium. I took the . . . liberty of keeping these in their shielded container until I could deliver them to you personally."

Two of the doctor's tentacles, hovering menacingly near the Gentleman's head, suddenly darted downward to grab the old man by the lapels of his jacket. "'Liberty' is right. I ought to kill you a thousand times for every minute you kept them locked up out of my control."

"Easy, Doctor!" This from Beck. "Can't you even loosen up long enough to be grateful to the man for rescuing them in the first place?"

Octavius practically spat the word: "No."

The Gentleman acknowledged that with a nod. "I did not think so, either. Even if your obstinance is beginning to frustrate your allies. But, Doctor, may I at least make one final point before you task those limbs to rend mine?"

42

"Choose it wisely."

"Consider: if I can orchestrate the prison breakouts that brought you all together, and the liberation of your mechanical arms, and a commitment to ten million dollars apiece, just on the chance you'll agree to my terms, don't you think I can also deliver everything else I've promised? A plan that will bring this city—and through it, the world—to its knees? Wealth beyond your wildest imaginations? The humiliation and defeat of Spider-Man? Even if you reject the idea of any moral obligation to me, don't you at least owe it to yourself to see what I have in mind?"

The next ten seconds seemed to last forever.

Then the two tentacles holding the Gentleman withdrew, and the two tentacles holding Octavius aloft gently lowered him to the ground. Octavius took a step back, glowered, grimaced from the massive effort involved in acknowledging that another human being had just made a legitimate point, and managed, "This is not finished, old man. I don't trust you."

"And I don't trust you. But mutual suspicion is conducive to mutual profit, yes?" The Gentleman chuckled. "And there will be a substantial profit, here. I promise you."

Octavius merely muttered to himself.

The other men in the room glanced at each other meaningfully. They didn't have to speak out loud for everybody to know what all the others were thinking. Octavius had always been the most volatile of their number; he was not known for backing down from anybody. But the Gentleman had just faced Octavius down, without showing a single iota of fear . . .

The man placed his cigar on the edge of the mantelpiece, straightened his collar and tie, ran a hand over his crown of thinning white hair, and said, "So. Very well. I believe that's everybody . . ."

"Not quite," Beck said.

"Oh?"

"If this *is* supposed to be the return of the Sinister Six . . . I still count only five of us. Who's the sixth member? You?"

The Gentleman wrinkled his nose with genuine distaste, as if he'd just been offered a plate of food too rancid to stomach. "Heaven forbid. No." His arm swung in a violent arc that stopped only when arm and hand and index finger were all aimed at the wan young woman still silently petting the canary on the other side of the room. "Her."

With the exception of Dillon, who had been sneaking glances at her all through the conversation, they had almost forgotten her existence. From the looks of her, the amnesia was mutual: utterly lost in her communion with the canary, she'd almost completely shut off the rest of the world. Even so, at the bark of her master's voice, she stood at attention at once, her eyes very wide, very round, and very lost.

The canary hopped about on the palm of her hand, cocking its head quizzically. In another context, the gesture might have been cute.

Beck said: "You've got to be kidding me."

"She doesn't look like much," Toomes said. He glanced at the Gentleman. "What can she do?"

"Much more than you'd expect. I will happily have her give you all a demonstration, in a minute. But even before that, a testament to her sense of dedication—"

Pity's eyes went eloquently moist with pleading.

Dillon, the first to realize what was happening, rose halfway out of his chair. "Oh, man, don't make her—"

And the Gentleman's voice turned to blood. "Do it."

She closed her hand into a fist and squeezed. The canary had just enough time to emit a single squeal of terror and pain—so eloquent that every man in the room, even the notoriously insensitive Octavius, perceived that it knew how brutally it had been betrayed. They all saw the look in Pity's eyes as its back broke. They saw how she shuddered when she felt it die—the heartbreak, the self-loathing, the awareness that moments like this were all she had to expect out of life.

Beck seemed to enjoy the spectacle. Smerdyakov remained as unreadable as ever. Octavius no doubt admired the Gentleman's hold over this mysterious young woman. Toomes, on the other hand, clearly burned with fury—though whether his sympathies lay with Pity or the bird, was a subject open for interpretation. And Dillon was devastated. The man who'd repeatedly terrorized the city under the code-name Electro was in fact so outraged by this one moment of simple psychological cruelty that he actually flashed lightning from his eyes and cried out: "Why, you miserable, sadistic—"

The Gentleman's chuckle, which remained totally devoid of fear, stopped him in mid-step. "Forgive an old man's sense of theatre. I just wanted to establish that it would be a serious mistake to underestimate her. She is not a cute young thing. She is a ruthless killer. And she is mine..."

CHAPTER TWO

Aerodynamically speaking, there's no reason the common bumblebee should be able to fly. Its wings are not large enough to carry it.

It flies anyway.

Why? Well, there's a long and involved explanation involving patterns of vibration, but it all boils down to: because its designer wants it to.

Similarly, there's no reason an aircraft carrier should be able to fly. It weighs thousands of tons, it's as streamlined as a huge metallic brick, and it contains so many moving parts that even the slightest breakdown brings it closer to a smashing cataclysmic reintroduction to the ground.

The SAFE Helicarrier, which at five stories high and four city blocks long is a lot like a tremendous anvil hovering about New York twenty-four hours a day, is supported only by a combination of hovercraft, jet, and helicopter technology, dominated by the huge spinning rotor that juts out from one side like a gigantic pizza cutter.

It flies anyway.

Why?

Again, there's a long and involved explanation involving lightweight metals, the precise manipulation of air currents, the big rotor itself, the smaller rotors deployed around the sides, and certain highly classified techniques that might as well be written off as magic—but again, it all boils down to, because its designer wanted it to.

The first Helicarrier, designed by billionaire industrialist Tony Stark, had been built years earlier, for the international law-enforcement agency known as S.H.I.E.L.D. They'd been through several. This particular Helicarrier had in fact belonged to S.H.I.E.L.D. once upon a time, before they came into a little budgetary surplus and upgraded to an even more elaborate species of huge floating bathtub. Now, only slightly the worse for wear, it belonged to the little-known domestic anti-terrorism agency known as SAFE, an acronym for Strategic Action for Emergencies.

In a world where major population centers are subject to almost weekly assault by terrorists, extraterrestrials, demons, sorcerers, Atlantean hordes, and giant robots—not to mention the odd costumed super-villain, who are so common by now that they're practically not worth mentioning—it makes perfect military sense to maintain a paramilitary strike force within reach at all times. It also makes sense to equip them with a base that can itself be moved, on a moment's notice, to any location where rapid deployment can save lives.

The downside is that Helicarriers do, sometimes, crash.

This is unfortunate.

One Helicarrier crashed in San Francisco, under the assault of a giant radioactively-mutated tyrannosaur. Another crashed in the desert, thanks to sabotage by a swarm of super-intelligent cockroaches. This very Helicarrier currently being used by SAFE, reeling from damage wrought by a gamma-radiated man-monster known as the Abomination, came within minutes of crashing into the Russian Embassy not too long ago. It says a lot about the facts of life in Manhattan that the incident went almost unnoticed, without a public outcry about the dangerously unstable object the authorities allow to hover above the city twenty-four hours a day; it says a lot about SAFE that when they weren't specifically needed elsewhere, they kept the Helicarrier positioned above the East River and not the teeming streets of the city.

Despite that, the Helicarrier does possess one major advantage that deserved to be mentioned: discounting the occasional super-villain or cabal of Hydra assassins, who just had to be dealt with, it was a pretty safe bet that anybody actually capable of getting aboard was authorized to be there.

The Amazing Spider-Man was not accustomed to receiving respect.

Yes, he saved lives every day; yes, he saved the whole city on an almost monthly basis; yes, he'd even been known to save the world and had, on a smaller number of occasions, even saved the universe. But New York's biggest tabloid still called him a menace, New York's constabulary still couldn't make up its collective mind which side he was supposed to be on, and New York's citizens still weren't sure whether to cheer or hurl epithets as he swung across the sky high over their heads. He couldn't even trust most of his fellow super heroes to remember all the battles he'd fought at their sides, since, with a few notable exceptions, the rest were all too willing to join the collective lynch mob every time somebody like Norman Osborn or the Kingpin tried the old but always reliable "Let's frame Spider-Man for Murder!" trick.

Spider-Man was, in fact, so very accustomed to being denied his due that genuine gestures of good will, like the salute he received from a SAFE technician upon disembarking the noontime transport, tended to floor him.

Temporarily at a loss over what to do, he snapped a salute back.

His escort, Special Agent Doug Deeley, a tall black man whose perpetually bemused expression testified to the various unlikelihoods he encountered in the course of a typical working day, said: "Nice going, webhead. But I'm afraid it doesn't really work, coming from you. Not in that outfit."

He referred to Spider-Man's costume, an all-concealing bodysuit dominated by dark blue tights, a spider-shaped chest emblem, a red stocking mask, and red shoulders and sleeves patterned with a lattice designed to mimic the webbing of the common spider. Though Spider-Man had worn other costumes, and even resorted to other aliases, from time to time, it was so much a part of him that he was occasionally surprised to hear that even people like Deeley, who wear skintight blue battle suits to work, were capable of thinking it looked funny. Embarrassed, Spider-Man said: "Sorry. I guess I'm just not used to gestures like that."

"Officially?" Deeley said, as he led Spider-Man from the shuttle hangar into the narrower corridors of the Helicarrier's administration offices. "You're not supposed to get any. On the record, the government stills regards you as an unknown quantity, not to be trusted."

Spider-Man immediately thought of the last ten times he'd saved the world. *No, forget the world: how about just the city?* "Oh, good. I was starting to think that someone up there likes me," he said with practiced sarcasm.

"Keep in mind that this is the same government that always worries about what the newspapers are going to say in the morning. And you're not exactly beloved by the press." This being a reference to the *Daily Bugle*, which under the guidance of its crusading publisher J. Jonah Jameson had spent years blaming Spider-Man for everything from street crime to global warming. "However," Deeley continued, "off the record, there are any number of people here who remember how many times you've put yourselves on the line for us. Here, at least, you're considered one of the good guys. Hence the salute."

"I'm touched," Spider-Man said. Meaning it, because he still wasn't used to being appreciated.

"Of course," Deeley said, the amusement creeping back into his voice, "it's also possible that it was just a sneaky way of getting you to raise your hand, so he could see whether you still wore that flexible webbing under your arms. The techies here have been arguing about it for weeks."

Spider-Man grinned wryly beneath his mask. Even distracted by a personal errand so important to him that it reduced most other considerations to background details, he appreciated being nailed by a good zinger. It reminded him that all glory was fleeting, all respect was illusory, and all inflated egos subject to immediate puncturing. If any of that ever changed, he'd probably be too stunned to function.

As Deeley led him from the Helicarrier's internal landing pad into a narrower corridor leading to the Administration offices of SAFE, high-tech gave way to rubber ferns and faux-paneling designed to make the interior resemble a mid-range law firm. There were plenty of agents strolling the hallway in SAFE battle armor, but just as many dressed in conservative suits and ties. Some of those nodded at Deeley and Spider-Man as they passed by, so casual in their reaction to their super-powered visitor that Spider-Man wondered if SAFE had organizational directives against double-takes. He came up with another theory entirely at the intersection where a squad of six agents in green Guardsman exoskeletons marched by, escorting a chained six-foot...something...that seemed to be all matted fur and gaping fanged mouth. Its eyes narrowed as it saw Spider-Man, evidently wondering how he'd taste. Watching it recede down the corridor, knowing that Deeley wasn't about to volunteer any explanations, and perversely denying himself the temptation to ask, Spider-Man knew the story behind that one would be long, involved, and filled with triumph and tragedy; he also knew that any organization dealing with such things with any degree of regularity was also capable of dealing with the occasional friendly neighborhood super hero in its stride.

Still, the sight gave him one of the occasional moments of total temporal dislocation that sometimes ambushed him with the realization of just how much his life had changed over the years.

Once upon a time, before the lab accident that had made him what he was, even gym class was a challenge. Once upon a time, as the lonely teenage boy named Peter Parker, he'd been just another adolescent bookworm, living a quiet life in Forest Hills, Queens, his only family the elderly aunt and uncle who'd raised him since the plane crash that had claimed his parents. Once upon a time he'd been so overprotected that he'd needed to carry a sweater every time the temperature outside dipped below seventy. Had he been told back then that in just a few short years he'd look back on those days from the perspective of a veteran masked super hero with the proportionate strength and agility of a spider—a man who had been to other planets and other eras and all over the world fighting for stakes that were sometimes beyond even his own capacity to imagine—he would have wondered just what the storyteller had been drinking.

Of course, if he could have been persuaded that this glimpse into his future was true, the young Peter Parker would have considered it extremely cool. And it was, most of the time. But the young Peter would not have known about the price. He would not have understood the painful lesson that had driven every moment of his life since his failure to use his powers to stop a petty thief left that very same thug free to later put a bullet in the heart of Peter's beloved Uncle Ben. He would not have known the epiphany that ever since echoed through his days and nights like a refrain: With Great Power, Comes Great Responsibility.

And had he somehow been able to understand that, without living it, would the young Peter also have understood the terrible truths that came with it? Would he have understood that just as the responsibility never went away, neither did the dying? After all, even a man with the ability to climb walls, jump four stories straight up, and take punishment that would flatten almost anybody else—a man who had done more good for more people than he would ever be able to count—cannot protect everybody all the time; he just feels every death as if he caused it himself. Whether it was friends like George Stacy, who had been crushed by fallen rubble . . . or Gwen Stacy, whose neck had snapped . . . or Harry Osborne, who had been consumed by the legacy of his insane father . . . or Ned Leeds, who had been killed by assassins . . . or Ben Reilly, who had perished from a bomb blast . . . or for that matter any of the strangers who Spider-Man had not been fast enough or smart enough or strong enough or good enough to save . . . they were all hash marks on his conscience, whose faces tended to loom before him with no prior warning. He was able to deal with them only because he was also aware of all the good he had done. But sometimes, it was a very, very close call.

"Spider-Man?" It was Doug Deeley again. He'd apparently had to repeat himself more than once. The web-slinger jolted out of his reverie.

They'd reached a bullpen of sorts, where half a dozen clerk-typists determined to treat their famous visitor with equanimity typed away at monochrome word processors. The man he'd come to see, Colonel Sean Morgan, sat behind at a cluttered desk behind an open door at the far end of the chamber. Even as Spider-Man met his eyes, Morgan grimaced. It could have been impatience, annoyance, or a welcoming smile; they were all the same thing, where Morgan was concerned.

Colonel Sean Morgan was not colorful, not flamboyant, and not perversely likeable, like some of the other paramilitary super-spy types the wall-crawler knew. Giving him credit, he did not try to be any of the three. He was just a consummate professional, who refused to allow anything—even a discernable sense of humor—to come between himself and his duty. He operated with machinelike precision, his slate-gray eyes constantly measuring everything around him as if it were a potential battle situation. He sat on an institutional metal desk, in no way fancier than the government-issue desks used by his subordinates—in part because he wasn't the type to see the point in frivolous luxuries like fancy office furniture, in part because his desk was so completely covered with paper that he probably never got to see it anyway. No doubt, Spider-Man supposed, some of the documents there had to do with payroll, health benefits, externally mandated regulations and intelligence requests from other agencies; many had to be reports on potential crises currently being monitored or infiltrated by SAFE personnel. It was not the kind of job suitable for folks who had problems dealing with stress.

Even though Morgan watched them approach all the way across the bullpen, Deeley still knocked on the open office door. "Colonel? I just brought your two o'clock on the last shuttle from midtown. You ready for him yet?"

"I can give him twenty minutes," Morgan said briefly. "Hello, Spider-Man."

"Colonel," Spider-Man nodded.

"Want me to stick around?" Deeley asked.

"No, thanks," Morgan said. "Just finish up the report on the Arnim Zola operation. I needed that three days ago."

"Sorry, chief. Had to wait for Nefertiti to come in from the field."

Morgan acknowledged that with a nod. "Fair enough. Just close the door when you leave. The hero and I have things to discuss."

Deeley nodded and left them alone. Spider-Man hopped in, scrambled onto a spot midway up the one blank wall in Morgan's office, and crouched there. Trying his best to be ingratiating, which was relatively unusual with him and authority types, Spider-Man said: "Well. Good to see you, Colonel. See they're keeping you busy."

"No more than usual," Morgan said briefly. He gestured at one of the chairs opposite his desk. "Sit there, please."

Spider-Man was perfectly comfortable crouching on the wall. "That's okay."

Morgan sighed heavily. "No, it's not. Use the chair."

Spider-Man almost obeyed, just to be polite, but some perverse part of him insisted on pressing the point. "Does this really bother you, Colonel?"

"Not at all. If I actually needed the chair for somebody

else, I'd appreciate the effort. But since it's just you and me, and I have a perfectly good chair right in front of me, clinging to the wall is just showing off for no good reason."

"It's not showing off, Colonel. Honest. I'm just more comfortable this way."

Morgan's jaw worked. "All right. If you insist. At least you're not making any damned jokes this time."

Spider-Man cocked his head. "After the way you've reacted in the past, I wouldn't dare."

Morgan seemed to appreciate that; his congenitally straight line of a mouth seemed to come within a couple of millimeters of smiling. After a moment, he nodded. "Actually, I ought to give you credit for impressive response time. I didn't expect even you to hear the news until later on today."

"What news?"

"The breakouts."

"What breakouts?"

Morgan rubbed his temples. "You're beginning to give me a headache, Spider-Man. You're saying you don't know."

"Know what?"

"I thought you got my message."

Spider-Man shrugged expressively. "I would say what message if I didn't think you'd belt me."

Morgan's mouth was not only a straight line again, but it was in danger of curving downward. "All right. Let's get on the same page here. Less than three hours ago, I made contacting you a triple-A priority. I had all my Manhattan Field Agents on the job. Failing that, I thought this morning's news breaks would prompt you to seek me out. Do you honestly mean to say that your visit's just a coincidence?"

Spider-Man shrugged again. "I'm afraid so, Colonel. I wanted to see you anyway, so I swung on down to your

Times Square liaison office and told the lady on duty that I needed transport to the Helicarrier. I guess she just assumed I got the word. What's up?"

"He doesn't know," Morgan told the wall. "He doesn't know." Grimacing, he dumped all the papers on the right side of his desk into an overflowing basket on the left side of his desk. The action revealed a touch pad with four buttons. Morgan tapped one of the buttons and the entire wall behind him slid into a housing, revealing a bank of monitor screens. "All right, Spider-Man. I'm glad you came anyway. Because we have a situation here, and I don't need my best analysts to know that you're going to be in the middle of it."

"I always am." He would have said more, but that would have taken him dangerously close to the vicinity of a quip. And Morgan didn't do quips.

"All right. I'll start with the material you know." Morgan clicked one of the buttons; the monitors suddenly lit up to form one giant still image of Spider-Man himself, fighting robot sharks in a flooded Broadway theatre. "Point One: you spent most of the past week fighting your old enemy Quentin Beck, aka Mysterio. The two of you tangled three or four times, in various locations in and around Manhattan, before you and some wannabe in a pig costume finally managed to bring him down. This is accurate, right?"

Spider-Man nodded, thinking only that he had a very bad feeling about this. Mysterio's crazed vendetta against his old showbiz colleagues had left three dead and hundreds injured; only some last-minute assistance from "the wannabe in a pig costume"—a regional Arkansan super hero known as Razorback—had prevented Mysterio's attack on a movie set from adding dozens of additional casualties to that list. Spider-Man had hoped to go six months or a year without hearing Mysterio's name again. But he supposed it wasn't to be; part of the legacy of being Spider-Man was being exactly four times as busy as anybody else.

"Point Two," Morgan said. "Just about one week ago, when your Mysterio situation was still heating up, police were summoned to an apartment building in Washington Heights, after several local thugs were severely beaten by an old man they were trying to shake down for money. Although severely outnumbered, the old man incapacitated three of the juveniles and crippled the fourth for life. He fled the premises before the police showed up, but witnesses said they saw a huge green bird fly out of a fifth-floor apartment, carrying a man in its claws. Fingerprints at the apartment confirm that the old man was in fact Adrian Toomes, better known as—"

"The Vulture." Spider-Man said it even as the wall of screens formed an old news photo of a scowling Toomes soaring above the city in his familiar winged costume. The photo, which must have been taken from a nearby helicopter, made Toomes look like the bird of prey he was: powerful, cruel, pitiless, deadly—everything a bird could be, except for majestic. Nothing Toomes had ever done had been that.

"Yes," Morgan said. "We don't know for certain that he's involved in what happened next, but given his associations with the others we do see a high degree of probability." He faced the screens, clicked the button, and replaced the image with another one of a glowing man backlit by lightning bolts. "Point Three: the very next day, even as you fought Mysterio at the Brick Johnson funeral, a man disguised as a project scientist walked into a top-secret government facility and walked out with Max Dillon, better known as Electro. They left a double-digit body count behind them."

The grimace behind Spider-Man's mask was becoming a near-duplicate of Morgan's own. "That was probably Electro's doing. He's always been a murderous thug, but he's been downright crazy since his latest powerup."

"Since several of the bodies were fried to a crisp, I am inclined to agree. Electro probably did kill everybody his confederate, who was almost certainly the Chameleon, didn't just up and shoot. But I don't think you could give either one of the murdering bastards a trophy for respect for human life." Morgan clicked the touch pad again, revealing the image of a man Spider-Man had particularly dreaded seeing in this little slide show. "Point Four: Sometime after that, an individual disguised as me—also probably the Chameleon—entered the maximum-security prison we call the Vault, flashed a forged signature from the President, and walked out with Dr. Otto Octavius."

The screens displayed a famous news photo of Octavius, taken on Wall Street several years earlier: surrounded by flames, laughing insanely, using two of his prosthetic limbs to hurl a gasoline truck high over his head preparatory to hurling it at an attacking SWAT team. Spider-Man remembered the incident well; he'd shown up only a heartbeat later. "This is bad, Colonel. Really bad."

Morgan nodded. "That, as I don't have to remind you, is beyond bad. The Doctor's schemes have gotten so nasty in the last few years that we count him as worse than all the others put together; he regularly endangers millions, sometimes hundreds of millions of people. The others, bad as they are, are police matters; he's the one whose escape's gotten us involved. Even so, I trust you see where this is going."

"And how." Spider-Man ticked them off on his fingers. "Doctor Octopus. The Chameleon. Electro. And the Vulture. That's two-thirds of the Sinister Six right there."

"I'm afraid it's more than that, Spider-Man." Morgan clicked the touch pad, and the screens behind him merged to form a giant image of the caped, helmeted master of illusion known as Mysterio. "Point Five. Quentin Beck escaped custody only two days after you put him away. He walked out the front door of Ryker's Island, disguised as the warden. Our analysts believe he may have never been in custody at all—that the man behind bars was always the Chameleon, taking his place to keep Mysterio's escape under wraps for a little while longer."

Unable to take any more, Spider-Man dropped off the wall and landed on his feet on the ground. "Damn it, Colonel! I busted my butt for a whole week to catch that guy! Now you tell me it was all for nothing!"

A moment of silence passed between them.

Then Spider-Man sat down. This time, almost without realizing it, in the chair. The urge to bolt from Morgan's office and spend the whole night searching the streets of Manhattan for the men he'd fought so many times was overwhelming. But he stayed where he was, and muttered, "Man. Sometimes this line of work is so . . . frustrating."

"For me, too, wallcrawler. But we have to focus on the matter at hand. Starting with just who they may have recruited for that empty sixth slot."

Spider-Man closed his eyes and tried to concentrate. "All right. Not the Hobgoblin. Jason MacCorkendale is dead—"

". . . and as of bedcheck this morning, Roderick Kingsley, the original Hobgoblin, is still relaxing on a Caribbean resort island. I know. We sent an agent to secretly get a sample of Kingsley's DNA to make sure it wasn't the Chameleon taking his place. The DNA confirmed it's him all right. We still have an agent watching him, just in case."

"That's a relief," Spider-Man said. "Except that whoever else they're recruiting is probably just as bad."

"We've eliminated the Sandman—"

Spider-Man spoke a little too quickly. "Couldn't be him anyway. He's reformed."

"I know, but we had to be thorough. After all, he was a steady member in the past, and they have been known to coerce his involvement. But he has been confirmed to be in Tunisia, working with his employer Silver Sable. Ought to like it in the desert, I suppose; he'd fit right in. In any event, when we informed him that his old buddies in the Sinister Six were probably getting together again, he was downright eager to fly back to help you. Unfortunately, Sable wouldn't give him the leave of absence."

"She's a tough boss."

"I've been tougher," Morgan said. "For what it's worth, he made himself available for long-distance consultation, if we happen to need him. And he sent you a personal message— 'give 'em hell.' He wishes he could be here."

Although there was no way Morgan could see it, Spider-Man still found himself smiling ruefully. Both on his own and as a member of the Sinister Six, the Sandman had for years on end been a brutal thug so contemptible in his disregard for human life that the mere thought of his rehabilitation would have been laughable. When all that changed, almost without warning, Spider-Man had initially been as suspicious of the man's sudden new leaf as anybody else. But it had turned out to be real; against all odds, the ruthless criminal had turned out to possess a genuinely good soul underneath. One who, given their shared past, sometimes went overboard with his anxiety to prove himself Spider-Man's ally and friend.

Spider-Man sometimes wished the same could be accomplished with Doc Ock, the Vulture, and the other members of the Sinister Six; certainly, he'd daydreamed more than once about how easy his life would be if they just woke up one day to the same kind of life-altering epiphany that had so completely changed their erstwhile teammate. But he knew it was just a daydream. Flint Marko's reformation had been a wonder and a miracle. Another five were probably too much to expect.

He shook his head. "Guessing's probably a waste of time, Colonel. Whatever they're planning, there are any number of people they could recruit for that sixth slot. Hydro-Man, Jack O'Lantern, Boomerang, the Rhino . . . even more if you consider folks I only fought a couple of times, like Sabretooth or the Trapster or, please, I don't even wanna consider it, the Juggernaut."

Morgan grunted. "I hadn't even thought of him. Thanks for giving me something new to worry about."

"Sorry."

"He's unlikely, anyway. Not a team player. And historically far more likely to go after the Hulk or the X-Men than yourself. In any event, we're going through all our files to your personal history to see who's still at large. It's a depressingly large number."

"Would be a smaller one if the authorities just figured out a way to keep them locked up once I dropped 'em off."

"If it were up to me," Sean Morgan said, and left the thought hanging. It was clear enough what he would do to the likes of the Six if the law he served left the decisions up to him.

Spider-Man said: "And we don't know it's anybody I've seen before, anyway. It could be somebody brand new." *Somebody who's going to be bad news no matter what way we choose to slice it.*

Morgan darkened just enough to indicate that he was thinking the same thing. "In any event, we'll want you to keep in touch until this breaks. We won't ask you to carry a beeper, since you wouldn't anyway, but it would be helpful if you shared information and contacted us, let's say, three times a day, to see what we've come up with, and vice versa. Even if it's nothing."

Spider-Man stood up. "No problem."

Morgan stood as well. "And when the crisis comes . . . as I'm sure it will . . . don't forget us. We want to coordinate our efforts if possible."

"Again, no problem."

Morgan offered his hand. "I have to give you credit, Spider-Man. Most people in your fraternity would have taken this opportunity to assure me they were capable of dealing with this all by themselves. I wouldn't have thought you capable of being such a team player."

Spider-Man took the offered handshake. Under other circumstances, Morgan would have been absolutely right. Aside from very brief tenures with the Avengers and the Fantastic Four, Spider-Man had never been much for group efforts, apart from the occasional team-up. But he'd worked with SAFE on several occasions—including the last time Doc Ock got loose—and he'd come to respect the organization and its commander quite a bit.

In response to Morgan's comment, he said, "I'm usually not, Colonel. But one of your guys saluted me, before. It must have gone to my head."

Spider-Man saw from the wry twist of Colonel Morgan's lips that he had actually succeeded in coming up with a joke the leader of SAFE regarded with frank approval. Probably because it was military humor; maybe because Morgan happened to be in what was, for him, a good mood. Maybe because he knew the Sinister Six was on the loose and he didn't want to alienate such a valuable unpaid resource. In any event, it was a first, and Spider-Man was not about to push it.

He was about to leave when Morgan said: "Okay, you heard my problem. What's yours?"

Spider-Man hesitated in the doorway. "What?"

"You said you had your own reason for seeing me today. Before you knew about my summons, or the breakouts. What is it?"

Embarrassed he'd forgotten, Spider-Man closed the door and returned to his seat. "Sorry. Must be too many blows to the head from megalomaniacs with super-strength." It had actually been driven out of his head by the news that he'd probably have to face six of his personal nightmares all at once; that kind of weight on his head tended to toss all personal considerations on the backburner. But since he'd been reminded: "I kinda need a personal favor."

Morgan was immediately guarded. "This isn't quid pro quo, Spider-Man."

Spider-Man was genuinely insulted by that. "Hey, I didn't say it was. I've been doing this kind of stuff for free for years now."

There was a moment of silence between them.

Then Morgan grunted. "All right. Ask."

"I need access to the personnel files of two deceased intelligence agents."

"Why?"

Spider-Man hesitated. "That's personal."

"And their names?"

"That's also personal. I just need access to the records so I can look them up. I promise it's for a good reason, and I promise I won't take advantage."

Morgan stared at him for several seconds, as if trying to

read his face through the all-concealing red hood, and then shook his head. "Sorry. No can do. Not under those conditions."

"It's important to me," Spider-Man said.

"Nobody would ask that kind of favor unless it was. But since this is going to be an inter-agency request, I need to be able to justify that kind of information outlay. And I can't without information you're not willing to provide." Morgan actually looked regretful, as if he needed more of an excuse to oblige him. "If you'd just tell me something. Anything . . ."

Spider-Man truly wished he could. But he couldn't. He couldn't say that his parents had been Richard and Mary Parker, a pair of covert operatives in the international spy agency that would someday become S.H.I.E.L.D., and that he'd recently stumbled onto photographic evidence that seemed to suggest he hadn't been their first child. He couldn't say that he needed to examine their personal files to determine if it was true . . . and beyond that, what had happened to the baby girl in his mother's arms. He couldn't say that his true reason for coming here was finding out where his sister was . . . and whether she was still alive.

So instead he just stood up and went to the door again. "Understood, Colonel. Don't worry about it. I have another source."

For a moment, before the stern professional mask took over his features once again, Sean Morgan seemed almost human. "And I hope it pans out for you, Spider-Man. Whatever it is . . ."

Somewhere, in a dream, a little girl walked through the world of light.

It was a bright and colorful world: a world filled with blue skies and smiling faces and warm arms to hide in. A world defined by two faces that, now, seemed permanently obscured by haze: the faces of the man and woman who had always made her feel safe and loved. She remembered the man telling funny stories, though she was never able to recall what those stories were; she remembered the woman singing soft lullabies into her ear, though the music itself had fled into the mists of time.

As always, when she dreamed this dream, she also remembered the happiness, without being able to recall what that forgotten emotion had been like.

She was too busy feeling dread. Knowing that this brief taste of normality was all she'd ever have, and that the dream replayed it now only to set the scene for the terrible time when He would come to take it all away.

The little girl knew who He was, of course. She had to. She'd lived this nightmare so many times that everything in it had become as familiar as her last breath. She knew what would happen next as certainly as she knew that the sun would rise the next morning.

The Dream played itself out in different ways. Sometimes her mother and father burst into flame, browning and curling at the edges like paper tossed into a fireplace; sometimes the earth itself rose to swallow them; sometimes the hand of some monstrous godlike figure reached down from the sky to obliterate them with a single malevolent slap. Sometimes she was even able to remember what really happened, though the truth vanished like smoke whenever she woke.

The only thing that never changed was Him. Because as soon as they were dead, He appeared, to repaint the world in His image.

In the dream she perceived Him not as a man . . . but as cold, yawning absence, destroying all light, all warmth, all love, all hope, all chances at future happiness. He rose up out of the earth like something that had been buried there since the dawn of time, so large He blotted out the sky, so overwhelming that there was no chance of even trying to defy him. In the dream He was a black void, swallowing up everything good she'd ever known ... taking away the faces who'd looked upon her with love and replacing them with His own, which was always cruel, always demanding, always incapable of being satisfied with anything she did. In the process, He turned all the bright promise she'd known before and left behind an existence punctuated only by horror and death.

The dream echoed with all the jokes he'd made about the name he'd forced her to wear: *I call you Pity because you'll never know love. I call you Pity because that's all you're worth. I call you Pity because it's all you'll ever have.*

I call you Pity because you're mine ...

Then he spoke her name for real, in a voice like shards of glass.

She woke instantly, realizing in a hateful moment of all-consuming vertigo that the dream lied. She was no longer a little girl. She hadn't been a little girl for more than twenty years. She was a grown woman, who had committed crimes beyond redemption, and who hated herself as much as she hated everything her life had become.

The room was still dark, of course, darker than it could have been, if it were just a question of lights turned out. Nothing penetrated this blackness—not ambient light from elsewhere in the house, not even the phantom light perceived by eyes starved for something to see. She flicked a switch in her mind and the absolute blackness went away, replaced by the more mundane shadows of a dark room partially lit by an open door.

The Gentleman stood in that doorway, backlit by the

hallway. As she'd slept on the hard wood floor—her usual place—he seemed unnaturally tall; although his face remained in shadows, the light made his wispy white hair light up like a halo. She secretly thought of him that way: as her own personal dark angel, as beyond compassion as the stars were beyond man.

"Downstairs," he said. "We have formulated the plan for phase one."

Of course. She was not to be permitted any input, but she did need to know what was expected of her. Some, she knew, would sicken her. It didn't matter. She did what she was told. She wiped her eyes free of tears and sleep, and nodded her understanding.

He almost turned away, but then he paused, a smile tugging at the corners of his lips. "Bad dreams?" he asked, approvingly.

She did not want to meet his gaze. She averted her eyes.

The Gentleman did not need her to speak, though. He already had his answer.

And before he turned away, he spoke the single word that expressed his habitual reaction to anything that denied her a moment of peace.

"Excellent . . ."

CHAPTER THREE

When they made him, they broke the mold.

It was a cliché that had been spoken about any number of men, for any number of different reasons.

But in the case of Captain America, those words were almost literal.

There had never been another like him. There would never be another.

And in the many years since he'd first taken up his indestructible shield and star-spangled costume to fight for the American Dream, the world had been fortunate indeed that one of him . . . had so far been enough.

Spider-Man began and ended his search for the seemingly immortal super-soldier at the Fifth Avenue landmark once called Stark Manor and now better known as Avengers Mansion, for the world-famous super hero team which had long been headquartered there. Individually and collectively, the Avengers had saved the world even more often than Spider-Man himself; indeed, they specialized in battles on that scale, and he figured they were more than welcome to that gig, because he had always been more comfortable saving a little piece of the planet at a time. After all, life as a friendly neighborhood super hero was difficult enough; he didn't see any pressing reason to seek more than the reservist status they'd taken so many years to finally bestow upon him. (Even if he did occasionally take out the membership card they'd issued him, and look at it, and try to fight off the chill that came with the knowledge that yes, it actually was his adopted identity printed there.)

Unlike Spider-Man, whose Avengers membership was essentially a trivia question, Captain America was such an integral part of the group that they'd retroactively declared him a founding member, even though he'd joined several months after their charter. Indeed, he was currently the Chairman . . . and though he still spent most of his time criss-crossing the globe on his own, battling one band of international terrorists or another, looking for him at the mansion was still a logical first step.

Edwin Jarvis, the group's unflappable butler (*and wouldn't it be nice,* Spider-Man wondered forlornly, *to be the kind of super hero who could afford a butler?*) greeted him with the front door with the perfect equanimity of a man who'd greeted many far stranger visitors over the years. Jarvis was a compact, balding gentleman whose British reserve masked both warmth and a wry sense of humor. "Ah, yes. You're in luck. Captain America is indeed here today."

Spider-Man was floored by his luck. "Really? But this trick never works!"

"If by that," Jarvis remarked as he ushered the wall-crawler into the gleamingly immaculate foyer, "you mean that the Active Avengers are usually elsewhere, fighting their own battles, whenever you come here seeking their aid against some menace you initially believe too large for you to handle. . . yes, it is unfortunate that circumstance has all too often turned out that way. However, from what I discern in the more reliable newspapers, The *Bugle* of course being beyond the pale, you usually prove equal to the challenge anyway. I do hope this isn't a life-threatening emergency of some kind."

Spider-Man felt a totally irrational urge to say something like pish-tosh. "Uh, no. Not this time. Just came to ask him something."

"I see," Jarvis sighed. "I suppose it's similar to the phenomenon of only being able to find a member of the local constabulary when you don't really need one. Please walk this way."

Jarvis led him to the gymnasium, entering through a door on the second level running track. Like most things associated with Tony Stark or the Avengers, it was a state-of-the-art facility, with brand new gymnastics equipment, weights, climbing ropes, and rings; in addition, the special exercise needs of the individuals who used this room were met by more exotic equipment like kevlar gym mats, solid-lead medicine balls, and barbells linked by heavy cables to adjustable hundred-ton counterweights in the building foundations. An ugly-looking crater in one wall provided sufficient testimony that sometimes even this wasn't enough to contain the forces that were so often honed in this room.

Jarvis and Spider-Man found Captain America training in his familiar red-white-and-blue costume, half leotard, half chain-mail, with the star on his chest and vertical red and white stripes girding his waist. His exercise equipment consisted of two dozen floating platforms, all of which remained in constant motion, bobbing up and down, sliding in random directions, or even upending; Captain America was in constant motion as well, leaping and somersaulting from one to another as cannons in all four walls targeted him in a cross-fire of razor-sharp flechettes. The regimen would have been suicidal for a normal man and insanely dangerous for most experienced combat soldiers. For Spider-Man, who'd left normality behind many years ago, the routine would have been survivable but it not exactly his idea of a fun way to spend his afternoon. But Captain America was clearly in his element; as he dodged one deadly volley by leaping straight up, performing dizzying pirouettes in mid-air, and batting aside a multidirectional blizzard of gleaming knives with swats from his famously indestructible star-spangled shield, he was even—frighteningly enough—smiling.

As Spider-Man watched, the flechettes scattered over the gymnasium floor were being gathered up by a fleet of servitor robots that then carried them through sliding panels at ground level. To be fired again, he supposed. Captain America would naturally be a heavy supporter of recycling.

"Wow," said Spider-Man. "Jarvis, how long has he been at this?"

"A couple of hours at this setting. Give or take fifty years, of course."

Another good reason for the recycling; at the rate the flechettes were being fired, it wouldn't have taken very long to fill this entire gymnasium to waist-level. Spider-Man shook his head. Strictly speaking, he was many times stronger, faster, more agile, and more tireless than the living legend before him; he was, after all, superhuman, and Captain America was merely (*merely!*) the pinnacle of human potential, polished by decades of experience. Strictly speaking, Spider-Man could handle everything Captain America could, and probably (*heresy!*) a number of things Captain America could not. But even so, watching Captain America always gave him a major case of imposter syndrome. Spider-

Man was just dumb luck and raw talent. Captain America was diamond-edged perfection.

Jarvis tapped an intercom set by the entrance. "Captain? Master Spider-Man is here to see you."

"I see that!" Cap shouted, without missing a beat. "Hello, Spider-Man!"

Spider-Man found himself suddenly, perversely certain that saying "Hi!" at the wrong moment would throw Captain America off his stride just enough to expose him to the one deadly flechette with his name on it. But not saying "Hi!" might do the same thing . . . "Hey, Cap! Lookin' good!"

"I'll be done in a jiffy!" Cap called. He hurled his shield—his only source of protection from those deadly knives—away with all his might. Moving with a speed that reduced it to a streak of primary-colored light, it ricocheted off the floor with a loud *thwong*, rebounded off the ceiling, bounced off the floor again, and (not perceptibly slowed down), impacted a red failsafe button in the corner. The cannons ceased fire. The floating platforms disappeared. Captain America dropped to the floor, landed on his feet, and extended his arm just in time to slip his hand through the straps of his returning shield.

Cap was one of the few people on Earth capable of performing such an insanely complicated manuever casually. As well as one of the few remaining human beings capable of using the word "jiffy" without corniness or ironic intent.

Another unusual thing about Cap: his welcoming smile, as he leaped and somersaulted his way onto the second-level running track, was absolutely genuine. Spider-Man didn't always get along with his fellow super heroes; too many of them either bought into the whole public-enemy thing, or, like Sean Morgan, simply had problems with his nails-on-a-blackboard wisecracking style. Captain America was one of a small handful of exceptions; having established to his own satisfaction that the wallcrawler fought on the side of the angels, Cap had absolutely no difficulty treating him with totally unguarded fellowship.

Just thinking on that gave Spider-Man another of those disconcerting moments of forced perspective. For just a heartbeat, he was once again the scrawny teenage kid who was always the last one picked for a team in gym class. And he thought, Hey. *I* am friends with Captain Am*erica*. I am *friends* with Captain America. I am friends with *Captain America*. I am *friends* with Captain America.

Cool.

Captain America shook his hand and said: "Good to see you, son. This a social visit?"

"I wish it were, Cap."

An understanding nod from the super-soldier. "Sean Morgan faxed us a complete report on the potential Sinister Six situation, a couple of hours ago. I was set to fly off to Tokyo on another matter, later today, but that one can wait; if you'd like my help, I'll stick around town as long as you need me."

Touched, Spider-Man said, "I appreciate that. But we don't know if they're really getting together, or for that matter whether they'll make their move tomorrow, next week, or six months from now. Besides, I've been able to deal with them before, and you always have plenty of other things to do. I'm here for another reason."

There was no surprise in Cap's nod. The offer had clearly been a serious one, and he would have backed it up in a second if asked, but he just as clearly hadn't expected Spider-Man to accept it, for exactly the reasons stated. Coming from somebody like Cap, that was a major compliment.

Jarvis coughed. "Gentlemen, I have refreshments waiting

in the other room. I set them out for the good Captain alone, but there is enough for both of you. If you'll just follow me . . ."

"We'd be lost without you, Jarvis." Cap followed Jarvis and Spider-Man into a small locker room off the running track. The floors were pure marble, the walls polished tile; doors to a sauna, a steam bath, and a shower room stood clearly marked along one wall. Even here, there were indications that this wasn't exactly a normal athletic club; among them a sign outside the sauna warning that the chamber contained controls not only for heat but also for varying spectra of electromagnetic radiation. However, as promised, there was also a selection of freshly-baked cookies still warm from the oven, and freshly-squeezed fruit juices set on a table against one wall. Edwin Jarvis proved he was a butler with an impeccable memory by immediately turning toward the percolator for the benefit of Spider-Man, who on previous visits to the mansion had established himself as a caffeine fiend extraordinaire.

Captain America gave his shield its own chair, then poured himself some celery juice, taking exactly one cookie as if to establish that he still possessed some human frailty. Taking a bite, he said: "So if it's not the Six situation, web-slinger, what does bring you here?"

"I was wondering . . ." Spider-Man hesitated. He considered the matter somewhat delicate, and it was a bit more difficult to bring up with Jarvis here. What he finally blurted out surprised him: ". . . what you do about hood hair?"

Jarvis did a double-take. Captain America stopped chewing, and said: "I beg your pardon?"

"Hood hair," Spider-Man said, helplessly. It was like watching himself in a slow-motion car-wreck; he couldn't stop the process once started, and he had to see it through.

"You know, when you take off your hood, and static makes all your hair stand straight up on end . . . I find that incredibly annoying, don't you? How do you handle it?"

Captain America and Jarvis exchanged bemused glances. Jarvis hurriedly returned to his work at the percolator, and a now guardedly amused Cap swallowed his cookie, sipped his juice, and said: "Somehow, Spidey, I don't really believe that's why you came here today . . ."

Spider-Man's face, under the mask, was as red as the cloth itself. "Well, no, not really . . . but I've been thinking about it, and as long as I did have to drop by . . ."

As Jarvis handed Spidey his coffee—a particularly fine Colombian blend that smelled like it tasted the way most coffee tastes only in dreams—Cap scratched an errant itch on his chin, "Absolutely no problem. I suppose we ought to hold support group meetings every once in a while, just to nail down these minor but practical issues that somehow never come up when we're out in the field. If you really want to know, son, it's never been that much of a difficulty for me. Back in World War II, I wore a crewcut and grooming wasn't really that much of an issue. More recently, I use a special hair tonic Tony Stark developed just for people in our industry with our unusual sartorial problems. Jarvis can probably hook you up with a bottle or two, if you want . . ."

"Uh. Okay. Thanks." He knew Cap was joking, or at least he thought he was—it wasn't easy to tell with a straight-shooter like Cap. Spider-Man pulled the cloth of his mask away from his mouth, hooking it over the tip of his nose so he could sip his coffee. It still left the mask on over most of his face.

"And now that we've gotten that out of the way," Cap said, with an unwavering smile that nevertheless betrayed awareness that everything beforehand had just been a psychological delaying tactic, "why are you really here?"

Spider-Man, realizing now that Jarvis probably knew enough personal stuff about the Avengers to keep gossip columnists busy for years yet would die before revealing any of it, repeated the same request he'd made of Sean Morgan.

Cap nodded sympathetically, with a level of understanding that suggested he suspected a personal, perhaps even family relationship between Spider-Man and the two deceased government agents. When Spider-Man was done, Cap glanced at Jarvis—who, ever the perfect butler, pretended to be invisible—and said: "No problem, webhead. I know you've got your reasons. And after all the times we've teamed up, I owe this to you ten times over."

Captain America owes me.

Cool.

Only anxiety over what he was likely to learn from his parents' records kept Spider-Man from doing a triple-somersault with glee. "You can get me access?"

Cap shook his head. "Not directly. The government does allow Avengers into its main databases, but only under specific guidelines. Specifically, the clearances in question are only open to Active Members. Reservists or Inactives—especially, I'm sorry to say, those greeted with as much official suspicion as the Sandman and yourself—have to make their requests through us. Which means I'll have to look up the files for you."

Spider-Man's crest fell. "So I have to tell you their names."

"Yes," Cap said. "You do." His eyes narrowed slightly; the look of a man habitually ten steps ahead of everybody else, whose suspicions, if any, had been supported by Spider-

Man's hesitation. He spoke softly, "Not that I'll ever ask you why you need this information, Spider-Man. You have the right to your secrets."

Across the room, Jarvis cleared his throat. "Captain? Spider-Man? I'm afraid I have urgent matters that suddenly require attention in the kitchen. If you'll excuse me?"

Captain America nodded, without taking his eyes off Spider-Man.

And that should have been enough. But even as Jarvis exited in a burst of discretionary propriety, Spider-Man found himself hesitating. He didn't know why. Of course, giving Cap the names of his parents came perilously close to revealing that they were his parents, but what was the problem with that? This was Cap. Cap: the most trusted man in America. Cap: the man who'd practically displaced the bald eagle as the most prominent symbol of his country. Cap: the man who'd always played straight with him, who always played straight with everybody. Cap: the man Spider-Man would have trusted with his life in a heartbeat. If Cap didn't deserve custody of the single most revelatory clue to Spider-Man's identity, then who did?

It was such a little thing, when you considered all the other people who'd ferreted out his secret identity over the years. Daredevil . . . Captain Stacy . . . Mary Jane, who'd figured it out years before he got up the nerve to tell her . . . Aunt May, who hadn't even revealed that she'd figured it out until right before she died . . . even that dying little boy in the cancer ward. They'd all kept the secret. Then there was Joe Robertson, the managing editor at the *Daily Bugle* . . . who might or might not know but had certainly dropped enough provocative hints over the years. And several members of the X-Men: specifically Jean Grey, Professor X, Wolverine, and Bishop. They'd kept the secret. Hell, if it came down to that, even Venom and Puma had kept the secret, which was pretty impressive for a couple of murderers who would rip out his spleen as soon as look at him. If they could know, without telling anybody, why couldn't he tell Cap? Didn't Cap deserve to know?

Then Spider-Man thought of Norman Osborn. Who had found Peter Parker's face beneath Spider-Man's mask and immediately declared war on everybody in Peter's life. Norman Osborn, who had killed a woman Peter Parker loved, and murdered a man Peter Parker considered brother.

It was ridiculous. Merely mentioning Norman Osborn and Captain America in the same sentence was an injustice. After all, one was evil incarnate; one was one of the most heroic men ever to walk the earth. But Osborn was always there, standing over the Secret he had turned into a murder weapon ... and deliberately revealing that Secret, even to a trusted friend like Cap, meant first having to look that ghost in the eyes.

Spider-Man, considering it, remained silent for all of ten seconds.

And when those ten seconds were over he was sincerely ready to tell Cap everything.

But by then his hesitation had spoken as eloquently as any words ... and Cap had placed a single hand on his shoulder.

"Don't worry about it, son. You have other avenues. Find out on your own, if you can. If it doesn't work out, I'll always be willing to help."

Spider-Man was glad his hood hid his face, because his cheeks were burning with shame. "Cap ... I ..."

"I said don't worry about it," Captain America said, with no irony at all. "We're in a secretive business, you and I. All of us. Two of the best friends I ever made in this line didn't tell me their true identities until I found out by accident, years after we started fighting side by side. I didn't take it personally from them. And I don't take it personally from you." He turned, retrieved his star-spangled shield, and slipped his arm through the straps on the interior side. He flexed his gloved fist once, twice, then three times, and smiled. "Do me one favor, though? Without telling me any more than you're comfortable with—do let me know, at least yes or know, whether everything turns out all right."

"I'll do that," Spider-Man said gratefully.

Captain America waved. "You can show yourself out, right? I have to pack for Tokyo."

"No prob, Cap. And thanks."

And then he was gone.

Spider-Man took one last sip of his nearly untouched coffee and found a well of bitterness that belied its previously sweet flavor.

He knew Cap didn't take it personally. Cap was, after all, Cap; respect for other people was a large part of what made him the man he was.

But that didn't change how Spider-Man now felt about himself.

And the thought was still there, echoing in the otherwise silent room: *Good going, webhead. You just told a friend he was a stranger. You just told the most trustworthy man on the planet you didn't trust him. You just insulted a living legend.*

Pretty good score for one conversation . . .

After the planning session, the Gentleman indulged himself with a brisk afternoon walk—invigorating despite the necessity of sharing his sidewalk with the slack-jawed, uncouth barbarians who laughably considered theirs the greatest civilization in the history of this earth. He was unable to discern a thought or a noble impulse in any of the faces he saw, finding naught but bovine self-interest in most. It was not the America he'd known on his last visit, which had been distasteful for any number of other reasons, including its rudeness, its witlessness, its pretensions and its filth; the America he found now seemed to have given up most of its cultural memory and its higher reasoning ability as well. As far as the Gentleman was considered, it was a land already well on its way to devolving back to the caves—a land that well deserved the immediate future he had arranged.

He was still glowing with the awareness of his own innate superiority when he returned to the townhouse to check on the preparations.

It was a different gathering. The townhouse he'd left had been a cauldron of excitement, as five of the world's most dangerous men hammered out a course of action capable of dovetailing with the first phase of what he expected from them. They'd bickered, insulted each other, come to agreement, suggested novel ways of inflicting terror on the city and highly detailed disfigurements to be inflicted upon the person of Spider-Man; they'd come up with a suitably vile plan; and they'd expressed their anticipation of the moment when they'd be able to start playing their new game.

The townhouse was a much quieter place now. Beck was gone; as usual with his schemes, his part in the drama to come would require significant advance preparation, which would occupy his every waking moment both tonight and tomorrow. He deserved credit for being able to make his arrangements in less than forty-eight hours, instead of the months it might have taken entire work crews of ordinary men. Smerdyakov was also gone; his own task may have seen comparatively simple, but it also needed several hours of night work dealing with explosives and timers under the most demanding of stealth conditions. They had both pledged to be back at the townhouse by this time tomorrow, freeing the stage for the grand announcement to follow twenty-four hours later. Toomes' own part was childishly easy—he didn't need anything but his own talents—but he was gone too, either to pursue his own interests, or to help either of his aforementioned colleagues in their labors.

That left Dillon, Octavius, and Pity.

Octavius was moving around in the kitchen, no doubt—if his physiognomy was any indication—preparing himself something with plenty of starch. His voice was clearly audible from the foyer; like many in his line of endeavor, the man ranted about his genius even when he thought he was alone. Dillon was sprawled on one of the easy chairs, his right leg draped over the corresponding armrest; the sullen look he flashed at the Gentleman as he entered offered mute confirmation that he'd probably spent most of the past couple of hours casting ardent stares at Pity. Pity herself was sitting motionless in the corner, eyes downcast, lips tremulous. The Gentleman knew she hadn't moved since he'd left. He had told her to stay, and she'd stayed, from all appearances totally withdrawn, but in actuality alert enough to monitor her new teammates for any signs of incipient betrayal. It was, of course, far too early for genuine treason; though he'd already blessed them with one major detail, they still did not know the entirety of the plan. But it was never too soon to let the dogs know that their master was vigilant.

The Gentleman nodded at Dillon. "They also serve, eh? You should have gone to help your friend Beck. I imagine your talents would have been significantly useful, redirecting so much municipal power."

Dillon grunted. "Toomes is helping him. I wanted to stay here."

"You're not still sulking over your rather . . . behind the scenes . . . part of the plan?"

"No. I know I'll get to fight the bugman sooner or later. I . . . just wanted to stay here."

The Gentleman glanced at Pity, then smirked to demonstrate that he understood exactly why Dillon had stayed. "I see."

Dillon saw how transparent he'd been, and reddened. "I tried to talk to her. Make friends."

"I told you. She does not speak."

"I once shared a cell with a mute guy. It was still possible to communicate with him. She acts like she's afraid to admit she even hears me."

The Gentleman looked pleased by that. He crossed the room and tapped her on the knee with the tip of his walking stick. Only then did Pity look up, her eyes wide and pleading. He spoke coldly: "You may get yourself a small drink of water. Warm, from the tap. But no more than half a cup, and you will return to this corner to drink it."

Pity leaped up at once, hurrying into the kitchen like a small dog scolded for being bad.

Dillon watched her retreat. "What is she? Your robot?"

"You know she's not," the Gentleman said. "She's as flesh and blood as you are. And no doubt she heard everything you said to her. She may even like you; stranger things are possible. But her wants, and needs, and preferences are not important. Mine are. This was made clear to her years ago, through the most persuasive conditioning techniques available at the time, and is now as much a part of her being as her . . . ah . . . unusual genetic resources."

Dillon's face twisted with a degree of empathy that most of his court-appointed psychiatric evaluators would have considered alien to him. "That's a pretty good definition of slavery, mister."

"A much underrated institution," the Gentleman said. He withdrew a Corona from his jacket pocket and sniffed it. "Human beings have always been a marketable commodity. This century may be the first where the majority of civilized nations have become too feeble of will to accommodate the trade. Fortunately, I have no such limitations."

Dillon stood up and crossed the room in three angry steps, delivering his response in a harsh crackling whisper: "You know, I've only known you a few hours, and I already don't like you."

Most men would have cowered, afraid of the powers commanded by the man better known as Electro. The Gentleman, who had faced down worse, merely smirked, and spoke in a voice just as controlled: "You feel sorry for her, eh?"

"Yes. Yes, I do."

"Appropriate, after all," the Gentleman said. "Her name is Pity."

Dillon's eyes flashed like circuitry on fire. "Do you get some kind of sick thrill from terrorizing her?"

"Not at all," the Gentleman sniffed. "She is nothing to me. As you and the others are nothing to me. Just another resource, to be used as long as I find profit—or pleasure—in the association. Of course, if my treatment of her truly offends you enough to endanger our enterprise, then her usefulness is placed in question." He mimed serious consideration. "Perhaps I'll order her to kill herself. Or . . . or . . ."

Pity had returned, still holding her untouched cup of water. She did not return to the corner, as previously commanded; instead, observing the confrontation between Dil-

Ion and her master, she drew close, her expression blank but for eyes as moist and vulnerable as ever. The room grew noticably dimmer, and shadows on all four sides seemed to elongate . . .

The Gentleman glanced at her, and leered maliciously. "Ah. Here is an idea. Perhaps I will offer her to you as an incentive bonus. Perhaps, when our enterprise is successfully concluded, I shall simply abandon her to your care, so you may treat her in a manner that better suits your compassionate sensibilities. I am certain that you shall, initially at least, be a perfect . . . if you deign to excuse the expression . . . gentleman." He smirked. "But she will never consider you a friend. Or a man to love. You will always be . . . just the one who gives orders."

Pity looked even more stricken than usual.

Dillon, of course, couldn't help notice that. As the Gentleman meant him to. "I oughta fry your butt right now."

"Another option," the Gentleman said. "Of course, if you took it, you would not only sacrifice everything that rides on our enterprise, but you would also render the lady in question your mortal enemy. And you don't want her as an enemy, do you? You like her too much."

Dillon crackled at the edges, but backed down, his eyes burning.

It was a dangerous game the Gentleman played, but it was the game he always played: his field, the petty fears, ambitions and desires that drove the majority of the people on the planet, his game pieces, the dance between their need for him and their hatred of his manipulations. He was driven to this game like most men are driven to breathe; his own lifelong disappointment with humanity demanded it. For lesser men, it would be foolish to court the hatred of a creature like Electro, but for the Gentleman, it was merely that part of the game that kept things interesting. He particularly enjoyed the way Dillon glowered when a snap of his fingers signaled Pity, showing no evident spontaneity or affection, to move close to the Gentleman, stand on tippy-toes so she could reach the taller man, and plant a dutiful kiss on his cheek. He took pleasure in permitting Dillon to see that this little act terrified her, humiliated her, and made her skin crawl.

Dillon was one of the most powerful men on the planet. His dynamo of a body made him as potentially deadly as any bomb dropped from any plane. He was a valuable catspaw—and in some ways, though it was not yet time to tell him, the most important to the Gentleman's plan. The final phase of this operation could not possibly work without him.

But he was still just a man. And in terms of intellect, a sadly limited man. The Gentleman had survived the hatred of worse.

Still grinning, he looked over Dillon's shoulder at the pudgy, tentacled figure filling up the doorway to the kitchen. A man accustomed to being in charge, who chafed at being a hired hand. A man of intellect and breeding, whose suspicious glare was a far more pressing source of concern—whose idiotic soup bowl haircut utterly failed to hide the intensity of the thoughts that roiled beneath.

Dr. Octopus.

Yes, the Gentleman thought, enjoying himself. *As I expected.*

He is the one who most bears watching.

CHAPTER FOUR

On cursory examination, the townhouse in Manhattan and the small white house in Forest Hills, Queens, could not have seemed more different.

The townhouse sat on a narrow side street on the West Side; it was made of stone and covered with ivy and set off by an elegantly wrought iron gate that was less a deterrent to criminals than a discreet symbol of the wealth that sat cloistered within.

The white house sat in an aging suburban neighborhood, among wide streets and scrupulously mowed lawns. It was a modest clapboard home, with a white shingled exterior and a sloping black roof, on a half-acre lot shaded by trees and contained by a freshly painted white picket fence. Though clearly one of the older houses in the area—where many of its contemporaries had been torn down and replaced with homes of newer vintage—it seemed more quaint than decrepit, a tribute to the good old days that never really existed but which everybody of a certain age seems to remember anyway.

They were two houses separated not only by a river, and miles of geographical distance, but also by worlds. One house bespoke the privileges of wealth, the other bespoke the simpler ambitions of the lower middle class. If they had anything in common, it was that they both seemed peaceful enough; there was no signposts capable of alerting the casual passerby that there was anything extraordinary about the people in either of them.

But the townhouse was home to a gathering of monsters.

And the modest clapboard house was home to the hero who fought them.

Spider-Man's commute home was as discreet as any approach by a man in a red and blue bodysuit possibly could be. In his case, that was pretty discreet. He came in over the suburban rooftops, taking refuge wherever he could find it— sometimes behind big brick chimneys, sometimes in the upper branches of trees, sometimes in tiny patches of shadow lengthening beneath the late afternoon sun. Sometimes, when his uncanny spider-sense warned him that he was danger of being spotted by his neighbors, he froze in place for as long as a minute at a time; but it wasn't long before they looked away and he was able to leap or scramble to the next place of concealment. It was a handy thing, this spider-sense; despite these delays, and despite his impatience for streets that were not (for him, at least) nearly as conducive to rapid transit as the concrete canyons of Manhattan, he still moved through the neighborhood faster than most people were willing to drive—and despite streets that were inhabited with shouting children or pedestrians trudging home from the bus stop or the train, he was still able to pass over their heads and across their backyards without even once being spotted by anybody.

He sometimes wondered if he was the only super hero

who commuted—if, for instance, the Avengers had somebody who showed up fifteen minutes late for battles with Kang or Attuma and complained that it was all the fault of the damn LIRR strike. Maybe they carpooled. In civvies, he hoped.

Tonight, as he hopped over the head of an unsuspecting grandpa gathering up all the plastic toys strewn about the backyard swings, landed on the old man's roof, and immediately launched himself into a leap that completely cleared the two remaining backyards between himself and the palatial Parker estate, he found himself wishing for the transporter booths and secret underground access tunnels that certain misinformed sources claimed typical accessories of the average super hero's lifestyle. He wasn't sure he could ever rely on such conveniences—especially since he genuinely enjoyed web-slinging—but they would sure be tempting on days like today, when the temperature was only a degree or two above freezing.

The big old tree that sheltered the Parkers' backyard, that in summer provided so much cover that he barely needed his stealth to stay hidden in its upper branches, was this time of year denuded and bare. He scrambled across the branch that shadowed the attic window, hopped down, and slipped inside so quickly that even somebody looking directly at him might have discerned nothing but a flash of red color.

Mary Jane had left his brown terrycloth bathrobe—ratty but still a favorite—hanging on a hook just inside the window. As he changed, he heard soft classical music filtering up from the first-floor living room, and smiled. He could usually read his wife's moods by the kind of music she played. She preferred loud rock when club hopping, or when she had chores to take care of at home, but she used jazz when she was feeling maudlin and classical when she wanted to relax. He loved her in all her moods, but had been in a soft classical mood himself. He called to her in an outrageous parody of a Cuban accent: "Looooseee! I'm home!"

"Ricky!" she shouted back.

The Lucy-Ricky bit was a shtick they'd been using to amuse each other for a couple of days now. It would pass, like stupid private jokes usually did—but until then, he was determined to enjoy it.

He climbed down one flight of stairs, took a hot shower as much to get the winter chill out of his bones as to scrape off the detritus of a day's webslinging, then donned a t-shirt and jeans and descended to the living room.

Mary Jane was curled up on the couch, facing a coffee table littered with envelopes large and small. He could tell she'd been home a while by the way she was dressed; always stunningly fashionable when out in the world, as her career as a model-actress demanded, she sometimes—but not very often—compensated by going as far as possible in the other direction at home. Today, she'd dressed in faded jeans, an oversized Empire State University sweatshirt that would have qualified as shapeless on anybody else, and a pair of battered pink bunny slippers that somebody—maybe Betty Brant, maybe Jill Stacy—had presented her as a gag gift on her last birthday. Her long, luxurious red hair, which normally cascaded around her head and shoulders like a flamboyant corona cast by the beautiful face at its center, had today been tied back behind her head, but for a few rebellious strands that insisted on feathering her cheeks instead.

The pleasant irony of all this was that Mary Jane's occasional attempts to be casual about her appearance were always entirely ineffective. She couldn't help herself; she was always stunning. The very first time he'd met her, at the start of a blind date he'd been trying to duck for months, she'd greeted him with "Face it, Tiger: you just hit the jackpot." He'd seen no reason no quarrel with that assessment. Today, as he bent over to kiss her, he still didn't.

After about a minute, she said: "So. Hero. Save the world yet today?" A question that in some marriages might have been sarcasm, but which in theirs was simple idle curiosity.

"Naah," he said, hopping over the back of the couch to land beside her. "Too cold. I bet even Doctor Doom's at home, cocooning."

"With who?"

"Ummm. Good point. I don't think there's a Mrs. Doom."

She snuggled up. "What about your family research? Any luck with that?"

"Not yet. Nothing but dead ends." Changing the subject a little too quickly, because he didn't want to burden her with the news about the Sinister Six just yet, he asked, "Anything interesting in the mail?"

"A check for one day's work on *Fatal Action IV*," she said, referring to her starring role in a motion picture that had been delayed indefinitely due to Mysterio's attack on the cast and crew. "A card from Aunt Anna, with the same old 'what's new' from Florida. Bills, bills, and more bills—but most of them only first notices, so we're in pretty good shape for a change. Spent the bulk of the day reading scripts."

He raised an eyebrow. "Really."

"Uh-huh. Seems that my conduct during the Mysterio mess enhanced my rep as a real trooper. At least," she said, her lovely face curling into a scowl, "among the kind of producers who value the publicity so much they don't even bother to see if I can act or not."

He winced. "That bad?"

"Well, let's put it this way: I started them all. And managed to get fifteen pages into one of them." She shuddered. "Tiger, mind answering a question for me? You're a man, right?"

"Uh, right. Though I kinda hoped my lovely wife would have considered that an established fact by now."

She gave him a squeeze. "You're so cute when you're insecure. No. Really, you know very well that wasn't the question I meant. Can you answer this as a man? Can you please tell me the appeal of a Women-In-Prison movie? I mean, not a sensitive character-driven drama of the conditions faced by women behind bars, but the kind of story where, less than five pages into the script, a riot in the yard has us all scrabbling around in the dirt pulling each other's hair while the guards take bets?"

He winced. "That was one of them?"

"That was three of them."

"Ouch."

"Ouch is right. What's frightening is that when I took a look at the creepy state of our bank account I almost considered taking one. So tell me. You're a man. What's the appeal?"

"I plead the fifth?" he ventured.

"May the record show that the male who regularly battles alien symbiotes and guys dressed up in rhino suits flees in terror from a interrogation regarding the various disturbing peculiarities of his gender."

"Absolutely," he said. "Give me Galactus over a redhead with an embarrassing question any day."

"I don't know, Peter. I like acting, but not because of the notoriety—I'm serious about it. It means something to me. But some of the roles I've been offered lately would humiliate Barbara Ann Boopstein. I'm torn between wanting to take something, anything, just to stay active—and not incidentally, help to bring a little more money into this chronically strapped household—and thinking I should keep saying no until I get an offer with a little dignity. What do you think?"

He didn't hesitate at all. "I think that you've always been very good about not doing anything that made you uncomfortable. And I think you should listen to your instincts."

"I know, I know, but the money—"

"What was it you once said to me? That you don't want our finances to pressure you into doing something you'd be embarrassed to find on a video shelf five years from now? I think that's a good way to go. We'll get along, just like we always have."

"Which," she said, kissing him, "is exactly what I thought you'd say."

"Glad to be of service, milady."

"Now." Her green eyes narrowed. "What are you trying so hard not to tell me?"

As Spider-Man, Peter had seen the escapes of Electro, Mysterio, and Doctor Octopus hit the moving headlines on the news building in Times Square. He said: "I take it you haven't seen the news today."

"Huh? No, too busy reading. What's up?"

He told her. Predictably, Mary Jane stiffened with each new revelation. Part of her visceral response was no doubt due to her own personal history with various members of the Sinister Six. She had, after all, at various times in her life, been kidnapped by an imposter disguised as the Vulture, forced to use a baseball bat to defend herself against the Chameleon, and only a few days ago survived the murderous intentions of Mysterio. And the entire membership of the Sinister Six had been involved in a previous incident on the set of the *Fatal Action* film prior to the one Mysterio had just ruined all by himself. Too, Mysterio had just terrorized and murdered a close friend of hers, and she'd allowed herself to believe that he'd been brought to justice for that crime. Now, it was impossible to avoid the awareness that Mysterio could now keep his promise to seek vengeance on her. But most of it was the knowledge that each of these men was a significant danger to everyone who lived—and that the man she loved would be once again forced to take insane risks to live up to a responsibility greater than anybody should ever have to burden.

She said: "Do me a favor. I know you can't duck this situation, but you don't have to go it alone. Do you trust this Colonel Morgan?"

He thought about it. "I don't really trust any authority figure unconditionally. After all, if the suits ever ordered him to go after me, he'd have to do it without question. But do I think he's a good guy? Do I think he'll keep his word? Yes."

"Then if the man wants to help you, let him help you. Take any advantage you can get against those people."

"I intend to," Peter said. "I may be crazy, but I'm not stupid."

"I'm serious. I don't like seeing you come home all bloody and bruised, more dead than alive. I know it's part of the price I have to pay for being your wife, and I usually pay it without complaint. Well, without much complaint, anyway. But I'm not going to let you take bigger risks than you have to, just because you feel more heroic dealing with people like the Six alone. If Morgan wants to help you, don't throw it back it in his face."

"I won't," he repeated. "I promise."

"You sure?"

"Yes, I'm sure."

She prodded him. "Then why do you look like you just swallowed a lemon?"

"Well, as long as he's gonna help me with that, I only wish he'd help me with this other thing. Access to my parents' files." He told Mary Jane about all of Spider-Man's failed attempts to exploit his contacts in the superheroic and law-enforcement communities. Morgan and Captain America had been only a small part of it; the webslinger had tried half a dozen other sources, before and after, and was each time either refused or asked for qualifying information capable of putting his secret identity at risk. "It burns me," he said finally. "It really does. After everything Spidey's done for this city—for this world!—I can't even call in a simple favor! I—" He frowned. "What's so funny?"

There was a knowing smile tugging at the corners of Mary Jane's lips. "I warn you, tiger, you're going to feel really stupid when you find out."

"I feel stupid already," he said. "Your point?"

"Specifically, that you spend way too much time in that super hero suit."

It was such a nonsequitur he had to stare at her. "Probably."

"So much time, in fact, that you've begun to think as Peter Parker as the disguise worn by Spider-Man, instead of the other way around."

He knit his eyebrows warily. "Oh?"

"No," she laughed and bopped him over the head with a cushion. "Don't worry! This is not a lead-in to that old argument! It's a simple observation! And it's the reason you can't find what you're looking for—at least, not the way you're looking!"

"What do you mean?"

She spoke with exaggerated slowness. "Don't you get it? You're not investigating Spider-Man's parents. You're investigating Peter Parker's."

His mouth fell open.

She continued: "And it's Peter Parker who should be asking the questions."

He did feel stupid.

"After all," she said, "nobody's going to be suspicious about why you want to know . . ."

She might have said more, but that's when he kissed her.

As the sun retreated low over the horizon, the shadows in the concrete canyons grew longer, bearing with them the first hints of night. The air turned even more bitter as the last vestiges of the day's warmth began to fade; all over the city, the people who called this city home felt the cold rake their throats, saw their breath puff from their lips like steam from locomotive engines, and shuffled off to the indoor places where the glories of modern civilization had managed to keep a little warmth caged for their benefit.

It began to snow. Not a lot: not enough to stick in Manhattan, which was always a little more resistant than the lands that surrounded it. But enough to flit about at skyscraper level, teasing the streets below with the possibility of harsher storms yet to come.

In the Presidential Suite of the Plaza Hotel, the architect of one of those storms sat in an easy chair before an expansive picture window, sipping a truly superb cognac as he watched the city batten down for night.

It was not a perfect view. The window overlooked Central Park, which may have been scenic enough, but was nevertheless not the part of the city that would be hardest hit by the final stages of this enterprise. The Gentleman would have much preferred a view overlooking the great centers of business, or perhaps the towering condominiums inhabited by the city's pathetic and self-absorbed wealthy; it would have been amusing to gaze out at their little enclaves and think about all the doomed complacent people unaware that the entire fabric of their civilization was about to come tumbling down all around their heads.

But he supposed he couldn't complain. The view notwithstanding, it had still been a productive day. His negotiations with the super-powered miscreants had gone extraordinarily well; they'd accepted his terms, and were even now making final arrangements for Phase One.

Better yet, they even imagined themselves in control of the situation. Even those not entirely swayed by greed were still operating within estimated parameters; the smitten Dillon allowing the manipulation of his emotions, the snarling Octavius ignorant of the precautions that had been taken against him. The rest of them actually seemed to believe that they'd emerge from this partnership with anything but the taste of ashes.

The Gentleman smirked. *How surprised they would be, when the final accounts were tallied! How impotently enraged!*

And as for the other one . . . the self-proclaimed hero, himself . . .

The Gentleman raised his glass toward an imaginary befuddled Spider-Man crouched on the balcony window. It was not precisely the same mental image that Octavius or the others would have conjured up, in that this Spider-Man wore everything but his mask. This one wore instead of that ridiculous hood the face of the normal man the freakish wall-crawler sometimes pretended to be: a man whose life the Gentleman had already shattered once.

It was a distinction that none of the current members of the Sinister Six could claim. The Gentleman had already reached deep into the young man's life and taken that which could never be replaced; had in fact taken even more than the young man knew he was missing.

Or, to put it another way: he had always been Peter Parker's enemy. Only magical, marvelous fate, many years later, had also made him Spider-Man's.

And now they were about to meet.

Ah, Peter, Peter, Peter. If you truly had any clue what I have in store for your greatest enemies, you might not try so hard to stop me. You might just let it happen, if only to see the betrayed expressions on their faces.

He sipped his cognac. Let it warm his belly, as the next thought warmed his heart.

Of course, by then, you'll probably be as dead as your mother and father.

CHAPTER FIVE

The next day, as it happened, there were absolutely no developments involving the Sinister Six.

Super hero life could be messy that way, sometimes. Menace B didn't always wait until you were finished with Menace A; sometimes you were all geared up to fight one bunch of sociopaths and it turned out you had to deal with another bunch of sociopaths first.

In this particular case, Spider-Man had to contend with a hairy situation on Fifth Avenue, involving not one but three villains of the undearingly lame variety, all of whom attempted to rob a Swiss currency exchange of its francs, marks, and guilders. One was the skateboard-riding miscreant known as the Rocket Racer, whose speed and agility might have been formidable if he wasn't so easy to knock off his chosen form of transportation; another was a recently recurring nuisance known as the Candy Man, who today came armed with a peppermint-stick bazooka; and a third was a long-inactive guy called the Black Hole, who might have been blessed with the ability to make things disappear but who was so incompetent that he had once been defeated by the girlfriend of a little humanoid duck. In terms of general concept, aesthetic sensibility, and all-around cluelessless, these three made perfect partners for each other. Spider-Man took them out so quickly that a witness with a camcorder later won grand prize on *America's Funniest Home Videos.*

Later, Peter Parker was able to meet Mary Jane for dinner, and actually finish the meal at his leisure without an unexpected crisis requiring a sudden change to Spider-Man. They got to go listen to some fine jazz in the Village, and made it home in time for a nice, quiet, romantic evening before the fire. If he spent some of the wee hours after Mary Jane fell asleep making a quick rooftop-level circuit of Manhattan hoping for the telltale spider-sense buzz that might alert him to the whereabouts of the Six, it was still, pretty much, a good day.

Which was a good thing. Because the next day would be not quite as good.

And the day after that would be even worse . . .

Early afternoon.

The *Daily Bugle* took a lot of abuse, even for a newspaper. Forget the inevitable libel suits from politicians horrified at being quoted accurately; forget the angry letters to the editor from readers who thought it was too liberal or too right-wing or too controversial or too soft on the issues or too hard on certain friendly neighborhood super heroes; forget America's tendency to demonize the press for the bad news it delivers; forget the occasional attacks made on its reporters and editorial staff, both on and off the job, by people like Tombstone and Carnage and the Scorpion and the Green Goblin and Jack O'Lantern and Mr. Hyde; forget even the fallout of more exotic disasters like the plague of demons sent by the Norse fire-giant Surtur. Forget all that ... and consider just the daily torrents of multi-directional abuse that emanate from the mouth of its perpetually aggravated publisher.

Peter Parker had it on good authority, from colleagues who worked in the city room all day, that J. Jonah Jameson was not actually yelling every moment from his arrival first thing in the morning to his departure sometime after the first copies of the next day's edition rolled off the presses early each evening. *Be serious*, they said. *If he yelled that way all day long, how would anybody get any work done? It's just your luck, that's all. For some reason, you always walk in just as he's starting to rant. Trust us: you just see him at his worst, that's all.*

Intellectually, Peter knew this had to be true. He even knew it in his heart. Despite all the intense aggravation he and his wall-crawling alter ego had taken from Jonah over the years, he'd seen the man's human side just often enough to confirm to his own satisfaction that it did, in fact, exist. Certainly anybody capable of earning the loyalty of Editor-In-Chief Joe Robertson—who was, in Peter's opinion, to newspapermen what Captain America was to super heroes—had to have something going for him. But working at the *Bugle* still meant dealing with a whole lot of yelling.

As Peter ambled through the double doors to tenth-floor city room, he waved to various people he knew: the embittered advice columnist Auntie Esther, who was both chain-smoking and sneering with her trademark existential nausea as she picked up the day's mail from readers who needed her to help run their lives; his old friend Betty Brant, who sat at her desk tapping a coffee cup with a pencil as she whispered urgently into a phone ("No, Flash. Not now, Flash. I'm at work, Flash. No, I don't have the time for this, Flash."); the rhyming but otherwise unrelated Glory Grant, who ran past him shouting a quick *Hi-Pete-How're-You-Doing-Pete* as she carried a thick stack of papers out the double doors to the elevators. Although Jolly Jonah's voice was clearly audible— yelling incessantly from one of the offices on the far side of the city room—the man himself was blessedly not visible. Neither was Joe Robertson, who was obliged to spend so much time witnessing Jonah's insane tirades that it was sometimes a wonder the paper ever got printed at all.

Peter scanned the faces and saw the one he'd come to see.

Ben Urich was a thin sandy-haired man in his mid-forties, who was absolutely nobody's nomination for Mr. Physical Fitness. He smoked incessantly, coughed whenever he was between cigarettes, wore suits that hung limply on his underweight frame, and seemed to live on takeout coffee and hot dogs scarfed down in a hurry whenever he was on his way to another interview. Though he seemed to have an inexhaustible supply of energy, when it came to ferreting out the facts for one of his stories, the weariness and cynicism born of the various things he'd discovered had etched deep lines in his face, making him look easily ten years older than he was; it was all too easy to mistake him for a case of incipient burnout. In fact, he was something else entirely: the single best reporter Peter had ever known. Among those in the know, Urich was widely believed to be able to find out anything—and, more than that, to have personally buried more than one story he personally believed better off untold.

Ben Urich would probably never be rich, or for that matter famous. At least not to the *Bugle*'s readers, who usually failed to register his byline. But in the corridors of municipal power, and in the oak-paneled offices of the corporations, and in the back rooms of organized crime—wherever the system strained at the edges, and the venal and corrupt sat like ticks growing fat on the life blood of the people—he was watched with a respect that sometimes bordered on fear. He'd had his hand broken, his home invaded, and his wife attacked — but he'd always come back, sometimes with graphs capable of shaking empires.

It was a measure of Urich's worth that the *Bugle* actually indulged his aversion to computer keyboards and allowed him to type his stories on paper, using an old manual Olivetti he'd reportedly won in a bet from a similarly cyber-phobic science fiction writer in Sherman Oaks, California. As Peter approached, Urich was busily tapping away at his latest, leaning so close to the typewriter that he peppered the story itself with ash from his Camel. Without looking up or missing a keystroke, he said: "Peter."

"Ben." Peter winced as a fresh wave of Jamesonian invective, audible but too distorted for comprehension by its journey across the clattering keyboards and other ambient sounds of the city room, echoed past himself and Ben as attractively as a bad rumor. He said: "What's our peerless publisher so peeved at today?"

Urich puffed a cloud at the last graphs of his story. "The *Globe* beat us to a story about a certain alderman who's been caught taking kickbacks on new housing starts."

"That's the reason for the tantrum?"

"It's today's reason," Urich said. He puffed a second cloud to join the first: "You know Jonah: he needs his anger."

Peter smiled. "I notice I've never seen him angry at you."

A darkness passed over Urich's haggard features. "Well, in my case, he found something that intimidates me more than his anger."

"Oh, really? What?"

"His disappointment." Urich rubbed his right wrist, and

winced, clearly experiencing a phantom pain from long ago. He did not elaborate, though—merely rolled his chair over to a battered personal filing cabinet beside his desk. As he unlocked the bottom drawer with a key, he said: "You're in luck. In most cases, the federal government being the bureaucratic octopus we all know and loathe, a request of this kind would have taken weeks to process. But after you called me the other night, I spent part of yesterday morning calling in some favors with an old source at the National Security Council. He pulled some strings and overnighted the files you were looking for." He opened the drawer and removed a pair of thick manila folders bound by rubber bands, which he immediately handed to Peter. "From what little I saw, just collating, they seem fairly complete."

Peter stared dumbfounded at the thickness of the stack Urich had just given him. "Holy Hannah. Ben—you're a miracle worker."

"Not really." Urich peered at him curiously. "After all, aside from expediting the request, I didn't do anything you couldn't have done."

"But—"

"Come on. Peter. Do you really mean to tell me that an accomplished photojournalist with your knack for getting the impossible shot needed my help in basic reporting technique? Haven't you ever heard of the Freedom of Information Act?"

Peter's cheeks burned. *Actually, Ben, the reason I get so many impossible shots is that I'm usually part of the story myself. Most of my rep comes from Spider-Man shots, and those are all self-portraits shot with automatic timers. If it wasn't for that, my "accomplishments" would be mediocre at best. Of course, if it wasn't for that, I'd have probably gotten my doctorate and been a biophysicist by now . . . so there are disadvantages too.* He made light of it: "Aw, I've never been any good at that bureaucratic stuff, Ben. You know that."

"Uh huh." Urich stubbed out his cigarette and immediately looked regretful, like a man who'd just had to put the beloved family dog to sleep. He turned back to the typewriter and said: "Meanwhile, I have five minutes to finish this puff piece before I need to run out the door to make a genuinely important interview I've been trying to set up for three weeks."

"I'll let you get to that," Peter said. "And Ben—thanks."

Urich granted him a dismissive wave as he plunged back into his story. Peter couldn't help but feel relief; if his suspicions ever got genuinely aroused, a guy like Urich stood a good shot of actually uncovering the face behind the spider-mask.

Shuddering, Peter walked past Betty Brant (who was still on the phone, exasperatedly telling good old Flash that she didn't have time for him now), and made his way to a row of unoccupied desks adjacent to the locked office supplies closet. They were reserved for the use of "floaters"—i.e. freelancers and stringers and new employees who had not yet merited a space of their own, but nevertheless occasionally needed a place to complete the work they did in-house. Despite his many years at the *Bugle*, Peter's freelancer status still placed him in this category. He sat down at the floater desk next to one currently occupied by one of the newer employees, Billy Walters, an affable kid with long brown hair and a goatee, who possessed smarts not easy to discern behind his excessive enthusiasm and the kind of personality that expressed itself by calling everybody *dude*.

Whatever Billy was working on had his full attention; he limited his usual chatty hello to a quick "Hey, dude!" without a pause in his typing.

"Hey dude, yourself!" Peter said. "Jameson got you working on anything interesting?"

"No dull stories, man. Just . . ."

". . . dull reporters," Peter finished. It had been the Jameson rant of the day two weeks ago.

Billy grinned. "I hope it's not true, man . . . because this is about a tenant's rights meeting in the Village, and from what I can tell so far, I must be a really boring guy, cause I can't make this story sing to save my life. Listen, can we shelve the talk 'til later? I gotta boogie on this."

"Sure thing, bud." Peter, secretly relieved—he liked Billy, but didn't have the time for him right now—plopped his folders down on the desk, abandoned them just long enough to get himself a cup of the *Bugle*'s notoriously awful coffee, and sat down to read.

He soon discovered that one of the files was dedicated to his mother and one to his father, although their married status did result in a fair degree of redundancy. He was surprised by how much data there was, and supposed that the exhaustiveness of the data had a lot to do with the background checks they must have undergone to qualify for their jobs as intelligence agents. There were birth certificates, records of the various public schools they'd attended as children, high school and college transcripts—even a term paper his father had done as an ivy league sophomore majoring in political science. Both his parents had enjoyed exemplary scholastic records, ending most of their semesters on the Dean's List. His father had served with honors in the special forces, his mother (then Mary Fitzpatrick) had traveled extensively in Europe before getting her security clearance and settling down in Washington as a translator and data analyst for the Central Intelligence Agency. There were photocopies of both passports, none of which recorded trips to anywhere more exotic than London or Paris.

The first genuinely interesting item was a set of transfer papers drafting Richard Parker into the agency that would someday become S.H.I.E.L.D.—said papers signed by none other than Colonel Nick Fury himself. There was also a CIA employee evaluation praising his mother's work and recommending her for transfer to same multi-national espionage agency. Peter felt a chill as he imagined their first meeting. He wondered if they liked each other right away, if they met cute, or if it took them a while to sense the brewing chemistry; it was a shame the dry facts were capable of recording such things.

He shook his head and continued filing through the papers, finding his mother's promotion to field work, finding his father's transfer to an liaison office in Rome, his mother's several travel vouchers for trips there. He found their wedding announcement, and even one blurry second-generation copy of a group shot that included not only his mother and father in full bride-and-groom regalia but also the ebullient forms of Peter's Uncle Ben and Aunt May. Even in those shots, his aunt and uncle looked startlingly old next to the couple of the hour—younger than Peter usually thought of them, but still well into their fifties. Ben Parker had been almost a quarter-century older than his kid brother Richard, who must have been a change-of-life baby...thus leading to the odd phenomenon of one brother edging toward retirement while another was just beginning to rise in his chosen career. Alas, neither was fated for a natural death.

Peter ignored the lump that threatened to rise in his throat and pushed on.

After a few more minutes, he found part of what he was

looking for, in a subsection originally stamped A-1 Clearance but later marked Declassified. Detailing his parents' activities starting from a point about one year after they were married, it documented some sixteen months they'd lived in a boarding house in Prague. Photostats of the passports they were using at the time revealed that they were living as resident aliens under the names of Felix and Lisa Mendelsohn. There were other documents, including bank statements and drivers' licenses and stamped visas, that also provided the Mendelsohn identities. Peter could not help noticing that the period coincided with the recently discovered dated photographs of his mother, imminently pregnant before an eastern-European cityscape.

Peter's heart was already pounding.

Even so, he was, emotionally, totally unprepared for the photostat of a birth certificate.

The little girl had been born at 4:23 A.M. on a cold winter morning, weighing in at 7 pounds 3 ounces. She'd had blue eyes and blonde hair—both of which told him nothing, as both could have darkened over time—and she'd been given the name Carla May Mendelsohn. (The middle name, an apparent tribute to his Aunt, made Peter close his eyes.) A change-of-address form dated three months later, and an apartment lease shortly after that, documented the Mendelsohn family's subsequent relocation to Paris, France.

When the Parkers returned to the United States a year later, the baby girl was no longer with them. There was no record of what had happened to her. No death certificate, no adoption papers, nothing.

Peter stopped reading long enough to reflect on what he'd found so far. He'd always harbored unresolved feelings about his parents. He loved them, of course—but only because he was supposed to; the fact of the matter was that he barely remembered them. Even as a toddler, he'd known them only as a kind, playful couple who disappeared for months at a time, leaving him in the able hands of Uncle Ben and Aunt May. He'd understood that they were his Mom and Dad, and had even loved them as his Mom and Dad, but had known them as people who were gone more often than they were around. They'd disappeared for good long time before he was old enough to understand why.

Uncle Ben and Aunt May had been the best substitute parents any child could have hoped for. They'd given him a home and made sure he knew he was loved. But every once in a while, musing about his real mother and father, Peter sometimes found himself resenting a virtual abandonment that had begun long before they died.

The revelation that he'd probably had an older sister—and, more than that, that she'd been born while his parents were living undercover—put an entirely new spin on that resentment. Peter didn't even need to know the details to concede that their business in Prague and Paris, whatever it may have been, must have been important to national security. So important that she didn't even come out of deep cover to have her baby? So important that they even incorporated their firstborn in the lie their life had become? So important that the little girl entered the world with a false name and a false past and no future beyond the lie she was too young and innocent to understand?

It was horrifying. Peter knew espionage was a filthy business . . . and that his parents had been hip-deep in it . . . but he had never before allowed himself to implicate them in the darker side of their craft.

There were other issues, too. The little girl named Carla May Mendelsohn had gone with her parents to Paris but had not returned with them to the States. What had happened to her? Had she been caught in the crossfire of her parents' deadly occupation? Had she disappeared or died? Was whatever led to her absence on the plane flight home the reason Richard and Mary Parker so carefully kept their second child, Peter, so completely segregated from their professional activities? Had they learned that their lives as secret agents made them absolutely the wrong people to be a daily presence in the life of their children?

The mere thought was enough to make Peter sick.

Is that the kind of people you were? So caught up in the cloak and dagger thing that you first endangered your daughter and then abandoned your son?

If that's so, Peter thought, *I wasted my love on you.*

Please, don't let that be true.

He ran his hand over Carla May's birth certificate, and thought: *As for you . . . my sister . . . if that's what you are . . . I don't know you. I don't know whether you're alive or dead. But I will find you, either way. I will find out what happened to you . . . and I will not abandon your memory.*

I will not . . .

He blinked.

His spider-sense had kicked in.

It was a minor buzz, of the intensity reserved for potential dangers rather than immediate ones. But it was still enough to get his attention. He immediately looked up from the folders and searched the room for the source.

He saw it immediately.

There was a tall, thin, well-dressed old man—Peter estimated eighty or ninety years old—standing at the back of the city room, just inside the sliding doors. He wore an expensive camelhair coat and carried an elegant silver-tipped walking stick, and though he stood stock-still, staring at Peter, amidst the usual chaos that defined the city room on any working day, he somehow remained totally unnoticed by anybody. His smile, meant for Peter's eyes alone, was cruel, arrogant, and knowing, in a manner that gave even Peter—who'd looked evil in the eye a thousand times before—chills down his spine.

It took Peter almost a full second to place him as the same old man who had engaged his spider-sense about a week ago. Spider-Man had been fighting Mysterio in a Broadway theatre during a production of the hit musical *Submarine!* The old man had been sitting in private box seats, watching the panic below with absolute aplomb. He'd been smiling the same way then.

Spider-Man had been too busy trying to save the audience from Mysterio's terrorism to follow up his vaguely sinister impressions of an unknown old man. Until this moment, Peter had forgotten all about him.

But now . . .

Peter stood and faced him.

They faced each other from opposite ends of the city room. There were any number of people between them, working on their various stories—and Jonah, bless him, was still audible somewhere on this floor, ranting at great length about all the people who insisted on continuing to take advantage of his generosity—but at this one moment, without knowing it, they had all been reduced to a distant irrelevancy. There was nothing important in the room except for the young man with the secret life and the old man with the malevolent smile.

Peter took a single step toward the aged stranger, expecting him to run away. The old man stood his ground. Peter moved faster, passing between the cubicles, keeping the old man in sight, unwilling to look away lest the old man disappear the moment of Peter's first wayward glance.

Unfortunately, the urgency must have shown on his face, because even as he passed Betty Brant, she saw at once that something was wrong. She clasped a hand against the receiver of her phone and said: "Peter! What's wrong?"

It should not have stopped him. Not by itself.

But from the way his spider-sense was tingling, the danger was not potential anymore. It was immediate. And it was not just coming from the old man anymore: it was all around them, coming from somewhere outside the building.

The old man nodded, tipped his hat, and walked out the swinging doors.

"Peter!" Betty said. "Can you hear me! What's wrong?"

Peter's spider-sense flared. The danger was approaching fast. And it was now coming from a single direction: namely, from somewhere outside the building face, just beyond Jolly Jonah's office...

"Peter?" Betty said.

It was too late to change to his costume. Whatever this was, it was going down now.

Peter said, "Something—"

And then all hell broke loose.

The first sound was Jameson yelling. It was an entirely different sound from his previous yelling—that had been Jameson in his element, this was Jameson in mortal terror. The transition lasted only a fraction of a second, but everybody in the city room perceived it at once, even before it was drowned out by the sounds of breaking glass and smashing furniture. For another heartbeat it was impossible to see what was going on through the drawn blinds of Jameson's office door. Then the wall exploded outward in a cloud of dust and splintered wood and shattered glass. The door flew off its hinges, and debris pelted the city room, cratering walls, smashing computer screens, sending most of the reporters and other employees diving for cover behind their desks.

A white-shirted, charcoal-gray-panted missile flew out of the blast zone with a velocity that carried it most of the way across the city room. Most of the *Bugle* employees present had time to recognize the object hurtling through the air as a human being. Some might have recognized that human being as the spindly, irascible J. Jonah Jameson himself. Only one could have reacted quickly enough to realize that Jameson had been thrown too hard, too fast, to survive his impact with the first solid object in his way.

Fortunately, by the time Jameson started to lose altitude, something else was in his path.

Namely, Peter Parker.

Intercepting Jameson was the easy part; as Spider-Man, Peter had caught much faster-moving objects. Intercepting Jameson in a manner Jameson could survive, without giving up his own identity as Spider-Man, was considerably more difficult. Peter managed it by absorbing the impact, allowing it to knock him off his feet, pretending absolutely no control at all as he allowed the force to carry himself and Jameson backward over one of the desks. They landed together on a desk blotter, Peter deliberately taking most of the impact with the small of his back. The desk blotter slid across the smooth metal surface like a sled moving across ice. Clutching Jameson tightly—in a manner meant to grant Jameson the impression of a terrified reflex—Peter pressed his other hand against the desktop, and used his adhesive grip to slow their shared momentum by more than two-thirds. Then he let go and, still gripping Jameson, tumbled over the edge of the desk, making sure that Jameson landed on top of him.

The impact knocked the breath out of J. Jonah Jameson.

It barely stung Peter Parker, who had to force himself to gasp in simulated pain. "Jonah? You all right?"

Jonah said: "Gaaaaaahhhh." Which was all right, since that was a word he said often even on his best days.

All over the newsroom, people were screaming in realization.

Betty, who was closest, yelled: "Peter! Mr. Jameson!"

Billy Walters cried out: "What the hell was that? An explosion?"

Auntie Esther shouted something unprintable.

"We're . . . okay!" Peter gasped, forcing the ragged, breathless quality in his voice. "What's happening?"

Over by Jameson's office, something smashed to pieces, prompting another chorus of gasps and screams. Peter struggled out from under Jameson—holding himself back just enough to make it look like he was struggling with the old man's weight, when the truth was that he could have thrown Jameson just as hard—then lurched to his feet, to confront the sight that had his spider-sense screaming like a siren in his head.

The Sinister Six.

They were here.

Doctor Octopus, grinning maliciously as his adamantium tentacles carried him past the wreckage of Jameson's office.

The Vulture, cold and predatory in his armored green bird costume, his wings keeping him aloft like a raptor riding a high-altitude updraft.

Electro, who had once worn a mask but no longer felt the need, scowling furiously as he marched in behind the others, his eyes flashing brilliant bursts of light to indicate all the lightning at bay within him.

The Chameleon, wearing street clothes and inexpressive

white mask, nevertheless managing to grin as he stepped over the shattered doorframe.

Mysterio, shrouded by smoke, chuckling softly to himself, whipping his long billowing green cape like a hellish curtain.

And one other.

At first glance, Peter thought she was a kid. She was certainly small enough: thin, girlish, only a hair over five feet tall, dressed in a loose-fitting all-white costume with a sash at her waist. It was only as she stepped forward, away from the shrouding effect of Mysterio's smoke, that Peter was able to see that she was considerably older than he'd first believed: from her features, she must have been in her mid-to-late twenties. Even so, there was nothing at all obviously threatening about her. Her sleeves were puffy and diaphanous, her hair, a modest black bob, her expression, pained and wan and regretful. Even the vertical scars on both cheeks failed to make her look menacing, instead imparting an almost pathetic vulnerability. The only reason Peter could accept her as a member of the Six is that she happened to be standing with them; otherwise, she seemed absurdly innocuous. So much so that he found himself, against his better judgement, genuinely sorry for her.

As Peter surveyed the city room to see if everybody else was okay, he saw that most of the people here seemed to have immediately put together the same impression. Shocked as they were, terrified as they were, none of them could reconcile this young woman and the monsters she associated with. The very thought was instinctively repellent.

The young lady aside, the various members of the Sinister Six all looked exceedingly comfortable with their surroundings. And why not? They'd all been here before, some of them several times. At various times, over the years, Electro had tried to extort millions from the paper; Mysterio had used Jameson's legendary knack for backing the wrong horse to promote himself as a hero; and Octavius had attempted to poison a third of New York by slipping a deadly nerve toxin into the printer's ink. Peter would have been tempted to consider this string of persecution a major factor in Jolly Jonah's less-than-sterling disposition, but he'd known Jameson before any of this became a common occurrence, and the guy had always possessed a serious attitude problem. Still, that was no reason to just go attacking the man. As Peter helped Jameson up, he whispered, "You okay, Jonah?"

"Guhguh," Jameson said. He was not usually very good in crisis situations. Which was okay. If he could say *guhguh*, he'd recover.

The dust was settling now, allowing Peter and the others their first good look at the pile of wreckage that had been Jameson's office. The outer wall had been completely ripped away, leaving the room open to the cold winter air. Typical super-villain behavior, especially for the Sinister Six: they had about as much respect for walls as they had for laws. Or each other, for that matter. They were monsters. They made their own doors.

Doctor Octopus grinned nastily as he moved past trainee reporter Billy Walters, who was wide-eyed and aghast but trying very hard not to show fear, and chain-smoking city editor Kathryn Cushing, who was not so much terrified as irritated. Ben Urich, on the other hand, was pressed against the wall so hard he might have eventually succeeded in becoming part of it; Ben had tremendous courage on paper, but didn't deal well with physical danger in person.

And Betty Brant looked outraged . . . not flinching even as Dr. Octopus paused before her to run one of his tentacles over her cheek.

"Ms. Brant," he nodded. "It has been far too long since last we met. You were, I must admit, one of the most cooperative people I ever took hostage."

Betty practically spat the words. "I was a frightened teenage girl, Octavius. Did that make you feel strong and powerful?"

"Actually, yes. How considerate of you to ask." His eyes flickered across the crowd, and focused on Peter, who immediately tensed, prepared to defend himself if necessary. But Octopus was not interested in attacking him: "Ah. The illustrious Mr. Parker, who so gallantly—and foolishly—tried to play hero that day. I heard about your dear Aunt's death, my boy. I know this comes rather late, and may seem less than apropos under the circumstances, but please accept my sympathies. She was a kind and gentle woman, and one who was always rather . . . precious to me."

Peter remembered another day, many years earlier, when he'd burst into a church to discover Otto Octavius and May Parker about to be declared man and wife. It was not one of his fuzzier memories. "Keep your condolences, Doctor. She never knew you. She never understood the kind of man you are. If she was ever kind to you, it was because you fooled her."

Octavius raised an eyebrow. "And is that what you tell yourself, that lets you remember her as a paragon of virtue? That she was deaf and blind and stupid and incapable of following current events? How do you know she wasn't bored and stifled as an elderly suburban matron? How do you know she didn't know exactly what I am? That she didn't find something devilishly attractive about my outlaw status?"

"Why, you—"

Somebody placed a restraining hand on Peter's shoulder. Peter could have shrugged off that grip in an instant, with a strength capable of shattering every bone in that hand; but the second he recognized the touch as Joe Robertson's, Peter backed down. Robbie's level-headedness was, as always, contagious. Whether he knew Peter was Spider-Man or not, he was still right. This was not the time or place.

Backing down, averting his eyes, Peter thought: *But I owe you one, Octavius. That's a promise.*

Behind Octopus, Electro rolled his eyes and shot off some sparks. "And now that we got the Springer show out of the way, Doc, can we just get on with the reason we came here in the first place?"

Irritation flashed in the Doctor's eyes; the kind of irritation that, in his case, could have conceivably led to murder as a punishment for effrontery. After a moment, it faded. "I suppose you're correct, Max. Tempting as it might be, this is not the time or place for catching up with old friends. Ladies and gentlemen of the Press, the various esteemed members of the Sinister Six have gathered together today to announce the latest Chapter of our righteous war against the vigilante known as Spider-Man." He smacked his lips. "We are declaring tomorrow . . . a city-wide commemorative Day of Terror."

The buzz was immediate, even over the gasps and the tears and the pervasive atmosphere of fear. After all, the *Daily Bugle* was still a newspaper, in the business of reporting news . . . and everybody in the room knew an exclusive when they heard it.

If that seemed an awfully cold reaction, it wasn't. Not really. After all, their shared relief had a lot to do with it. Because if the Sinister Six wanted the *Bugle* to get out the word, then they probably weren't here to kill everybody in the building.

Billy Walters asked the obvious question: "Day of Terror?"

Mysterio glided through the air on a platform of smoke. "You heard him right, young man. Consider it . . . an exercise in corrective PR."

"For years," Octopus snarled, "the wall-crawling freak has taken inordinate pride in saving the lives of innocents. He has even earned a reputation (despite the heroic corrective efforts of this newspaper), as one of the best in that pathetically self-aggrandizing field. But my friends and I know both claims to be exaggerated. Specifically, we know that there have been any number of cases where the arachnid tried to preserve life, and failed; cases where, despite all his obvious physical advantages, he was still not strong enough, or fast enough, or smart enough, to prevail; cases where death still claimed those unlucky enough to be under his incompetent protection. And it is our contention that those cases have not received nearly as much attention as they deserve."

"Yeah, that's right, people!" Electro laughed nastily. "It's time for an editorial reply!"

Octopus grimaced at that, clearly unhappy about any contribution that stole the spotlight from himself. "Which is why we have decided to devote all day tomorrow to commemorating the deaths that occurred on Spider-Man's watch. We shall visit just a few of the sites where blood was spilled because he bumbled the job—and we shall, between us, make it our business to increase the casualty list a hundredfold." He paused to let that figure sink in. "Of course, being men of honor—"

Electro, appearing stricken, cleared his throat at that.

Octopus grimaced, then glanced at Pity—who looked away, as if unable to take his gaze. After a moment, Octopus acknowledged the legitimacy of Electro's point with a nod. "Excuse me, Max. Once again, you are correct. Men and women of honor. Being men and women of honor, we will play fair. At each site, Spider-Man will have a reasonable chance to stop us. But at each site, if he fails, the streets will run crimson with the blood of the slaughtered."

"And he is going to fail," the Chameleon said, in the voice of the well-known shock jock he had become just for this moment. "Fail, as even he has never failed before."

"By this time tomorrow," the Vulture put in, with the unholy glee of a man who took pleasure in little except his own maliciousness, "the City of New York will be able to fill a cemetery with more of Spider-Man's failures."

"It shall begin with the first," Doctor Octopus said. "And it shall end . . . where it began." He scanned the crowd, sought out the still-recovering Jameson, and smiled. "You should be proud, fool. After all . . . it was your headlines that gave us the idea."

Several of them laughed, then—the only exceptions being the Vulture, who probably never laughed at anything, and the young lady in white, who still hadn't made a sound. The shared laughter was loud, and insane, and totally lacking in mirth. It went on so long that Peter Parker, whose heart was already raging at the thought of all the people who were about to be endangered in his name, wanted to scream; it went on even as they all turned to leave through the great gaping crater they'd made in the wall of what had once been Jameson's office. The Vulture flew away first, carrying the Chameleon; then Mysterio floated away on a pillar of smoke, and Electro rocketed after him on a crashing wave of lightning. The young lady seemed prepared to just leap out the window, much as Spider-Man himself would have done. Doctor Octopus lingered behind them for a second or two, as if considering whether there was anything else he wanted to say; then, he, turned to leave, his long sinuous adamantium tentacles bearing him as carefully as a new mother carries her beloved firstborn.

Nobody wanted to say anything. Nobody wanted to make a sound. They were all too aware that they'd survived this long, and that in a matter of seconds the nightmare would be over.

Everybody, that is, except for Billy Walters, who shouted: "Hey! Wait! Doc! Come back!"

In the silence, the main shared thought among everybody in the room was disbelief that anybody could be so incredibly stupid. Another two seconds and the monsters would have been gone: what possible profit in calling them back?

Octopus, who seemed equally baffled, turned with extreme deliberateness. "Young man, I do hope, for your sake, that this is not an attempt to appeal to my sense of morality. I do not take well to people who waste my time."

"No, man! I'm not crazy! I just wanted to say—for the story, y'know—you forgot to introduce your new member! We all recognized the rest of you—but who's she?"

The pause that followed was long enough for the shifting of continents. Nobody wanted to see what happened next; they were all sure that Walters was about to torn to bloody gobbets, and they wanted to remain silent enough to avoid being next.

Peter, tensing for action in case he had to leap to Billy's aid, couldn't help noticing that the young lady herself, who had not yet followed her other teammates out the window, was one of the several people who averted their eyes. Why? Shyness? Shame?

And when it was done, Octopus actually smiled. "Congratulations, young man. Of all these timid, frightened sheep, you were the only one who retained the instincts of your chosen profession. Whatever pittance Jameson is paying you, he ought to double it. Her name, for your information, is Pity. P-I-T-Y, like the emotion." He turned to go, but, being the man he was, could not resist one more remark as he left: "Though I assure you that when it comes to supporting us in this grand endeavor, she will show no pity at all."

CHAPTER SIX

Up the stairs.

Forget about your friends and co-workers, consoling each other in the wake of their brush with madness.

Forget about the hugs, the assurances that everything was going to be all right, the first aid for those injured when the wall exploded into the city room. Forget about Joe Robertson calling 911 and a rapidly-recovering Jameson already slanting the story to display his own courage in the face of evil. Forget about making excuses for your own hurry to get the hell out of there. Just pick the one moment when nobody happens to be looking directly at you—and disappear.

Out the door. Down the hall. Into the stairwell.

Up.

Ripping off your shirt, tearing off your shoes, kicking off your pants, revealing the red and blue costume underneath. Pulling on the hood. Clicking the web-shooters into place, inserting fresh cartridges so you'll have plenty of web-fluid to chase the monsters all over the city if necessary. Knowing that however much you have probably won't be enough. Doing all of this as you leap a zigzag path from one wall to another, cursing the concrete and metal staircase that keeps you from running the entire distance in a straight line, feeling yourself slowed down even as you take the eight flights faster than any human being has a right to take them.

Up.

Aware, even as you go, that you're about to face at least five—and, though you can't say for sure because you don't yet know the woman's capabilities, almost certainly six—of the deadliest people on the face of the planet.

And not frightened because you might get killed.

Frightened because they have the power to keep their promises. . .

Spider-Man burst through the door to the roof, wincing as the first thing to greet him was not an enraged super-villain but a blast of freezing winter air. It cut through the thicker material of his winter costume so quickly that he might as well have been wearing nothing at all—a feeling that experience told him would go away as soon as he had to devote all his energies to fighting super-powered maniacs at rooftop level. That sort of thing tended to keep a body warm.

It seemed quiet enough, for the moment. The wind was light, the horns and other traffic noises filtering up from street level were no more than background noise, and the hum of the air intakes was so soft it was almost subliminal. As always, when Spider-Man left the building via this route, the corporate logo at the roof's edge glared back at him in reversed lettering four feet tall—E L G U B Y L I A D. In lighter moments, he'd reflected that this phrase was a perfect summation of his life since the spider-bite: an Elgub Iliad. Nonsensically Epic. Now, with who-knew-how-many innocent people endangered just because some super-powered reprobates wanted to pick a fight, he was in no mood for such whimsies. He just wanted to find them.

Then his spider-sense screamed at him, and he knew they'd found him.

He whirled, and saw a familiar green figure swooping down from above. It was the Vulture, his wings spread wide, grinning as he dove toward the wall-crawler with the speed of a runaway train. The worst thing about his smile was not its maliciousness, but its ugliness: Toomes still had most of his teeth, and actually deserved sympathy for that; they were stubby and irregularly spaced and less like teeth than standing gravestones. The wall-crawler had often wondered if the Vulture's mad-on for the world would have been alleviated by a good dentist. The thought was always banished by a good look at the Vulture's eyes. This guy didn't need excuses. Hostility just came naturally to him.

Spider-Man ducked as the Vulture went for him, barely avoiding the razor-sharp steel tips of the old man's wings; he knew from experience that they were honed to cut flesh, and could probably cut him in half if allowed to strike at a sufficiently lethal angle. He managed to throw a punch at the Vulture's stomach at that instant. The punch connected, but not solidly, and the Vulture flew off not visibly shaken by the experience.

Spider-Man would have gone after him, but another spasm of painful tingling at the back of his neck forced him to leap ten feet to his right. A cornice-stone heavy enough to have crushed his skull shattered to pieces on the spot where he had stood. He caught a glimpse of Dr. Octopus, using his tentacles to race along the edge of the roof at a speed that would have been respectable for highway driving. The Doctor glided twenty feet above the concrete, totally unconcerned with the height as his tentacles carried him along with a cold mechanical grace. Mysterio, bobbing in mid-air behind the Doctor, his cape flapping majestically, his helmet amplifiers broadcasting his usual crazed maniacal laughter—which Spider-Man had often suspected he played from a tape loop—tossed a handful of concussion grenades; a line of them went off in sequence, creating a barrier of flame and smoke that for an instant shielded both Octopus and himself from view.

Oddly, neither one of them pressed the attack.

The hair prickled on the base of Spider-Man's neck. His spider-sense flared, and he leaped away just as a bolt of lightning fused the place where he'd been. He somersaulted, flipped, spotted Electro hovering just above him on a crackling arc of sheer energy. Not having any better ideas, Spider-Man shot a webline at Electro's face. It never even touched the man; Electro's eyes flared like neon, and the energies at play all around him boiled off the approaching webline before it even got close.

Then Electro smiled, and arcs of crackling power flashed between his teeth.

"Not yet, webhead. Check with your friends at the *Bugle*. We've already set the time and place."

"No reason to wait, sparky! Not as long as you caught me free!" Spider-Man leaped at Electro, hoping for some way to knock Dillon out without frying himself in the bargain.

But Electro, who'd become a lot faster since his latest power-up, zipped away faster than even Spider-Man could move. "You heard me, you wall-crawling freak! There'll be plenty of time to kill you tomorrow! Besides, somebody else has claimed first licks!"

Spider-Man spun in mid-air, and landed on his feet in time to see that the various members of the Sinister Six were serious about not wanting to fight today. The streak of light that Electro had become was already a speck, zig-zagging uptown at skyscraper height; Mysterio was ascending on a pillar of smoke, to lose himself in the clouds; The Vulture was maintaining a westward course high above rooftop level, and Doctor Octopus, carried by his amazing adamantium arms, was skittering across the glass face of an office building two blocks away, moving east at his greatest possible speed. Spider-Man didn't see the Chameleon or this Pity woman anywhere, but the picture was already crystal clear. They had split up so there was no way Spider-Man could go after one without letting the other five go.

For a moment, so brief that most observers would have been hard-pressed to recognize any hesitation at all, he wavered. After all, they were all ruthless killers; even if he could defeat and capture one of them, that still left all the others free to spread their personal brand of terror. Which one took priority? Who should he go after?

He almost decided on Electro, who was clearly the most dangerous in terms of raw power; after his last upgrade, the guy could blow up a whole city block just by pointing at it. It was even the kind of thing he was likely to do.

But even being able to blow up a city block was a far cry from being willing to blow up the world. And possessing both the genius and the madness to make it happen. Dr. Octopus had demonstrated both many times.

Spider-Man whirled toward the east, already prepared for the battle of his life.

He was not prepared for the sudden wave of all-concealing darkness that passed over the rooftop like a shroud. Or the tingle on the back of his neck that warned him he was about to be attacked. Or the pain as something slammed heavily into the side of his face.

The blow would have been strong enough to break his neck if his spider-sense hadn't given him the chance to roll with the blow. Still surrounded by darkness, wondering just which idiot had turned off the lights, he spun, somersaulted, landed on his feet, and—sensing another attack headed directly at him—leaped forty feet straight up, hoping to carry himself out of the zone of darkness.

It was only at the apex of his leap that he suddenly found himself emerging into the late afternoon light again. The *Bugle* roof, far below him, had become a field of blackness as dense as an oil slick. He focused his spider-sense as hard as he could and located a specific nexus of the danger moving beneath that shroud as invisibly as a shark prowling inky-black Pacific waters.

It was a nexus about the size of a human being.

By process of elimination: the woman.

They'd called her Pity.

He reached the top of his leap and fell, descending once again into the darkness.

His spider-sense flared, warning that the source of the danger was rising fast to meet him. He threw a punch, pulling it considerably, the way he usually did when he didn't know a foe's resiliency. It was effortlessly batted aside. Pity, if it was Pity, also managed to kick him between the shoulders as he fell past her. The kick was perfectly placed, and powerful enough to hurt. She was strong, this one. And agile, too. Probably his equal in every way except, he hoped, experience.

He landed on his feet, rolled, scrambled up the side of the stairwell housing, and called out to her: "Got to give you credit, sister! I'm impressed! But I came equipped with a nightlight!" He flicked on his belt-buckle signal light, the one that cast a spotlight-sized image of his Spider-Man mask. But nothing happened. Though he could tell from the heat beneath his gloved fingertips that the bulb was working, Pity's darkness swallowed the light from the lamp as easily as it had swallowed up the light of the day.

He grimaced. "Hey, niiice powers! You must stub your toe a lot!"

He sensed her moving along the rooftop, keeping her distance but preparing to attack him again at any moment. He didn't need his spider-sense to know that the darkness wouldn't be impeding her vision at all.

It was time to give her another obstacle.

He fired both web-shooters at once, casting lines at the ground to either side of her. The web-cables hardened at once, not penning her in but giving her something to trip over if she moved too fast without thinking.

Strangely, he no longer sensed any movement from her at all. His spider-sense impression of her was fading, becoming vaguer, more ill-defined.

Whatever else she might have been doing right now, she must have decided not to press her attack. That complicated things. He wished he could temporarily trade the spider-sense for an equivalent radar sense, such as the one possessed by another rooftop hero of his acquaintance; that fellow would have taken her light-devouring powers in his stride. (Indeed, the guy might have had some difficulty figuring out that she had light-devouring powers at all.)

But being Spider-Man was pretty cool, too. Spider-Man proved it by firing another dozen web-lines in rapid succession, until the roof was crisscrossed with slanting barriers anchored from his position. Even in absolute darkness, his spider-sense would give him a clear fix on where they were at all times. He strafed another webline along what would have been his line of sight, hoping to hear the soft impact as it hit her.

Then he heard something scrape along the rooftop, at about three o'clock from his position. Only a couple of feet away, far closer than she had a right to be. Whoever she was, wherever she'd come from, she was good: so good that for the first time since discovering that the Sinister Six intended her to be his sole opponent today, he began to suspect he might be in serious trouble.

He tensed, waiting for the moment.

Then his spider-sense screamed at him. He ducked just in time to feel the rush of air as a powerful blow whistled past his ear. The force of it would have been enough to crush his skull. He passed beneath the blow, and kicked, sweeping her legs out from under her. She must have expected the move, because she flipped, and without even hitting the ground, was suddenly above him, slamming the heels of both feet into his shoulders. It was another solid blow, powerful enough to do him some real damage. Blinded by pain, he whuffed, fell backward off the stairwell housing, sprayed a wide stream of web fluid at the place where he thought she'd been, and once again managed to land on his feet.

Just in time to realize that his spider-sense had lost her again.

Despite himself, he felt like Inigo Montoya, fighting Westley in *The Princess Bride*. "Who are you?"

She didn't answer. Another voice did: this one aged, male, arrogant, tinged with an unidentifiable continental accent, and far colder than the frigid air that surrounded them: "I suppose we ought to ... enlighten the man, my dear. If not for his benefit, then at least for mine."

The lights came back on. It was that sudden: as if some

crazed god had just seen fit to flick a switch. Spider-Man's eyes, which had grown accustomed to darkness, watered painfully for a second or two, nevertheless recovering almost immediately, one of the benefits of superhuman recuperative powers being that even minor annoyances like light sensitivity tended to go away in seconds. The *Bugle* roof was still much the same as it had been before the darkness descended, except that weblines were strung to and fro like a chaotic cat's cradle, and the silent young woman in the loose-fitting white costume was standing atop the stairwell housing. Considering how much trouble she'd given Spider-Man, it was a bit of a shock to be reminded of just how short she was: if not for the maturity of her features, it would have been easy to mistake her for a girl in her early teens. Her expression was strange; Spider-Man would have expected the standard super-villainous scowl, but if anything she seemed regretful, almost sad, in a manner that, again, perversely, made him feel sorry for her.

There was a patch of webbing dangling from her right arm. He'd tagged her, then. But not in any manner that would slow her down.

The well-dressed old man who had stared down Peter Parker downstairs stood beside the letter "Y" in the *Daily Bugle* sign, massaging the bridge of his nose. "Ah," he said. "That's much better. I'm afraid these old eyes aren't quite as resilient as they used to be."

Spider-Man glanced at Pity, and then at the old man. It didn't make sense. Pity was the threat. But his spider-sense was reacting more to the old man: the way it would to a dangerous predator, just loosed from its cage. He said: "Yeah, and you can't buy a comic book for a dime anymore, either. I'm sure you used to walk five miles to school in the snow, too. What's your point?"

"The point, my dear boy, is that I wanted to introduce myself downstairs, but supposed a meeting up here would be far more discreet."

Downstairs . . . Spider-Man already had the awful feeling he knew what the old man was getting at, but postponed the realization for one more conversational exchange by saying: "You must have me confused with somebody else, pops. I just got here."

The old man frowned, and removed a cigar from his jacket pocket. "Pity? The wall-crawler is insulting my intelligence. Please chastise him. Briefly."

Pity leaped on him. Spider-Man didn't evade her attack this time, but instead faced it head-on, clutching her by both wrists even as he allowed himself to go limp beneath the force of her leap. As he fell backward, he encouraged her angular momentum with a little toss of his own. She went flying over his head. He caught a glimpse of her expression as she flew out of sight: it was wan, helpless, heartbreakingly unhappy. It would have been easy to hate himself for being so cruel to her.

But when he somersaulted back to a standing position, he found her already on her feet and waiting for him.

Who was she?

Spider-Man and Pity faced each other from twenty feet apart, two unstoppable forces ready for their next encounter.

"Clearly," the old man said, "I know your real name and your real face. There is no profit in pretending otherwise; forcing me to confirm my knowledge about your pathetic box of a home in Forest Hills, your dead-end career as a photographer, and your wife the unbearably perky actress in execrable z-movies, accomplishes nothing but wasting energy we can devote on more profitable discussion. I have never possessed a high opinion of your intelligence, my dear boy, but if you refrain from treating me like an idiot I shall endeavor to show you the same courtesy."

Spider-Man gritted his teeth. First the troubling questions about his parents, and then the attack of the Sinister Six, and now this guy. It was not shaping up to be a good day. "Yeah, you're right. Let's be civil about why you're trying to kill me. Who are you?"

Pity charged again. Her attack was sudden, savage, and utterly without warning—his spider-sense warned him only at the very last instant, barely in time for a quick leap up to carry him out of her way. As it happened, she also leaped to intercept him. She threw close to two dozen punches just in the time the pair of them matched trajectories in mid-air; Spider-Man managed to block almost all of them, but was pummeled to the point of breathlessness by the few that got past his defenses. As he and Pity fell to the rooftop again, he grabbed hold of her wrists, spun her around in mid-air, and pulled both of her arms behind her back; though the move caught her by surprise, she still had enough presence of mind to fling her head backward, hammering his nose with a force that staggered him. It was not enough to make him let go.

They landed together, both with the grace of cats, both still grappling with all the strength available to them. Spider-Man shifted position, tightened the grip he had with his left hand, and released the one he had with his right. She was inhumanly strong, too strong to hold fast with only arm, but he only needed a heartbeat for this next part. He used his right hand to web her pinned arms to her back, releasing the grip he had with his left hand only when he had to avoid gluing it in place as well. He would have immediately sought a more secure grip on her upper arms, but she kicked down hard on his right foot, spun around with dizzying speed, and knocked him thirty feet across the rooftop with a perfectly-placed kick to the right of his head.

Again, he landed on his feet, regarding her with increased respect. She faced him in a perfect battle stance that appeared no less dangerous despite the two arms now securely webbed behind her back. Varying shades of darkness radiated from her in waves.

Despite her dangerousness and proven capacity for savagery, she still looked heartbroken and wan. Again, Spider-Man felt sorry for her.

Across the roof, the old man sniffed his cigar appraisingly. "A most gratifying performance, my dear. I'm tempted to say, almost adequate. She's quite impressive, isn't she, Spider-Man? And totally, absolutely, under my thrall."

Spider-Man wanted to dribble this obnoxious guy's head off the blacktop a few dozen times. "Thrall? Are you talking mind control?"

"More like psychological conditioning. I obtained her very early in her life, recognized early on what she was, and from that moment on took all the available steps—psychological, hypnotic, and pharmaceutical—to ensure that she was incapable of any personal ambitions beyond obeying me in all things. In that, I feel I succeeded admirably."

Spider-Man grimaced behind his mask. "If you're into that kind of thing."

The old man snipped the tip off his cigar with a tiny knife from his coat pocket. "You only need to see her habitual stricken expression to know that her heart rebels at everything I require her to do—and that she would still eagerly die a thousand deaths before disappointing me in any fashion."

Spider-Man's heart sank as he measured this explanation against his personal instinctive reaction to the dangerous young woman—and realized it was true. "You're a real sick puppy, you know that?"

"Indeed I do. In fact, your friend Electro said as much to me just the other day. I find it delicious that two individuals with such a long history of mutual hatred as yourselves can be so perfectly united in their feelings on this one issue."

"Swell," Spider-Man muttered.

Pity feinted. Spider-Man reacted at once; the two of them went for each other, passed in mid-air, pummeled each other with almost identical kicks, and landed at the same moment, having accomplished nothing but trading places.

Spider-Man said: "So answer the question already, will ya, Pops? What's your name?"

"You will find out my real name if you survive the next twenty-four hours. You will also find out my precise connection to your personal life, which will probably shatter you. But until then," the old man sniffed, as if he found this next part unbearably gauche, "you may call me the Gentleman. It will present a more than serviceable alias, for now."

Spider-Man shot a webline at Pity's ankles, intending to bind her legs as he'd bound her arms. She cleared the incoming webline easily, leaping, somersaulting, and landing on her feet on the stairwell housing. Temporarily losing the use of her arms had affected her balance not at all; she landed with perfect poise, staring down at Spider-Man with a nightotal lack of concern over whatever he intended to do next.

Not taking his eyes off her for a moment, Spider-Man addressed the Gentleman: "So what's the story, bunkie? If you don't want to tell me anything today, why are you even here?"

"Oh," the Gentleman said, with apparent amusement, "I do have a number of things I wanted to tell you today. The first, of course, was that I know who you are. The second is that I have been your mortal enemy for more years than you could possibly guess, and that I have already taken more from you than all your other enemies put together. The third—though I hasten to tell that journalistic percentage of your split personality that this is not for publication—is that in this latest endeavor of theirs, the Sinister Six are acting as my hired agents. I solicited them, I outfitted them, I provided them with their operating budget and their safe house. I wanted you to know that our shared agenda is a good deal larger than simply terrorizing you with your failures. Our intentions are . . . global." The Gentleman bowed slightly. "I sense an imminent interruption, so that will have to be enough for now. Have a good evening, Spider-Man. I look forward to continuing this discussion tomorrow."

At which point, two things happened simultaneously.

The door to the stairwell swung open. Betty Brant and Billy Walters burst out onto the roof, their eyes widening even as they registered the webbing strewn everywhere, made eye contact with the opaque lenses of Spider-Man's mask, and realized that they'd both done more than simply chase down a breaking story. They'd waltzed into ground zero. Billy, who was no photographer, carried a camera anyway, probably because he'd been the only one available at the moment. Billy, Betty, and Spider-Man all cried out simultaneously, Billy saying, "You were right, he's up here, he's—", Betty, who'd been in a significantly higher number of these situations, shouting, "My God, it's not over, get—," and Spider-Man, already leaping toward them, shouting, "Get down, you two, it's not—"

Even as all of that happened, Pity's darkness descended upon all of them.

Spider-Man had been so concerned about getting his

friends to safe cover that keeping track of the newest member of the Sinister Six had become a distant second priority. She took advantage of his inattention now, planting another solid kick against his jaw. The force of the blow drove him back; in the fraction of a second they were both still in the air, she landed on his chest and rode him like a surfboard all the way to his painful landing on the rooftop. He rolled away the second they hit, but she kept pace with him, pursuing him, repeatedly kicking him in the ribs and the shoulder blades and the back of his head. They were solid kicks, too: any one of them capable of killing an ordinary man.

Somewhere nearby, Billy said: "The light, something's happened to—"

It took Spider-Man several seconds to anticipate one of those kicks, seize Pity by the ankle, and twist. She had a choice between falling down, or allowing her leg to be broken. She fell down. Her other foot slammed against Spider-Man's forehead, stunning him enough to make him let go. As he sensed her scrambling backward, he aimed his web-shooters and fired, but she was leaping out of range again.

As the danger she represented receded away from him, he got the distinct impression that she was racing toward the edge of the roof.

A retreat. Leaping over the barrier weblines with no difficulty at all.

With every bone in his body aching, Spider-Man leaped to his feet and pursued her at top speed. "Oh, no you don't, lady! We're not finished with this yet!"

Somewhere, Betty said: "He's fighting somebody! I can hear them!"

Billy said: "Yeah, but who uses darkness? You think Mysterio—"

Considering how close Pity had come to beating him

with both hands literally tied behind her back, Spider-Man had mixed feelings about his success in taking her down with a flying tackle. Especially since she not only seemed to expect it, but was more than willing to take advantage of it, choosing that moment for a powerful leap that merely added her own momentum to his. The two of them, still grappling, slammed into the huge letters of the *Daily Bugle* sign, smashing the last two letters of the newspaper's name to kindling as they passed over the edge of the roof and out of Pity's zone of darkness.

As the pair of them fell toward the pavement sixteen stories below, Spider-Man's automatic concern for the safety of the innocent bystanders below forced him to shoot a look at the damage their little battle had done to the sign on the top of the *Daily Bugle*. He saw three chunks of falling debris large enough to be dangerous and devoted half a second's effort—all the time in the world, with his reflexes—to casting a pair of web-nets that would catch them before they hit the street.

He was aware that later, if there was a later, he might have the opportunity to be amused by the memory—since, until fixed, the sign would now read *Daily Bug*. This was of course an alteration destined to thrill the arachnid-hating J. Jonah Jameson no end.

But there was no time for amusement now—not with Pity kicking her way free of him and becoming a separate body plunging to a messy death on the streets below.

Even as he fired web-shooters with both hands, snagging her belt-buckle with one webline and a convenient, frequently-used cornice stone with the other, he shouted at her: "Don't be crazy, Pits! I'm the only one who can catch you!"

She said nothing. Of course.

The webline to the cornice-stone drew taut, adjusting their angle of fall. He let go of it immediately, and fired another webline, this time at a flagpole he used almost as often to the cornice-stone. As he had learned, to his eternal sorrow, on one of the most tragic days of his life, it wasn't enough to simply arrest the fall of a tumbling body: he had to adjust the angular momentum with great care to make sure that the potential victim's spine was able to survive the rescue. If not, he would have to relive the tragedy of Gwen Stacy, who he'd loved, and who he'd snagged with a webline as she fell from the Brooklyn Bridge. He'd have to be haunted again by the terrible sound of cracking vertebrae as it echoed across the water . . . and the awful stillness of her form as he cradled her broken-necked corpse.

Spider-Man would not let that happen again, to friend or enemy.

It took a series of strategically-aimed weblines to transform terminal velocity, straight down, to a zig-zag course that passed within two stories of the street before he was confident enough to completely halt their shared downward plunge. In that instant, he was overcome by the usual overwhelming sense of relief that always washed over him whenever he succeeded in saving another life. But Pity, looking up at him, as they hit the bottom of their shared swing and began to ascend toward a planned landing on the fifth-floor ledge of a bank building still half a block away, did not seem grateful. If anything, she seemed about to cry.

His next words came as a surprise to him. "My . . . God. Lady! I don't even know who you are. But what did that monster do to you?"

Pity said nothing. Of course.

But this time his spider-sense, screaming sudden extreme danger from just above and just behind him, answered very eloquently for her. He spun, just barely avoiding the electrical explosion that lit up the air where he'd been. A wave of hot ozone buffeted him, driving him back, but not forcing him to let go of Pity. He shot another webline and spun away, desperate to gain altitude, knowing that it was his only chance to hold on to his prisoner and still stay ahead of the human powerhouse Max Dillon had become.

As always, Electro's voice crackled, like a cat entangled in a high-tension wire. But there was a new quality to it, something Spider-Man had rarely, if ever, heard there before; simple concern for another human being. "Don't worry, babe! I got ya!"

Oh. Swell. The lug's been smitten.

Spider-Man scrambled up another webline, Pity in tow. He climbed the line even faster than his swinging trajectory carried him toward the pavement. In an instant, he gained a net sixty feet of altitude. This was something he frequently needed to do to prevent his passages across the cityscape from taking him lower and lower with each swing — a trick that had taken the young Spidey, with his amazing reflexes, only a few short weeks to learn. It was, alas, not quite so easy to do when he was holding on to one squirming bad guy and trying to evade the deadly lightning bolts of another. If he could only find some safe place to stash Pity, so he could face Electro alone—

—but he didn't have a chance.

His spider-sense flared again, too late to stop a slash from the Vulture's razor-sharp wings from severing the webline. Gravity took over. Spider-Man fell, knowing that he'd almost certainly be able to save himself but that this low to the ground he might not be able to arrest his own fall in time to catch Pity again.

He heard the Vulture say: "Tsk. Don't worry, my dear. I won't let you fall." All in a tone Spider-Man had never heard from the embittered old man named Adrian Toomes. A concerned and loving tone, even a solicitous one. "I hope he didn't hurt you. After all, I know the way he can be . . ."

Oh. It figures. They've all been smitten.

Spider-Man hurled an adhesive spider-tracer, hoping to snag the Vulture's costume; the signal it broadcast on the same frequency as his spider-sense would enable him to track Toomes to the hiding place he must have shared with the other members of the Six. But the backwind from the old man's wings threw off the toss by just enough to make the adhesive device miss. And a fresh zap of lightning—striking just close enough to knock the breath out of him—blinded Spider-Man enough to prevent another try.

"Uh uh!" Electro howled. "Not 'til tomorrow, bug-man!"

By the time Spider-Man landed on his feet on passing bus and leaped after them, it was too late. The Vulture had transferred Pity to a seated position on his back. Openly contemptuous of Spider-Man's pursuit, the bird-suited criminal flew a course straight up, past the rooftops, taking himself and Pity well out of webslinging range before changing course for some unknown destination downtown. Electro, gallantly showing off for Pity, demonstrated his superior speed by literally flying circles around the Vulture every foot of the way.

Spider-Man kept up for a while, but lost them when the three bad guys dipped low behind some rooftops a mile up ahead.

He wasted more than half an hour looking for them, before he was willing to admit that they'd escaped. By the time he returned to the *Bugle*, both the zone of darkness and the Gentleman had vanished as if they'd never been there at all . . . leaving both the Sinister Six, and their mysterious patron, at full fighting strength for their scheduled Day of Terror.

Spider-Man knew only that whatever happened, he was not looking forward to tomorrow.

CHAPTER SEVEN

History is filled with times when the whole world seems to hold its breath.

For New York City, the night before the Day of Terror was one of those times.

The word spread quickly, as it tends to do; between the rumor mill and the six o'clock news and the radio reportage of the front page story of the next day's *Daily Bugle*, almost everybody in New York who paid attention to anything knew what was going on by nightfall. Some commuters made plans to take the next day off; some parents decided that maybe their children might be better off kept home from school. Local police departments cancelled days off, local insurance carriers trembled with concern for the avalanche of claims to come, and all over the city, fueled by talk radio and street-corner commentary, the battle to come gradually became the overwhelming topic of conversation.

There was not much outright panic, mostly because this was New York City, a tough place to live even with the super hero battles that seemed to take place here three or four times a week. (After Galactus, it was easy to be jaded.) But there was still intense, city-wide emotional involvement.

After all, Spider-Man may have been a strange guy—and whether he was a super hero or a dangerous menace depended on what paper you read—but he was still the home team. And whether or not he was as creepy as Jameson liked to say he was, nobody had any doubt at all where the Sinister Six stood.

New Yorkers did what New Yorkers always do. They came out to support the home team—especially if they can make a buck or two at it. As it was far too cold for t-shirts, the knockoff entrepreneurs did the next best thing. The first (unauthorized) GO SPIDEY buttons were rolling off the presses by six.

7:22 P.M.

The heating system had failed under the increased demands caused by the destructive additions to tenth-floor cross-ventilation, and most members on the night desk were shivering profusely as they typed up their stories in full winter gear. A cleanup crew sent by Damage Control, the city's number-one specialist in repairing the wreckage left by super-villain activity, was still busily sweeping up the mess. Betty Brant, Billy Walters, and Ben Urich, all of whom had been assigned specific aspects of the breaking story, had departed to pursue their assignments; nobody seemed to be able to locate Peter Parker, whose past accomplishments made him an obvious natural for a photo assignment.

Joe Robertson and J. Jonah Jameson, both smoking furiously as they stood around shivering in their bulkiest winter coats, looked glum as they surveyed the wreckage of their beloved city room. It was a forlorn moment for both of them, and they both looked forward to getting home to their respective wives.

At long last, the sniffling Jameson exhaled all of his prodigious rage in a long plume of malodorous smoke. "At least there's one good thing about this. Everybody's going to see that web-headed weasel for the phony he is."

It was a full ten seconds before Joe Robertson answered, in a voice so controlled it betrayed none of the feelings behind it: "Would that really be a good thing, Jonah?"

"Of course! I'm surprised you ask! After all, it's something this paper's been trying to tell people for years!"

Robertson's pipe matched Jameson's cigar puff by puff. "And if the only way for you to prove yourself right is for people to die?"

Despite himself, Jameson looked chastened. "I—no! Robbie, you know me better than that! Or you should, anyway!"

"Then," Robertson said, "you better hope that everything you've ever written about Spider-Man is wrong. Because Doctor Octopus was right. You did give those maniacs the idea for this. And if Spider-Man is not a better man than you think . . . then the next editorial you write, congratulating yourself for being right, will be dancing on an awful lot of graves . . ."

8:10 P.M.

Peter Parker was back home in Forest Hills. He could have been back at the *Bugle*, hustling for the photo assignments that would no doubt he hot commodities come tomorrow; or he might have been criss-crossing the city, searching for the spider-sense signal that would lead him to the Sinister

Six, or he might have been soliciting help from the Avengers or the Fantastic Four or anybody else crazy enough to work in this insane line of work. But for the moment, he was doing none of these things.

He was holding on tight to Mary Jane. And she was holding on tight to him. Each one of them with the fierce desperation of people who'd learned the hard way just how fragile their lives together were.

Maybe later, before he was forced to leave again, she would mention just how scared she was. Maybe he would tell her he'd handled the Six before, and maybe he'd admit that he was scared too.

But right now they were between words.

And they both found some comfort there.

8:47 P.M.

Betty Brant, shivering despite her three layers of clothing, her bulkiest winter coat, and a pair of kerosene-powered space heaters that rendered the rooftop alcove merely uncomfortable, smiled gratefully as Billy Walters clambered over the alley fire escape and handed her a pair of thermoses. "Hot Jamaican Blend," he said, with his usual enthusiasm. "And piping-hot clam chowder, fresh from the Original Soup Kitchen."

"Thanks," she said, meaning it.

"We're going to have to take frequent breaks inside the stairwell, anyway. Space heaters or not, this is frostbite weather out here."

"No argument," she said.

He hesitated, and pressed on. "Are you sure we're not, like, just wasting our time? I mean, spending the night here?

The Sinister Six said they weren't even going to do anything until tomorrow morning."

"Some of what they're going to do," Betty said, "is probably going to take a lot of advance preparation. If we can get there early, maybe we can catch them in the act."

"And what if we just freeze our butts off and find out in the morning that they picked another location?"

"That won't happen," Betty said. She took out her night vision glasses and peered at the building across the street. It was a small squat structure of no particular distinction: three stories of brick and mortar and wire-glass windows. There was no way of telling that anything remarkable had ever happened there, that once upon a time a costumed hero had fought a monster in a battle that had led to the sudden shocking death of an innocent man. The monster that time had been Dr. Octopus; the agent of death had been a cornice-stone, shattered by a blow from the madman's thrashing metallic arms; the victim had been a heroic police captain named George Stacy, whose last act had been rescuing a little boy in the path of the falling rubble. Stacy had succeeded in propelling the boy out of the way. He had not been quite fast enough to get out of the way himself. It was one of the greatest known tragedies of Spider-Man's career, and one Betty suspected the wall-crawler had taken especially hard. She surveyed that fateful rooftop, lingering especially long on its long-since repaired cornice.

Billy said: "Hey, I'm sure you know what you're doing, and all. But, uh . . . how can you be sure?"

Betty did not take offense. She said: "I once spent almost a full day as that maniac's prisoner. I spoke to him. I saw him for the kind of man he was. I even got to know him, God help me."

"And?"

"He's the kind of man who measures himself by the amount of terror he inflicts. I'm betting you that he's proud of what happened here. And that he'll want to come back to do it again."

Billy nodded a bit too long at that. He took a sip of coffee from the thermos, winced as it burned going down his throat, and asked the real question that had been going through his mind. "What about Spidey? I mean, don't get me wrong. I think he rocks, totally."

"He does," Betty said, surprised to find herself smiling.

"But, you know, he'll be awfully busy. How can you be sure he'll show up in time to save us, if Ock arrives and things go wrong?"

Betty put down the night-vision glasses and faced him. The condensation of her breath glowed visibly in the light of distant neon as she said: "You know, once upon a time, when I was even younger than you are now, I hated Spider-Man almost as much as I hate Octavius. I thought he was just a selfish, maniacal thrill-seeker, who fought people like Dr. Octopus out of some twisted sense of fun. I thought he didn't really care about the people he saved—that he was only doing it to enjoy himself. A couple of times, when I saw him close-up, fighting bad guys in the city room, I heard all those stupid wisecracks he makes and decided that he was probably also completely out of his mind."

"And now?"

Betty thought of telling Billy all she now owed Spider-Man. And demurred: not because it was too personal, but because the story would probably last all night. She peered through the night-vision goggles again, and once again saw no change. "Let's just say he grew on me. Don't you fret, he'll be here. Hey, did you bring me my Altoids?"

9:15 P.M.

Ben Urich's eyes were burning.

Stuck in the *Daily Bugle* morgue, paging through page after page of the *Bugle*'s incessant crusades against Spider-Man, was not his idea of a fun evening. Read one after the other, Jameson's rants were even more repetitive in print than the man himself was in person; they were the journalistic equivalent of Mad Libs, with the dominant formula being accusations that the citywide crisis just past had been Spider-Man's fault all along. At best, Jameson's conclusions were open to debate; at worst, they required factual misinterpretations bordering on outright lunacy. Urich had often been tempted to do some freelance research into the reasons for his publisher's single-minded hatred for the wall-crawler; the urge was so particularly strong now that he wrote himself a mental note to spend some time lying down until the feeling went away. Some stories you just didn't want to know.

Besides, Jameson's neuroses weren't the issue, now.

The issue, thanks to the Sinister Six, was just how many times Spider-Man had tried to save lives, and come up short. Urich was certain that the press had only documented a small number of these, but he was still disturbed by just how many there were. He knew about Captain George Stacy, of course; everybody at all interested in the subject knew about what happened to George Stacy. And Stacy's daughter, Gwen, only a few months later: that one had been so horrific the *Bugle* had made it front-page news for a week. But there were too many others: from the fireman horribly burned by a collapsing wall while Spider-Man and the hero for hire Luke Cage helped fight the same tenement blaze, to the elderly woman who had just recently suffered a fatal heart attack in the wake of Spider-Man's battle with Mysterio.

Urich couldn't blame the wall-crawler for trying. After all, the list of lives Spider-Man had saved was much, much longer: according to some of Urich's sources in the super-hero community, possibly even planetary in scale. The people he'd failed to save were probably an infinitesimal fraction of a percent of the number of people still walking around thanks to him.

But that wasn't the point. Not now.

The point was, first of all, with the list of fatalities as long as it was, there was absolutely no way to foretell where the Sinister Six planned to strike.

And second of all, from Urich's personal perspective as a man who'd been saved by Spider-Man more than once: if even superhumans could fail, what chance did mere humans have?

He lit his latest cigarette from the burning embers of the old, and shivered.

11:13 P.M.

The Gentleman had always preferred dining near midnight; he had always felt that the final meal of the day should be the capstone of that day's accomplishments, and that any dinner earlier in the evening was testimony only to a criminal lack of ambition. He could not understand the state of affairs in America, where people approaching his age often dined between four and five P.M. at places advertising inexpensive "Early Bird Specials"; he had sampled such an establishment out of perverse curiosity and had seen naught but a room filled with people so demoralized and decrepit that they could not wait to declare their days over and done. He, fortunately, was made of sterner stuff.

Following recent habit, he dined at the Macchiavelli Club,

an exclusive establishment catering to men and women possessing a certain species of vision. Founded in the late 1890s
by a certain London mathematician, and joinable only by
specific invitation, its halls had been graced by figures ranging from the infamous mercenary terrorists known as the
Gruber Brothers to munitions magnate Justin Hammer; from
promising newcomers like the German Herr Taubman to the
Wrightsville billionaire Diedrich Van Horn, from powerful
crimelords like Wilson Fisk to the scarred wheelchair-bound
man who went by the name Ernst.

The Gentleman, who planned to dine alone as always,
nodded to Ras, chatted with Soze, declined a taste of Hanni-
bal's appetizer, complimented Carmen on her new slouch
hat, endured another rhapsody on myth and comic book art
from Mr. Glass, and pretended to be impressed by the outra-
geously purple tuxedo recently purchased by Napier. He
hated all of them, of course, just as most of them hated him.
But that was all right. This was the Macchiavelli Club. It was
neutral territory. And custom dictated that as soon as he sat
down he would be left alone, precisely as he preferred.

Alas, custom, this time, was violated; almost as soon as
he presented his order, he was accosted by the two idiot
brothers who he had hoped to avoid. He had long despised
them because they didn't really belong in the Macchiavelli at
all; they may have been ruthless, greedy, and utterly contemptuous of the rights of others, which might have seemed
to qualify them, but only within the narrow confines of ordinary everyday capitalism. Though they'd both reached their
seventies, it could not be said that they'd ever, even once,
taken that last additional step which would ever make them
true Macchiavelli stock. The Gentleman could only wonder
just who they'd bribed for their membership invitation. But
the Gentleman had to be courteous, and so he nodded as the

pair of them slid into the seats opposite his. "Randolph. Mortimer. The years have been kind."

"To you, too," Mortimer said, his black eyes gleaming. "We had feared you lost—or, worse, retired."

"Never," the Gentleman sniffed. "I am simply . . . more discreet, these days. And I must say that I am surprised to see you here; the last I heard, you were both totally wiped out in that commodities scheme of yours."

"We went through some difficult years," Mortimer admitted, a strange darkness passing over his features.

"In fact, the last I heard, you were homeless."

"We were," Randolph said, with considerable tension. "But we came into some new seed money. I suppose you could call it . . . a grant from a visiting African dignitary."

"Indeed. And aside from vague curiosity, why should I care?"

Randolph and Mortimer met each other's eyes. Mortimer spoke: "This Sinister Six business—"

The Gentleman made the kind of face he usually reserved for finding live things his soufflé. "I am certain I have absolutely no idea what you're talking about."

"Oh, please." Mortimer took a breadstick from the basket and bit it noisily. "We watch the news. We saw what happened at the *Bugle*. We know about the challenge thrown down by the Sinister Six. And we know that the new lady member of that team of degenerate ruffians happens to be named Pity. All this, in light of your recent return to America, and your long-simmering grudge against Spider-Man . . . well, my old friend, it was not precisely difficult to see your organizing hand."

"And even assuming you're correct about this? What, precisely, do you want from me?"

The two elderly brothers glanced at each other. Mortimer

nodded, and Randolph said: "You may not be aware of this, but certain elements in this city's gambling community have been already placing bets on the outcome of tomorrow's . . . festivities. Specifically, just how many people the Six will succeed in killing before defeating Spider-Man or, failing that, being defeated themselves. Most of the bets are running over three figures. We were wondering if you would be willing to part with any . . . inside information?"

The Gentleman regarded them thoughtfully. "Inside information? Again? I would have thought you'd learned your lesson dealing in orange futures."

"Last time we relied on a middleman. This time we are obtaining our information ourselves."

"Ah," the Gentleman nodded. He studied them carefully for several seconds, and then said: "If I give you my best personal guess, will you go away?"

"In a minute," said Mortimer.

"Right away," said Randolph.

The Gentleman nodded, removed a cigar from his vest pocket, snipped off the tip, and lit it from the candle burning in the center of the table. He blew a cloud of smoke at the faces of the two churlish brothers, smiled, and named a figure in the upper six figures . . .

12:35 A.M.

The woman known as Pity stood by a window in a darkened room, watching the snow flurry past the streetlights. It was a light snow: not the blizzard the city had been expecting, but a dusting that would leave the morning tinged with a thin layer of white. She stood so close to the window that each fresh exhalation fogged the glass before her, making the city outside look less like a real thing and more like a dream she would never know. She pressed her palm against the glass, felt its coldness, and practiced shrouding the streetlights in darkness; they seemed to pulse on and off, like slow-motion strobe lights, illuminating a world that sometimes seemed real and sometimes seemed like an illusion she had the ability to banish at will.

She knew when Octavius entered the room behind her, and also knew that he believed he believed he'd entered unnoticed. She reacted to his presence not at all, keeping her own counsel, as she'd always been commanded to do.

He spoke in a voice as soft as velvet, that pretended warmth while containing nothing but ice: "Do you know? You are very beautiful."

His face was a crescent of light, illuminated by the street light, bisected by the shadows of the frames between the window panes. His tentacles, writhing all around him, like snakes constantly searching the air itself for threats, glimmered wherever they caught the light, an effect that made them look much more real than he was.

Pity said nothing. Of course.

He said: "Providence was wise, when it gave you power over darkness. Because the darkness becomes you. You should be its mistress, not its servant. You should be the queen of any place you choose to walk."

It was probably meant to charm her. But it was the phraseology of a man who knows words, but cannot connect them to the feelings they are meant to convey; she was relieved to find she could not discern any sincerity behind them. She waited, and did not look at him.

He said: "I know he treats you like a slave. I know you are not happy under his yoke. If you decide to work for me instead, I promise I will make you the queen you deserve to be. And all you have to do is tell me what that old man's not telling us. Who he is, and what he's really after."

Her reaction to that was in danger of showing on her face. She drew a curtain of darkness over her features, and then around her entire self, feeling it wrap her as cozily as a favorite coat. Shrouded like that, she might have smiled. It would have been a sad smile, entirely without mirth—but it would have been a genuine smile nevertheless, since she knew the darkness better than she knew any human being, and it comforted her in the way few other things in this life could.

Somewhere, outside that zone of darkness, Octavius snarled. "Very well. This is not over. Remember that."

And then he was gone.

Leaving Pity where she had always preferred to be: alone and in the dark.

2:20 A.M.

Adrian Toomes, aka the Vulture, sat up in bed, a fresh scowl twisting his aged but predatory features.

He had hoped to get an unbroken night's sleep tonight. It was his policy before committing especially grandiose crimes; he was, after all, not exactly a spring chicken anymore.

He had not expected to wake up with tear-tracks staining his cheeks, and the last of a sob dying in his throat.

It shouldn't have surprised him; after all, he frequently experienced that dream, which he never remembered except for a single unanswerable question and an impression of overwhelming grief. He didn't have the nightmare every night, but it had returned at least once every week or so since he was a young man. And though he had never been able to answer the question, he never felt the need to explore it further than a few curses muttered beneath his breath.

The question was: *How come nobody's ever loved you?*

The answer, at least in recent years, had always been: *Who cares? I'm the Vulture. It's enough that they're afraid.*

But tonight . . . that did not seem like enough.

He muttered to himself, rolled over, and went back to sleep.

3:15 A.M.

Max Dillon, aka Electro, lay awake on top of the covers, staring up the ceiling, using a single glowing fingertip to draw lightning-pictures in the darkness all around him.

Even considering the unusual medium—jagged strokes of light that faded into purple afterimages as soon as he created them—he was not a very good artist. He had very little talent, and almost no knowledge of the fundamentals.

But it wouldn't have taken an art expert to recognize that the fleeting, ephemeral images were portraits of Pity.

3:30 A.M.

Anatoly Smerdyakov, aka the Chameleon, did not even make a pretense of sleep.

He sat in a soft leather easy chair in the corner of the bedroom that had been assigned to him, leaning forward slightly as he rested his chin on folded hands. Lost in thought, he might or might not have been aware that the malleable features of his mask were altering every few seconds or so to reflect the subjects of his brooding obsessions; or that the churning maelstrom of his thoughts were reducing even those false faces to grim, distorted caricatures. Toomes, Dillon, Beck, and Octavius all appeared there, only to disappear almost immediately; so did J. Jonah Jameson, Ben Urich, Peter Parker, and Billy Walters, mostly because they were individuals he'd seen at the *Bugle* that day, whose faces were foremost in his recent memories. He also transformed to the perennial superhero sidekick Rick Jones, who had once been one of his disguises; to an elderly news vendor who had recently sold Smerdyakov a *Daily Bugle*, and whose craggy visage Smerdyakov had especially admired; and to a variety of entirely imaginary faces he had used to disguise himself at one time or another.

But the face that appeared most often belonged to the Gentleman . . . who was each time blanching in abject defeat.

Smerdyakov, who had his own agenda, smoked one cigarette after another, and occasionally chuckled to himself.

3:50 A.M.

Quentin Beck, aka Mysterio, slept like a baby, his harsh features enjoying a rare moment of total relaxation. His dreams, which were sweet, had nothing to do with his criminal life, or with his ambition of destroying Spider-Man, or with his long list of other enemies, or for that matter, with the kind of ridiculous schoolboy crush that he had earlier realized Toomes and Dillon harbored for their newest teammate; Beck had been cruelly amused by that little observation, and had enjoyed the feeling of superiority that came from the awareness that he was never moved by such passions. No; these dreams were set at the Dorothy Chandler Pavillion in Los Angeles, and featured the hugely successful Writer/ Director Quentin Beck, this year's winner of twelve Academy

Awards for his five-hour epic version of his own life. His acceptance speech was a brilliant denunciation of everybody in the audience for taking so long to come to the shared realization that their overrated talents were miniscule sparks of light compared to the glorious conflagration that was his. In his dream, the audience of thousands, which included not only the living but also the great names of the past like Griffith and Hitchcock and Ford and Chaplin and Sturges and Kurosawa, applauded every fresh outpouring of abuse from Beck's lips, their smiles fixed but sincere, overflowing with awe at the depth and breadth of his accomplishments. They knew they were nothing next to him. They didn't care. They were just content to admire him, and shower him with praise.

Much later, after he woke up, Beck would think back on the vision and realize, to his chagrin, that all the Oscar statuettes on the podium before him had been wearing little Spider-Man suits.

4:00 A.M.

Mary Jane Watson-Parker watched through slitted eyes as her husband, moving with a superhuman grace possibly only for an incredibly agile super hero who believes his wife to be asleep, rose, donned his familiar red-and-blue costume, and moved toward the window. He had mentioned needing to make a rendezvous before the day's promised insanity started in earnest; he had just as clearly spent the past four hours pretending to be asleep instead lying wide awake, unwilling to aggravate her apprehension with his own. In this, he was being typically Peter, but also typically naive: for she had spent those four hours also wide-awake, listening to the soft rumble of his breath, trying not to think about the horrors that awaited him. She hadn't revealed herself to be awake because she'd known that he would need all his strength for the ordeal to come; and he hadn't revealed himself to be awake because he'd known that she would need hers just as badly.

It was a transparent charade for both of them: one they'd both playacted before, during previous crises.

The pretending stopped only after he clipped his fresh web-cartridges in place, pulled up the lower half of his mask, and leaned over the bed to kiss her. "I'll see you tonight," he whispered. "I promise."

She sat up and hugged him. "Don't be late. I'm making stroganoff."

"Oboy. What a motivator. Poor Ock won't stand a chance." He kissed her again. "I love you, Red."

He didn't give her a chance to say anything else. A heartbeat later, he was gone.

Mary Jane collapsed against the pillow, her vision blurring. She hated this: it was like being a cop's wife, only a thousand times worse; every parting bore with it the terrible suspicion that this time it might be the last one. She'd had to prepare to mourn her husband almost every night of her life.

And she still wouldn't have traded him for anybody else.

She went back to sleep—or rather, to pretending to be asleep—and spent what remained of that night staring up at the ceiling, trying not to hear the phantom sounds of fisticuffs and lightning bolts and explosions.

It wouldn't be until almost sunrise that she remembered something the worries of the night before had completely driven from her mind, something that seemed unbearably trivial now but which the rational part of her knew she simply could not afford to forget . . .

. . . her job interview . . . .

5:30 A.M.

The last calm before the storm.

Spider-Man and Colonel Sean Morgan stood on the roof of a small four-story apartment building in Chelsea. There was nothing special about the building, no particular reason that it should have been selected as the site of their rendezvous; it had been chosen at random, by a city map in SAFE's computers. Morgan had commented that a site chosen completely at random would be most unlikely to attract premature attention from the Sinister Six. Spider-Man had allowed as how this sounded like a good idea and not mentioned that he'd once rented a skylight apartment just down the block.

It was a bitterly cold morning, with a light dusting of snow. Spider-Man had worn one of his best thermal uniforms and he could still feel the air sucking the warmth from his bones. Morgan, clad in a SAFE kevlar jumpsuit, didn't seem to feel the temperature at all. Either he was even more of a robot than he pretended or SAFE had some kind of fabric that really kept in the heat. Spider-Man had thought of asking him for details, but quickly forgot as circumstances turned their conversation toward the subject of death.

Specifically, the people Spider-Man had been unable to save.

Even Spider-Man, who habitually felt his failures like physical wounds, was aghast not only by just how many he was able to list, but also how many he'd almost forgotten. He had already gone over the George Stacy incident, the Gwen Stacy incident, an incident involving a innocent woman murdered by the super-strong serial killer known as the Rooftop Ripper, an incident involving a fireman and a collapsing wall, several incidents involving the psychotic symbiote known as Carnage, and others. By the time he got to the story of the murderer known as the Sin-Eater, the weight of all that death had turned his voice hollow and despairing.

He clenched his fists and continued: "It didn't stop when I beat him to within an inch of his life; it didn't stop when I turned him into the cops; it didn't even stop when the police were bringing him up the steps of City Hall for his arraignment. He'd killed a lot of people by then—including one I knew and respected, a good cop named Jean DeWolff." He hesitated. "Jean. She was a friend. I don't think we ever used that word to describe our relationship when she was alive. But she was a friend. I liked her a lot.

"The street in front of City Hall was mobbed with people who wanted the Sin-Eater's blood. Somehow, in the confusion, he broke loose, and got his hands on a double-barrelled shotgun, I swung down to stop him. He fired it directly at me, point blank."

Here, Spider-Man hesitated, his head bowed. "But of course," he said, more loudly, his tone bitter and self-accusatory, "I have the proportionate speed and agility of a spider! That's no threat to me! I just leaped over the blast! What a slick move! What a great thing for the swashbuckling hero to do! So what if there were people behind me, and the innocent civilian who took the brunt of it died on his way to the hospital? At least I beat up the bad guy! That made everything better again, didn't it?"

"City Hall," Morgan noted, using his light-pen to write this into an electronic notepad. "Seems a natural target, for the Six; it's public and it's dramatic and any terrorist strike there will only exacerbate any panic or chaos affecting the rest of the city. I'll have spotters there, too."

Spider-Man didn't answer him a long time. Then he nodded, his voice hollow. "City Hall."

Morgan ruminated that a little longer. "We can't say it's a certainty, though. The Six wants to keep you guessing. Since I agree with your assessment that they'll probably consider the Brooklyn Bridge, site of the Gwen Stacy murder, almost mandatory—the witnesses we've interviewed all say it seemed to hit you pretty hard—we have to go by the assumption that they'll devote some of their attention on less obvious targets. We have to spread our people around, so we can provide logistical and even tactical support wherever we're needed."

Spider-Man, nodding, rested his elbows on the parapet and stared down at the street. "Aren't you afraid of running out of spotters, covering all the places I've let people down?"

"Negative," Morgan said, giving him no sympathy at all. "This is a full-scale operation. I can assign as many people as I need."

"Swell. With all the possibilities I've come up with, I was afraid you'd have to call in the other armed services! Maybe even leave all our military bases unguarded!" He was unable to keep the bitterness out of his voice: "We would feel pretty damn stupid if you used so many people covering all my failures that the Sinister Six was able to walk away with the country!"

Sean Morgan snapped his notepad closed, and clapped a hand on Spider-Man's shoulder. The web-slinger, who had felt no warning from his spider-sense, whirled, ready for an attack, instead seeing nothing but the Colonel's look of grim determination.

"Shut up," the Colonel said, quietly.

"What?"

"I said, 'Shut up.' You're not doing this operation any good."

"The operation?" Spider-Man was incredulous. "Is that all this is to you?"

The Colonel stepped closer, facing Spider-Man from across a gulf of inches. "Did you really imagine that you long-underwear types are special? That you're the only people who walk around feeling the weight of your own personal body count? I have news for you, mister. Every doctor who ever watched a patient die on the operating table, every ambulance driver who couldn't get to the hospital in time, every cop who answered a 911 call too late, every commanding officer who had to order soldiers to take the next hill, and every—" The colonel hesitated, squeezed his eyes tightly shut, then opened them again and finished the thought, "—hell, every parent whose kids ever got hurt in a stupid, pointless accident. They all feel the blood on their hands. They all think about how they could have been faster, or stronger, or tougher, or on time. All of them!"

Troubled, as much by the colonel's demeanor as what he was saying, Spider-Man said: "But there are so many in my case. So many failures . . ."

"And you know why, web-slinger? Because you do what so many other people don't even bother to do. You try."

"I—"

"Most people give up in advance. They let other people suffer and die because they figure there's nothing they can do. You have failures because you try—because you're out there taking the responsibility every day. If you never went out there and tried, if you never attempted the impossible every time you put on that stupid costume, if you just acted like Ock and his friends and used your powers to resign from the human race, you wouldn't have all of this coming down on your head. You'd just have a whole lot of dead people who never even had somebody like you trying to help them. The only difference is that there'd be a whole lot more of them! If my figures are right, enough to fill this city a dozen times over!"

On a purely intellectual level, Spider-Man knew Morgan was right; if anything, the SAFE man was understating the case. The Time's Arrow affair with Kang the Conqueror alongside the X-Men, just a few months earlier, had saved the lives of everybody in this plane of reality. But Spider-Man wouldn't have been the man he was if his heart permitted him to see the figures that way. He said: "I'm sorry. I know it doesn't make sense. It's just that—just to fail at all, with everything else I can do—all my power—"

"To hell with sense. To hell with power." Morgan turned his index finger into a club, jabbing his points at Spider-Man's chest. "I command enough weaponry to turn this whole island into a smoking cinder. The Hulk is so strong he makes you look like a maiden aunt. We're both more powerful than anybody has a right to be. Does it make sense that neither one of us could save my kid from a stupid car wreck? Does it make sense that we both still feel the guilt?"

Spider-Man hadn't known. Hesitantly, he ventured, "Morgan, I—"

"This is not a bonding moment, Spider-Man!" It was the first time Morgan had even raised his voice. "We are not friends. We will never be friends. We may be getting along better than we used to, but I still don't like you."

"Then what's your point of bringing up your son?"

"The point? That we all live with our failures. We all

wish we could rewrite history, win where we lost, and take back what we can't. If the deaths are on your head, and I'm certain they are, then that's because you're the one who bothered to take the responsibility for trying to prevent them. And if you let the Sinister Six trick you into thinking that this is all your fault . . . then you're giving those murderous scumbags exactly what they want. Because they *want* you to torture yourself. They *want* you to think that it's you putting people in danger. They *want* you to forget that this is really only about a bunch of lowlife murdering psychopaths who have lucked into power and who think this entitles them to rob and kill and terrorize anybody they want. It's about how if they weren't doing this, they'd be doing something else just as bad." The colonel let that thought reverberate into the cold January air. Somewhere, down on the streets below, a siren wailed; the colonel let it fade in the distance, then faced the dim light just beginning to light up the sky in the east. "And it's about how much it bothers them that one man has always stood in their way."

7:30 A.M.

Showing a rare concern for management-labor relations, the Gentleman had arrived at the townhouse with a bag of steaming hot croissants. He allowed Pity to eat. He deflected hostility from Octavius. He made sure Mysterio's own extensive preparations were ready. He wished the Vulture luck. He passed a few private words with the Chameleon. He assured Electro that his own secret agenda today was critical to the success of the larger plan. He reminded them all about their rendezvous at the end of the day. He watched with approval as his pawns descended into the basement, to use the access tunnel that led to the nearest subway line and points beyond.

Throughout all this, his smile never changed: it was very white and very nasty, like a picket fence dipped in venom.

Karl, he thought. *I have not forgotten you.*

CHAPTER EIGHT

8: 36 A.M.

The Vulture had done this before.

Despite his chosen sobriquet, he was a bird of prey, not a creature who fed on carrion. His unique flight harness, powered by a battery strapped to his back, allowed him to slice through the air with a velocity much more reminiscent of the common hummingbird; though he much preferred slower speeds, for conveying the impression of deliberate, unhurried deadliness, he was at full acceleration little more than a terrifying green blur, moving faster than most human eyes could track him. This speed was invaluable on those frequent occasions when he had to fight Spider-Man, and an unstoppable advantage when he directed his aggression against ordinary people.

Moving that quickly, he could swoop down to the street, skimming the rush hour crowds. He could seize some civilian at random, drop him unharmed on a rooftop . . . and repeat the process ten more times before his first victim even had time to think of trying to get away.

He could grab another ten victims in the time the last few were starting to panic. He could accumulate hostages faster than they could climb through the windows or down the fire escapes or over the adjacent rooftops; he could even take his time about it because there would always be some so terrified of heights that they curled up into a ball, unable to muster the necessary will to save themselves. He could recapture the most defiant among them several times in rapid succession, laughing at their repeated attempts to escape, exhausting them so badly that soon they, too, were hopeless, quivering, and defeated.

He had done this on previous occasions just to gain Spider-Man's attention.

It had worked.

He saw no reason not to try it again.

After all, why not? In some ways, the web-slinger was so predictable . . .

8:39 A.M.

Spider-Man had spent the past two hours on a triangular course that took him from Macy's at Herald Square, to the Museum of Natural History at Central Park West, to the Chrysler Building, and then back to Macy's, before repeating the route a second, third, and fourth time. He had done most of this travelling without benefit of web-fluid, figuring that he'd probably need all he had, later; instead, he'd hopped from rooftop to rooftop across the narrow streets, taking the wider avenues in dizzying leaps off the tops of buses. Bereft of any solid indication of the Six's plans, needing to move because the alternative was to drive himself crazy by waiting, he had hoped to maybe get a jump on their first attack by picking up a quick spider-sense impression somewhere along the way—but all he accomplished, in these frigid temperatures, was keeping warm for the battles to come.

And maybe something else.

He'd taken the Colonel's words to heart, and used them to transform an entire career's worth of regrets into a nice, piping-hot mad.

He'd thought of all the people who were going to be endangered today, just because the Sinister Six wanted to make some kind of twisted point . . . of how little that meant to them, and how much it meant to him . . . of everything the Colonel had said . . . and he felt it building, in a white-hot knot of concentrated anger roiling in the pit of his belly. They had no right to do this. And he intended to teach them that lesson, in the most persuasive manner available to him.

That is, if they ever announced themselves . . .

(He had an idea for a poster. *What if they gave a super-villain battle and nobody came?* Probably sell a million copies, that. Or at least five. The kids at Xavier's School would probably want to put it up in their dorm rooms . . .)

His right ear vibrated—not a manifestation of his spider-sense, but an incoming message from a borrowed SAFE communicator now tucked into his right ear. Its presence was distracting as hell, even with Doug Deeley's voice coming in as big as life: "Spider-Man! Spider-Man! Do you copy?"

Feeling ridiculously self-conscious—he'd never voluntarily submitted himself to the input of a dispatcher before, but he knew it was probably necessary in this case—Spider-Man tapped his throat mike and said: "No! I just take thorough notes! Over!"

"We have a confirmed hostage situation involving the Vulture in the diamond district!" Deeley gave the exact street and address, then went on: "He's snatching people right off the street, taking them up to the rooftops! Specifically, Yeganeh Treasures and Precious Stones! Does that place mean *anything* to you? Over!"

As Spider-Man altered course, heading toward the neighborhood in question, he frowned beneath his mask, trying to place the vaguely familiar name. It was all of two seconds—and most of a crosstown block—before he groaned in remembered pain. *No. No, not that place.* He hadn't even considered that place. If the Six was starting there, it meant their itinerary wasn't going to be predictable. He said: "Something bad happened there, a long time ago! Over!"

"The NYPD already has uniformed officers there, trying to keep people off the streets! Do you copy?"

"Nothing trademarked! Over!"

Deeley's voice lost some of its military precision, and took on a bemused edge. "You do know I'm going to have to eventually type all this up in a complete transcript for Colonel Morgan? He'll go ballistic. Over."

"I have no problem with that, Deeley! Not as long as you tell me where to point him! Out!"

Leaping from building to building with a speed that devoured the blocks like candy, Spider-Man was not nearly in as light-hearted a mood as he wanted Deeley to believe. His eyes were burning at the unexpected reminder of a dark, rainy night he would have liked to forget.

Yeganeh Treasures and Precious Stones, owned and operated by Sabra Israelis, had joined the neighborhood less than six months previously. Having never shopped there, or broken up any robberies at that establishment, Spider-Man never would have noticed the transaction—had he not also had specific reason to note the departure of the previous merchant in that space, a venerable family firm known as

Stockbridge Jewelers. Specifically: late one night many, many years ago, shortly after first donning his costume, he'd interrupted two brothers named Wayne and Kent Weisinger in the act of trying to break in through the roof. The routine burglary had been the kind of crime Spider-Man should have been able to stop with his eyes closed. A little more experience, and he would have been able to stop what happened next: as Kent, who had always hated his brother, took advantage of the distraction caused by Spider-Man's sudden appearance to push Wayne off the roof.

Wayne had fallen five stories and died on impact.

Spider-Man, taken by surprise, had not reacted in time to save him.

The incident had provided Spider-Man his first real taste of tragic failure.

His first . . .

He suddenly remembered what Octopus had said, during their impromptu press conference. *It shall begin with the first.* Of course. They had practically drawn him a map.

Of course, he'd been younger then . . . and he hadn't even thought of the incident for years, having been distracted by more recent tragedies.

But the Vulture, in his malicious wisdom, had just reopened a wound.

He was going to pay for that.

At the moment, the Vulture was mostly concerned about upping the ante.

There were now close to three dozen people huddled on the roof of Yeganeh's. He had selected a fine cross-section of humanity from the pedestrians on the streets below; bearded hassidim in heavy woolen coats, on their way to jobs at one jeweler or another; a couple of teen-aged bike messengers, clad in form-fitting warmups; several elegantly-dressed young woman in mink; a somewhat older rich lady with a face stretched taut by cosmetic surgery; a uniformed policewoman who the Vulture had found pathetically easy to disarm; several raggedy homeless, including one still asleep who didn't seem to realize that he'd been snatched off his heating grate; and an obese man straining the material of his black suit, who the Vulture had chosen just to demonstrate that nobody was too heavy to be snatched. And more. There were others, of course—even if you didn't count those not currently in the act of fleeing—but they would do. They were the Vulture's favorites.

It was easy to hem them in. He just flew around them in a circle, at shoulder-height, in a low banking turn that kept the razor-sharp tip of his right wing only inches above the surface of the roof. He revolved around them so quickly that nobody among them could work up the nerve to even try to get past him; they all knew that anybody who made the attempt and was even a fraction of a second off ran the risk of being sliced in half by his next pass. This did not stop them from screaming or cowering or huddling together in a pathetic attempt at mutual protection—the sole exceptions being the policewoman, who though clearly terrified kept asking him what he wanted, and the most deranged member of the homeless contingent, whose steady stream of profanity really did deserve credit for its creative use of imagery.

But no Spider-Man. Not yet.

The Vulture took in the screams of the witnesses in all the offices across the street, the wail of sirens in the streets below, the police sharpshooters gathering on all the neighborhood rooftops, the *whup-whup-whup* of distant news choppers already beginning to converge on the neighborhood, and even the unpleasant numbness in his ears brought on by the beastly cold weather, and decided he'd had enough. It was time for them to die, as years ago Wayne Weisinger had died.

He changed course, gained altitude, performed a perfect loop high above them, and attacked them head-on. From their screams, they must have been certain they were all about to die. This was an accurate assessment, but he had no intention of killing them the way they probably imagined; he was not in the mood for the mess using his wingtips on that many people would generate. Instead, he slowed, hovered vertically, and spread his wings as far as they would go, using them as scoops, to drive the hapless, cowlike civilians back toward the edge of the roof.

They cried out all the obvious things: "No! Don't!" and "Please! I have children!" and "Oh god oh god, I don't want to die." A few even took swings at him. But the blows were puny things, that rolled off him like spring rain.

As they stumbled back, herded toward oblivion by the power in his wings, some even retreated faster than they had to, preferring the five-story drop to the icy ruthlessness of his advance. Two of the Chassidim went over. Then the policewoman. Then the obese man. Then crazy homeless guy, who held his nose before leaping, as if believing himself at a municipal swimming pool. Then the bike messengers and the young women in furs and the rich lady and the rest, all falling without a sound, their screams halted by their own sheer disbelief at where their fate had brought them.

When they were all gone, the Vulture frowned. That had been stupid, using up all his hostages like that. Killing one or two, as a demonstration of his intentions—that was always good policy. But all of them? Wasteful. He would now have to start all over again, getting some more.

Still, drawn by morbid curiosity, he peered over the edge of the parapet, to see the mess they'd made on the street.

There was no mess.

There was just a wide expanse of gray webbing, stretching across the street, one story up—and a wriggling, entangled mass of erstwhile hostages, still bouncing from the initial impact. The Vulture scowled as he considered just what that meant, tensed as he tried to figure just where the attack was coming from, and said, "Oh", as for the most fleeting instant, his entire field of vision was taken up by a flash of red in the shape of a red boot.

The kick to the face was a solid one. It dazed the Vulture, knocking him back ten feet. Spider-Man rode the Vulture's fall as far as he could, standing with his left foot on the Vulture's chest and his right foot still pressed firmly against the Vulture's now even more unlovely nose. He flipped off only when the old man snarled and grabbed at his ankles. Not that the Vulture's hands were all that much of a threat—but the wings attached to his arms were. The move had made those razor-sharp wings curl up and around Spider-Man's body like the leaves of a hungry carnivorous plant.

Spider-Man spun, leaped off the parapet, rebounded off an air-conditioning unit, and leaped at the Vulture again. "Got to hand it to you, Vulchy! Just when I think you've sunk as far as you can go, you get back in there and dig yourself a new sub-basement!"

The Vulture recovered in time to evade the attack, flying a spiral course around Spider-Man's leap. Two of his wing-blades scraped the rooftop, raising sparks. "I'm so glad you're here, Spider-Man! I was looking forward to ripping your spine out through your throat!"

"Now *that's* a charming image!" Spider-Man gibed. He landed, leaped straight up, and fired two weblines that both missed by the Vulture by inches. "I gotta give you credit, Vulchy—that's much better than the kind of stuff you used to come up with! You must have started practicing in front of the mirror at night—though with what you have to look at, I wouldn't blame you for not wanting to!"

The Vulture banked, changed course so suddenly that the turn was indistinguishable from a right angle, and rocketed straight up. Spider-Man, who knew his tactics well, didn't even bother trying to leap after him; he just watched, warily, as the old man leveled off, circled high above, then dove toward him. It was a textbook strafing run, much like the early biplanes used to attack civilians on the ground, except that in this case the attacker was a nasty-looking old guy in a feathery green bird suit.

Spider-Man simply remained where he was. If he dodged too early, the Vulture would have time to alter course. Too far, and the Vulture would miss him by a mile. Too close, and the impact would probably knock them both silly. Too late, and J. Jonah Jameson would have had the headline he'd lusted after all these years.

Timing this just right, on the other hand . . .

. . . that would be special.

At the very last second, rocketing toward Spider-Man at waist-height, the Vulture seemed to realize that his foe had no intention of dodging. He saw Spider-Man winding up for a punch, and his eyes widened as he instantly calculated the results of adding the force of own significant momentum to the superhuman strength behind Spider-Man's blow. He gasped and tried to gain altitude.

"Wax on!" Spider-Man cried, as he swung. "Wax off!"

The Vulture's wings tilted perpendicular to the ground,

catching the air, slowing him down just enough to make the punch a glancing one. It still freight-trained the Vulture's jaw, and rattled the brain in his skull, and set him up for a follow-up punch to the ribs which didn't look like much fun either, but it was unfortunately not enough to knock him out; he was still able to recover in time to thrash his right wing at Spider-Man's face, forcing the wall-crawler back.

"A . . . lucky blow!" the Vulture managed. "But it will be your last!"

Spider-Man took his time advancing on him. "You've got it all wrong, Vulchy! Y'ever notice that whenever you yeggs band together I seem to have less trouble taking you on than I do when you attack me one at a time? You ever wonder why that is?"

The Vulture feinted with his left wing again, cutting the air bare inches in front of Spider-Man's face.

Spider-Man dodged, but only a little; according to his spider-sense, the slash hadn't been in any real danger of connecting. "Come on!" he said. "Don't you wanna know the answer to that question, Vulchy? Don't you wanna know why I've almost got you beat already?"

The Vulture bellowed and charged, attacking Spider-Man with his bare fists. One punch connected on the right side of Spider-Man's face; the next on his left. Both landed solidly, and both hurt. Next the Vulture drove his knee into Spider-Man's belly, driving the wind from the wall-crawler's lungs. That hurt, too. The trick, Spider-Man knew, was not minding that it hurt: accepting the moment of pain as the price of an opportunity to strike back. He grunted, slapped aside another pair of punches with a of pair lightning-fast jabs to the Vulture's wrists, then took advantage of the moment's opportunity to slam his fist into the Vulture's solar plexus.

Thanks to his strength he derived from his flight harness, Adrian Toomes had always been an extraordinarily powerful foe, especially for a man his age. He could take the punch, especially in light of the way his costume absorbed impact.

But this particular blow was so strong his grandmother must have felt it.

The Vulture staggered back, gasping.

"Wanna listen now?" Spider-Man asked.

"I will kill you," the old man raged. "I will see you a broken rag doll, shattered by a fall from a height!"

"Little chance of that, Vulchy! Y'see—what I've been trying to tell you is—when I fight you guys one at a time I have time to worry about not hurting you too badly! When you guys band together, and pull a stupid stunt like today's, I don't have that luxury! I can't hold back anymore! I've got to show you how easily I could take you down if I was really trying!"

There was a moment of silence, as the Vulture digested that, his eyes narrow and disbelieving.

Then, outraged, he leaped.

The cutting edge of the Vulture's right wing sliced the air where Spider-Man had been. Spider-Man dodged, but set himself up for an equally deadly slash from the left. He did not, quite, manage to get out of the way of that one. He avoided the cutting edge, but was struck head on by the flat, the impact a lot like a smash in the face with a two-by-four. Spider-Man staggered back, already raising his hands to ward off the inevitable follow-up attack.

There was none. The Vulture had taken flight.

This time, Spider-Man knew, he wasn't just getting into position for another attack; he was fleeing, to lick his wounds, rendezvous with the rest of the Six, and find some more civilians to terrorize. Spider-Man leaped, matching the

Vulture's rate of ascent just long enough to fire another webline. This one, aimed at the Vulture's ankles, connected solidly, binding them tightly together. There was a surreal moment when the line fluttered, thanks to a midair u-turn which gave it plenty of slack—but then the Vulture decided where he was going and the line drew taut with a bone-jarring tug.

The Vulture cackled. "You were correct, Spider-Man! With a solid surface beneath you, the advantage is yours! But here, in the sky—the Vulture is king!"

Now being towed along like a kiddy toy at the end of a string, through air now rendered even more frigid by wind chill, Spider-Man knew that his old enemy was right. At ground-level, trading punches, the Vulture was a dangerous but essentially quantifiable risk; in the sky, he had gravity and the city's architecture on his side. Up here, Spider-Man's little speech about holding back became nothing but wishful thinking. Spider-Man had to take him down quickly. He gripped the long looping webline more tightly and began pulling himself toward the Vulture hand-over-hand.

"Spider-Man!" This from Doug Deeley, via the SAFE communication device in the web-slinger's right ear. "We have unconfirmed reports of an explosion at City Hall and a developing hostage situation at the Brooklyn Bridge! Do you copy?"

"I copy, I copy!" Spider-Man groaned, doubling over into a ball to avoid being smashed into the wall of a nearby sky-scraper. "I'm just a little busy now, do you mind?"

The Vulture had seized upon his strategy—now that he had Spider-Man dangling at the end of a webline, he was going to play crack-the-whip against the Manhattan skyline. The first few collisions were almost playful, as the old man perfected his technique: Spider-Man skidded along office windows hard enough to make the lexar wobble, rebounded off, spun helplessly, then felt the webline snap taut again as another familiar building loomed like a forty-story hand about to slap him in the face.

Entire city blocks turned into blurs as the Vulture raced through the concrete canyons, slamming Spidey against the McGraw-Hill building, heading north to batter him against the G.E. building, then making a sudden turn to the right to descend so low over the Avenue of the Americas that the latest obstacle threatening to smash the web-slinger flat was an approaching double-decker tour bus. Spider-Man calculated his chances of surviving this large-scale reenact-ment of the bug-on-a-windshield trick (not large), kicked off against the pavement directly below him hard enough to gain himself some altitude, and was yanked in between the two rows of rooftop seats for the amusement of some twenty fascinated tourists thrilled that their guide had man-aged to arrange such an intimate encounter with one of New York's best-known citizens.

As a demonstration of the human animal's endless capacity to think the oddest thoughts in the most stressful situations, Spider-Man caught a glimpse of one mid-western tourist with the presence of mind to snap his picture, and thought: *Whaddaya know. I have that camera, too.*

Up ahead, the Vulture changed course again, aiming himself directly at the open air above the canyons of steel and concrete and glass. Still gripping the webline with his right hand, Spider-Man used his left hand to fire another one at the thirtieth story of a skyscraper housing a well-known advertising agency. This second webline stuck, and Spider-Man held on tight with both hands, hoping to arrest the Vulture's flight with nothing but the considerable strength of his own two arms. He gritted his teeth, awaiting what would certainly be a painful jerk when both lines snapped taut.

They did not snap taut.

The Vulture, spotting the maneuver, had looped around to sever the second webline with a single pass of his razor-sharp wings. "It won't be that easy, wall-crawler! I already know your tricks! If this is to be the final battle between us, it will be at a site of my own choosing!"

"How about Lindelmann's Deli? I can really use some hot hazelnut coffee!" Spider-Man somersaulted, attempting to use the Vulture's looping flight path to guide himself to a landing on the villain's back. In this he failed; the Vulture had altered course again, heading southeast. The path carried them over Park, north of Grand Central, facing the place where the road split to become a pair of tunnels running beneath an elegant Helmsley hotel and then around the great broad expanse of the Met-Life Building. As usual, the bifurcated avenue was packed with bumper-to-bumper traffic, much of it yellow cabs. The Vulture was headed directly toward the northbound exit, apparently intending to take them both through that narrow opening, flying against traffic. In that constricted space, with the Vulture controlling his trajectory, it was going to be next to impossible for Spider-Man to avoid a deadly collision with a windshield or a tunnel wall.

Forget that. It was time he started making his fair share of the navigation decisions.

He released the webline tethering him to the Vulture's ankles, and simultaneously fired another pair at each of the Vulture's wings. Both connected. Spider-Man tugged hard on both, forcing both wings to draw back, catching the air, resulting in a a course change toward the sky.

The Helmsley Building loomed before them, then passed

by underneath—replaced by the far greater expanse of the Met Life building, which seemed far too close to avoid. The Vulture banked of his own volition, headed east again; centrifugal force swung Spider-Man into a painful belly flop against the unbreakable glass windows. The impact would have shattered every bone in the body of any other man. As Spider-Man slid across the glass on his stomach, still holding on to the weblines with both hands, proximity made it possible for him to see the startled faces of the white-collar workers in the offices inside. He wondered if any of them had imagined they were having a tough morning—copier jammed, phones busy, boss perhaps a little cranky—and decided he had absolutely no sympathy. *Try this sometime, okay?*

"Spider-Man!" This a transmission from Doug Deeley. "The City Hall bomb threat was a prank—just a couple of Yancy Street kids who thought they could horn in on the act! But the Brooklyn Bridge sighting is a definite! Electro is on the bridge! Repeat! *Electro is on the bridge!*"

"Th-thanks," Spider-Man managed. "You're really helpful, you know that?" Gritting his teeth, he renewed his grip on the two weblines and once again focused all his concentration on reaching the Vulture before the old man could batter him with another building.

The Vulture changed course again, heading north, swallowing the blocks like candy. They had close encounters with the Waldorf Astoria, its close neighbor the Marriott Eastside Hotel, and the Seagram Building. They even passed through a fifty-story office building under construction on Lex, the Vulture looping around the bare girders in an attempt to shake Spider-Man off. This was, of course, a tactical mistake: construction sites were more Spider-Man's territory than the Vulture's. Spider-Man let go of the weblines, scrambled over a pair of girders, launched himself ahead of the Vulture's arc, and grabbed the pair of weblines again.

"You again!" the Vulture cried. "I thought I'd lost you!"

"Don't know why you're so surprised, cuddles! After all, who else were you expecting to meet, up here?"

The tower looming up ahead now, recognizable by its wedge-shaped roof, was the Citicorp Center: another perfect place to play crack-the-whip. Also the perfect place for Spider-Man to pull off the maneuver he'd finally concocted to put an end to this insanity.

The Vulture flew within ten feet of the skyscraper's glass walls before veering off. Spider-Man, headed for another bone-rattling impact, flipped in mid-air and hit the building with the soles of his feet. The Vulture was going so fast that Spider-Man slid almost fifteen feet across the side of the building, in a position best described as vertical water-skiing, before the remarkable adhesive abilities of the wall-crawler's extremities finally kicked in.

Spider-Man screeched to a halt.

The Vulture kept going until the weblines attached to both his wings suddenly snapped taut. At which point simple physics brought him up short, conserving his angular momentum with a fresh trajectory defined by his speed and the limits of the web-cables tethering him. He changed course against his will, screamed, and slammed into the side of the Citicorp Center at full speed.

Had the windows been true glass, the Vulture might have broken right through, leading to a new phase of battle occupying the offices inside. But these windows were lexar. They vibrated, but held. Flattened against the wall, the Vulture looked like he was going to stick there. "S-savage!" he managed, through a jaw forcibly slammed shut. "You hurt me!"

"Oh," Spider-Man said. "Like we're playing fair now. Excuse me?'"

"It ... will end ... where it began! Mark my words! Where it began!"

Spider-Man was about to finish mopping up the Vulture when his ear-phone crackled again, bringing another frenzied update from Deeley. "Spider-Man! We have a developing situation on the Brooklyn Bridge! Electro has seized hostages! Are you ready to engage?"

"Engage," Spider-Man muttered. "Where's the Borg?"

Gravity peeled the Vulture loose. He fluttered backward, knocked silly but still kept aloft by the sophisticated technology of his flight suit; he might have just bobbed along motionlessly, but some atavistic refusal to give up allowed him to continue flapping his wings, enabling a slow and painful retreat to the west. Spider-Man considered going after him again. The man was, after all, pretty close to defeat now; it would only take another couple of minutes to take him out completely, web him up, and consider him written out of the rest of today's festivities. But a couple of minutes was a long time. And the Brooklyn Bridge was way downtown, near the southern tip of the island. And Electro was one of the two most dangerous members of the Six. And he had hostages.

Deeley said: "Spider-Man? We estimate about two hundred seventy civilians."

The Vulture was ascending now. Slowly, painfully ... but already almost a hundred feet higher than the nearest tall building. Spider-Man could probably get him now if he really tried. But what of Electro? He was the guy who'd once tried to blow up a city block just to make a point. Would he be inclined to show mercy toward people he'd made his prisoners?

Spider-Man realized he had no choice. The Vulture was dangerous; Electro was a potential city-killer.

And besides—he had to admit this to himself—after that terrible day with Gwen Stacy, the Brooklyn Bridge carried a particularly terrible weight. He didn't think he could bear to risk anybody else being hurt or killed there.

He tapped his throat-mike. "All right. I'm on my way."

"Good." Deeley said grimly. "Because I don't get the impression this dude is into waiting . . ."

CHAPTER NINE

9:53 A.M.

At 27, Jay Sein was programming director and morning drive time personality on WMRV, the only station devoted to 24-hour-a-day coverage of developments in the superheroic, super-villainous, and similarly paranormal arenas. This may have been an unusual marketing niche, but it provided a vital service in a city where invasions from Atlantis took place almost as frequently as transit strikes. In the past few years alone, his award-winning lineup had included weekly discussions of Super Hero Case Law hosted by former District Attorney Franklin Nelson, regular (heated) debates on the mutant question between Senator Robert Kelly and Dr. Charles Xavier, and a one-shot half-scholarly, half-speculative analysis of super hero marriages by Dr. Ruth Westheimer.

Still, most of the station's programming had always focused on hard news: from which bad guys were at large at any given time, to traffic reports for commuters needing to avoid the neighborhood being trashed any given day.

Unsurprisingly, Jay had directed heavy airtime for the conflict between Spider-Man and the Sinister Six.

"So the bugman beats the birdman," he said, in the half-wry, half-somber voice that had made him popular among standup comedians looking for somebody to imitate. "That was a no-brainer. I mean, I'm sure he's dangerous and everything, but if the Sinister Six were the Beatles the Vulture would have to be Ringo. What do you think, Cosmo?"

This a cue to Jay's sidekick, Cosmo the K, self-proclaimed coolest man in the universe, and owner of the world's most frightening eraser-shaped hairstyle. Cosmo bit on his pipe, puffed out a cloud of ruminative smoke, and said, "I'm gonna have to differ with you there, Jaybee. Sure, nobody really expected the Vulture to win, but it's still a formidable first strike by the Six, in that he was able to keep Spider-Man on the defensive for almost a half hour. One can only assume they deliberately scheduled the Vulture's play for first, just to wear out the web-slinger before they brought out Octopus, who has traditionally been considered their toughest gun."

"A situation that might change," Jay pointed out, "considering recent indications that Electro's upgraded his act."

"That's true, Jay. Spider-Man has defeated this new and improved Electro before—most recently when that shocking individual tried to threaten the city's water supply—but we've yet to see if he can pull off that trick when kept off balance by the rest of the team. Electro does bear watching. Still, Doctor Octopus has always been the key player in the Six before, and we have no reason to believe that he'll been anything but that, now. If I were a betting man, I'd put my money on him."

"Not that we're rooting for him," Jay prodded.

"Uh . . . no. Right. Not that we are."

"We'll be right back, with more coverage of the ongoing Sinister Six crisis, right after these words from Stereo City."

9:57 A.M.

The Brooklyn Bridge had become a prison, bordered by lightning.

Great electrical explosions, both exquisitely timed, had cut off both ends of the roadway, trapping the cars and buses then in the act of crossing the East River. Curtains of glowing electrical energy had descended from both the eastern and western towers, forming a barrier only a madman bent on suicide would have dared to challenge; arcs of crackling, blindingly bright lightning now raced up and down the supporting cables, and over the heads of the stranded motorists themselves, none of whom—unusually enough for Manhattan—were foolhardy enough to risk abandoning their cars. Nor could they drive to safety, since the monster had also used his uncanny control of electricity to drain their batteries. Protected from immediate electrocution by the insulating effect of their rubber tires, the almost three hundred people in the cars and buses craned their necks, trying to catch a glimpse of the madman—or was it mad god?—who stood atop the Manhattan-side tower, laughing at their plight.

He wore a green jumpsuit with two cartoon representations of lightning-bolts crossing over his chest in a V shape. It may have been a silly outfit, but the design wasn't all that easy to see, anyway: the man glowed like a miniature sun, and had eyes that roared like turbines. His laugh, amplified so loud that everybody on the bridge could hear it, was cold, merciless, and insane. It was easy to believe that he would actually kill everybody on the bridge, as he'd repeatedly threatened; just as easy to believe that the several sled-like flying machines visibly circling the bridge at a safe distance, (which a very small number of the captives recognized as belonging to the same government guys responsible for that helicarrier thing that was always hovering over the water just past the southern tip of Manhattan), were holding back only because they knew they were helpless in the face of his raw elemental power.

There was only one thing that nobody understood.

Namely, the woman.

The beautiful young blond woman, in short skirt and pale green windbreaker, who seemed to repeatedly tumble from the Brooklyn-side Tower, as silently and bonelessly as a rag doll . . .

10:02 A.M.

Heading downtown fast, hopping from building to building in a series of apartment complexes overlooking the East River Park and FDR Drive, just a few blocks north of the Williamsburg Bridge, Spider-Man was brought up short by a fresh buzz from his SAFE communicator. This time, it wasn't his official liaison Deeley, but Sean Morgan himself, his voice as sharp as a knife-edge drawn across flesh. "Spider-Man! Stop what you're doing! We have a problem!"

Caught in mid-air, between one building and the next, Spider-Man back flipped, shot a web at a fire escape, looped around, and landed in a crouch on the nearest wall. "Gee, that's a novelty!"

The nearly imperceptible pause was probably the sound of Morgan parsing the humor, finding it irrelevant, and moving on. "Dr. Octopus. The roof of an office building on West 20th! Specifically, the building where—"

Spider-Man didn't need reminding. "Captain Stacy." He winced as his mind replayed a slow-motion animation of the way the bricks had tumbled and spun as they fell toward the child frozen with fear on the street below . . . only to miss that child and strike down the brave old man whose last act in life was to protect that child from harm. Doctor Octopus had been the catalyst behind that tragedy; the thought of him deliberately staging a replay, as if out of some twisted form of pride, was enough to stoke the anger Spider-Man already felt at Electro's desecration of the place where the Captain's daughter Gwen had died. Which was probably the whole point. He muttered: "It figures. They're not even taking turns."

"No, they're not. Did you expect them to?"

Spider-Man almost replied that there was no reason not to; after all, they'd used that bone-headed method of teaming up more than once in the past. Alas, this time, they seemed prepared to take advantage of their superior numbers. He said: "What about Electro?"

"He can wait," Morgan said.

"But his hostages—"

"We have room to maneuver here. We have paranormal neutralization experts and combat tacticians in place on the Manhattan Bridge. We have aircars marking off a perimeter, and submarine units converging on the site in the water. We're even pulling our analysts from some of the other potential locations to plan an assault. We'll keep an eye on the situation, hold back as long as it remains stable, and prepare to go in ourselves if we have to. The Octavius situation, on the other hand —taking place as it does in the middle of a crowded neighborhood, with the usual mobs of rubber-neckers—can only benefit from a smaller, more concentrated assault, like yourself. We need you there."

Spider-Man refrained from asking Morgan whether he was sure his agents could handle Electro. He hadn't often seen SAFE's people in action, but he'd seen enough of Sean Morgan to estimate the quality of the people under the man's command. Still, he had one remaining concern: "I don't like turning my back on this, Colonel. Ock has fifty hostages. Electro has a couple of hundred."

"He does," Morgan said. "Unfortunately, even with that factored in, the hostages are secondary. Apprehending Octavius has to be our top priority, and you know it."

Spider-Man knew it, all right. He hated it, but he knew it. Dr. Octopus wasn't the most powerful member of the Sinister Six—not since Electro's power up, he wasn't—but his brilliantly twisted mind still rendered him a menace to all civilization. Every second he was loose, the world teetered on the brink without knowing it . . . rendering Electro, for all his awesome power, just a nasty neighborhood problem by comparison.

He realized he'd formed a pair of white-knuckled fists without knowing it. "On my way," he said.

10:10 A.M.

Mark Twain once wrote that it was easy to quit smoking; after all, he'd done it hundreds of times.

As she sat in the outer office of the Performing Arts Dean of Empire State University, feeling stifled in her conservative regular job interview suit, and trying not to make eye contact with the four virtually identical tweedy, sandy-haired, cardigan-wearing young men who occupied each of the other seats, Mary Jane Watson-Parker could only admire Twain's knack for the great eternal truths. She'd started and quit smoking in her teens, started and quit again when playing a small supporting role on a cop show out in Los Angeles, then started and quit again during her marriage to Peter. She hadn't touched the filthy things in a long time now, but still felt the cravings especially hard during moments of extreme stress—which were not uncommon in the life of a woman married to a guy who battled the forces of evil on a daily basis.

Now, waiting for an important job interview, and struggling not to show more than academic interest in the distressing regular updates Jay Sein and Cosmo the K provided through the receptionist's desk radio, she flirted with the thought of taking up the bad habit again, if only to provide her with something to do with her hands other than wring them in constant, helpless frustration.

The dean's door opened, and a dejected tweedy man, identical to each of the other four, shuffled out, wearing the look common to everybody who has ever known a job interview had just ended with a resounding flush. Ian Farnswell, a tall, gray-haired man who was predictably also wearing what seemed to be the official department uniform, poked his head out the door, scanned the applicants, consulted the resume in his right hand, and spoke in the lightest trace of an oxford accent: "Ahh, I suppose I don't need to ask which one of you is Mary Jane. Can you step in here, please?"

Mary Jane gathered her things and followed the dean inside, wondering distantly why she felt more nervous at this interview than she did when auditioning for major motion pictures. Inside, she found the kind of office that was not so much decorated as accumulated: the hundreds of books, most of which were leather editions stuffed with handwritten notes on yellowing paper, which sat stacked four-deep on institutional-design metal shelves, had to compete against a lifetime's sediment of beloved knick-knackery for every inch of shelf space. There were twenty snowglobes alone, ranging from one that seemed to be a replica of the famous prop from *Citizen Kane* to the more recent bloody murder scene snow-globe offered as a premium with video-cassettes of the Cohen Brothers masterpiece, *Fargo*. The photographs on the outer wall, most of which were signed WITH DEEPEST RESPECT AND AFFECTION or somesuch variant, depicted Farnswell with Lee Strasburg, Orson Welles, Peter Ustinov, Helen Hayes, Simon Williams, and President John Kennedy, among a host of other, equivalently familiar faces.

It looked like a comfortable room. If you were part of the history.

If you weren't part of the history, it was next to impossible to sit in this room without feeling small.

Farnswell gestured her to a chair, then sat on his side of a huge mahogany desk, leaning back so far in his chair that the back of his head almost brushed the hernia-inducing *Complete Shakespeare* open to *Macbeth* on the podium behind him. "I must say," he remarked, "it's awfully sporting of you to brave the city today, with all this Sinister Six rot wreaking such chaos with public transit. I had a dozen other qualified applicants, not quite as hardy as yourself, call to cancel their appointments. Tea?"

"Yes, thank you." As Farnswell poured from a silver pot, Mary Jane said: "I just figured . . . if you think a super-villain battle's sufficient excuse for not showing up, you shouldn't try to get a job in New York."

"Or in the theatre," he said, giving that exalted word three syllables. "The show must go on, you know."

She sipped. "I think I've heard that once or twice."

"Yes. I was fourteen years old, working my apprenticeship for the Royal Shakespeare Company, when the Blitz hit London, and unless somebody specifically told me a performance was cancelled, I still arrived in costume in time to stand on the parapet and try to keep a straight face holding the spear." A nostalgic smile tugged at the corners of his lips. "Once, we had a near miss. A bomb went off so close it shook the rafters. A six-inch chunk of plaster fell from the ceiling and knocked me unconscious. I recovered in time for the curtain call, and won a louder ovation than that night's Hamlet. I think back on those hard times and wonder why you Yanks allow a few costumed ruffians like the Sinister Six throw the whole city into such a tizzy."

Mary Jane couldn't believe she was being drawn into this conversation. "Well, sir, they are dangerous people . . ."

"This," Farnswell smiled, "coming from the brave young lady who I've been told practically defeated Mysterio all on her own just one week ago?"

Mary Jane winced at the realization that this respected and distinguished academician probably obtained all of his news from the *Daily Bugle*. "It wasn't quite like that, sir. Spider-Man and Razorback deserve all the credit. I just survived the crossfire."

"Mmm. Razorback. Yes, I remember now. He made a strange front page, didn't he? Ionesco would have loved him. In any event, my dear, how much do you know about this proposed position?"

"Only that you're expanding your evening Acting Workshops."

"Indeed," Farnswell said, lighting his meershaum pipe. "The University ran into an unexpected budget surplus and decided—miracle of miracles—to plow the funds back into our evening community extension classes. But these are advanced workshops, and we are looking for instructors with background in classical theatre. Precisely which roles would you say qualify you for this position?"

Mary Jane had been a recurring player in a hit cop show starring her late friend Brick Johnson, voice talent for two seasons of a Saturday morning cartoon show called *The Hypernauts*, lead actress on a daytime soap opera *Secret Hospital*, and star of several direct-to-video action movies. They—and a significant number of commercials and modeling gigs—may have rendered her recognizable, but weren't exactly designed to impress an aging Shakespearean who had worked alongside Burton and Olivier. So she said: "Two years ago, I did a limited run as Nora in Ibsen's *A Doll's House*."

"One of my favorites. Do go on."

"In college I did Kate in *The Taming of the Shrew*."

Farnswell narrowed his eyes appraisingly. "I find it difficult to picture the formidable specimen of manliness they would have needed to cast as your triumphant suitor in that production. Any others?"

"Ummm ... well ... I freely admit that the production itself was one of the most wrongheaded ideas any producer ever had, but I also played Wilhemina Loman in the Bleeker Street Experimental Actor's Workship production of *Death of A Saleswoman*."

Farnswell winced. "I've heard of that one."

Her spirits sank. "Really?"

"Yes. I had hoped it was one of those unfortunate urban legends, like the Mexican pet or the poodle in the microwave. But I trust you out-shined the butchering of the source material. Is there anything else?"

Mary Jane found herself drawing a blank.

"Very well, then," Farnswell said. He tapped the head of his model Maltese Falcon, ruminated the interview so far over several clouds of cherry-scented smoke, and leaned forward in his chair. His eyebrows seemed to hover a full inch ahead of his brow as he asked, "I suppose you won't mind if I ask you a leading question. When you played Emma Steel in *Fatal Action III*, which I must say I rented only because it was your name on the video box, was that really you performing that leap through that second story window into that speeding convertible in on the ground? I examined that scene frame by frame on my VCR, and I could not discern any obvious doubling or substitutions. It was a moment worthy of Jet Li, Sammo Hung, or any of the other great action stars of Hong Kong, and I found it simply dazzling, the greatest moment of your *ouevre* so far. If you don't mind, would you mind telling me how it was done?"

It was one of the unexpectedly surreal moments that comes from even the slightest measure of fame, and it took Mary Jane entirely by surprise. She blinked several times before managing a response. "The entire interior of the convertible was an inflated stunt bag. We switched to a regular car for the fight scene in the back seat. But that isn't really my main area of interest, sir. I have a grounding in—"

"Ms. Watson-Parker," Farnswell said sternly. "This is an evening workshop, run for profit, geared toward the general community instead of the matriculated student body. A little way to raise funds, if you will. Who do you think is more likely to attract the most paying students? One of those fine theorists in tweed, who have been putting me to sleep for the past week of interviews? Or the beautiful, charming, and apparently courageous star of *Fatal Action III*, who's gotten more real acting work—and more varied acting work—than all the rest of them put together? I'm surprised you even feel you need to come in for an interview. Shall we discuss terms?"

Mary Jane's tension evaporated. She broke out into a wide grin, thinking of all the bills she and Peter would be able to pay with the added income. They might even get to remind themselves what it was like to pay all their bills on their time, instead of selecting a few that were safe to delay until the sternly-worded third notice.

The smile faltered almost immediately.

She'd just thought of Peter.

10:15 A.M.

There's a very old, and very bad, joke about the child who looks out the window of an airplane and says, *Wow. We're so high up the people look like ants.* Whereupon his sister looks out the same window and says, *We haven't even taken off, stupid. Those* are *ants.*

Doctor Otto Octavius was not the kind of man who appreciated humor of any kind, unless it was the special kind of hilarity he always derived from terrified people fleeing in the face of his superior might. But ever since childhood, he'd always treasured that little two-liner, in much the same way a zen philosopher might treasure a particularly profound koan. It spoke to the attitude he'd always harbored toward the rest of humanity, even before the acquisition of his wondrous mechanical arms: that wherever he stood in life, whatever ambitions he might choose to pursue, or whatever means he might choose to pursue them, he was always so far above the great mewling mass of the species, just by virtue of his own advanced intellect alone, that it was impossible not to regard them as ants infesting a world rightfully his.

It was a particularly painful irony of his life that fate had mocked him with an enemy who was himself modeled on an insect.

No, he mentally corrected himself. *Not insect. Arachnid.*

I will not be corrected by that cretin again.

Not during our battle today.

And after I rip him to bloody shreds, sometime in the next few minutes, not ever again.

Captain Anthony Scibelli of Manhattan South, who had been placed in charge of municipal response to the hostage situation on the West Side, licked his wind-chapped lips as he stared at the nightmare up above. He stood in the center of the street, exhaling so much condensation he looked like a man breathing fire; already shadowed by the overcast light, his face changed colors every fraction of a second or so, courtesy of the almost two dozen squad cars flashing their dome lights on all sides of him. As the only cop in sight not taking cover behind a prowler, or leveling his weapon at the roof of the office building, he was as much the center of attention as the monster they'd all come here to stop.

Somewhere up above, Doctor Octopus shouted: "I am still waiting for the arachnid! Assure me he's on the way!"

Scibelli spoke through a megaphone: "We're working on it, Doctor! We need more time!"

"The hostages don't have time!" Octopus shouted.

"We're doing the best we can, Doctor! Understand me! It's not like the wall-crawler and this department have ever been on the best of terms!"

Octavius cackled. "True! As I recall, you initially blamed him for the death that took place on this very spot! But your delaying tactics will have limited effect on me, Captain! I am not some addle-pated political terrorist, capable of being manipulated by the procedures in your rulebook! I am Octavius! I give you five minutes to produce the wall-crawler!"

Scibelli was neither impressed or intimidated. A thirty-year veteran, twice hospitalized for gunshot wounds, thrice decorated for courage above and beyond the call of duty, he was a fiftyish, jowly black man with narrow eyes and a handlebar moustache several shades darker than his graying (but still reasonably full) set of hair. He had long been considered the department's best hand at deploying massive uniformed response to those situations where the routine violence of the city escalated to a level best compared to all-out war—a wide spectrum of possible scenarios which in this city ranged from riots, and terrorist attacks on skyscrapers to invasions from marauding Skrulls. Scibelli's demeanor in such crises would have surprised civilians who only knew people of his profession from media portrayals. In the first place, he did not wear a look of constantly simmering rage; his habitual expression being closer to a great, soul-devouring weariness at the horrors men can inflict upon other men. And in the second place, unlike movie and TV cops of his age (and—it had not failed to escape his notice—color), he did not moan constantly about being only one week from retirement. Nor did he complain about being too old for this crap. He would know when he was too old, namely, when they closed the lid on his box.

He had no intention of allowing the likes of Dr. Octopus to hasten that day. But he couldn't deny that this crisis made him feel significantly older than most.

Less than half an hour earlier, Octopus had appeared atop this battered brick warehouse, using two of his tentacles to carry his pudgy form back and forth across the room, and two others to imprison a young man and woman whose helplessness in the face of the strength did not prevent them from screaming and struggling to the point of exhaustion. Dr. Octopus wore a double-breasted white suit specially tailored to fit the ring-shaped harness that held his tentacles fast to his body. Even so, it barely contained him, and it would have rendered him comical if not for the liquid, sinuous deadliness of the adamantium tentacles that seemed as much a part of him as his own limbs. Hurling a couple of cinderblocks to the sidewalks below—crushing one parked car, and destroying a fire hydrant that was still flooding the street in protest—Octopus had wasted no time in announcing that he had approximately fifty more workers locked inside a storeroom down below. "If I don't see Spider-Man," he'd shouted, using hidden amplification systems that rendered his voice audible for blocks in every direction, "I will collapse the roof and kill them all!"

Scibelli, who'd worked with Captain George Stacy, had considered him a friend, and had never been able to drive by this particular building without feeling a twinge of remembered pain, had expected Octopus to choose this as the site of his demented commemoration, and had done his best to prepare for the siege. He'd ordered the site—a five-story brick building with sooty windows and no doubt cramped offices—placed under surveillance, stationed sharpshooters in the windows of the office building across the street, even placed four members of SWAT in the building's security force. The sharpshooters were still in place, unable to fire as long as Octavius was still holding civilians in his arms; the SWAT officers were reputedly among the hostages locked inside the storeroom; and the officers who'd been stationed in unmarked cars across the street had been quickly spotted by Octavius, and would not be able to join the small army now training their guns on the building until the fire department first succeeded in prying them loose with the Jaws of Life. How Octopus had gotten into the neighborhood without being spotted, in the face of such tremendous surveillance, remained a mystery. Scibelli was certain he'd kick himself once he found out.

In the meantime, he hadn't been idle; the surrounding

streets were now filled with hundreds of officers and dozens of prowlers and armored vans. The firepower trained on Octavius was enough to reduce him to a thin red mist—but not even a direct hit by a nuclear bomb would have tarnished his indestructible tentacles, and even a perfect head shot capable of eliminating Octavius immediately would have caused those tentacles to constrict at once, dooming both hostages to an agonizing death.

Of course, New York City being New York City, this crisis had attracted a crowd worthy of the Macy's Thanksgiving Day Parade. The crowd barriers placed at every intersection in a two block radius were teeming with shouting and grinning civilians, some of whom carried signs that read WE LOVE YOU SPIDEY! Most of those barriers served as the backdrop for reporters from the broadcast media, who intoned their usual banalities about *New York At Siege* while jubilant civilians jostled and shoved for their moment on camera. Inspecting one of those barriers, earlier, observing a gang of ten teenagers sticking out their tongues for the camera, while one of the newswomen recited the names of people known to be employees of the paper company in question, Scibelli had wondered if there would ever be a story so horrifying that New Yorkers wouldn't be more excited about the prospect of being on camera.

Up on the roof, Octopus was shouting another endless tirade about his unappreciated genius. Scibelli turned off his megaphone and spoke with his immediate subordinate, Lieutenant Philip Gerard. "God save me from the underwear types. Does he write this stuff down first, or does he just rattle it off extemporaneously?"

Gerard, who was famed department-wide for his complete lack of a sense of humor, replied in his disconcerting Texas accent: "I don't see as how it matters, sir."

"I suppose you're right. How's the deployment going?"

"There's a couple of rooftops we haven't accessed yet." Gerard pointed out two of them. "Some of them we don't need. That one up there: we didn't see the point, since it's not quite as tall and the shooting position is not quite as good. Besides, we don't have enough men to cover all the surrounding structures as it is. If you want, I could redeploy—"

"Not necessary," Scibelli said. They had more than adequate coverage of lines-of-sight as it was. "What about tear gas launchers?"

"We have several of those in place, too, but nobody thinks they'll do any good. Octavius—"

"I know." Tear gas had been tried against Octavius before, on several occasions. It had always been totally ineffective; the man was capable of whirling his tentacles fast enough to fan away any noxious fumes. Scibelli said, "Maybe we ought to—"

He heard the vast, communal gasp of breath before he registered the gunshot.

"Oh, God," he said. "No—"

It had come from somewhere at ground level; one of the uniformed officers had, either by accident or sheer panic, squeezed off a shot. The sound was so loud, and so unexpected, that Scibelli's heart skipped; for a fraction of a second he was terribly afraid that the rest of his people would take it as a cue and pepper the rooftop with a fusillade that might not get Octopus but would certainly cut the man's two prisoners to pieces. But his people, showing almost superhuman restraint, continued to hold their fire, instead shouting at each other in anger, demanding to know who among them had been stupid enough to initiate this potentially very lethal contact.

Gerard moaned. "Aw, no! It was Kranz!" He used the

word the same way a child of seven, learning what his Mommy had prepared for dinner, would say, "Aw no! It's liver!"

Scibelli caught a glimpse of the patrolman in question, a rookie who had been in firing position behind the door of his squad car who now stood in the center of a maelstrom of accusatory faces, stammering something about being sorry. As Gerard ran toward that prowler to relieve the dumb-head from duty, Scibelli raised his megaphone, intent on making sure that Octavius didn't interpret this momentary lapse as the beginning of an all-out assault.

In this, he was too late.

Because Octavius was among them.

Still lugging his hostages, a young man and young woman who both wore the shell-shocked expressions of people enjoying a premature glimpse of hell, Octavius had used his tentacles to descend the side of the building in two giant strides. He landed in the center of the street, in the middle of the cops, as if to demonstrate how little he was intimidated by their bullets. Supported by two tentacles, he swept the one clutching his male hostage across the street, tripping up seven officers with a single move. He used the end of the tentacle clutching his female hostage to tear off the front hood of a squad car, fling it aside, rip out the engine block, and hurl it through a earby wall. He grabbed a young policewoman by the collar and used her as a missile against another bunch of cops at that point mostly interested in getting out of his way. He even lashed at Scibelli, who was knocked to the snowy sidewalk from the most glancing of blows. Octavius shouted, "You think you can defeat Octavius with bullets? With bullets?"

At which point, answering in affirmative, the front of the Doctor's suit shredded from several shots to the abdomen.

They made metallic sounds when they hit, as did the ones stopped by his whirling tentacles.

"Hold your fire!" Scibelli shouted, in a voice that carried despite his failure to use his megaphone. "You'll shred the hostages with the ricochets!"

Most of his people listened. Most.

Predictably, since he'd already screwed up big-time today, Kranz was one of the ones who didn't. He probably wanted to redeem himself by being the one who brought down Doctor Octopus. Either that, or he was just too scared to think straight.

Or, for that matter, to shoot straight.

The round raised a cloud of brick dust on the outer wall of the paper warehouse, well away away from where Octavius happened to be rampaging at the time. It did, however, gain the not-so-good Doctor's attention. Snarling, shouting something about demanding the respect that a man of his intellect deserved, Octavius whirled and descended upon the hapless rookie. Kranz did not have the time to scream before he was grabbed by both tentacles and lifted into the air.

He'll be torn to pieces, Scibelli thought. Ignoring his own order, he leveled his service revolver.

But Octavius merely stuffed Kranz through the driver's-side window of a squad car, took a step back, and with one of his whirling tentacles (the one already imprisoning his female hostage), lifted the car high in the air. He held it on its side, shaking it violently, the terrified Kranz bouncing up and down on the seat holding on to the steering wheel for dear life.

Then Octavius froze. Scanned the rooftops in the distance. And, distressingly, smiled.

"Well, well, well," he said. "This is just too perfect."

Gerard groaned. Kranz screamed and begged. The tentacles of Dr. Octopus loosened just enough for the stunned hostages to fall to the pavement. As members of the SWAT team scrambled in and pulled those hostages to relative safety, Dr. Octopus laughed, drew back, and hurled the police car as hard as only he could.

Despite the hysterical entreaties of the poor officer inside, it was still rising as it sailed past the next intersection.

By then it was five stories above the pavement.

And carrying not one, but two passengers.

CHAPTER TEN

10:23 A.M.

The crisis on the Brooklyn Bridge had not appreciably changed. The Bridge was still cut off by the blinding coruscating energy that burned at both ends. Lightning still raced up and down the girders. The cars and buses trapped on the span were still immobile, Electro still paced the East Tower in a ball of light, and the young blonde woman in the miniskirt still plummeted from the West Tower, again and again, each time almost hitting the water before flickering, disappearing, and reappearing at the apex of her plunge.

The municipal and SAFE response had been massive. Acting on the assumption that if Electro did blow up the bridge, nothing nearby would be safe from the inevitable wave of collateral damage, the police had closed off many nearby thoroughfares, including the FDR Drive and the Manhattan Bridge, to all but emergency vehicles. As they had also closed that section of the East River to all but police cruisers, this was a quadruple whammy that wreaked havoc on traffic patterns and basic services in two boroughs. The police had also deployed long-range snipers atop several of the major skyscrapers that lined the Manhattan waterfront southwest of the bridge. SAFE, which had been handed procedural jurisdiction, had used helicopters to fly in a modular command center, about the size of a house trailer, and secure it to the Manhattan-side tower of the Manhattan bridge; the command center, staffed with techs and equipped with millions of dollars worth of state-of-the-art sensor and surveillance, was keeping a constant watch on Electro and the massive energy barriers he'd used to turn the Brooklyn Bridge into a cage.

Doug Deeley was piloting one of the three SAFE aircars flying constant half-mile circles around the bridge. It was a "flying ashtray" model—essentially a floating convertible, powered by helicarrier technology, with sides tall enough to come up to a standing passenger's waist. There was no hood, side windows, or windshield, leaving the entire vehicle open to the air, but the passengers within were still protected by an invisible ionic shield that spared its passengers what would have been debilitating wind and cold. The temperature inside, thanks to Colonel Morgan's preferences, was actually uncomfortably warm. But that didn't stop Deeley from experiencing a chill as he surveyed the macabre death scene being played again and again far below. He muttered to himself: "Gwen Stacy. Murdered by the Green Goblin, as Spider-Man tried to save her."

Colonel Sean Morgan, currently biting his lower lip almost but not quite hard enough to draw blood, shot his subordinate a harsh look. "I'm aware of that. It is the reason Electro chose this site, after all."

"I know, sir." Deeley spoke mildly, with no trace of defensiveness. "I'm reminding myself, not you. That hologram's so realistic that every time she falls I have to restrain myself from breaking formation to rescue her."

Morgan nodded. He felt the same way; it was such a clear, vivid, powerful image of a doomed innocent that his awareness she had passed into the realm of history didn't prevent him from wishing the same. He didn't need a major investigation to know that Mysterio must have been involved in its creation. What he did want to know is why that was ringing alarm bells up and down his spine.

Morgan's ear mike buzzed. He tapped his throat. "Morgan here. Talk to me."

"Palminetti here, sir." One of SAFE's best tactical planners, the quadriplegic Vince Palminetti could probably figure out a way to bust into Heaven without any of the angels noticing. He commanded the techs at the modular command center. "I've run the analysis."

"So? Talk to me."

"First off, our instruments indicate that Dillon is not bluffing about the electrical field surrounding the bridge. It's enough to power twenty square blocks, and potentially deadly if he decides to use it for anything other than hostage containment. It not only blocks the Manhattan and Brooklyn sides, and lateral access, but also—we've confirmed this—the narrow gap between the eastbound and westbound spans. Secondly, any aerial approach will probably result in Electro taking retaliatory action directly against his hostages, probably by firing explosive energy bolts at the automobiles. Assuming we obtain a shooting solution and succeed in taking him down within, conservatively, ten seconds of entering his airspace, he will still have time to explode both buses and at least four of the cars. Civilian casualties will run between eighty and a hundred, with approximately two more for each additional second we need to take him out."

Morgan closed his eyes, trying to remember the last time a Palminetti Casualty Estimate had been off by more than ten percent. It had involved a certain terrorist stronghold, and a cache of nerve gas nobody had known about. He said: "What about a frontal assault on foot? Breaching the energy barriers in insulated suits?"

"Numbers would be roughly the same, except that we'd shift approximately half the casualty list to our own people."

Still unacceptable. Morgan grimaced. "All right. Third option. A marine approach. We deploy elite forces via submersibles, surfacing directly under the bridge where the span itself can shield us from view. We climb up the supports and anchor ourselves on the underside of the roadway."

"No problem there. It would take maybe twenty minutes to get that many people into position. The main hitch is that Electro's patrolling the air in small circles and is bound to notice any attempt to climb up and over."

"Not if we set shaped explosives beneath the pedestrian walkways. Worst comes to worst, we distract Electro with our aerial maneuvers, then blast our way up from below, and take him out from a distance before he can realize he's being attacked on two fronts. Will that work?"

There was a moment of stunned silence. Morgan didn't need to see Palminetti to see his expression; it must have been nearly identical to the aghast stare on Deeley's.

After a moment, Palminetti said: "You'd need several simultaneous points of entry, to provide a crossfire for any possible Electro position. Each one would require an explosion large enough to blow a wide-open hole in the bottom of a major suspension bridge. The brunt of the debris would be absorbed by the nearest automobiles, shattering the windows and therefore injuring or possibly killing some of the civilians we're trying to save. In addition, the explosions would all have to be positioned near the sides of the bridge, to avoid coming up under a vehicle . . . so we'd have to be absolutely accurate in calculating the force of our charge, or risk serious or fatal damage to the support cables. If we made a sufficiently serious mistake, we could conceivably lose the entire structure and everybody on it—with the certain exception of Electro himself, who can fly."

Morgan nodded. "What are the chances of such a screw-up?"

"Well, we do have state-of-the-art demolitions people, but it's an old bridge, and with all the unknown factors . . . I'd say up to one percent."

"And if the odds pan out? If we do place the explosives properly?"

Palminetti considered that at great length. Over at the Brooklyn Bridge, the glowing figure of Electro flew circles around both towers, while the hologram of Gwen Stacy fell to her death, only to reappear and fall, reappear and fall. After a long time, Palminetti spoke again, an unmistakable reluctance coloring his voice. "We would lose between one and two dozen civilians just blasting through and getting into position. We would also almost certainly succeed in taking out Electro on our first volley. According to all the standard rules of the game . . . that's acceptable breakage."

Morgan felt like he'd swallowed a burning stone. He knew the concept of acceptable breakage and understood that there were some situations where it had absolute tactical validity. He also knew that the bland words hid a legacy of dead innocents, ruined lives, grieving families, and a historical verdict that would no doubt brand him as an uncaring, out-of-control martinet at least as guilty as Electro himself.

Still: less than two dozen lives. Against up to a hundred, by any other method . . . and maybe as many as three hundred, if Electro went for the hostages before Morgan could get his people into position.

And Spider-Man might not be back in time to make a difference.

Deeley saw the shift in his facial expression and said: "You're not going to do this."

"Yes," Morgan said, with infinite regret, "I am." He tapped his throat mike again, and began to give orders.

10:25 A.M.

Trapped in the hurtling squad car, as it sailed upward into the sky, gripping the steering wheel for dear life, rookie cop Steve Kranz knew that he was going to die. He knew this with such absolute certainty that everything else he'd ever said or done in his life had contracted to that one pitiless, indivisible thought. It repeated itself with a lightning rapidity that almost but not quite kept pace with the constantly changing view through the windshield*: I'm going to die* (street) *I'm going to die* (sky) *I'm going to die* (street) *I'm going to die* (sky) *Ohmigod please please please I don't wanna dieeeee . . .*

The squad car somersaulted over the city streets forever. Hours. Days. Lifetimes.

Maybe, a couple of seconds. If that.

Then the entire interior of the car was swallowed by the sound of tearing metal, and Kranz almost died of sheer fright, believing that the fatal crash had come.

When a pair of red-gloved hands reached down and

grabbed him under his arms, Kranz, still operating under the momentary assumption that he was dead, cried out, horribly certain that he'd just been sent to The Other Place.

Then a blast of freezing wind hit him in the face, and he caught a glimpse of the hurtling squad car, now far below him, plunging toward an empty lot. Only the sight of the car informed him that he was no longer inside it. The roof of the vehicle had been peeled back, like the lid of a can of sardines: he could look right down into the empty driver's seat, and see a tumbling clipboard which was following the car toward its crash landing, like a puppy insistent on following its master toward the end. The perspective made no sense to Kranz, especially since he was actually gaining altitude. He heard a strange, unidentifiable sound (*thwip*), felt a painful spinal realignment as his own trajectory abruptly altered to a more lateral course, saw the wall of an office building passing by uncomfortably close, and only then, registered that somebody was carrying him.

"D-daredevil?" he ventured.

The answer was wry: "That does it. I have *got* to print up some business cards."

A blessedly solid, unmoving rooftop, covered with a light dusting of snow, appeared beneath his feet. Released, Kranz sank to his knees, glanced at his rescuer, and said, "S-spider-Man."

"That, without the stutter, is me. Are you okay?"

Kranz thought of having to face Captain Scibelli later, and decided he wasn't. But he nodded anyway. "Yeah. Th-thanks. You're going to go after Octavius now, right?"

"That's the plan," Spider-Man said.

"Get him good, okay? Just—get him."

"Well," Spider-Man said, "since you asked . . ."

Kranz did not see him go. There was no moment of transition, no place to mark the borderland between Spider-Man being there and Spider-Man being gone. There was just his own determination to go into a safer line of work.

10:26 A.M.

The two men had warred as often as some hostile nations—from the early days of their mutual careers, through all the many years that followed, forging a special kind of adversarial relationship that went beyond fear, beyond hatred, and beyond the mere tally of their respective triumphs and defeats. It would have been too facile to call them twisted doppelgangers, or even assume that they each fully understood the other. But they did know each other, in the way of stage actors who have been playing the same script so long that it was no longer a drama but a frequently-performed dance.

Dr. Octopus scrambled up the side of the office building and rushed to attack Spider-Man head-on. Two of his tentacles carried him, two probed the air ahead like hungry snakes sensing an invisible mouse. There was nothing clumsy or mechanical in the way they moved; they were too sinuous to be machines, too liquid to be snakes. They were alive, and they were part of him.

When Spider-Man attempted to leap through the questing tentacles to reach the vulnerable man at their center, they had absolutely no difficulty batting him aside, slamming into his chest, and hurling him against the nearest brick wall.

The reeling Spider-Man was only barely able to leap out of the way a fraction of a second before another tentacle, hurtling downward with the speed of thought, shattered that section of wall into wreckage. Octopus crowed: "I have been looking forward to this, Spider-Man! I always wanted to tear you limb-from-limb at the site of your greatest failure!"

Spider-Man leaped and somersaulted from one section of rooftop to another, barely avoiding the smashing tentacles that came down like hammer blows. "Really? Gee! Maybe you oughta get out more!" A tentacle curled around him to cut off a planned leap. "No, sorry! Strike that! You get out more than enough as it is!"

"Keep running your mouth, web-slinger! It only reminds me how much I hate you!"

"Really?" Spider-Man asked, as he was once again knocked back. "Seems to me you were remembering that pretty good even without my help!" He corkscrewed into the air, contorted, and fired twin web-lines: one behind his back, and one (when he was bent almost completely double) between his knees. They both impacted against Ock's adamantium tentacles, and they both slid off without achieving any adhesion whatsoever.

"My latest masterstroke!" Ock crowed. "An experimental chemical coating which repels all adhesives! Your pathetic weblines won't stick there anymore!"

"Big deal! I'm supposed to be impressed by a new use for PAM?"

Spider-Man was struck again, this time a glancing blow against the side of his head. The impact was hard enough to be paralyzingly painful, and he moved a little less gracefully when he leaped over a narrow side-street to another rooftop. He was running away because he already needed time to recover, but the retreat didn't help much, since Dr. Octopus was able to scramble down the side of the first building, take two giant steps across the street, and ascend the second building in less than five seconds.

Keeping on the move, dodging one tentacle attack after

another, but unable to get past them to the vulnerable man beyond, Spider-Man cried: "Isn't this a bit of a comedown for you, anyway? The internationally feared terrorist, and would-be world conqueror, regressing to what he used to be? A neighborhood bully with a grudge?"

"There will be time enough for conquering—when you are dead!"

"I don't believe you, Ockie! You always have one eye on the big picture! Why are you suddenly working for somebody like the Gentleman? What are you really after?"

Doctor Octopus laughed cruelly. "As always, webslinger, my agenda is my own! The Gentleman will find that out soon enough! As will you!"

As Spider-Man attempted another leap past the whirling tentacles, one looped around from behind and grabbed him. The pincers bit deep into his upper arm, drawing blood. Spider-Man wrested himself free only by sacrificing a chunk of flesh. Another tentacle came around and grabbed for his neck. Still dizzy from the blow to the head, Spider-Man dropped to the rooftop and scuttled away, rolling, twisting, somersaulting, and jumping, but completely unable to stay more than a fraction of a second ahead of the adamantium death machines. Then three of them slammed against the floor on both sides of him, shattering the rooftop. Spider-Man tumbled into the darkness, and Doctor Octopus followed.

10:37 A.M.

Though the battle had moved inside one of the evacuated office buildings across the street from the one Octavius had originally seized, out of sight of any of the police officers at street level, nobody had any difficulty determining that it was still in progress. Not only were the smashing and crashing noises emanating from the building in question loud enough to be heard by everybody within a two block radius, but the effects of the battle announced themselves in the manner that dust and furniture and other debris kept sailing from shattered windows. This went on for minutes on end, so long it seemed eternal.

Observing from another nearby rooftop, Billy Walters watched the embattled structure through field glasses while Betty Brant used her cellular phone to relay the blow-by-blow to the *Bugle*. The chilly air up here made puffs of vapor burst from his lips to accentuate every word. "Another bunch of SWAT guys—ten, I think—just ran into the building where Ock has the hostages."

"What are they carrying?" Betty wanted to know.

"I make flak gear, bolt cutters, and blast shields." He hesitated. "Bomb squad. You think Ock has the door to that storeroom wired?"

"I wouldn't put it past him," Betty said. "You see a whole bunch of people come running out of there in a hurry, get down and cover your face. I guarantee you, he's not the kind to go in for controlled explosions." She relayed this latest information to Urich for rewrite, winced as a particularly huge cloud of plaster dust billowed from the shattered windows of the building now under siege, remembered that awful day years before when she'd been the madman's prisoner, and silently gave thanks to Spider-Man for luring the madman away from the hostages.

As if on cue, Billy Walters inhaled suddenly. "Oh, man. Like, tell me this isn't happening. You still got your cell phone?"

"What's wrong?"

"The name of that cop in charge down there. You said you recognized him?"

"Sure," Betty said. "It's Anthony Scibelli. What about him?"

"We have to call and warn him. I just spotted something."

10:42 A.M.

The interior of the unfortunate building where Spider-Man and Dr. Octopus had taken their battle was now a maze of shattered floors, cratered walls, splintered furniture, and sparking light fixtures. The cross-draft created by newly created ventilation in all four of its outer walls had stirred up reams of paper liberated by a shattered filing cabinet; the hallway where they now fought was a blizzard of documents and invoices, filling the space between the two men as they hurled endless blows at each other.

The fight was not going well for Spider-Man. Already battered and bruised from his roller-coaster ride with the Vulture, he'd been struck more than a dozen additional serious blows during this fight, including not only the previous one to the head but two more to the ribs that had left a constant throbbing pain in his side; he'd clipped Ock maybe twice, each time only a glancing blow that did nothing more than leave the man gasping for breath. It was the most difficult factor, fighting Octopus: his arms protected him too well.

There was another factor, too: fatigue. Spider-Man didn't get tired easily, but he'd just experienced almost twenty minutes of constant frenetic effort, at his peak level of performance, and he desperately needed a breather. Ock, on the other hand, was fresh as a daisy—if dusty from plaster and other debris. He wasn't even winded. After all, it was not actually his body getting all this exercise. His tentacles were extensions of him, but they were not him. Creatures of metal and not flesh and blood, they could fight on forever, without requiring any caloric input from the man whose orders they obeyed. The longer this fight went on, the greater the advantage Ock enjoyed—and Ock knew it. The madman crowed at him: "You're slowing, wall-crawler! Getting sloppy! Before long you'll make a fatal mistake, and I'll be able to rip your still-beating heart from your chest!"

"As long as you don't take the spleen!" Spider-Man cried. "Venom keeps telling me he gets first dibs on that!" He flung a mahogany desk which Octopus shattered to splinters, decided that the closed quarters had lived out their allure, and dove through a double-helix of questing tentacles out a window leading to the alley.

The entire side wall of the building shattered behind him as Doctor Octopus followed close in pursuit. Too close for the Doctor's own good: alighting on the opposite side of the alley, Spider-Man had ripped a six-story fire escape from its moorings and swung it like a club.

Startled, Doctor Octopus shielded himself with three of his tentacles, easily saving his vulnerable human body from the full force of the blow...but the impact was still enough to shatter the section of wall where he'd anchored himself, and send him tumbling toward the pavement in a shower of wreckage.

Meanwhile, Captain Scibelli was daring himself to believe that things were going well.

He had just gotten a report that the bomb squad and SWAT team had succeeded in breaking into the storeroom were Dr. Octopus had barricaded his prisoners. As surmised, Octopus had wired the door to that room with a firebomb powerful enough to vaporize everything and anybody unlucky enough to be in the building; the bomb squad had bypassed the bomb by breaking through a rear wall. They were now in the act of leading the hostages out an emergency exit, an operation which would take several minutes thanks to the shambles Octopus had made of the interior.

Everything would be okay as long as Spider-Man kept Octopus away from the rescue. And as long as there were no other developments to complicate things.

He winced at the thought, realizing that it was the sort of sentiment that tempted fate.

Lieutenant Gerard said, "Sir."

Scibelli said, "What?"

Gerard extended the radio. "The dispatcher's patching through a 911 call from somebody on the block. It sounds like you ought to hear this."

"Somebody on the block? But we evacuated!"

"Take the radio, sir."

Scibelli took it, covering his other ear to filter out the crashing and smashing sounds that would otherwise make a sensible conversation impossible. "Captain Scibelli here. What's the problem?"

It was the voice of a young woman: "Captain, my name's Betty Brant. I'm a reporter from the *Daily Bugle*, and I'm calling you from a rooftop less than fifty yards southeast of your position."

Startled, Scibelli scanned the skyline until he saw two young people, a man and a woman, frantically waving from a rooftop down the street. "Get the hell out of there!" he shouted angrily. "Don't you know this whole neighborhood's in the line of fire?—Phil, get somebody up there to—"

"Captain, listen to me. Please. This is an emergency."

Scibelli, who like many cops possessed a keen dislike of journalists and reporters, heard something urgent in the woman's voice, and shut up immediately. "Go ahead."

"You've all been so busy watching the rooftops that you haven't been paying attention to anything that's been going on at street level. And my associate here," (the distant man waved, a little too jauntily), "just spotted a young boy, approximately ten years old, sneak past all your people, and cut into the alley just east of your position. From where we sit, he's still visible hiding behind the dumpster. My guess is he's hoping to see some of the fight. You have to get him out of there before—"

By the time she finished the sentence, Scibelli had started to run.

At the same time, batted off the side of the building by the tremendous weight of the fire escape, Dr. Octopus was still able to catch himself within a fraction of a second. He accomplished this minor miracle by extending his tentacles against the alley wall and using them to brake his fall ... but the maneuver rendered him temporarily unable to protect himself from the rest of the falling debris. A hail of bricks slammed against his chest and forehead. None hit quite hard enough to knock him out, but he was left dizzied and stunned. Gasping, aware of the blood spurting from a fresh gash over his right eye, he snarled: "Blast you, webslinger! You'll pay for that!"

Spider-Man, leaping down at him, said: "Oh, I'm so sorry to hear that. And we were such close friends up 'til now!"

Dr. Octopus batted Spider-Man aside with a casual swipe of a tentacle. "Jokes! Jokes! It's always jokes with you, isn't it? Well, I have a better idea!"

By the time Spider-Man recovered enough to follow him again, Octopus had descended all the way to the alley floor. His tentacles, operating at full extension, easily carried him over the heads of the police officers taking potshots at him as he headed back to the building where he'd left his hostages. Although several of their rounds impacted against his shielded midsection, further shredding his white suit, he didn't seem to notice them at all: they were just irrelevancies, beneath the notice of a man incapable of allowing anything to stand between him and his chosen goal.

Spider-Man traveled the same distance in two great leaps, slowed down only by the necessity of evading some of the police fire himself. He had no way of knowing whether the rounds were stray fire, intended for Octopus, or deliberately aimed reflections of the NYPD's official policy regarding his own humble self. And he didn't care. He had the terrible idea he knew what Ock was up to, and he needed to reach that rooftop first.

Climbing toward the roof, Octopus cried: "Remember this building, Spider-Man? I remember it well—because it was the few places I ever got you to stop making those inane witticisms! I should have learned my lesson then! Because if it takes the deaths of innocents to shut you up—then innocent deaths is what you'll have!"

Octopus punctuated this threat by using two of his tentacles to smash six-foot chunks of wall from the building; separating into pieces as they fell, the debris sailed across the street and impacted against the police position, shattering prowler windshields and sending helpless cops running for cover.

"Ock—" Spider-Man said, his voice a warning.

"You still don't get it?" Octopus crowed, his tentacles closing around a familiar cornice-stone—a replacement for the one that, years before, had toppled to the street and crushed Captain George Stacy to death. "The hostages inside were just bait, to get you here! I came here as part of our Day of Terror, to commemorate the death of Captain Stacy— by toppling this entire building onto the police positions below! The street's far too narrow for them to run for cover! I can take out dozens of his law-enforcement colleagues, with you helpless to save them, exactly as before!"

As if in punctuation, he smashed the cornice and flung it toward the street.

And exactly as he had all those years before, Spider-Man darted toward the edge and shouted "No!", only to see the debris falling directly toward a young boy who'd wandered into the line of fire.

Watching from their vantage point down the street, both Betty Brant and Billy Walters could only gasp in horror.

The boy had evaded Captain Scibelli by shimmying through the narrow space between the dumpster and the wall. Running from the middle-aged cop, considering it a game, he'd emerged onto the street before Scibelli could realize what was doing . . . and had stopped to stare at the battle just as Octopus sent a hurtling cloud of debris raining toward him.

The kid saw his death approaching and froze in place, too scared to move.

In that same instant, Scibelli emerged from the alley, saw the kid, saw what was happening, and ran to intercept.

It all took place in a heartbeat. Neither Betty or Billy had time to say anything. But they both remembered how Captain Stacy had died. And if they could have expressed what was going through their minds in that moment, they would have thought: *Oh, God. Please don't let this happen again.*

Captain Anthony Scibelli was not fast. He'd never been fast, not even as a rookie. Purse-snatchers and smash-and-grabbers had enjoyed a spectacular advantage, outrunning him; he'd watched so many recede in the distance, laughing at him, that only his genius at leadership had been able to salvage his career. And that was decades ago. These days, he didn't even jog. There was no way he'd ever be able to out-race something as primal as gravity.

But he'd been a friend of Captain Stacy.

And he remembered how Captain Stacy had died.

And he refused to let it happen again.

He focused on the back of that stupid kid's even stupider jacket, and he ran across a sidewalk growing dark with the shadows of the masonry toppling from up above, and he knew that there there was no chance on Earth he was going to survive this, not fighting history, not battling an inevitabil-ity, no, not at all, not even remotely.

His feet grew wings and he took the rest of the distance in one desperate leap, knocking the kid out of the way, impossibly tumbling to safety himself just as enough masonry to crush them both flat shattered to powder in the empty space behind them.

Doctor Octopus, peering over the side of the roof, sneered: "A disappointment. I had hoped for history to repeat itself, But perhaps a more, ah, hand's-on approach—"

His words were clearly a blatant attempt to make the wall-crawler angry, to fool him into forsaking all caution and attempting a suicidal frontal attack.

In that, they worked.

The results, however, were not precisely what Octopus had envisioned.

Because this time, as his tentacles looped around to deflect Spider-Man's inevitable outraged leap, Spider-Man merely twisted in mid-air, grabbed them both . . . and held them apart just long enough to deliver a vicious kick at the Doctor's chest.

For Octavius, the kick was a lot like what being hit by one of Ock's tentacles was like for Spider-Man, except that the flesh-and-blood part of Octopus had never been a fighter and was not able to take it.

He clutched at Spider-Man with all four tentacles and succeeded only in clutching empty air. "Impudent . . . fool! You . . . hurt . . . me . . ."

"Yeah, the Vulture said something like that, too! And like you, he had the nerve to be surprised! And you say *I* don't get it?" Spider-Man fired a wide spray of webbing at a pile of fallen bricks, yanking it off the ground and hurling it at Octopus like a club. The package was smashed to debris as soon as it was deflected by the Doctor's whirling tentacles . . . but that was the whole point. Brick shrapnel peppered the Doctor's face and chest. Dodging the blind, even desperate gropings of Ock's tentacles, dancing over and around and beneath them as if they were no impediment at all, Spider-Man shouted: "I'm not even begun hurting you, Doc Ock! I'm sick of dealing with you! I'm sick of you endangering people to get at me! No more jokes, no more rules! I'm going to deal with you the way I should have dealt with you years ago! I'm going to tear those arms of yours out by the roots!"

As he flailed away, barely evading Spider-Man's punches and kicks, Octopus managed to hold on to the ghost of his previous sneer. "You've . . . done that before, Spider-Man! I remember well . . . how much it hurt! But that's . . . why I changed the metallic makeup of my arms! They're . . . indestructible now! You can't do . . . anything to them!"

"You misunderstand me, chuckles. I'm not talking about your mechanical arms. Taking those away from you never did any good. This time I'm talking about the ones you were born with. You love your tentacles so much that this time I'm going to make sure they're the only arms you have!"

And with that, Spider-Man leaped straight through the cat's cradle of deadly thrashing adamantium, to the man at their heart: hurling a punch that dislocated Dr. Octopus' shoulder with a sickening audible crack.

Octopus screamed.

Once again, he sent his tentacles after Spider-Man. And once again, by the time the pincers at their tips grasped at the place where Spider-Man had been, the web-slinger was somewhere else. Only, by now, it was not so much of a surprise, to either combatant; the adamantium tentacles, which had seemed so unstoppable, had been reduced to clumsy, groping things, slowed by the desperate agony of the man who commanded them.

As for Spider-Man himself, pressing his attack, darting past that undulating barrier again and again and again, taunting Octopus with increasingly more graphic and creative descriptions of all the physical damage he was ready to inflict, he seemed to have suddenly become ten times the fighter he'd been mere minutes before. He was empowered by righteous anger, and thoroughly unstoppable.

An uninjured Octopus might have continued to fight anyway; this time he decided that discretion was the better part of valor, and launched himself off the roof, fleeing toward the street below. He landed on his feet, reared up and clubbed the pavement with all four tentacles at once. The shock wave was enough to send every cop in sight tumbling to the ground. It was also enough to send a twenty-foot section of sidewalk collapsing into the subway tunnel below.

"Oh, no you don't!" Spider-Man cried. He was racing down the side of the building several times faster than the fastest Olympic athlete can run.

Octopus used a tentacle to hurl an unoccupied cop car at Spider-Man. Spider-Man leaped away just in time to evade the vehicle before it smashed into the warehouse wall. He flipped, snagged a lamppost with a webline, and dropped to the street a fraction of a second after what was left of the car did. By which time Dr. Octopus had already disappeared into the subway tunnel. That didn't matter. Spider-Man was fully prepared to go after him, and finish this once and for all.

Whereupon his SAFE communicator crackled. "Spider-Man! Stop!"

Though the signal stopped him from pursuing Octopus, it was still several seconds before he got himself under enough control to tap his throat mike and respond. His voice was breathless and ragged. "Deeley . . . you have got to get yourself a life, man."

"This is the nineties, web-slinger. Who needs a life?"

"You were watching me, right?"

"We've tapped into the police blow-by-blow. I've got to give you credit, webs . . . I never thought this thing would go the distance."

"And I wuv you too," Spider-Man said, startling the cops who were just now beginning to approach him. There was a groan behind his voice; now that the adrenalin rush was fading, his head felt like it had been massaged with falling cinderblocks. His eyes were burning. Every bone in his body felt like it had just gone ten rounds with Tyson. There may have been a spot on his elbow that didn't hurt, but he didn't feel like probing it to push his luck. On top of everything else, his sudden inactivity made it possible for the cold to penetrate a costume now sopping-wet with perspiration; he had to suppress a shiver as he asked, "Why did you stop me from going after Ock?"

"There's too much going on. Citywide, we have seven incidents of homeless men being beaten by citizens who suspected them of being the Chameleon. Unconfirmed sightings of the Vulture over Central Park and Mysterio at Madison Square Garden, both of which are being checked out by our people. And we still have this major situation at the bridge. We're hoping you can get here before we have to go in ourselves; we're pretty sure we can take out Electro, but not without a major fatality rate among the hostages."

"Swell," Spider-Man muttered. He thought about the way he'd so blithely declined Captain America's offer of help. That had been a smart move, all right. The way things were going today, he would have welcomed assistance from Fabian Stankowicz.

He let Deeley know he was on the way, then tapped his throat mike, looked up, and made eye contact with Captain Anthony Scibelli, who had approached to within three feet of him. His own completely concealing mask couldn't have been any more enigmatic than the blank, ambiguous look on the face of the captain. Scibelli may have been grateful, annoyed, angry, or just working up enough nerve to try to arrest him. After a moment, Spider-Man decided that he must have been wrestling with all of those impulses at once—an ambivalence with which he sympathized.

Spider-Man said, "What time is it?"

The surprised Scibelli checked his watch. "Almost eleven."

"Man oh man," said Spider-Man, swaying a little as he aimed his web-shooter at the battered rooftops. "This is shaping up to be one hell of a stressful day."

Scibelli grabbed him by the wrist. "You don't actually think you're going anywhere, do you?"

Spider-Man moaned. "Oh, come on, Captain. This is no time to play blame-the-web-slinger again."

"I'm not," Scibelli said. "I think you've done a good job.

And I know you have to rush to the bridge. But I don't think you're ready to go fighting anybody else right now. Or aren't you aware just how much you're bleeding?"

Spider-Man just stared at him dumbly, not taking his meaning. Then he reached up with one hand, touched the cloth on the top of his hood, and felt something sticky and wet.

That clip Ock gave me across the temple, he thought. *No wonder my eyes are burning; I'm bleeding from the forehead.*

He pushed Scibelli aside, intent on making for the rooftops anyway.

Then the darkness lingering at the edges of his vision swallowed him whole, and he pitched forward into the startled police captain's arms.

CHAPTER ELEVEN

11:04 A.M.

"We have an update!" shouted Jay Sein, whose switchboard was ringing off the hook. "Spider-Man has whupped the tar out of Dr. Octopus! Repeat, Spidey has whupped the tar out of Dr. Octopus! That leaves us with a second-inning score of Spidey 2, Sinister Six 0!"

Cosmo the K said: "An excellent early showing for the wall-crawler, with only minor civilian injuries. I will repeat our previous retraction, given at the top of the hour: Stephen Kranz, the police officer previously reported as murdered by Dr. Octopus, was in fact rescued—repeat, rescued—by Spider-Man, in a spectacular mid-air retrieval that's going to go down in the record books as one of the most memorable of the webslinger's career. We are still awaiting an official statement on the condition of the Doctor's other hostages, but our sources at the NYPD have indicated a completely successful rescue operation. Let's hope that's true, Jay."

"I hear you there, Coz. We can only hope that Spider-Man continues this remarkably successful early showing. In the meantime, we do have an incoming statement from the Mayor's Commission on Super-Villain Activities, urging citizens in affected areas to remain indoors for the duration of the conflict. Those forced to evacuate are instructed to gather their immediate belongings and move swiftly and in an orderly manner to the nearest Paranormal Crisis Shelter. If you don't know the location of your shelter, call your local precinct for an update. Do not use 911 for routine queries. We'll be right back, with further developments, after this word."

He inserted a cartridge and pressed play. Cosmo's voice came on. *"Are you a homeowner in the city of New York? Have you experienced difficulty obtaining property insurance due to repeated damage by paranormal rampage? Then Timely Underwriters is the company for you! Timely offers reasonable rates, a minimal deductible, and expert consultation on villain-proofing your home!"*

A woman's voice interjected. *"My apartment building was levelled twice, once by the Hulk, and once by Count Nefaria when he fought the Avengers! Timely helped me get a fast, easy settlement, and paid for my motel accomodations while the landlord rebuilt! Thank you, Timely!"*

"The Juggernaut just walked right through my building," another man said. *"We lost the entire east wall. Timely paid for renovations, and got them done quickly! Thank you, Timely!"*

A third voice said: *"You said it, brother! When the Hulk knocked the Rhino through my living room, I thought that was bad enough—but when the Hulk's body came flying through the other way, I lost the kitchen and the laundry room too! Timely put me back on my feet again!"*

Cosmo the K returned, *"That's Timely Underwriters, People. A necessity for living in the city of New York. Call 1 (800) FYTSCEN. That's 1 (800) FYTSCEN. And tell them Cosmo the K sent you.*

Removing the cartridge, Jay said, "Now, let's go back to our all-day coverage of the Spider-Man/Sinister Six battle, starting with these words of friendly reassurance from the Manhattan Visitors and Convention Bureau . . ."

11:07 A.M.

The most difficult thing about being a super-hero's wife was forcing yourself to pretend interest in your everyday activities. Errands, job interviews, the mundane or not-so-mundane problems of friends or co-workers, even simply walking down the street at a rate that projected normalcy instead of barely repressed panic, required a degree of acting skill that should have earned Mary Jane a hundred Oscars and about fifty Tonys every single day crises required her husband's presence. But hiding her concern, extreme as it may have been, wasn't always as difficult as just finding the strength to go on with her life.

Case in point: Upon the conclusion of her successful interview in which Mary Jane accepted the job, Dean Farnswell had urged Mary Jane to check out an all-day acting seminar currently taking place in the Liberal Arts building. It was one of a special series of extracurricular workshops, using campus facilities currently shut down for winter break; though not officially affiliated with the college, but with a semi-professional acting society incorporating many local members of the theatre community, it had been held on campus property for as long as ESU had possessed a Theatre Arts department. Attendance actually increased slightly during school vacations, thanks to students remaining on campus who figured it was as good a way to pass time as any. Farnswell believed Mary Jane might be able to observe a few hours of the seminar for some ideas on how to run her workshop.

It was not that bad an idea, actually. Of course, he couldn't possibly have known that at the moment, with her husband busily swinging around town risking his life in mortal combat against murderers and megalomaniacs, Mary Jane couldn't think of many things she was less motivated to do. But since the only immediate alternative was going home to Queens and driving herself crazy with the TV coverage, she decided to take him up on the suggestion.

Her face fell when she walked into the back of a darkened auditorium filled with maybe fifty or sixty students, half of whom were lying on stage, crooning breathless noises at the rafters. Mary Jane, who had always regarded acting as 50% instinct, 40% empathy, and at most 10% technique, had never had harbored any sympathy for workshops like this that seemed to stress sheer lunatic insanity over any of the aforementioned ingredients; she'd attended more run by coaches capable of gulling their students into the belief that standing around in circles shouting, "Mwah!" at each other was an invaluable way to find one's center, whatever that was. She'd been to some that forced students to hop around like frogs, or carry each other around like suitcases, or sit totally motionless pretending they were rocks—only to stand up at the end of class and once again shout, "Mwah!" at each other for fifteen minutes. She'd spent a lot of good money attending such workshops, never once learning anything of any real substance, before realizing that the best way to learn how to act was to act; to practice every day, join amateur productions, and give performances to the mirror, being brutally frank with herself about what tricks worked and what tricks did not. She'd met several famous, talented, respected actors who swore by the silly exercises of the "Mwah!" classes; she'd met just as many who'd confided that the greatest service that particular species of workshop provided was gathering together, and forever isolating, all the people capable of taking such *mishegos* seriously.

Either way, given everything else she had to worry about today, she decided that pretending polite interest was more than she'd be willing to handle. She almost turned around and walked out—but then she spotted somebody she knew, waving at her from the fifth row.

Matt Gordon had orange hair with purple streaks, a stud through his tongue, three hoops in each ear, enough rings on his eyebrows to hold together a loose-leaf notebook, and bright blue tattoo flames flaring up his neck and around the edges of his jaw. Despite years of pounding the pavement, and a formidable acting talent, he had never succeeded in fulfilling his lifelong dream of getting cast in Sondheim musicals. He had only worked a couple of times, mostly playing Thug Two or Thug Three in movies about kung fu heroes; Mary Jane's character Emma Steele had knocked him through a plate-glass window in FATAL ACTION III. She waved, hurried down the aisle, and made her way to a seat directly behind him. "How's it going?" she whispered.

"Fine!" He whispered back. "Got a callback for a new Broadway musical about Emile Zola! You know, the 19th-century novelist?"

"*J'accuse*, right?"

"Right! I'm up for the part of the accused spy, Alfred Dreyfuss! I think I got a lock!"

Mary Jane tried to picture Matt playing a prig of 19th-century French military officer sent to Devil's Island on trumped-up charges. It was certainly creative casting. She whispered: "Good luck! I hope you get it!"

The short girl sitting next to Matt was Fern Rosen, another face Mary Jane knew from multiple auditions; she had golden blonde hair, eyes so pale that the irises were almost indistinguishable from the whites, and an ethereal voice that cultivated the impression she was constantly in danger of running out of breath before she reached the end of her next sentence. The combination virtually ensured instant typecasting as a dumb bimbo—which is why she deserved credit for always wanting to hold out for something better. Her eyes brightened as she noticed Mary Jane. "Midge!" she cried, demonstrating her unfortunate tendency to burden her friends with cute nicknames. "How are you? I read about that Mysterio thing in the *Bugle*! Nice going!"

"Thanks!" Mary Jane whispered back, "but I wasn't exactly trying for publicity! It just happened!"

Up on stage, ten students were standing in two rows, their backs to each other, chanting "Why? *Why?* WHY? *WHY?* WHY?" as the teacher, a muscular crewcut blond man in yellow turtleneck and blue jeans, walked around them in circles, evaluating their respective performances, praising this one or that one for their centeredness. At one point he stopped before a track star Mary Jane vaguely recognized, whose biggest sin was difficulty maintaining a straight face, and snapped at him sharply. The track star immediately changed the tempo of his whys. Mary Jane didn't see the point of this, of course, despite the fact that *why* seemed as appropriate a word as any.

Matt indicated the instructor. "That's Claudio Guzman. He's a genius. I can't tell you how much I've learned since he took over this class!"

"*That's* Guzman?" Mary Jane couldn't believe it; this may

have been the first time she'd laid eyes on the man, but she'd heard nothing but good things about Guzman, a classically-trained actor whose recent performance of Iago had supposedly been the only worthwhile element of a wildly uneven off-off-off Broadway production of *Othello*. He was supposed to be an excellent actor and an absolutely first-rate acting teacher. She wondered, for a moment, if she'd misjudged the importance of Mwaaaah exercises; if somebody like Guzman endorsed them, then perhaps they had merit after all . . . even if they'd never worked for her.

She watched him more closely, searching for some, you should only excuse the expression, method to his madness . . . but finding nothing but pretentiousness and silliness. When Guzman led all the actors participating in the exercise in a synchronized bunny-hop from stage left to stage right, she had to fight hard to suppress an appalled giggle. She whispered to Matt: "Is he always like this?"

Fern answered instead, "Naaah. This is the wackiest and wildest he's been in some time. He does some experimental stuff, just to loosen things up, but it's mostly emphasis on body language and line readings, with some technical info on regional accents."

In other words, Mary Jane noted, revising her opinion of Guzman up yet another notch, precisely the skills that most beginning actors needed. She leaned back in her seat, forcing herself to keep an open mind as much as she would have preferred to do otherwise. After all, she wasn't a great actress, merely a capable one; maybe she didn't have the right to cop such an attitude. Maybe there was something she could learn here.

Up on stage, the various students completed their frenzied hopping. Guzman directed them to applaud themselves—which they did, with both enthusiasm and sustained whooping—then asked them to take their seats in the audience again. When everybody was seated, he took a spot at stage center and said: "*Whoo.* Thank you, everybody. That was new and different. Those of you who find such exercises silly and pointless should be apprised that this is precisely the point; as working actors, much of what you'll be called upon to do will be silly and pointless, from treating certain brands of toothpaste as if they're mankind's most important achievement, to reciting dialogue that sometimes may not resemble anything any human being has ever said to another human being outside of some sticky-floor mall cineplex. If any of you ever succeed in building a career more substantial than something to call yourself when you're waiting on tables, you'll learn that silly and pointless exercises like the one you just witnessed are so much a part of this profession, these days, that 'meaningful' and 'relevant' should be treated as an aberration instead of the rule. The trick is to build the skills that permit you to perform even the silly and pointless with absolute conviction—so that you may, in time, have the chance of possibly adding something meaningful and relevant to your resumé." He paused meaningfully, then scanned the auditorium (giving Mary Jane the spooky feeling that he'd known exactly what she'd been thinking, and therefore directed his comments, and his gaze, at her), and said, "That established, we have another hour before lunch, and therefore enough time for a somewhat more substantial exercise. This one is designed to build your improvisational skill, and will involve a little field trip to another part of the campus. You'll need to put on your coats."

"Oh, poo," Fern said, amid the buzz of dozens of acting students scrambling to get into their boots and goose-down jackets. "I hate cold."

Matt was already putting on his gloves and zipping into a heavy leather jacket dangling enough chains to restrain a fifty-foot ape recently captured on Monster Island. "Not me, babe. I used to be into cross-country skiing. C'mon, it'll be fun."

Mary Jane, who hadn't ever gotten around to taking off her own coat, knew only that the butterflies in her belly had returned; she naturally attributed this to leftover concern for her husband, who was probably well into the thick of things right now. It didn't occur to her that she might be, too . . . or that the butterflies might be an early manifestation of the sixth-sense that comes from being taken hostage more frequently than most people order out for pizza. It was not spider-sense, like Peter's. But it was something almost as reliable. It was the being-married-to-the-guy-with-spider-sense sense.

Too bad Mary Jane wouldn't realize until too late what it was.

11:25 A.M.

The janitorial closet was kept locked when not in use, mostly because students liked to raid it for cleaning supplies they could use to keep their dorm rooms, if not as pristine as their parents would have liked, then at least within an acceptable degree of filth. The janitor assigned to this particular building wouldn't be back on-campus until early this evening, which meant that the darkness within would remain undisturbed until several hours after the Sinister Six's commemorative Day of Terror. The air in there smelled vaguely of soap, disinfectant, and ammonia . . .

. . . and fear.

The source of this last odor lay in a rear corner, beneath a utility sink, partially hidden by a yellow bucket on casters; though fully conscious, and largely unharmed but for a nasty bump at the base of his skull, he wasn't about to go anywhere in a hurry, since his arms were handcuffed to the drain pipe behind his back, and his legs had been chained together at the ankles, after first forced to straddle the heavy bucket on rollers. The bucket had been filled to the brim with sealed cans of cleansing powder, to ensure that the man would not have the strength or the leverage to bang it around and thus summon help; though his captors had resisted blindfolding him, probably on the grounds that the lights were going to be out in the closet anyway, the lower half of his face, including his mouth, had still been prudently sealed off with duct tape.

The man's name was Claudio Guzman.

And despite his familiarity with The Method, Motivation was not currently one of his problems. He had plenty of Motivation. He had Motivation coming out his ears.

What he didn't have was the ability to do anything about it.

Colonel Sean Morgan stood at the head of a SAFE aircar hovering twenty yards above the water a couple of blocks north of the Brooklyn Bridge, and monitored the deployment through enhanced long-range binoculars. His people had acted with all the efficiency and professionalism he demanded; inserted with submersibles, they'd climbed the support towers in seconds, and massed in place along the girders on the underside of the bridge. The demolitions crew, targeting a closed lane, had set shaped charges at three separate locations; they now needed only his green light to break through and assault Electro from three separate vantage points.

"Take us back up," he told Deeley.

Deeley piloted the aircar upward, rejoining the formation of other SAFE aircars circling the bridge. Nothing had changed. The span was still ablaze with arcs of paranormally-induced electricity; their master Electro was still flying around above the tower on the Manhattan-side, firing random bolts of ball lightning for emphasis; the repeating hologram of the doomed Gwen Stacy was still tumbling again and again from the tower on the Queens side. If there'd been a change at all, it was a rapid increase in the number of news-media helicopters filming the standoff at a discreet distance. An unworthy part of Sean Morgan wished that one of those helicopters would fly closer than was strictly safe; he was too much of a professional to want anybody to die, but it would be nice for an unplanned dunking in the east river to teach those reporters the value of keeping their distance.

Deeley said, "Our forces have been holding for more than half an hour, sir. The longer we delay the greater the chances of Electro noticing them."

"I know," Morgan said. "Tell them to keep holding. Where's the web-slinger?"

"Latest word from NYPD," Deeley said, "is that he's being treated by paramedics. Nobody's willing to hazard any guesses about his condition. Meanwhile, the hostages—"

"I know," Morgan said. The longer they were left unattended, the greater the chances that panic or stress could start taking a toll. If their number included any senior citizens with heart conditions, or people who needed specialized medication in order to stay alive, the wait alone could prove deadly. That, alone, was enough to argue against further delays. But there were other things to consider. "This stinks like day-old fish."

"The entire situation does, Colonel. What specifically do you have in mind?"

"Him." Morgan pointed at the distant, glowing figure of Electro. "All this waiting. You haven't spent as much time around these long-underwear types as I have, so you might not have noticed—but hero or villain, they all seem to have the same thing in common: namely, the attention span of two-year-olds. They all want confrontation now, not later."

"That's not really fair to Spider-Man. Or Captain America. Or any of the others I've—"

"All right, all right. Give them credit for another couple of years of maturity. But the point's still valid. They're not folks known for their patience. And Electro's pretty hyperactive even by their standards. He's strictly instant gratification. It doesn't make sense for him to just float there for this much time, calmly waiting for the wall-crawler to show up; the Electro in my dossier would have started blowing up things an hour ago, no matter what the plan was. Whatever else is going on here, we're missing something."

"I've been getting that feeling myself," Deeley admitted. "Unfortunately, that still puts our people at risk."

Morgan wavered for less than a second before turning several degrees additionally grim, tapping his throat mike and barking: "Get Palminetti back on the line!"

11:37 A.M.

Empire State University's Maria Stark Memorial Stadium is surprisingly spacious for a college in the middle of New York City; more than just the muddy field and rickety set of retractable bleachers that the crowded local real estate would lead any reasonable university in its position to expect, it's an honest-to-god permanent sports complex, with enough seats for several thousand spectators. There are concessions, locker rooms for both teams, vast underground storage space, and even a broadcast booth emblazoned with the call letters of ESU's low-wattage campus radio station.

For insurance reasons, the stadium was usually kept locked behind gates when not in use. That didn't seem to bother Claudio Guzman, who used a key to unlock the stadium doors behind the box office. He ushered his forty chattering students inside, walked them down the stairs to the field entrance, then brought them out onto the field and gathered them together on the fifty yard line.

"It's cold," Fern complained.

"It's bracing," Guzman replied, the wind ruffling his crewcut not at all. All around him, would-be actors and winter break residents attending his workshop just out of need for something to do huddled together in varying states of excitement or misery, hopping up and down or hugging themselves the warmth. The grass beneath their feet was crunchy with frozen dew. He said, "Some of you, if you're lucky, may have a chance to perform in venues even larger than this; the key, for you, will be learning to project your emotions to fill any available space. That will be part of this exercise."

Somebody sneezed. Mary Jane didn't blame her.

"We will try to keep this brief, so we can get back inside in time for lunch. I need everybody to gather over there," Guzman said, indicating the ESU end zone. He pointed to the Visitor's goalpost. "I will take up position on the opposite end of the field, over there. You'll hear the rules of this exercise when we're exactly one hundred yards apart."

"That's gonna take some pretty loud yelling," Matt Gordon remarked.

"I have a remote to the P.A.," Guzman said, waving a

small mike which had just miraculously appeared in his right hand. "Come on, everybody. Hurry up. The sooner we get into position the sooner we can warm things up a bit."

There was some grumbling at this, but Guzman clapped his hands, and the assembled students began to make their way toward the ESU endzone. There was plenty of joking and flirting along the way, among those invigorated by the cold; like any students cooped up inside musty buildings, who suddenly enjoy the freedom of a field trip, they enjoyed the change of routine so much that none among them took this moment to ask any questions. As for those who weren't enjoying the cold, who wanted only to get this over with so they could luxuriate in central heating again, they were mostly just going along with the others, to avoid looking like quitters or crybabies. If anybody felt the same vague sense of unease that now afflicted Mary Jane—who still hadn't distinguished her sense that something was wrong from her ongoing concern about Peter—they did not speak up any more than she did. They all walked like sheep toward their slaughter.

The students huddled together beneath the home team goalpost, shivering and clapping their hands and staring expectantly at the opposite end of the field.

"This is not good," Mary Jane murmured. She did not know why she'd said that.

One hundred yards away, Claudio Guzman knelt beside the visitor's goal. He tugged at a spot on the field, opened up a concealed trap door, and stood a second later bearing the treasure he must have planted there before this exercise: an AK-47 assault rifle. Most of the assembled acting students were still chuckling among themselves in disbelief, misidentifying the weapon as a prop or a fake, when Mary Jane realized she knew exactly what was going to happen next. It wasn't hard to guess, after all; even from this distance, she had no trouble seeing the shimmer effect as it wiped the teacher's face clean.

Her blood turned to ice. "Smerdyakov," she whispered.

Half a dozen faces turned toward hers. "Who?"

She didn't have time to respond before the stadium's public address system came to life and rang with the sound of mad, malignant laughter.

"Typical Americans!" the Chameleon laughed. "So stupid! So gullible!"

A murmur rose among the acting students, just now beginning to realize that something was terribly wrong. Fern said, "Mary Jane, who's—"

"Shut up!" Mary Jane snapped, more harshly than she intended. "You want to live, let him waste time by ranting!"

Fern recoiled, stunned by this side of the normally affable MJ.

Mary Jane Watson-Parker didn't have the time or the luxury to feel bad about it. She could only concentrate furiously, filtering out the sounds of disbelief, denial, and incipient panic among all the innocents around her, and completely ignoring the opening words of the Chameleon's rant, as he established his name and his credentials and delivered his usual polemic about the perceived wrongs done to him by Spider-Man. She'd heard that kind of speech so many times before that it practically went without saying; she didn't need to pay direct attention to it.

What mattered more, was understanding what the rest of her fellow hostages did not.

About a year ago, after many years of using his uncanny powers of disguise to make life difficult for Spider-Man however he could, the Chameleon had finally succeeded in uncovering the identity of the man behind the mask. His subsequent campaign of terror had culminated in a particularly nasty night where he captured and caged Spider-Man, then returned to the Parker home in Forest Hills, disguised as Peter, plotting to murder Mary Jane only after first taking full conjugal advantage of his bogus face and identity.

It may not have been the worst thing any super-villain had ever tried to do to her, but it certainly was the sleaziest.

It also showed very little understanding of women, or faith in Mary Jane's ability to recognize a phony when she saw one.

She'd kissed the false Peter, realized at once that the flavorless, rubbery, dead-mackerel kiss she received in return could not have come from her husband, understood from the context of recent events that the smirking man in her bedroom could only have been Smerdyakov, then slinked off to the other room to "change into something more comfortable" and returned bearing a baseball bat instead of a warm inviting smile.

Smerdyakov, still showing very little understanding of women—not surprising, given his personality—dropped his disguise, leered, and tried to press the issue anyway.

This was a bad mistake.

A really, really, *really* bad mistake.

One that had probably put him off his feed for a long time.

Smerdyakov's main asset as a criminal had always been subterfuge, not direct physical confrontation; indeed, the biggest problem Spider-Man, and the handful of other super heroes who'd encountered him over the years, had ever experienced in dealing with him had always been chasing him down and unmasking him, rather than defeating him when the fight actually began. He was, in fact, a terrible fighter. As a result, Spidey and his colleagues hadn't ever needed extreme force to subdue him: usually, a punch or two, at most.

But then, they were super heroes, and Mary Jane was just a thoroughly enraged wife dealing with the sleazebag who had tried to trick her into cheating on her husband.

It almost went without saying that Mary Jane had not stopped after a mere walloping or two.

She may have inflicted more damage on the creep in those five minutes than he'd suffered in a lifetime worth of defeats at the hands of Spider-Man, Captain America, Daredevil, and the Hulk.

And though she hadn't realized this until after telling Peter what she'd done, she'd had a damn fine time doing it too. Though Smerdyakov had managed to escape with his life, beating him up had been cathartic, almost therapeutic—a perfect antidote for all the occasions where being Spider-Man's wife had forced her to feel helpless in the face of more formidable dangers.

Unfortunately, like most of these situations, it left fallout.

Because not long after that, Smerdyakov was attacked by one of his own old enemies, and left for dead with a bullet in his brain. He'd recovered with all of his evil cunning and malicious nature intact, but with only the vaguest memories of his recent past—losing, among other things, his knowledge of Peter's secret identity. And though this seemed a rare stroke of good luck for the Parker clan, the Chameleon's amnesia had proved to be spotty at most. There was always the chance that he'd remember Peter's identity, or his vow of vengeance against the woman who'd provided him the single most humiliating night of his life.

In his guise as Claudio Guzman, the Chameleon had not yet offered any indication that he recognized her.

The second he did, she was dead.

* * *

SAFE's dispatch unit was able to patch Sean Morgan's crisis analyst, Palminetti, onto the line within thirty seconds. "Yes, sir?"

Morgan glowered at the glowing man flying in tight controlled circles above the Brooklyn Bridge. "I want you to assume an x-factor we haven't counted on. Specifically, the possibility that Electro is actively counting on our involvement, that he wants us to break this standoff, that he has a surprise of some kind waiting for us. Estimate the approximate breakage resulting from an assault beginning now."

There was a pause. Then Palminetti said, "I'm afraid there's no way of knowing precisely, sir—not without identifying the x-factor in question—but if that's what's going on, we can probably add another sixty or seventy corpses to the day's total. Maybe more. We might be fortunate to save only a small minority."

Deeley, piloting the aircar, turned around and raised his eyebrows.

"Damn," he said.

Morgan grimaced. "Yeah." He tapped his throat mike. "Morgan to all units. Maintain readiness. Be ready to go at my signal. But *only* on my signal." He leaned against the railing of the aircar and swore with an eloquence that surprised him.

C'mon, Spider-Man. Snap out of it.

11:53 A.M.

The preliminaries (establishing his identity, persuading the fools that the weapon in his hand was real, that the entire stadium was rigged with enough explosives to totally incinerate anybody foolish enough to flee, and that their best chance of survival was listening to what he had to say) took the Chameleon only a couple of minutes. They were college students, after all; they were accustomed to absorbing information quickly. Even if they were now, mostly, clinging to each other in helplessness and fear; even if some of the more hysterical types had broken down into messy sobbing, they had calmed down enough to listen. Some of them, as far as he could tell from this distance, even looked determined. *Hero-types,* he assumed. *Probably the first to die.*

Good.

Hero-types didn't die often enough.

He raised the microphone to the mouth-slit in his smooth white mask, and delivered his presentation to the cowering fools: "I was not lying before! This is indeed an acting exercise of sorts! This exercise is indeed designed to test your improvisational skill! Only, the stakes are not some vainglorious dreams of stage or screen, but your very lives.

"You may have heard that my colleagues and I are commemorating the many occasions where Spider-Man proved inadequate at saving civilian lives. You may not have known that this is the site of one of the lesser-known incidents.

"The victim on that day was Bradley Bolton, an ESU alumnus best known, in his student years, for being the best quarterback in this university's history. You need to know his past to fully understand his tragedy. He was expected to reach the pros. But then came the Saturday when Empire State played Metro for the League Championship. It was the last two minutes of the final quarter, in the last game of the season. Bolton gained control of the ball on his one-yard line, and heroically ran the entire length of the field toward the opposing goalposts—evading all the other team's attempts to bring him down, lunging around and past and sometimes through their defenses, remaining in motion despite a failed tackle that cracked his ribs on the fifty-yard line." The Chameleon paused. "It would have been the kind of touchdown that makes legends. Except that he did not, quite, reach his goal. He was finally brought down one foot from the goal line. Metro took possession on the next play, scored their own touchdown, and won the game."

The Chameleon paused again, savoring the rhythms of the story. He had one thing in common with these vain pups: he loved to act. Indeed, it was what he lived for. He just staged his performances in a worldwide arena, usually without a script, and in the service of an ongoing play where a moment's artificiality could lead to capture or defeat or death. He had sometimes wondered what it would be like to be the other kind of actor, but not for long. He did not thrive on applause. His skill was avoiding recognition, not seeking it.

Still, he was not incapable of enjoying a captive audience.

Continuing: "Bolton gave up football and turned all his attention to his engineering major. He married, had a lovely daughter, and pioneered a new computer technology years ahead of its time that would have revolutionized the tracking of Worldwide Habitual Offenders.

"As you may imagine, there were some parties who were naturally quite put out by this, who wanted to prevent this technology from being used.

"They kidnapped Bolton's daughter and demanded that he meet them here, in the place of his greatest defeat, to turn over his invention. He complied. But the kidnappers had no intention of honoring their half of the bargain. And as he and the heavily armed kidnappers stood at opposite ends of the field—facing each other from a hundred yards apart—they announced that they were going to keep the little girl for insurance against him going to the police.

"It was quite touching, really. Bolton ran the same hundred yards he had run twenty years earlier. He ran the entire length of the field toward the kidnappers, evading all their fire, lunging past and around and over the slugs as they tore up the grass at his feet, persisting even as automatic fire tore into his chest on the fifty-yard line. He kept going, elbowed the last of the hired thugs aside, tackled the main bad guy, and seized his daughter ... but by then he was already a dying man.

"Spider-Man, protector of innocents, showed up, literally, one second later.

"In time to beat up the kidnappers and save the girl. But just one heartbeat too late to save Bradley Bolton."

The Chameleon chuckled. He couldn't help it. He found that part of the story funny. He only wished he could have been there, to watch; the web-slinger must have been incensed. He allowed the laugh to roll out across the empty stadium, echoing across the seats, raining down upon the pampered college kids huddled together one hundred yards away, like an army intent on conquering it.

"We are here to reinact that terrible moment ... with all of you would-be Oliviers and Streeps playing the part of Bradley Bolton.

"The explosives I've placed beneath this stadium are set to go off in thirty minutes. They are unidirectional; they will reduce the infrastructure to rubble and kill anybody unlucky enough to be standing on your half of the field. The exits have all been sealed or booby-trapped—except for the one directly behind me. I will be standing here, with this quite reliable AK-47, ready to perforate anybody who tries to get past me. Survival, in other words, will require a courage and an agility that equals ... actually, given his unfortunate results, far exceeds ... that shown by Bradley Bolton all those years ago. I cannot believe that the typically lazy and indolent college students of your benighted country can possibly manage it, but I am willing to allow you to prove me wrong.

"Because I am guarantee you that Spider-Man is being kept far too busy to show up on time. Or even one second too late."

CHAPTER TWELVE

11:47 A.M.

Spider-Man awakened flat on his back to the sound of angry men yelling.

"Damn it, Scibelli, I'm telling you for the last time—"

"You told me for the last time four times ago! And the answer's still no!"

Spider-Man stirred, realized that he was strapped down. Leather straps. No big deal, really. He could snap those with a shrug of his shoulders. He just didn't feel like it at the moment, that's all. Not with his headache.

"You continue with this career suicide and I promise you—"

"Promise whatever you want! Threaten whatever you want! But you're not getting past me — and I promise I'll put you in the hospital if you try!"

Stop arguing and close the door. It's cold in here.

"Are you threatening me, Captain?"

273

"I'm doing my duty, Captain. Now get out of my face or I'll put you down."

Spider-Man winced at a sudden surge of pain between his eyes. He remembered fighting Dr. Octopus again. That was typical. He was always fighting Doctor Octopus. He wondered idly why he'd been fighting Doctor Octopus this time. Then the events of the past twenty-four hours all returned to him in a rush, and he sat bolt upright immediately, with an abruptness that not only broke the straps, but sent the buckles rebounding off the ceiling.

Somewhere right beside him, a woman cried: "Yow!"

Spider-Man focused. He was in an ambulance. The woman was a paramedic: short, compact, round-faced, cocoa-colored, and not the kind of person who startled easily. That was okay; he specialized in startling the kind of person who didn't startle easily. He nodded at her, then turned his attentions toward the open rear doors. Captain Anthony Scibelli and another plainclothes cop he didn't know stood framed in that square of light. The other cop was white and in his early thirties; he had a blonde crewcut with darker roots, a charcoal-gray Brooks Brothers suit several degrees fancier than anything most plainclothes officers could afford to wear on a regular basis, and pale blue eyes that went wide as saucers as Spider-Man struggled to his feet.

The lady paramedic said, "You shouldn't be getting up. Your head injury—"

He gently pushed her to one side. "—will be okay. I've always . . . healed faster than most people." He made a liar of himself by stumbling slightly as he moved toward the door. "I take it this argument is about me, Captain?"

"That's a no-brainer," Scibelli grumbled. He gestured toward the other captain, who was still struggling to regain his voice. "This mook here is Captain Chuck Mercier, of the

87th; a little far out of his territory, but he's still publicity-conscious enough to demand that I give him this opportunity to unmask you. He also wanted the paramedics to drug you insensate, for your trip to the jail ward at Bellevue."

Spider-Man cocked his head at Mercier, enjoying the way the guy winced from the attention. "Nice guy."

"Yeah, well," Scibelli said. "It was my well-considered position that since we have no current warrants out for you, and since Octavius and his fellow mooks are still out there causing trouble, harassing or arresting you at this time would not be in the interest of public safety. That is, in fact, in case you're wondering, why I made the paramedics treat you here; I didn't want you out of my sight in some emergency room somewhere, where I wouldn't be able to keep the med students from taking a pair of scissors to that stupid mask of yours."

"We had to peel the hood away from the top of your head," the lady paramedic volunteered.

"Yeah," Scibelli said. "They did that, to find the bleeder. They had to give you a couple of stitches. I made 'em put a sheet over your the rest of the face first so we wouldn't see any more than we had to."

Spider-Man felt his forehead and winced, as the mere touch caused a throb of pain. He took a deep breath, tested his balance, and found that it had mostly returned. He moved toward the door, smirking a little at how quickly Captain Mercier moved to let him through; it never failed to amaze him how the cops who took the hardest line about his humble self were also the first ones to trip over themselves getting out of his way.

Behind him, the lady paramedic said: "I don't think this is such a good idea, Spider-Man."

"Well," Spider-Man said, "it's not like somebody who

willingly goes off to fight people like Ock and Electro could be accused of using his head anyway. Thanks anyway." He took an especially deep breath as he stood at the edge of the ambulance. The street still looked like hell; there was rubble everywhere, and a number of smashed cop cars. He spotted Betty Brant and Billy Walters up the block, talking to a couple of the uniforms; Billy, noticing Spider-Man, gave him a hyper-enthused thumbs-up. Too distracted to wave back, Spider-Man glanced at Scibelli and said, simply: "I owe you one."

"Tell you what," Scibelli said. "Take care of that mook on the bridge, and we're even. Super hero fights are one thing, but from what I hear, that guy's really messing with the flow of traffic."

12:07P.M.

Racing across town, conserving webfluid by travelling the distance in leaps and more conventional acrobatics whenever possible, Spider-Man quickly realized that the paramedic was right; the skull-rattling blow on the head from Doctor Octopus had taken far more out of him than he liked. His moves were all a little off: many times beyond Olympic or even superhuman standards, but still noticeably slow and sloppy in comparison to his own peak performance. It was not surprising. The Vulture had slammed him against half the buildings in the city, and Doctor Octopus had given him one of the worst beatings he'd had in months. The exertion and the cold and the blood loss were also beginning to catch up with him, not enough to stop him, and probably not enough for anybody else to notice, but enough that he was not looking forward to battling a man who in terms of sheer power was probably more dangerous than Octopus and the Vulture put together.

Swinging past the New School for Social Research, he tapped his throat mike. "Morgan? Deeley? Cujo? Anybody there?"

"We're here and following your progress, web-slinger." This from Deeley. "Glad to hear you're up and around again. We were worried about you."

"Morgan was worried?"

"Okay, so I was worried about you. Are you all right?"

"Never better," Spider-Man responded, wincing as a slightly miscalculated trajectory forced him to land on his feet a little more heavily than he would have liked. It was a lie all right; from the way his reflexes were acting up, he was several degrees short of okay. But he couldn't tell Deeley that. He was back in the air again, somersaulting over a side street, before Deeley could have perceived any real hesitation in his voice. "Listen, you want to give me a hand, I've been thinking about how to get past Electro's energy-barriers and onto the bridge, and I could use a quick lift to get into position. Can you send one of your floating bathtubs to meet me halfway? Say, the roof of the Verizon building? I'll fill the pilot in when I get there—"

"You can fill me in," Deeley said. "I'll break formation and meet you there in two minutes." He clicked off.

Spider-Man hopped off a crosstown bus, landed against the third story of a seven-story mercantile building, and ran straight up. A frigid crosswind sliced through the thin material of his costume when he reached rooftop level; despite the exertion, which was usually enough to keep him reasonably warm even in temperatures like today's, he couldn't help an involuntary shiver as the freezing air played against the thin sheen of cold sweat that suddenly seemed to cover every inch of his body. He did not know how much of this uncharacteristic vulnerability was an honest reaction to the weather, how much he could attribute to his weakened state, and . . . given who was about to fight next . . . a little burst of commonsensical fear.

Oh, he'd handled Electro before. The man had always been dangerous, but he'd also, in times past, always been a bit of a jackass: the kind of bad guy who could be defeated by a bucket of water or some insulated sheeting. Once, an otherwise unremarkable college buddy of Peter Parker's had knocked Electro unconscious with a blow to the head with a metal figurine; another time, Spider-Man had shorted him out just by the simple expedient of forcing the man to touch his ankles with his fingers. It was hard to continue feeling awe for a villain's capabilities when you had that kind of memory walking around inside your head. Unfortunately, the man had undergone a physical and psychological trans-formation since those simpler days. And this Electro was not only several times more powerful than that Electro, but also several times crazier and several times more cunning.

Spider-Man could not be sure he was in any shape to handle him.

Of course, the biggest problem would be getting past the living lightning that reportedly blocked both ends of the bridge; Spider-Man supposed he could leap through it and trust in the protection he derived from not being grounded, but he knew Electro would be waiting for that. He'd con-tacted Deeley because he thought he needed an alternative Electro would not be looking for.

He was swinging past the NYU Student Housing off Bleeker Street when he spotted Deeley's aircar, coming in low to intercept him. Spider-Man certainly had to give those little suckers credit for being fast; he'd expected to have to wait for Deeley, at the Verizon building, but Deeley had flown right past that rendezvous to pick him up much sooner. Gratuitously, Deeley waved. Spider-Man waited for Deeley to "park"—a hovering position two stories above street level, well within sight of dozens of pedestrians eagerly pointing at the show—then flipped head over heels and landed on his feet in the back of the car.

Deeley piloted the vehicle straight up, then headed southeast over the rooftops. His brow wrinkled with concern as he glanced at Spider-Man. "Do you know you have bloodstains all over your hood? And on your right arm?"

That was where Ock's pincer had torn a chunk out of his arm. Spider-Man supposed he looked like hell—the blood was nothing, compared to all the plaster dust that had shrouded his familiar red and blue colors beneath a veil of gray. But he actually felt better than he had a second before; the aircar's ionic climate field made the vehicle as warm as toast. It was gonna be hard, jumping back out into the cold again. "It's my new, new costume, Deels. I wanna wreak not only fear but also disgust and revulsion in the hearts of evildoers. Where's Morgan?"

"He had to return to the stationary command post on the Manhattan Bridge to coordinate an investigation of a false sighting of the Vulture over by the Museum of Natural History. Heard on the way here that it was definitely nonsense: some tubby wannabe in a homemade feather suit, almost got himself shot by a SWAT team. Are you sure you're okay?"

"As okay as I'm gonna be, today. Don't worry about it. Listen, the wind's blowing east, right?"

"Yes, it is," Deeley said.

"All right. Take us out over the East River, southwest of the bridge. Someplace around the South Street Seaport might do it. But high up, over Electro's direct line of sight—and tell Morgan to order all your other aircars to circle the area as close to the water as they can. I want him watching them while I come down from above."

Deeley was concerned. "Come down how? By jumping? Shooting a webline?"

"Not exactly," said Spider-Man.

12:17 P.M.

After okaying the plan with Morgan, Deeley piloted the aircar to the location Spider-Man had specified: a holding pattern over the east river, one hundred meters west and one hundred meters above the crackling towers of the Brooklyn Bridge. The other SAFE aircars had, as specified, lowered their cruising altitude to only fifty feet above the two main spans; though they didn't decrease the radius of their constant circling flyby, they were bound to divert much of Electro's concentration.

Deeley's brow knit as he observed the changes in formation. "I don't like this, Spider-Man. Even if they do trick Electro into looking down, that's only going to make it more likely for him to notice all the people we have in position under the bridge."

"I know," Spider-Man said. "Which is one reason I'd better get a move on." He hopped up onto the rim of the aircar, facing the bridge, and for just a moment took in the unusual tingling sensation of the ionic field against his skin. It was a faintly pleasurable compromise between heat and cold; he would have to enjoy it while he could, since he was about to step into a high-altitude icebox. He calculated the distance and the wind velocity, wondered briefly just what he'd done in his past lives to deserve days like this . . .

. . . and began to work his web-shooters.

It was no webline he cast now; he fired the fluid straight up, in short, controlled bursts, weaving lines that crossed and intersected and began to form a mesh. Within seconds it was solid enough to hold its form. He began switching back and forth between one wrist-mounted web-shooter and the other, each time using the hand he had free to sculpt and form his creation as it grew from an unrecognizable irregular blob into something that had a framework, a support apparatus, and a purpose. He was still spinning the harness when the incredulous Deeley exploded: "You have got to be kidding me. A hang-glider?"

"No big deal," Spider-Man said. "I've done it before. Came in handy one time the Vulture dropped me a couple of miles over New Jersey. Thanks for the ride, Deels; I'll keep in touch." Spider-Man leaped from the hovering aircar, felt the sharp tug of his glider being caught by the wind, and set course toward the support tower on the Manhattan side.

He descended quickly, his unerring reflexes guiding him directly toward Electro's hovering form; even the distraction seemed to be working out precisely as planned, with the low-flying aircars keeping Electro's attention firmly focused on the water. Electro was even considerate enough to keep his back turned. The downside was that, now that Spider-Man was not only outside the aircar's protective ionic field, but above the radiant heat and wind-sheltering effects of Manhattan's concrete canyons, the frigid cold of the day was once again blasting him full-force. He grimaced, wondering why he couldn't have gone into this line of work someplace warmer. Miami, maybe.

Focus, web-slinger. Coming in low over the tower on the Manhattan side. Close enough to see through the glow of the energy field to the pale frightened faces of civilians in their cars down below. Most of the windshields were fogged up. It occurred to him, too late, that if all those batteries were drained, then the civilians had spent the last couple of hours trapped without heat. There was no telling how many of them might have already died just from that factor alone.

Electro, who was apparently tired of trying to figure out why the aircars were circling so low, rode a flash of lightning to a better vantage point directly over the water. This last-minute move brought him out of Spider-Man's path. Spider-Man didn't mind; he had allowed for sudden movements. As his web-glider passed twenty feet above the tower on the Manhattan-side, he slipped free of the harness and tumbled toward the tower, rebounded against stone and steel, and launched himself directly at Electro's back.

The high-powered criminal whirled in mid-air. "Nice try, creep! But I know you too well to let you sneak up on me!"

"You want to say you know me well, cuddles . . . how about telling me my shoe size?" Spider-Man dodged a pair of energy bolts blasting by on either side. The nearness of the electrical discharge made the hairs stand up on his arms—but his spider-sense failed to recognize any immediate danger until after they were safely past him. At that point, incredibly, his spider-sense warned him of a fresh attack coming from someplace behind him—too late to avoid the heavy skull-rattling blow that slammed into the base of his neck.

He tumbled toward the water, fired a webline at one of the support cables, swung down and then up in a wide loop that carried him back to tower level, and caught a glimpse of something that made the heart stop in his chest.

Gwen Stacy.

On the Brooklyn side.

Falling to her death again.

He watched as her whole body jerked, with an impact that made her head loll like a stone at the end of a limp rag, briefly doubted his sanity as he screamed inside that this couldn't possibly be happening again—then felt the anger flare up inside him as the distant hologram vanished, only to be replaced by a fresh vision of his one-time love falling to her pre-ordained death. He regained control of himself just in time to let go of his current webline and fired a fresh one angled to bring him back toward the Manhattan-side tower. Tapping his throat mike, he exploded: "Morgan! Deeley! Why the hell didn't you warn me about that hologram? I almost swung face-first into a cable!"

His earplug crackled, and Morgan came on: "Sorry, web-slinger. Should have realized how you'd react. I take full responsibility."

"Full responsibility?" Spider-Man echoed. "You and me are gonna have to work on our communication skills, colonel!" He flipped, fired another web-line, heard the little tell-tale click of the web-shooter on that side firing on empty, and compensating by scrambling extra quickly across the face of the Manhattan-side tower. Electro was clearly pursuing him; little explosions blew craters in the wall as Spider-Man, moving as fast as he could, stayed only one step ahead.

This was no good. Electro already had him on the defensive. Spider-Man did what he always did when he needed a breather: he jumped straight up, somersaulting at the peak of his leap to scan the lay of the battlefield.

Electro was looping around to a position directly above the Manhattan-side tower. "Did you like our little surprise, web-slinger?"

"About as much as I like typhoid!" Spider-Man shot back.

"She was an innocent young woman, Max! Is her death really that much of a joke to you?"

"What can I say, Spider-Man? If it causes you misery, it's a real crowd-pleaser!"

Spider-Man landed on the flat expanse of the Manhattan-side tower. Electro rocketed straight toward him, his hands grasping a cat's cradle of pure crackling energy. Spider-Man remained where he was, waiting, ready to leap again at the first telltale tingle that warned him of the next lightning-bolt to come.

But when the spider-sense warning came, it did not warn him of a lightning bolt.

Again, just like before, it warned him of another attack from someplace directly behind him.

He whirled, seizing the ankle of the leg a high kick had aimed at the base of his skull, twisting it, sending the green-clad form of Electro tumbling to the floor. Electro took the fall like a pro, flipping, rolling, back-flipping onto his feet so he could face Spider-Man again.

It was like no move Electro, who had never been a martial artist, had ever been able to make before.

And Spider-Man belatedly put it together: the notoriously impatient Electro, waiting all this time for him to show up. The Gwen Stacy hologram. The lightning bolts that failed to fully engage his spider-sense. Two unexpected assaults from behind at moments when Spider-Man had thought he could clearly see Electro in front of him. Electro suddenly showing the skill and dexterity of a Jackie Chan. The term, *crowd-pleaser.* Even the Gentleman, taunting him just last night that this Day of Terror was only a cover for a much bigger operation, something with, he had said, truly global implications.

At moments like this, when he saw how completely he'd

been played for a sucker, Spider-Man knew exactly what made more feral super heroes like Wolverine snarl.

He leaped right through an illusory lightning bolt, brought the bad guy down with a tackle, and snarled, "Nice fake-out, Mysterio!"

"Thank you," Mysterio said, this time in his own voice. "I certainly thought so." His Electro costume shimmered and turned to vapor, revealing the familiar caped, green-and purple jumpsuit with goldfish-bowl helmet that he used for his own costume. He seemed to turn insubstantial beneath Spider-Man's fists, reappearing several yards away, posing in the overcast light of midday as his cape billowed majestically behind him.

Unimpressed, Spider-Man advanced. "Where's the real Electro, mister? And what are you people really up to?"

"The same thing we were always up to," Mysterio said, in a bored tone of voice. "Revenge. We're just not going to be as obvious about it as you seemed willing to believe . . ."

12:18 P.M.

Governor's Island sits in the East River midway between Brooklyn and the southern tip of Manhattan. Federal territory in the process of being transferred to the state of New York, housing a small naval facility, it's so close to the Brooklyn Bridge that some of its off-duty residents were entertaining themselves by watching the excitement now taking place less than a mile north. Governor's Island is a quiet place, safely insulated from the bustle of the boroughs on either side; it is not, unfortunately, as isolated from the world of super-villain vendettas as its residents might like to think.

Governor's Island also happens to be home to a top-secret vault, hidden in a sub-basement of a building cunningly disguised to resemble a family residence. The facility occupies four separate sub-basements, each safeguarded by a series of timed locks and high-tech surveillance equipment; there are entire sections of hallway designed to be flooded with cyanide gas at a moment's notice. If the government of the City of New York were ever to discover just what was being stored on the first three sub-basements, it would be very put out at the federal government. Nobody would be persuaded by the federal government's protests that such horrors have to be stored somewhere, and that Governor's Island is more secure than most locations in large part because nobody would ever suspect even the federal government of being insane enough to place such items inside a city with millions of inhabitants. But even if that presented a legitimate excuse, then nobody could have possibly seen the intelligence of storing the item housed on the lowest level not only within range but within sight of the towers of Wall Street. That was totally insane.

The only conceivable excuses were unforgivable shortsightedness—always a possibility, when dealing with bureaucrats—or some paranoid fantasy of an eventuality so extreme that the United States would be forced to declare war on the center of its own economy. That, too, is a possibility, with bureaucrats. They'll believe anything.

In any event, the answer to Spider-Man's first question ("Where's Electro?") was "Not Far"; he was on that fourth sub-basement, pressed against a black wall, seeming to be part of that wall, invisible behind the shield of darkness cast by the teammate who stood pressed to the wall beside him.

He hadn't been happy about his mandated role in today's festivities; as the most powerful member of the Sinister Six, he should have been out and around in the open air, taking an active role in the incineration of Spider-Man. Indeed, he'd originally considered this somewhat less glamorous assignment a prime example of the criminal lack of respect he sometimes felt he received from people like Doctor Octopus and the insufferable, arrogant, you-don't-*need*-to-know-my-master-plan likes of the Gentleman. The only reason he hadn't put up more of an argument was his awareness that Pity was as central to this particular operation's success as he was; he'd have suffered far greater indignities than this just for a chance to get her alone, away from the others.

He liked her. He thought he could treat her right. And he was only waiting for the right moment to ask her to go out dancing with him, sometime after Spider-Man was dead.

The oscillating security camera completed its sweep of the wall. The shield of darkness faded. Pity led him around the corner to another area swept by cameras, waited for the proper amount, and again used her powers to disguise them both as an errant shadow. She acted with perfect professionalism, without hesitation, looking at Electro only to make sure he was following.

He really liked the way she moved. Sorta like a cat, but all sweet and vulnerable, too. But even watching her did not keep him from growing impatient.

Sure, he appreciated the plan. He knew that Mysterio's activities on the Brooklyn Bridge would be sufficiently close to Governor's Island to put all the naval personnel here on alert; he also knew that by disguising himself as Electro, Mysterio would help to ensure that any energy-spike anomalies on the island itself would be written off as stray voltage from the bridge. Electro also knew that the larger plan—the plan behind the Let's-Kill-Spider-Man Plan—absolutely required the theft here to be kept a secret for as long as possible. But he disliked stealth, and he usually didn't need it. He was Electro! He could blow up this whole island, and Manhattan too, with a twitch!

He took his humiliation quietly.

He didn't want Pity to be upset with him.

He didn't want her to be upset at all.

She was upset enough, the poor kid.

He wanted her to be happy.

The oscillating security camera completed its sweep. Pity withdrew her zone of darkness and beckoned Electro on. She moved by wall-crawling, just like Spider-Man—except, of course, that she was a lot more fun to watch than Spider-Man. To Electro, she moved with the grace of a ballerina. She motioned him to stop, gracefully slipped through a net of crisscrossing electric eyes, deactivated them by tapping a code into a numeric keypad on the wall, and gestured for him to follow. They moved through another sliding door—this one stainless-steel and three feet thick, not that Electro would have normally considered that all that impressive a barrier—and entered another darkened chamber, this one bearing a simple vault door.

She kept very clear of that door. She merely pointed. That one.

Beaming—because he'd been eagerly awaiting this moment, when he'd finally be able to prove himself useful to her—he strode toward that door. As instructed previously, he raised both hands, palm outward, and placed them on the metal walls on either side of that door. The high voltage that ran through those walls constantly, that would have been interrupted if anybody broke the circuit by opening the vault door, now used Electro's body to complete the circuit instead.

Pity slipped around him, taking special care to avoid the physical contact that at this moment would have almost certainly killed her. She pressed a hidden latch on the vault door. A rectangular section, less than half a meter across, slid open, revealing a shelf that bore only one item: a simple cannister. This was, in fact, the entire reason for the vault door, there being no actual chamber behind it; the latch to this tiny shelf was so cunningly concealed that only people who already knew it was there could find it. Even they couldn't access the sliding door without breaking the circuit and automatically firing off alarms at SAFE, the NSA, and the nearest army and naval bases. Only by employing Electro, in this particular way, could the cannister be removed without breaking the circuit; only by keeping this particular theft a secret for a while longer could the Gentleman keep the authorities from guessing too early what he was really up to. Everything else was, as Mysterio or Neil Gaiman would have said, only smoke and mirrors.

Pity flipped the latch again, to close the hidden panel. Then she nodded to Electro, indicating that he could let the walls complete their own circuit again.

Electro let go. He wanted to say something, of course. Even if it was just that he liked the way she moved. But he'd been warned to keep silent during this phase of the operation. So he contented herself with a knowing wink.

Wishful thinking allowed him to interpret her next expression as a smile.

CHAPTER THIRTEEN

12:23 P.M.

Colonel Sean Morgan had never been anybody's nomination for boss most likely to take a screwup well. In both cases, he was considerably far down the list—not quite as bad as the kind of super-villain crimelord who kept his underlings in line by executing anybody who failed, but still so uncomfortably close to that rarefied territory that the agents of SAFE sometimes wondered how close he was to ever incorporating such a policy himself.

Right now, to the agents manning the command post atop the Brooklyn-side tower of the Manhattan Bridge, he seemed only seconds away. "Mysterio?" he demanded, aghast. "How can it be Mysterio? All our instruments read massive energy barriers around that bridge!"

Most of the agents in the command post—there were five, the immobile Palminetti among them—wisely kept their mouths shut and their eyes on their monitor screens. They could not escape the sound of Morgan's wrath, not in a prefabricated oblong room storing millions of dollars worth of state of the art sensor and surveillance equipment, but they could try to escape the full effects of that wrath by redoubling their attention to their work, in the hopes of finding something that would enable them to correct the damage already done. That left Palminetti, who Morgan could not be too mean to, to speak for them all. "All our instruments are wrong," Palminetti said, between breaths from his respirator.

"You mean all our state-of-the-art technology—"

"—can be trusted only if we make the assumption that there's nobody out there who knows how to fool it. Yes."

Morgan glowered at a viewscreen which now displayed Spider-Man and Mysterio pummeling each other in all-out hand-to-hand combat. "And it's safe for our people to go in? Not blasting their way in, but directly through those illusory energy fields?"

"I suspect so. We won't know that until we know just how illusory they really are. We'll know the answer to that in a couple of minutes, as soon as our systems can finish re-evaluating the readings."

"So what you're saying," Morgan said, his voice dangerous, "is that until then we're still being held in check by a glorified magician."

"Absolutely. And one important lesson I learned from the writings of James Randi is that even trained scientists, and precisely-tuned scientific instruments, are easily fooled by sufficiently talented magicians."

"*How?*"

"Near as I can figure it, Colonel, he must have had the real Electro there at the onset, to drain the captive vehicles of power, and cut off traffic at both ends of the bridge; they then made the switch, and kept things going with holograms, electromagnetic pulses, stolen municipal power, and electrified cables, and a truly spectacular light show. That, and our belief that the man holding the bridge really was Electro, kept us interpreting our readings the way the Sinister Six wanted us to—and also, openly rejecting any data that momentarily suggested otherwise."

"I don't believe it," Morgan muttered. "Billions of dollars of cutting edge equipment and it's not worth a thing."

"Not next to a sufficiently devious mind, Colonel."

A little bit more than a week earlier, the Chameleon had busted Dr. Octopus out of prison by disguising himself as Colonel Morgan. That made today the second time the Sinister Six had made a laughingstock out of SAFE and everything it stood for. Standing there in his command post, unable to do anything but watch as an already injured Spider-Man fought for the lives of hundreds of civilians, Morgan made a decision. Whatever happened, however much of the burden Spider-Man would be forced to carry himself, The Sinister Six would not be able to take advantage of SAFE again. He said: "That does it. To hell with the instruments. We're going in. Only tell the troops under the bridge they won't have to risk blasting their way through; the rest of us are going to attack by air."

"Who are you going to designate to lead the assault, Colonel? Deeley? Jones? Strackman?"

"None of the above," Morgan said. "I'm sick of these bastards." He slapped an energy pack into his sidearm and stormed from the room.

He was in the air, leading the assault against Mysterio, before Palminetti received the first word of the explosions that had just utterly destroyed Maria Stark Memorial Stadium.

By then, of course, it was too late to rescue any of the ESU hostages.

Twenty minutes earlier.

The terrorized acting students huddled by the home team end zone were still in the first stages of panic. Some had tried crying out to their captor; others had cursed him; some had frozen with paralysis and others had collapsed in tears. Some had advocated waiting for either the police or Spider-Man; some had advocated trying to make it out through the allegedly booby-trapped grandstands; some sought comfort in each others' arms; two had bloodied each others' noses, arguing over what to do. A few were praying. Maybe a third of them remained calm enough to be useful. Mary Jane Watson-Parker, who'd silently listened to their furious brainstorming, simultaneously admiring their courage and mourning the days when she'd been able to show the same degree of naivete, said nothing. She just stood in place, her eyes shut and her brow furrowed in concentration.

She tried to find an alternative. She tried to persuade herself that Peter would be here in time. She tried to find inside herself enough self-involvement to just stay out of it and let somebody else do what had to be done.

She thought of Gwen Stacy. Ned Leeds. Ben Reilly. Brick Johnson.

All people she'd known who'd died because not even Spider-Man could always be there in the nick of time.

She even thought of Bradley Bolton, whose brutal murder the Chameleon had chosen to celebrate. Mary Jane remembered the night he'd died. It had been several years before she and Peter had married, long before she'd officially admitted to herself, and to Peter, that she knew the real reason the young man she called "Tiger" so frequently slipped away with the flimsiest of excuses. She and Peter had met Bolton for the first time, for a few fleeting seconds, in this very stadium, only a few hours earlier, when Peter had gone to help interview the famous alumnus for a *Daily Bugle* article. She remembered how Bolton had seemed like a decent, pleasant man, at peace with himself and with his world. And she remembered how, at that night's dance at the student center, when Peter's eyes took on the familiar troubled glaze that even then always seemed to come on him without warning, she'd given him merry hell about having to slip away from her again. The next thing she heard about Bradley Bolton was that he'd been machine-gunned to death in the stadium. Now, years later, when she was able to look back on that terrible night with the awareness of a woman who knew why Peter had been so desperate to slip away, it occurred to her too late that maybe, just maybe, it was having to make up an excuse for her that had delayed her future husband just long enough to arrive at the murder scene exactly one second too late.

That's the thing people like the Chameleon will never understand, she thought. *It's not just people like Spider-Man who bear responsibility.*

She raised her eyes to evaluate the panic of her fellow prisoners. Right now, everybody was listening to a lithe, track-star type she knew slightly: his name was Martin Anders, and he was trying very, very hard to be tough and brave. "We oughta spread out!" Anders cried. "One big line, so we can rush him all at once! Of course, he'll probably get a few of us, but if the rest of us can run fast enough . . ."

Mary Jane coughed. "Have you ever charged a AK-47 across an open field with no cover?"

She had spoken without raising her voice, but a dozen pairs of eyes immediately swiveled to focus on hers.

Martin, perhaps sensing the loss of his audience, glared at her accusingly. "Have you?"

"I'm standing here alive and breathing without holes in me, so it's pretty clear I haven't. Come on, don't you get it? If we rush him, he'll rip most of us in half in a single sweep. Most of the rest of us will be maimed for life, even before the bombs. If even one of us got through, it would be a miracle."

Fern was holding herself together by the thinnest of threads. "So what are you saying, Midge? That we just gotta stand here and die, without even trying?"

"No," Mary Jane said. "I'm not saying that." She looked down the field, and again without raising her voice, said: "Look. Some of you here have known me long enough to know that I've had a few experiences with people like this." *Even more than you think.* "And I'm telling you that we're facing a man who has no compunctions about murder, who is in fact looking forward to killing us, and who genuinely enjoys playing games with human lives. He doesn't think of us as real people, but as targets—game pieces, for his stupid grudge match against Spider-Man. The trick lies in changing that."

A short red-headed guy with an alarming constellation of freckles laughed bitterly. "And how are we gonna do that in the next fifteen minutes, lady? By linking hands and singing 'Kumbaya'?"

"No," Mary Jane said. "We want to give him less of a reason to shoot us. Not more of one."

Martin Anders made one last attempt at control. "This is crazy! She doesn't know what she's talking about—"

Matt Gordon glared at him. "Shut up and listen, will ya? Go on, Red."

"All right," she said, taking a deep breath, knowing both that she couldn't really afford the time it took the compose her thoughts, and that she'd have to if she was going the sell the craziest idea she'd ever had. "It's going to be hard," she said. "And dangerous. And it's going to take more courage than anybody's ever asked of any of you before."

"What?" Anders asked impatiently.

"Consider this," Mary Jane said. "If we rush him all at once, like you said, we're a giant faceless mob. We make it easy for him for him to see us as anonymous casualties instead of individuals. We allow him to mow us down without a twitch of conscience. But if we approach him one at a time, at a walk—hands out in plain view—then all of a sudden, we give every potential victim a human face. We stand a slim chance of making the carnage more than even a hardened killer like the Chameleon can stomach."

It took maybe five seconds for the implications to sink in.

"You're crazy!" Anders cried. "He'll shoot the first person who approaches him!"

"Probably," Mary Jane said levelly. "And probably the second and third, too. Maybe even the fourth and fifth. I told you this would take courage. But if we don't let that stop us from still taking turns approaching him, one at a time . . . if every one of us who falls down dead becomes the cue for the person after that to stand up and make the long walk alone . . . then I promise you, we'll unnerve him. He'll feel the impact of what he's doing. He'll learn the difference between cutting down a mob and being forced to look his victims in the eyes. He'll hesitate. He'll get spooked. He might even break down. It will become easier to get past him. Most of us will make it."

"You're insane!" somebody whispered.

Anders—to give him credit—was beginning to see the cold sense of it. "Even if you're right," he said, "who's going to be crazy enough to go first?"

"My idea," Mary Jane said. "I go."

"I take track," Anders protested. "I can run. Maybe if I get close enough I—"

Mary Jane shook her head. "You can be second. I have to go first."

"Midge," Fern said, so stunned by Mary Jane's proposal that she'd even stopped trembling from the cold. "Are you really that anxious to die?"

Mary Jane turned to face the sea of astonished, terrorized faces. "No. I have no intention of dying. I'm hoping to get close enough to say some things to him."

Matt Gordon stepped forward. "Mary Jane, I can't let you go first. There's—"

She surprised herself by giving him a tight hug. "We don't have the time to argue about this, Matt. The clock is ticking. And I have to do this."

She put everything she knew about being persuasive into that one sentence. To her ears it sounded pathetic and phony: the kind of declaration made by a would-be heroine who knew she'd talked herself into doing something fatally stupid and secretly hoped that somebody would be eloquent enough to talk her out of it. It didn't convince her and she knew that there was no way it could have convinced anybody else.

But, as she'd said, the clock was ticking.

So she turned around, faced the tiny masked figure one hundred yards away, and began to walk.

She made the first few steps with her eyes closed, less afraid of the Chameleon, at this moment, than she was of the sudden, panicking, restraining hand from behind. If her friends and fellow hostages pulled it together quickly enough to stop her from going, then the moment would be gone; they'd just continue arguing among themselves until the deadline drew so close that only blind, stampeding panic remained an option. If that was the way her last few minutes were going to run, then she did not want to be a part of them. She needed to take this chance.

The restraining hand from behind did not come.

Part of her could not help wishing it had.

Part of her wished she could turn around and nod at the others, even smile at them, just to stress that she was all right about doing this. But she couldn't.

Turning around would show too much weakness before the Chameleon.

She walked briskly toward the distant figure of the man who held her life and her death in his hands. He was at full alert now that he knew somebody was making a run for it; he'd even taken a few steps forward, onto the five-yard line, leveling his weapon. By the time she passed the ESU forty-yard line, she realized that she still didn't know what kind of range that thing had, or just how ace a shot he was. Could he hit her from where he was? Would she even know she'd been hit before what was left of her tumbled to the ground, providing an easy point of reference for the first person who screwed up his courage enough to follow her into the Chameleon's sights?

She forced herself to think of other things, and kept walking, cheeks flushing in the frigid cold.

How can you face them?

She'd asked her husband that once. She hadn't been talking about the Sinister Six in particular: she didn't even remember who she'd been talking about, but it had been some other super-powered monster out to cause terror and suffering and death.

How can you even look at them, knowing how powerful they are? Knowing they want to kill you?

His first answer had been, *Beats me, Red.* Then, seeing she really needed a considered answer, he said, *I guess I do a bunch of different things, depending on the day, or how badly I need my courage screwed up. I make jokes, or I think of Uncle Ben. But mostly I do what public speakers have to do, to avoid stage fright. They pretend the audience is naked.*

It helps you to imagine Doctor Octopus naked?

Peter had winced at the very thought. *All right. Spectacularly bad example. But I didn't mean it literally anyway, Red.*

What do you mean, then?

I mean that if you find yourself scared of something, you can handle it by reminding yourself just what makes it ridiculous. In Ock's case it's his ego. In Electro's case it's the stupidity of a guy who uses his powers to rob banks when he can make millions getting a job with the power company. In Venom's case, it's his slobbering tongue and his obsession with spleens. And so on. I fight these guys, and it's deadly serious most of the time—but if I can also remind myself just how ridiculous they are, I can forget to be afraid long enough to do what has to be done.

She thought of the Chameleon, coming after her in her bedroom, certain that a big bad super-villain would have no trouble subduing the redhead with the baseball bat.

She crossed the fifty-yard line.

She was close enough to see his face now: or at least the smooth white mask he possessed instead of a face. There was no sign that he recognized her, but he was still grinning widely, still raising the AK-47 at her midsection as she strode toward him. The terrible cold cut right through her fashionable black coat and the two layers of clothing she wore underneath; but she suppressed the urge to shiver, knowing that she could not afford even the semblance of fear.

Forty-yard line now.

The grass of the field crunching beneath her leather boots. The cold of the wind against her face. The distant sobs of her fellow hostages, who were so sure that they were about to see her die.

The Chameleon's eyes.

She knew he would not blithely allow her to pass. He'd murdered before and he'd murder again. Her life, and the lives of all those other young men and women, depended on the accuracy of her instincts: her ability to sense just how far she could walk before the invisible line that the rules of his twisted game designated as the place where he'd be allowed to kill her.

Thirty-yard line.

It couldn't be that far now. Surely she was living on borrowed time already.

She almost stopped.

But if she stopped she'd never find the strength to walk again.

So she kept walking.

The Chameleon, standing bolt-ready on the five-yard line, the assault rifle primed in his arms, leeringly obnoxious in his confidence, waiting for the very last minute so he could clearly see the expression on her face as he killed her.

How many more steps would he allow her to take? How many more before the burst of light, the spasm of pain, and silence?

Twenty-yard line.

The Chameleon tensed imperceptibly.

And the still-advancing Mary Jane suddenly knew.

Of course.

This was a football field, where the distances were precisely measured.

The Chameleon was on the five-yard line. Like all human beings—even sick, twisted, evil, murderous ones—he probably possessed a healthy preference round numbers. Whether or not he realized it, he could not avoid being influenced by that. He'd cut her down when she was exactly ten yards away.

One more step and she'd be crossing that line.

She stopped just short of the midpoint between the ten and twenty-yard lines, avoided a buckling of the knees by sheer force of will, and made the time-out signal with her hands.

If that surprised him, he did not show it. Instead, he shrugged. "Nice try," he said conversationally. "But I'm not interested in negotiating. Come any closer and you'll still be the first to die."

He betrayed no sign of recognizing her.

Mary Jane swallowed, a sound that to her seemed louder than anything else in the world. "I'm not interested in negotiating, either. I just wanted to ask a question."

"If it's an appeal to my conscience, I'll execute you where you stand."

"It's not," Mary Jane said. Her voice sounded tinny, tremulous. She reminded herself that this was not acceptable, that this was a stage as surely as any theatre floorboards she'd ever walked, that the only difference between those shows and this one was the stakes riding on the performance—and felt all the strength she had empower her voice like a deadly weapon.

The Chameleon waited.

And Mary Jane asked the one thing that he never could have expected: a scornful, disgusted, "Was this really the best you could come up with?"

12:25 P.M.

Across town, on the Manhattan-side tower of the Brooklyn Bridge, unaware that he'd just missed one hostage situation entirely, Spider-Man leaped into the cloud of billowing vapor Mysterio had just employed as camouflage. It was thick, black stuff, capable of swallowing light whole; it rendered Mysterio effectively invisible, even though that didn't provide much of a barrier to somebody with a compensatory spider-sense.

Spider-Man simply threw a punch where that spider-sense directed. His blow connected, eliciting a gasp that most insubstantial clouds find beyond their capabilities. Spider-Man accepted a glancing blow to the jaw in return; he had been able to tell, just from the tenor of the tingle at the base of his skull, that it represented no serious threat, and he made no attempt to evade it—though it was no fun for a guy whose head was throbbing as much as his. He was too busy focusing on his spider-sense, intent on finding Mysterio, propelling him somewhere out of this muck, and webbing him into a nice immobile package for SAFE or the NYPD.

Then his spider-sense went absolutely nuts, warning him of sudden intense danger directly beneath him, and he cursed himself for failing to remember Mysterio's penchant for deathtraps. All at once, the subfreezing temperatures that had been slowing Spider-Man down all day were washed away by a wave of searing heat. He leaped straight up a fraction of a second before the vertical incendiary jets Mysterio had used to mine the tower could barbecue him alive; an agonizing pain in his right calf warned him that he had not been quite fast enough. The first thing he saw when

305

he cleared Mysterio's smoke cloud was a spreading dark patch on his tights, right below the knee: the material there was not only smoking itself, but sprouting an ugly little flame all its own.

Somewhere below him, Mysterio was laughing. "It's like I've always told you, webslinger! Imagination has always been my key to victory!"

"I've seen your Hollywood work, Misty! Imagination and you aren't even distantly related!"

Spider-Man flipped head-over-heels as he reached the apex of his leap, firing not one but both webshooters at the burning flame on his costume. He did not tap the triggers delicately, to fire a perfectly-formed webline; he did not press them precisely or artistically, to form some more exotic structure like the hang-glider; he slammed those triggers hard, and held them all the way down, smothering the flame on his leg behind a messy glob of formless goo. His leg continued to feel like it was burning; only the lessening of his spider-sense buzz confirmed that he'd succeeded in damping the flame.

He landed in darkness again, immediately ascertained where Mysterio was now, faked a leap in that direction, then calculated where Mysterio was likely to dodge and leaped there instead. It was a sloppy jump; not only were his reflexes still suffering from his borderline concussion, but his injured leg spasmed just as he pushed off, throwing off his aim. He was still able to tackle Mysterio head-on. The two men tumbled head-over heels, back into daylight, throwing and blocking a dozen punches even before they came to rest on the tower's edge.

Spider-Man ripped off Mysterio's helmet, revealing the hate-filled face of Quentin Beck. Mysterio kneed Spider-Man in the belly. Spider-Man rammed Mysterio against the hard stone of the bridge. Mysterio magically produced a blade in a hand that had not been holding one before and drew a thin line of cold pain across Spider-Man's chest. Spider-Man backhanded Mysterio in his now-unprotected jaw—which should have knocked Beck silly, but which instead vividly demonstrated Spider-Man's own depleted condition by only splitting the man's lower lip.

He hesitated when he heard the shouting of troops down below. SAFE, taking the bridge and evacuating the hostages. He heard another sound directly above him, looked up, and saw Colonel Sean Morgan and Agents Rawlik and Siclari at the head of a SAFE aircar, grimly pointing their pulse rifles at Mysterio's head. The aircar piloted by Doug Deeley brought up the rear behind them; the affable pilot nodded as he brought his own weapon to bear.

Mysterio slumped, took a deep breath, and chuckled softly.

"Well, well, well," Spider-Man said. His voice sounded uncharacteristically ragged; he was no longer able to hide just how rocky he felt. "The cavalry. Good to see you, Colonel."

"From the looks of you, I don't doubt it," Morgan said, cementing his reputation as a man who never returned compliments. "Why don't you secure that guy so we can examine those wounds of yours?"

"My . . . pleasure," Spider-Man managed. He turned his attention back to Quentin Beck, who stared up him with the oddest expression on his face: not only his usual hate, but also amusement and—oddest of all, though Spider-Man did not quite want to think about it—affection. It was not the face of somebody who'd resigned himself to surrender. It was the face of a practical joker who was about to play his biggest trick yet.

Beck chuckled, and said: "Don't you remember what we promised you before? It will end . . . where it began."

Spider-sense screamed a warning.

And the Manhattan-side tower of the Brooklyn Bridge erupted with white light.

Spider-Man, who had sensed an immediate danger coming from Mysterio's costume but not known what it was going to be, rolled away from his captive in the instant before the flares built into the fabric went off. The glow was so intense that even an indirect glance brought painful tears to his eyes; he knew that a direct look, from point-blank range, might have done his vision permanent damage. Spider-Man recovered in time to examine the scene through a painful purple afterimage; he saw the helmetless Mysterio grin and scramble toward the edge of the bridge, dodging pulse bolts from SAFE's also temporarily blinded marksmen. Their fire struck the bridge to either side of the fleeing villain, carving little craters in the bridge but missing him entirely; he remained untouched when he leaped off the edge, trailing a thick black cloud of theatrical smoke.

Leaping right through the friendly fire, Spider-Man followed his old enemy over the edge and saw nothing but a spreading ripple in the waters below. The thought of actually following Mysterio into that near-freezing current was enough to make his legs go weak; he probably would have done it anyway if not for the sudden absolute silence from his spider-sense and the lesson born of bitter experience that Mysterio, master of illusion, probably hadn't even hit the water at all. So he flipped in mid-air and caught hold of the tower wall. As he climbed up he saw what looked like dozens of SAFE commandos, climbing over the road barriers on the sides of the bridge; they were passing right through the formidable energy barriers without any apparent diffi-culty, then spreading out to see to the civilians who had imagined themselves trapped in their cars. Some of the com-mandos were clearly medics, racing from car to car to find the people most in need of immediate attention for hypothermia. Spider-Man saw one wrap a heavy wool blan-ket around a pathetically shivering middle-aged woman as she stumbled out of her Yugo. The medic spotted Spider-Man and gave him a thumbs-up. Spider-Man was too affected by the vivid reminder that real people were suffer-ing today to be in any mood to respond.

Besides, the fresh wounds on his leg and across his chest were both killing him. Grimacing, he climbed back to the top of the tower.

Doug Deeley, who had set his own aircar on hover and hopped down to see if Spider-Man needed any help, kneeled and extended a hand when Spider-Man reached the top. Spider-Man was not quite shaken enough to need the assis-tance, but he appreciated the gesture and let Deeley help him up.

"You've picked up a couple more nasty-looking wounds since I saw you last," Deeley observed.

"What . . . can I say? I'm a completist. I want one of everything." Spider-Man peered down at the water. "He got away, of course. I'm batting 0 for 0 today."

"So are the Sinister Six, for what it's worth. Our intelli-gence confirms that you saved everybody held by Toomes and Octavius, and from what I see it looks pretty promising for all the people held by Beck."

Spider-Man had never been able to find comfort in assuring himself that at least the very worst hadn't hap-pened yet. "That . . . only gives them reason to keep them trying 'til they get it right."

"Or until you clean their collective clocks," Deeley said. "Like always."

"Yeah."

Morgan, whose irritated eyes were tearing furiously—making this, in Spider-Man's view, probably the first time the spit-and-polish character had cried since somebody took away his napalm in kindergarten—marched over and said: "We don't have time for self-pity or self-congratulation, people. This is still an active crisis."

"And we all know how important it is for crises to stay active," Spider-Man muttered. "They might get flabby and short of breath."

Morgan's glare indicated that he hadn't developed any more of a sense of gallows humor in the past few hours; he almost snapped at Spider-Man, then apparently thought better of it and directed his irritation at Deeley, who was trying, not entirely successfully, to suppress a laugh. "May I remind you people that Beck still left a real mess behind him? We have a couple of hundred people down there who need to be evacuated to someplace warm for medical evaluation while we clear this bridge of vehicles and sweep the structure for any leftover traps or gadgets.—Doug, I need to remain available to coordinate response to the next attack by the Six. I'm assigning you to take command here, make sure the source of that phony energy field is shut down, authorize the reopening of the East River waterway, the Manhattan Bridge and the FDR Drive, and interface with the NYPD to get their help restarting and relocating all those trapped cars."

"And then what?" Deeley asked with a straight face, perhaps proving that his time with the web-slinger had been a bad influence on him.

Ignoring him, Morgan reluctantly turned his attention

back to Spider-Man, "As for you, hero, we don't have any current reliable reports of Sinister Six activities, so I want you to swing over to the command post on the Manhattan Bridge for some first aid. I don't know how long this lull is going to last, but I prefer you to be a hundred percent when it's done."

"I don't think I'll be a hundred percent 'til Memorial Day, Colonel. And if I know the Six, they'll be at it again before your people can finish brewing the coffee."

"Nevertheless," Morgan said, "you do look like a man who's pushing his limits, and it's good policy for you to take some minimum basic care of yourself. Want one of my people to fly you over there?"

Spider-Man thought about it for all of two seconds. "Not a bad idea," he said. "But send that ride to the Brooklyn-side tower. I have something I want to do there first."

He turned and leaped off the tower before Morgan could present any arguments, landing on his feet on the roadway, taking the entire length of the bridge in three great leaps. Each time he landed his head felt like somebody was playing the cymbals in there, and his leg felt like an elf with an ice pick had savagely jabbed him there to keep time. He barely heard the screams of the civilians who thought they were being attacked again, or the cheers of those who didn't read the *Bugle* and could guess he'd played a role in saving them; he did notice SAFE giving oxygen to some of the frailer civilians, and cursed Mysterio for needing to feed his ego by bringing terror in the lives of so many.

He reached the top of the Brooklyn-side tower within seconds, just in time to see the holographic Gwen Stacy once again tumble over the edge. After all these years, the sight was still like a freshly-opened wound. It only took him a second of searching to find the hidden projector Mysterio had set to constantly replay that terrible moment on infinite loop; he ripped the device from its moorings, knelt beside it, raised both his fists over his head, and smashed it flat in an instant.

The hologram died, just as the woman had died all those years ago.

Spider-Man's head felt wobbly. He thought of a beautiful young woman, with hair so blonde it was almost white and a faith in people so extreme that it had once been capable ot taking his breath away. He thought of her laugh, which had been like wind chimes during a rainstorm . . . and he thought:

Gwendy.

When you were alive I thought that you were the only woman for me.

When you died I thought my world was over.

I was wrong on both counts, Gwendy. It took a long time, but I'm old enough now, and smart enough now, to know that whatever happened, things wouldn't have ever worked out between us. We were both young, and naive, and too much in love with being in love to realize that we were too different where it counted—you wanted a peaceful life, and I wanted crusades.

You wouldn't have been able to adjust to the kind of life I lead, the way Mary Jane has to each and every day.

That's not the only reason I'm madly in love with her; it's just one of the reasons why that love is possible.

But the way I feel about her now didn't stop me from loving you then, and it doesn't stop me from still missing you now.

I would have liked to still be friends with you, Gwendy.

I would have liked to see you live a long and happy life.

And whatever grudge they may have against me, the

animals I'm fighting today made a very big mistake by using your death like it was just the punchline of a sick joke.

I'm known for my wisecracks, Gwendy ... with and without my mask ... but I swear to you, right now, that this time I'm going to teach them the cost of dancing on your grave.

"Uh ... Spider-Man?"

The web-slinger, who had been kneeling by the smashed projector, turned around and saw a lady SAFE pilot, whose name badge read Annanayo, peering at him from the driver's seat of her hovering aircar. She seemed incredulous. "Are you ... praying?"

Spider-Man thought about it, and said: "Yeah. I guess I am. Let's go see your medic."

12:14 P.M.

Mary Jane had just asked the Chameleon if this was the best he could do.

His eyes narrowed suspiciously. "Are you actually insane enough to insult me?"

Encouraged by his failure to shoot her immediately for her impudence, Mary Jane pressed on: "No, really. I want to know. Doctor Octopus blackmails the world. Mysterio extorts millions from the rich and famous. Electro blows up entire city blocks at a time. And you just wave a gun at a bunch of unarmed kids, like any other psycho with a gun fetish? How is that supposed to measure up?"

"It will matter little to you when you're dead."

"Nice sinister comeback," she said neutrally. "But I'm serious. I must have spent half the morning overhearing radio bulletins about your buddy threatening to blow up the

Brooklyn Bridge. I live out in Queens, so you better believe that scares me. The commuter trains are crowded enough as it is. But really; how come you're not there threatening to blow up landmarks, like he is? How come you seem to be the only member of your little antisocial club who isn't out there in the streets fighting Spider-Man personally? How come you had to arrange things so your deadline would arrive when he was out there taking care of your bigger and tougher buddies? Are we really supposed to feel terror and awe of a guy whose great big master plan is to sneak onto a college campus and act like any other psychotic spree killer with a grudge?"

The cords in the Chameleon's throat had gone tight. "You're still going to die."

She snorted, beyond caution now, even beyond fear, pressing on recklessly in the awareness that she'd drawn blood. Whatever happened now, she'd succeeded in sinking a knife deep into the soft flesh of his deluded ego; her only chance to remain alive was to keep on twisting it. "I'll tell you what, dirtbag—" and it was not hard to power her voice with contempt, because the more she had to deal with this pig the more ridiculous he seemed; the myth of the honorable and noble super-villain with a code, so often espoused in some of the more pretentious paranormal-interest magazines who sometimes tried to hire her husband away from the *Bugle*, never seeming more wrongheaded than when she had to deal with somebody like the Chameleon to whom honor and nobility might as well be meaningless words in a language no longer spoken "—if you're going to kill us anyway, I'm not going to let you walk away from this believing in your own brilliance. I'm going to start walking again, and this time I'll keep walking until you let me go or shoot me. I'm going to show your master plan for everything it is." She spoke the next five words one at a time, like little explosions: "Petty. Shabby. Cowardly. Pointless. Pathetic."

It was 12:16.

There was no chance of Spider-Man, or any other rescuer, arriving in time to make a difference.

She resumed her advance.

The Chameleon leveled his AK-47 and fired.

CHAPTER FOURTEEN

Mary Jane shuddered when she heard the weapon go off. She was so certain that it was being emptied at her that for a heartbeat she also thought she felt the rounds cut into her flesh. She wondered if she would have time to know she was dying.

Then the evidence of her eyes caught up with her own immediate reaction to the sound, and she saw the reason she wasn't tumbling to the grass in a pool of blood. The Chameleon wasn't firing at her at all; he was firing over her head, strafing the grandstand to his right. She whirled automatically, and saw a distant figure—her multiply-pierced friend Matt Gordon—making himself as small as possible behind the first row of seats. Seat backs chipped and splintered as rounds struck home right over his head, but Matt was still moving at a speed-crawl toward the exit.

She didn't have time to figure out the long way what Matt was doing there, but the immediacy of the moment was such that the knowledge arrived by instantaneous revelation. Matt and the others had taken it upon themselves to amend her plan. They'd waited 'til the Chameleon's attention was fully focused on Mary Jane, then trusted in his momentary distraction to keep him from seeing a couple of people slipping into the stands. Those people, the fastest and the bravest, were risking the boobytraps the Chameleon had promised to try to slip past him and take him from behind. Mary Jane did not have time to scan the grandstand on the other side of the arena to confirm that there was probably another escape attempt going on over there; she only knew, with a cold and chilling certainty, that she had less than a heartbeat before one of the Chameleon's rounds found its mark in human flesh. Including, possibly, hers.

All that went through her mind in less than one second.

It was still 12:16.

Directly ahead of her, the Chameleon's eyes flickered toward her as he realized that she was the more immediate threat. He swung his weapon toward her, and sliced the air in half.

With time now slowed to almost nothing, Mary Jane dove low, beneath the plane of fire. She felt something hot zing through her flailing long red hair as she focused on the feet planted on the ground just ahead of her. Concussive fire struck the earth directly behind her as the Chameleon swung his weapon downward; speed-crawling now, aware that her life span was now measured not in seconds or in heartbeats but in the speed of thought, she launched herself forward, refusing to let the descending arc of fire catch up with her before she caught up with him.

12:17.

At the very last second, the Chameleon seemed to realize that her suicidal advance actually stood a chance of succeeding. He took a single step backward, without relaxing his grip on the trigger—but by then it was too late, because she was already upon him, directly beneath his rifle as he fired rounds over her head.

She came up screaming, less out of fear or rage than sheer disbelief that she might get away with this. Her hands closed around his wrists. Her long fingernails cut painfully into his skin, as she struggled with all her might to force his arms and his line of fire further into the cold winter air. In an instant man and woman were both face-to-face, battling for possession of a weapon held high above both their heads.

She could hear screams from the home team end zone: some of them recognizable as the sound of friends crying out her name.

She screamed her throat raw, "*Now! Run!*"

The Chameleon tried to wrench his arms free, so he could once again bring the rifle to bear. His strength—not superhuman but substantial—surprised her; the force of it jerked her partially off her feet. She came dangerously close to falling. She took a step to compensate, then jammed her knee into his most sensitive place. The Chameleon grunted and stumbled backward. Still holding on to his wrists, Mary Jane allowed him to pull her along a step or two before kneeing him again.

Something hot tumbled against her back, bounced off, then thudded softly on the grass behind her.

The rifle. He'd dropped it.

Somewhere far behind her, dozens of people screamed. The screams had the special quality of massed voices approaching at top speed; they'd be upon her and the Chameleon in seconds. This was the most dangerous moment; if she let him past her long enough to retrieve his weapon, he could drop bodies all over the field. She had to put him down and make sure he stayed down.

She tried to cripple him with a stomp to the foot, but miscalculated and stamped only brittle, dew-stiffened grass. He spun her around, breaking her grip on his wrists. It was a perfect opportunity for him to shove her aside and go for the gun, but the red-hot bloodlust was so much upon him now that he just groped for her neck. His fingers closed around her throat, and his thumbs pressed hard into her windpipe.

"You!" he cried.

Mary Jane stumbled backward, stunned by the single-mindedness of the hatred in his eyes. She could tell, without being told, that whatever damage had been done to his memory, whatever prognosis he had for full recovery, he now remembered (if only for this moment) how thoroughly she'd once humiliated him. At this one moment in the Chameleon's life, killing her was more important than anything else: more important than Spider-Man, more important than his partners, more important than his awareness that a mob of fleeing hostages would be upon him in seconds. The resolve gave him a maniacal strength he had never possessed before. The berserker rage in those hands was capable of anything—even breaking her neck.

"That does it!" he shouted at her. "I'm setting off those bombs right now!"

12:18.

Mary Jane made no attempt to pull those hands from her throat. Instead, she brought her own arms up and over, reached for his mask, and drove her thumbs into his eyeslits.

The Chameleon yowled, let go, wavered, stumbled backward, threw an ineffectual punch which she easily countered, and tried to dive for his weapon.

Some of the faster runners were passing by now, too

overcome by panic to even consider helping her. As she jumped ahead of the Chameleon, cutting him off, she saw that some of the others had changed course to come to her aid. They'd be here in a heartbeat. She heard a distant, muffled explosion, felt the shock wave travelling through the ground right through the soles of her fashionable black boots, and knew that it was the first of the bombs, going off. From the increased volume of the screams rising all around her, her fellow hostages knew it too.

What had he said? That nothing on the far side of the stadium was going to survive?

The Chameleon tried to tackle her.

She hauled off and punched him in the jaw, not once, not twice, but five times in rapid succession, winding up each blow even as the last one was striking home. It must have been the beating of his life, even by the standards of a guy who got beaten up regularly; the Chameleon kept trying to fall, but the force of her punches kept jerking him to his feet again.

A distant *whump*, and a ball of flame rose from the grandstand. Shock waves flew across the sod, sending some of the escapees flying. Two of those had been men rushing to her aid. Dazed rather than wounded, they got up, dazed, unsure what to do.

Another explosion; this one toppling the home team goalpost. Followed by another half dozen in rapid succession, turning the other half of the field into a rapidly expanding cloud of dust. Clods of dirt pelted the ground like artillery shells.

Her fellow hostages were really screaming now, this time with the awareness that the shrapnel was flying, and that their lives could be measured in the inches of difference between safety and ventilation by hurtling debris. Matt and Fern and a couple of others arrived beside her and tugged at her arm; she shouted at them, unsure that anybody else was still capable of hearing her, "*Never mind me, just keep running!*

"Mary Jane, he's down! You don't have to—"

"Just go!" she shouted. She had no intention of abandoning the Chameleon so he could get away again.

Another explosion, frighteningly close. She stumbled blindly to stay on her feet, and could not find her helpful friends in the clouds of dust that suddenly surrounded her on all sides. One running figure collided with her. She almost fell over, almost whirled with the certainty that it was another attack, then saw that it was one of the men, trying to drag her to safety. She brushed him aside, shouted, "*Go!*" and scanned the area for the Chameleon, who she'd just lost in the confusion. She couldn't see him. At least, she couldn't see anybody who looked like him; with all these shouting figures running for their lives, he could have been anybody. She took a step, stumbled as another shock wave hurled her to the ground, then shakily got to her feet as Matt Gordon stopped beside her to help her up.

Another explosion—the biggest yet—ripped a great big gaping crater in the grandstands, hurtling metal seats like missiles. Her sense of self-preservation took over. "We've got to get out of here!" she shouted. "The bombs will be going off directly underneath us next!"

Matt shouted back—"Come on, I'll help you!"—then surprised her by growling and going for her neck again.

It wasn't Matt.

She saw the attack coming and ducked beneath those grasping fingers. His hands caught hold of her long hair. She grimaced at the sudden pain and drove the heel of her boot into his knee. He fell, pulling her on top of him. She took advantage of the moment to drive both elbows into his belly. He released her hair. She pulled herself up, felt the heat from a closer explosion ripple unpleasantly against her back, and elbowed him in the midsection again and again, shouting in time: "I! Am! Thoroughly! Sick! Of! You! People!"

Another explosion—this one so close she could feel it in her teeth—reminded her she had to get out of here. She lurched away from the still struggling villain, evaded him as he grabbed for her again, and aimed herself at the exit beyond the goal post, a small rectangle of order in the midst of a universe of roiling chaos. It wasn't that far away, but she privately gave herself fifty-fifty odds of getting there.

When the real Matt Gordon met her halfway to help her find the way out, he could not know just much he owed to her capacity for thinking clearly even in crises. Had she not been able to reason that the Chameleon couldn't have gotten ahead of her again this quickly, she might very well have put the well-meaning young actor in the emergency room.

Not long after she and Matt got out—the last to get out—the genuinely heavy explosions began.

The Chameleon's piteous trapped screams remained audible until the structure collapsed in on itself, like a closing fist.

12:35 P.M.

Arnold Sibert, the movie reviewer and editor of the weekend entertainment supplement for the New York *Daily Bugle*, hummed to himself as he rode his employer's notoriously rickety elevator up to the tenth floor city room. He knew he shouldn't be as happy as he was: he'd had recent unpleasant history with the super-villain known as Mysterio, had just begun romancing a woman who had lost her father to the lunatic's last rampage, and had every reason to be terrified now both for himself and for her now that the nutball in question was back in town, wreaking havoc with five of his equally maladjusted friends. The Arnold Sibert of two weeks ago probably would have been on a flight to Bermuda by now. The Arnold Sibert of today felt so curiously fearless that at least two times this morning he'd had to restrain himself from walking and talking like John Wayne.

Walking like John Wayne, he knew, is always a mistake when you look more like Wallace Shawn. Even if, as in Sibert's case, you happen to be in the kind of mood where you don't care.

The elevator doors opened up onto the tenth floor city room, and a blast of cold air set Sibert's teeth to chattering. The security guard downstairs had warned him to keep his coat on: the outer wall shattered by the Sinister Six yesterday was still only a sheet of hastily-erected plastic sheeting today, and the temperature inside the city room, maintained by space heaters, remained, if not freezing, then at least twenty degrees colder than normal. The place was still the madhouse it always became during a volatile citywide crisis: as far as Sibert could see, people were shouting into phones, racing to and fro, and cursing their computers for the typos produced by clumsy hands. But they did it in coats, and sometimes in gloves, and more than one cubicle rang with the Dickensian sound of strained bronchial coughing. Sibert waved at the always-frightening advice columnist, Auntie Esther, who, suffering through the usual whining corre spondence from her readers, merely scowled back. As always, her pursed lips held a Marlboro dangling an unbroken ash of a length that testified to inertia being a more powerful force than gravity. Sibert would have stayed to witness just how long she could keep it up, but he had other places to be.

Further into the newsroom, he nodded at Billy Walters, typing away at one of the few unoccupied desks, and Ben Urich, who was on the phone pursuing a lead in the cagey, almost-whisper that indicated contact with his one of his legendarily impossible sources, and Betty Brant, who was currently demonstrating the veteran reporter's knack of being able to type first-draft prose at secretarial speeds while simultaneously engaged in a telephone conversation on a completely different subject entirely ("No, Flash. I'm busy, Flash. I have a deadline, Flash. Can you possibly call me back a little later, Flash?") Sibert hesitated at the center of this whirlwind of activity just long enough to triangulate the source of the muffled yelling that informed the scene like background music, determined that it was coming from the the rarely-used conference room, and immediately changed course to intercept.

Before he could get there, J. Jonah Jameson stomped from that room with all the delicacy of a rhino, his mood best discerned by the severity of his hunched-over posture. (When Jameson was happy about something, his stride resembled the letter "I"; when not, the diagonal slash "/".) His craggy, crewcut head preceded the rest of him like a battering ram intent on clearing a path for his matchstick shoulders; his usual cloud of cigar smoke trailed behind. His only concession to the cold was a thin gray sweater. "Spider-Man!" he shouted, the very word a curse inflicted upon the less-than-sympathetic heavens. "Spider-Man! Spider-Man! Spider-Man!"

The various reporters typing away at their desks didn't even look up at this interruption. They'd all heard it before. *Spider-Man. Yeah. Right. Sure. Thanks for the input.*

Joe Robertson, who had followed the irascible publisher out of the conference room, seemed perfectly calm. But then, he always was during Jameson's frequent tantrums; indeed some long-standing employees around the paper had been known to wonder whether his ability to maintain both his dignity and his air of equanimity qualified as a mutant power. He responded calmly, betraying no stress at all as he thumbed the fresh shag tobacco in his ever-present pipe. "Like it or not, Jonah, we do have to report the news, and he does seem to be the man of the hour. Some experts predicted dozens of dead today, but so far the man's driven off half the Sinister Six without a single casualty."

Jameson whirled on his heels. "And don't you find that awfully convenient, Robbie? Don't you see that the wall-crawler and his buddies in the Sinister Six must have choreographed this whole farce just to make him look good?"

As far as the eye could see, reporters remained focused on their typing. *All a Spider-Man plot. Yeah, right. Sure. Thanks for the input.*

Robertson remained focused on his pipe. "I'm not going with that angle, Jonah."

"I pay the bills around here, mister! And I tell you what angle we run!"

"You pay my salary," Robertson said, "to make sure our angle bears some resemblance to reality as we know it. And I'm afraid I can't allow this paper to take the position that the Sinister Six, who have together and separately tried to kill Spider-Man time and time again, are now calling so much attention to his occasional failures because they somehow think that's a way to make him look good. Whatever else you think of the wall-crawler, Jonah, that simply makes no logical sense at all."

Jameson exhaled a tiny mushroom cloud, his only concession to the explosion he might have preferred. "I don't care! I still won't run a headline glorifying that masked weasel for encouraging a grudge match that's torn apart half this city!"

Robertson refrained from pointing out that this way of describing the situation completely contradicted the spin Jameson had given it only a couple of conversational exchanges either. He merely lit his pipe, puffed out his own matching cloud, and said: "I don't see any evidence he encouraged it, but I suppose that's beside the point. In any event, you don't have to glorify him. You can take your usual anti-vigilante stance, if you have to. Even blame him for being the famous gunfighter the bad guys have to come to town to fight. Say he attracts trouble. I don't particularly agree with you, but at least that position can be reasonably argued." He puffed twice, and said: "Which still doesn't change the fact we can't avoid in our coverage—that, today, at least, he's the one who's been out there all day, stopping these maniacs from killing people."

"I don't want to make him a hero!" Jameson bellowed.

"*You* didn't," Robertson said softly.

It was the kind of answer Robertson could count on Jameson taking the wrong way, even as everybody else in earshot picked up its true meaning. As half a dozen nearby *Bugle* staffers covered their smiles with gloved hands, Robertson glanced at Sibert, who was at that moment manfully suppressing a grin of his own, and nodded.

Sibert nodded back, but didn't say anything; as confident as he felt today, this was still the *Bugle*, where one did not interrupt a Jamesonian rant unless one had damn good reason. So he just leaned against a composing desk and waited.

After a couple of seconds, Robertson said: "And there's something else you might want to consider today."

"What?" Jameson demanded.

"Something Octavius said last night—that your crusade against Spider-Man helped him come up with the idea for this Day of Terror. Do you really want to call undue attention to that, capitulating to those terrorist maniacs by making this the kind of story they specifically said they want?"

There was a moment of eloquent silence.

When Jameson spoke again, he was no less angry than before, but he'd clearly been dragged down to the frontiers of rationality by Robertson's steadying words. "I still don't like it," he muttered, so quietly that only Robertson and Sibert (who he hadn't noticed standing nearby) could hear him. "I don't care what angle we take on him—showboat, freak, or menace—the point is, the second you start glorifying a maniac like that, treating his grudge matches like they really matter, then you also start declaring everybody living a normal life just plain irrelevant."

Sibert didn't see how that followed at all, but he could see that Jameson believed it—and that the belief was powered by a wellspring of raw human emotion. For a moment, he sensed himself on the verge of understanding the obsession that had baffled most of Jameson's friends and associates for years.

Then Jameson came to a decision. "Bury him inside. If we can't attack him outright today, then at least we can find an angle without him."

"That's a tall order," Robertson said. "He's at the center of it."

"I don't care. Find something."

Sibert, taking his cue, covered his mouth with his hand and coughed.

Jameson's head swiveled, his eyes narrowing as he

noticed the hovering movie critic for the very first time. "Sibert," he said, with enough bemusement to leaven his usual kneejerk hostility. "What in creation are you doing here? Shouldn't you be in some screening room, reviewing some Czech film about a yak or something?"

For years, most of Jameson's gibes at Sibert had involved Czech films about yaks. This derived from separate coverage Sibert had once given a Czech film festival and a documentary about yaks; both stories had unfortunately run the same day, leaving Jameson, (who tended to nurture his prejudices like beloved family pets) the vague impression that Sibert was always cluttering up the entertainment page with stories about Czech yak movies. Sibert, who had long ago given up correcting him, said, "I wanted to propose a story about Mysterio."

Jameson grumped. "How can you do Mysterio without doing Spider-Man? And what do you think you're doing, suggesting stories when you don't work hard news?"

"I usually don't," Sibert agreed, "but the research I did during his last rampage is still valid, and I already have pages and pages of data on how his special effects illusions work. It only took me a couple of phone calls to my friends at Industrial Light and Magic to put together a pretty good model of how he probably managed his Brooklyn Bridge stunt; I can probably have the precise details by deadline. And as for how you can do Mysterio without doing Spider-Man . . . well, the man did manage to hold back both SAFE and the NYPD for hours, just on the basis of a spectacular bluff, and that strikes me as pretty significant."

Jameson looked hungry. "You may be on to something, there; a story like that can nail SAFE to the wall. Wasteful government spending, and all that . . ."

"Oh, come on!" Robertson protested. "We have no direct evidence of waste in SAFE's budget—"

"They spend billions keeping an aircraft carrier floating above a city already serviced by three major airports! If you don't think that's wasteful—"

"Mr. Jameson!" cried Vreni Byrne, as she rushed over from her desk.

Vreni was one of the *Bugle*'s younger but more talented reporters, whose accomplishments in the past had included exclusive coverage of an attempt to blow up the Space Shuttle. Sibert had been an avid follower of her series of articles on the federal grand jury handing down indictments against the now-imprisoned ringleaders of the racist/terrorist militia known as Liberty's Torch; as she had always struck him as a gutsy, level-headed observer, with little tendency to sensationalize the facts or inflate her stories until they seemed any more important than they inherently were, the stricken expression on her face could only be bad news.

Sibert, who had never quite managed to develop the psychological quirk that permits news people to relish the arrival of headline-quality awfulness, did not want to know what she was about to say.

Robertson looked apprehensive too. "What is it?"

"We just received a bulletin," Vreni said. She was far from hysterical—was not, in fact, the type to become hysterical—but the enormity of what she was about to report had shaken her. "The Chameleon just blew up the stadium at ESU."

The moment of silence that followed was not quite total: the newsroom was always clattering with ringing phones, clattering keyboards, and reporters scrambling to organize material that may have been exhaustively researched but was never quite complete. But in that moment, the assembled *Bugle* staffers all held their breath, caught in the familiar tug of war between appreciation of a major story and simple human apprehension over tragedies still in progress. Joe Robertson's voice turned uncharacteristically tight as he said, "Please tell me it wasn't filled with people."

"No," she managed. "My source on the bomb squad says he had about forty hostages trapped there, until somebody beat the tar out of him and rescued them all."

"Spider-Man again?" Robertson asked.

Sibert, who couldn't help noticing that J. Jonah Jameson seemed stricken by the very possibility, found himself freshly aghast at the degree to which his employer's hatred of the wall-crawler sometimes seemed to override all other human considerations. He almost snapped that he didn't care who the rescuer was, as long as the hostages were safe—an outburst that would have been totally at odds with his usual mild personality—but Vreni spoke before he had a chance:

"No. One of the hostages."

Sibert's anger died a-borning. "A hostage?"

Glory Grant, who had just returned from her latest errand in time to hear the news, repeated: "A hostage?"

Jameson could barely contain his glee. "What kind of hostage?"

"An off-duty cop?" Robertson mused. "A campus athlete?"

"Who cares?" Jameson clamped his cigar between his teeth and puffed out his most noxious cloud of the day. "It's an angle! A beautiful angle! We can run a front page about the courage of a common man with the moxie to stand up to Octavius and his goons! Byrne, I want the name of that hostage! And a head shot, too! I'm going to put him on page one!"

"The police haven't released the name yet," Vreni said.

Jameson's cigar flared. "You have two minutes to get it or you're fired."

Vreni, who, like most long-term employees of the *Bugle*, was well-used to being fired on a daily basis, merely blinked and said: "As long as you ask so nicely . . ." before rushing off to commit the usual miracle under the ax.

Jameson watched her until she hijacked a portable phone off the nearest desk, then puffed out another cloud, discovered Sibert again, looked momentarily confused, processed the information that he still had a program running in that window, and said, "Right. The SAFE story."

"I didn't propose a SAFE story," Sibert said. "I proposed a Mysterio story. The special effects he used to pull off that hoax at the bridge—"

"A worthwhile sidebar," Robertson said. "Nice thinking, Arnold."

Jameson switched tracks again. "Yeah. Nice going. You'll do ten grafs on the magic while we point Urich at the exposé. That sound good to you, Robbie?"

Robertson coughed. "Need to check, Jonah. Urich has a lot on his plate right now, but if we can clear him for this SAFE story in the wake of today's crises—"

"Do it," Jameson said. He puffed out yet another cloud and then discovered Sibert again. His internal hard drive whirred while he re-opened that window. "You," he said, as if astonished to discover that Sibert was still there. "Didn't we just authorize your story idea?"

Sibert, who had been momentarily stunned into immobility by Jameson's mercurial changes in mood, managed a stammering, "Well, I wasn't sure—"

"Get sure!" Jameson bellowed. "This is a newsroom, not some foreign twaddle about depressed yaks! I don't come equipped with subtitles so you can take notes while listening to me! Go get yourself to a desk and a phone and don't come back until you have a story I can use! Move! Move! Move!"

Sibert almost turned and ran. It was a galvanic response, spawned by some unholy connection between the specific raspy tenor of Jonah's voice and whatever part of his own neural hardwiring still remembered what it had been like, so many millions of years ago, to be an unusually intelligent tree shrew fleeing from the hungry jaws of larger predators. He might have taken the two flights to the entertainment reference library at a gallop, probably wondering every step of that distance why anybody sane would ever want to work for this man—but then he saw Vreni Byrne, who was returning from her desk with an even more shaken look on her face, and he froze before taking a single step, unable to leave until he heard the second shoe drop.

Robertson said: "What?"

Vreni was so dazed she could barely get the words out. "Jonah . . . I used up a couple of favors and got the name of that civilian."

"Well, don't just stand there!" Jameson snapped. "Tell us the guy's name!"

"It wasn't a guy. It was . . . Mary Jane Watson-Parker."

It was a perfect example of the annoying natural lulls that occur in any noisy environment, where ambient sound suddenly stops in time for a critical sentence to carry to every nearby set of ears. At least two people, drinking coffee at their desks, did spit-takes. The news was enough to knock even Jameson off his stride. He practically whispered: "*Our* Mary Jane? Peter's wife? The one who always calls him that stupid nickname, whatever it is? That one?"

"I'm not aware of any others, sir."

This time, astonishingly enough, Jameson beat Robertson to the paternal show of concern. "Is she alright?"

"Apparently, nothing more than minor bruises," Vreni said. "But, get this. From what my source says, the people she saved all agree they saw her giving the Chameleon the beating of his life."

There was another pause as the assembled *Bugle*'s staffers absorbed this. There were some laughs, some mutters of admiration, even a couple of high-fives—but the overwhelming shared emotion was retroactive relief. Somewhere in the hubbub, Glory Grant flashed the dazzling smile that had been a major asset during her own brief modeling career: "I do declare, I'm gonna have to go power shopping with that girl."

Jameson, on the other hand, was almost plaintive; the bluster that seemed to characterize his every waking moment had all fled him at once, replaced by the pained confusion of a man who needed all his concentration just to parse the impossible. He practically whined: "I don't get it, Robbie. She was involved in a couple of major fights with Mysterio a little more than a week ago. Now she's fighting the Chameleon. That's not supposed to be the kind of thing that happens to fashion models and actresses. What's with her, anyway?"

Sibert, who had witnessed Mary Jane in action during the chaos at Brick Johnson's funeral and would not have been surprised to hear that she'd successfully taken down Doctor Doom, attempted a joke: "Maybe she's really Spider-Man."

For one terrifying heartbeat, Jameson seemed to be giving that serious consideration. Then he rebelled, shaking his head with an insistence that suggested he was trying to ward off demons. "No. Absolutely not. Impossible. No way. I've seen both her and Spider-Man close up. They both wear skintight clothing. You can see . . . enough for me to know . . . you are not getting me to believe that he could manage that trick."

Auntie Esther, whose cigarette ash was now precisely

three times as long as the laws of physics permitted, wandered by with a coffee cup just in time to deliver the coup-de-grace: "You never know, Jonah. It might be a superpower we didn't know about."

She was gone before anybody realized that they didn't dare react.

Then Jameson, predictably enough, started yelling: "Gaaaaaaaaahhh! Thanks a lot, lady! Like I really needed that image ruining my appetite and disturbing my sleep for the rest of my life! And get those smirks off your face, everybody! We're still racing a deadline here!"

As Jameson and Robertson began distributing fresh assignments in light of the explosion at ESU, Sibert smiled and began to make his way toward the exit. He was glad he'd hung around long enough to hear Vreni's bombshell, and Jameson's reaction to it; not only did he now have the added Up of being able to feel inordinately proud of a friend, but he'd also—if only briefly—seen the human side that made it possible to regard Jameson as something more than just a perpetually shouting ogre. He was also looking forward to working on his story; hard news may not have been a venue he wanted to work every day, but he spent so much time in dark screening rooms watching movies for a living that he relished the occasional chance to exercise his rarely-used reportorial skills. He wondered what Angelique would say when—

—when—

—he stopped midway across the city room, uncomfortably aware that something was wrong.

He didn't know what it was.

But there was a strange old man standing in the swinging doors to the hallway.

The old man was very tall, and despite his age, which Sibert estimated to be somewhere in the late eighties, very hearty-looking; though he was standing completely still and therefore providing no context in which to judge, the silver-handled walking stick upon which he rested both delicate, liver-spotted hands seemed more an affectation of status than a physical requirement of infirmity. He was certainly prosperous-looking, as well; his precisely tailored black suit, his bejewelled fingers, and his fur-lined camel-hair coat, bespeaking a man who could spend more on what he wore on any given day than most people spent on rent in any given year. But that was not what had stopped Sibert cold, so much as the death's-head maliciousness of the old man's smile, or the murderous triumph in the old man's eyes.

Sibert, who had all-too recently seen a murderer brag about the death he had caused and the deaths he still intended to cause, had just enough time to recognize that he was once again looking into the face of evil. He almost cried out.

Then the world exploded.

A wave of hot air, striking him from behind, knocked him off his feet and to the newsroom floor. He heard screaming mingle with the sounds of shattered glass, heard somebody cry out, "Oh, no! Not again!" and, prone on the ground, surrounded by flying paper and frigid wind, belatedly remembered the grim promise Doctor Octopus had been reported to make just yesterday afternoon, in this very same room: *It shall end where it began.*

Nobody had put it together enough to realize that the Day of Terror had begun with the official announcement.

Here.

In this room.

Sibert grabbed his eyeglasses, which had not only fallen

off but popped out the frequently-wayward right lens, and placed them back on his nose again. Then he reached up, grabbed the corner of a nearby desk, and painfully pulled himself to his feet. What he saw was blurred not only by flying dust, and his own nearsightedness in one eye, and the fog that had misted the intact lens over the other, but also by unbidden tears. But he could see well enough to tell what was happening, behind the dust, and the bedlam, and all the terrified people so unsure that they were going to live past the new few seconds: five familiar figures, emerging from the wreckage that had been Jonah's office until their last invasion only one day before.

Mysterio, wafting in on a cloud of vapor: flapping his cape flamboyantly, like the showman he was.

Electro, riding in on a bolt of blinding light; chuckling to himself as he blackened a nearby desk just to prove he could.

The Vulture, flying in near the ceiling; licking his lips hungrily, as if anticipating a meal of fresh carrion.

The new member, Pity, somehow giving the impression of infinite reluctance even as she leaped past her teammates to cut off a pair of clerical workers who'd attempted to dart for the fire exit.

And Doctor Octopus, striding in on his own two feet, while directing his awful tentacles to begin gathering up hostages from all four corners of the room.

The temperature had dropped to near-freezing again, thanks to the shredding of the pathetic plastic sheeting Jonah had ordered erected over the crater torn in the wall only yesterday, but neither Sibert nor anybody else needed the cold as an excuse to shiver. Far from it. The story had just re-entered their own lives again. And as the pincers at the end of one of one of the Doctor's tentacles seized him by the wrist, and pulled him toward the terrified, sobbing mass of humanity that had just become imprisoned at the center of the room, Sibert had time to think only one determinedly upbeat thought, *At least there are only five of them. Mary Jane gave us that much. We only have to deal with five.*

Big deal.

Any individual one of them was powerful enough to kill everybody here.

CHAPTER FIFTEEN

1:35 P.M.

A lull in the fighting.

From one end of Manhattan to the other, the sound of paranormal combat had almost completely ceased. It never stopped completely, alas; in a city as filled with heroes and villains as Manhattan, there's always somebody beating up on somebody somewhere. As it happened, the Rhino was currently taking out his frustrations on a barroom jukebox in the Village, and the Avenger named Hawkeye was currently whupping the tar out of the recurring bad guy named the Candyman in Washington Heights. But the all-out chaos that had characterized the worst of this Day of Terror seemed to be taking a deep breath. Live coverage of the ongoing crisis had to content itself with updates on the cleanups at ESU and the Brooklyn Bridge, and occasional sexy clips of Mary Jane Watson-Parker playing Emma Steel in the last *Fatal Action* movie.

Some people began to wonder if it was over. Jay Sein and

Cosmo the K, bereft of new developments, found themselves resorting to banter about how come today's malefactors had called themselves the Sinister Six when only four of them had even bothered to do anything. "If these guys want to ruuuule the world," Cosmo opined, his famous voice dripping with sarcasm, "maybe they should first learn how to count."

Jay Sein chuckled. "You think?"

Very funny. "Dumb super-villain" jokes are always funny. The humor sections in bookstores are stocked with entire volumes of them.

But the lull was only a gathering of forces. It ended when, at 1:47, an impenetrable darkness swallowed the midtown offices of a certain major metropolitan newspaper.

Time for the final act.

2:03 P.M.

Riding a SAFE aircar to the site of the *Daily Bugle* building, Spider-Man couldn't remember the last time he'd felt quite this miserable.

Ninety minutes of taking it easy at the SAFE mobile command post, sipping coffee and enjoying Agent Clyde Fury's astonishingly tasty mulligatawney soup ("It's the way I grind the spices," Fury volunteered, as if expecting the injured super hero to take out a pad and pencil and scribble down the full recipe for future reference), should have left him energized, ready for anything; but the battering he'd taken all day long had instead left him washed-out, wasted, and as stiff as only several hours of being slammed into buildings can make a man in this line of work. His head was achy, he felt the beginnings of an ominous tickle at the back of his throat, his arm and his chest stung painfully from the places where Octopus and Mysterio had succeeded in drawing blood, and his right leg was badly blistered from the incendiaries on the Bridge.

He'd also heard about Mary Jane's adventure at ESU, and immediately pumped the agents tending him for confirmation that "all the hostages" were all right. Even when he'd found out Mary Jane was physically unharmed, he desperately wanted to go to her, and comfort her, and find some impossibly unhypocritical way to chide her for taking so many unnecessary risks. Instead, he'd been forced to content himself with a SAFE vid-link to the cops at the scene, who had after some prompting agreed to put Mary Jane on the phone so Spider-Man could "ask her some questions" about any information the Chameleon might have slipped before the bombs went off. Spider-Man and Mary Jane, both remaining in character as people who had met each other a couple of times in the past but were not even remotely friends, had drawn out this long-distance "interrogation" far longer than the exchange of tactical information could have possibly merited; the eventual conclusion, that the Chameleon hadn't said or done anything that seemed a relevant clue to the larger plan, must have seemed hardly worth the trouble to the cops and SAFE agents monitoring the whole thing. But then, they couldn't have known the real unspoken point of the conversation: *Thank God You're Okay. Thank God You Are Too. Be Careful. I Love You.*

Spider-Man knew she didn't get an adrenalin charge from danger, like he sometimes did. She'd pay for those few moments of incredible courage with shaking and tears later. It was another debt he looked forward to paying back to the Six.

With Deeley still occupied with the endless postmortems at the bridge, and Sean Morgan having flown ahead to check out the situation at the *Bugle*, Spider-Man's chauffeur on this particular flight was Walt Evans, a sandy-haired, bespectacled agent whose resemblance to a beefier Woody Allen had led him to the false conclusion that he had a workable sense of humor. Mindful of Spider-Man's jocular reputation, he kept up a steady stream of unfunny wisecracks throughout the entire flight, culminating in his reaction to the first sight of the jet-black monolith that seemed to have taken the place of the *Daily Bugle* building. "Bet you're happy about that," he said.

Spider-Man wanted to tell the guy to shut up. He wanted to protest that he had friends in there. But he knew he had no right to make self-righteous complaints about people who joked their way through deadly situations, so he merely said: "Uh huh."

The zone of darkness, no doubt cast by Pity, was as smooth as an obsidian wall, and affected an area extending ten feet into the street. Arcs of lightning, no doubt contributed by Electro, snaked jaggedly around the edges. As Evans headed for a landing, twenty yards from the place where the building's revolving front doors sat wrapped in blackness, Spider-Man saw that the entire surrounding block had been evacuated; crowds of heavily-dressed onlookers, hoping to see some action, were jostling each other behind police sawhorses at both opposing intersections. He saw several people filming his arrival with camcorders, several others holding up cardboard signs that expressed a wide variety of sentiments from support for Spider-Man to support for J. Jonah Jameson, to spiritual messages. There were even a couple of "Hi, Mom!" signs. The street itself had been cleared of civilian automobiles, and was now teeming with uniformed police officers, SAFE agents, and grim-looking people in suits. When Spider-Man spotted Sean Morgan shouting something unpleasantly official at a burly, moustached fireplug of a plainclothes officer who seemed about to belt him, he didn't wait for Agent Evans to find someplace to hover; he leaped from the aircar three stories above the pavement, rebounded off a lamppost, and landed in a crouch by the Colonel's side.

At both intersections, onlookers went, "Ooooooh," which made Spider-Man wince, since under the circumstances, putting on a show was the furthest thing from his mind. He nodded at Morgan, said, "Colonel," then acknowledged the red-faced fireplug of a cop with, "Detective."

The fireplug returned his nod, and greeted him in the same tone of voice: "Fruitcake."

Spider-Man, who should have been used to disrespect by now, was taken by surprise by that one. He said, "Sorry, you must be mistaken. I haven't been around nearly as long as most fruitcakes."

The fireplug looked him up and down. "Twinkie, then?"

Morgan, who appeared to have been more than slightly aggravated by this particular cop already, blew up. His words became little explosions of condensation as he shouted: "I have had more than enough divisive garbage out of you, Sipowicz! Like it or not, SAFE has been granted full tactical jurisdiction here, and Spider-Man has been operating with our full support! You will either treat him with respect or you will report back to your squad! Is that clear?"

"Ooooh," the fireplug said, "I'm shakin' in my booties. Lemme know when Lance Link shows up, okay?" But he withdrew, not completely off the site, but behind a squad car where he stood muttering derisively at the battle garb of the SAFE agents setting up a firing position directly across the street from the *Bugle*.

Morgan made sure he was gone before taking a deep

breath. "You don't have a lot of friends on the NYPD, you know that?"

"I have a few," Spider-Man said, mentally reminding himself to add this morning's Captain Anthony Scibelli to the short list. "What's the story here?"

"As near as we can piece together, Octavius and his cronies—excepting the Chameleon, who's apparently still missing in action from the explosions at ESU—seized the building an hour ago. They managed to keep it under wraps until they solidified their positions, then released everybody in the lower nine floors, keeping an unknown number of hostages in the tenth-floor city room. The zone of darkness went up about fifteen minutes ago; since then, they've been firing lightning bolts at anybody who approaches within ten feet of the front entrance. They say they'll start killing hostages the second anybody other than you tries to come in. They said that if you arrive you'll be allowed free passage through the front door . . . as long as you're not wearing the communicator we issued you."

"Swell," Spider-Man muttered. He rubbed his throbbing head, suppressed a shiver as a blast of cold air cut right through the thin cloth of his costume, and said, "Anything else?"

"This." Morgan fished a crumpled sheet of fax paper from a vest pocket of his battle suit. "They've spammed this e-mail press release to every newspaper, magazine, and TV station within fifty miles of here. It summarizes their mindset, if you can call it that, about as well as anything could."

Spider-Man took the wrinkled sheet and read it quickly. Nothing in it surprised him, given the people he was dealing with—but every word added to the bad feeling that had been growing in his belly since the moment he'd first learned just where the Six had decided to make their last stand.

* * *

The Daily Bugle *building has always been the scene of Spider-Man's greatest failure: his reputation. Here, in this place, the minions of Jameson spin the words that have kept him a hunted, friendless outcast. Here, we will bury the man in the place where the press has buried his dreams of glory.*

And then we shall execute everybody in the building.

It is unfair, we know; in light of the damage this place has done to Spider-Man's life, we his enemies should feel nothing but heartfelt gratitude. Indeed, we discussed the possibility of awarding Jameson the wall-crawler's head.

Alas, several of us have also been wronged by this place, in this place and we are all looking forward to the opportunity to rectify those injustices as well.

Here, it ends.

There were no signatures. None were needed.

Spider-Man was reading the fax a second time, searching for some kind of clue or giveaway reference that might help him survive the battle to come, when Morgan rumbled, "We've found an old utility tunnel linking the underground press room with the adjacent building. We could flood the offices with a harmless nerve gas that would render everybody in the entire structure unconscious in less than two minutes."

Spider-Man did not look up from the fax. "Except that Mysterio's costume comes equipped with its own air supply."

"Its own limited air supply. Which he only activates if he realizes what's happening to him."

"Right. But you know how long two minutes can be whenever lives are at stake. Even if we were lucky enough to catch Mysterio off-guard, the rest of the Six might still have enough time to realize what was happening. They'd be able to start killing people—or at the very least, bust out and start this whole nightmare all over again somewhere else."

"Yes," Morgan said. "That's the way I see it, too."

Spider-Man glanced at Morgan. It was a strange kind of eye contact, in that one of the participants was wearing one-way lenses set in a mask that hid every single detail of his face, and that the other was a hard man who rarely showed any feeling deeper than utmost professionalism, but the shared understanding was so total it was practically telepathic. "What was it you said this morning about not liking me?"

"Save those hostages," Morgan said, "and I'll keep a picture of you in my wallet."

Spider-Man handed back the fax, shook his head once to clear it, gathered up his resolve, and reached under his hood to remove his throat-mike and receiver. He handed both to Morgan, then, suppressing a limp, began to walk. He approached the building unhurriedly, paying absolutely no attention to the cops and SAFE agents shouting their best wishes at his back. He didn't even pay attention to the crowds now raising enthused sports-fan cheers at both sides of the block. Adulation may have been a treat that he'd tasted only rarely, and one he understandably preferred to the fear and distrust that was more frequently his lot, but he knew that whatever happened now, the cheers wouldn't last long; he had them now only because his day-long fight against the Six had been exhaustively covered by the media, and he'd lose them as soon as the public found its new thrill parade.

At moments like this, they were irrelevant anyway. Because cheers couldn't help him fight harder or better or with more bravery; they couldn't make the Sinister Six one iota less dangerous. And no amount of spin-doctoring, whether Jameson's endless crusade to paint him a menace, or a crowd's temporary willingness to see him as a hero, could possibly change the color of the blood that would spill if he failed.

All he really had behind him was the simple phrase he'd cried out on that terrible night so many years ago, when the meaning of being Spider-Man had been forcibly shoved in his face. The phrase that had come to define his purpose in life.

With Great Power Comes Great Responsibility.

2:07 P.M.

Jay Sein, watching the live coverage on TV, said: "This is an astounding moment, people. SAFE and the police have evidently decided to let the wall-crawler go in alone. And the man looks rocky and the man looks like he's been through a war, but he's going. What I wouldn't give to know what's going through his mind right now . . ."

Cosmo the K said: "Probably how he's going to survive more than thirty seconds after going inside. They're probably catch him in a crossfire as soon as he enters the lobby."

"Let's hope not," Jay Sein said, the jokey persona he used to describe superhero battles with a sense of ironic detachment having, at least temporarily, left him. "Let's hope that when the darkness around that building lifts . . . we won't prefer that darkness to anything that's there to see."

2:08 P.M.

Spider-Man was not used to entering tall buildings at ground level. He did it often enough as Peter Parker, usually when accompanying friends who would not have appreciated or been able to participate in his costumed habit of leaping out windows hundreds of feet about the pavement— but as Spider-Man it was a much rarer experience. With the *Daily Bugle* lobby both as silent as a tomb and as shrouded in Pity's all-encompassing darkness as the building exterior, it was a second before he could overcome his inevitable feeling of disorientation. He had to fight the sensation that this was a place he'd never been before, and rely on his spider-sense to guide him unerringly through the dark.

He didn't sense immediate danger anywhere. He only felt the low, almost subliminal buzz he always encountered whenever entering a place where danger lurked but was not quite ready to strike. He supposed he'd encounter a death-trap or two before the Six was ready to take him on—but if there were any, they were too faraway to pick up.

He hopped up onto the front security desk, wrinkling the paper on the clipboard where non-employees had to sign in. "What is this? A big game of hide-and-seek?"

A hateful voice answered, from somewhere out in the blackness. "Hardly, my dear boy. Just a little pause in the proceedings, while you and I get better acquainted."

Spider-Man narrowed his eyes behind his mask. "Gentleman? That you?"

"Indeed." The darkness vacated a space just against the building directory, where the dapper old man stood waiting for him. The Gentleman was dressed for the cold, as he'd been yesterday, but in the warmer confines of the lobby he wore his camelhair coat loosely draped around his shoulders; his gloved hands emerged from the unbuttoned confines of the coat to show his contempt with an insulting display of applause. "And I must commend you on your marvelous show of resiliency. I confess that quite a few times during today's violent festivities I truly feared we wouldn't have the chance to enjoy this meeting."

The wall-crawler's spider-sense still gave him nothing more than a background buzz. "I don't have the time for you, pops. I'm here for Ock and the others."

The Gentleman raised one aristocratic eyebrow. "I'm certain. But Ock, as you so sophomorically insist on calling him, has joined his fellows in kindly agreeing to permit you and I a quarter hour of undisturbed privacy for the purposes of this little chat."

"Given Ock's sweet personality, that must have taken some doing."

The Gentleman acknowledged that with a nod. "Indeed. He is far from the most obsequious of employees. Were it not for his special skills, which I shall require for the final phase of this enterprise, I daresay I would have been just as happy hiring somebody capable of understanding his place. However, since he is being well-compensated for his time, he was big enough to decide that there'd be no particular harm in indulging me on this one matter. The others felt the same way. I give you my solemn word that neither he nor his colleagues will take any further action against either yourself, or the unfortunate occupants of this building, until our discussion is concluded."

The old man's right hand disappeared inside the coat, and emerged with a fresh cigar. As he sniffed it, the zone of darkness receded still more; though darkness still shrouded the world outside the windows, everything from the front revolving door to the elevator bank was now normally lit, with only a few unnaturally-impenetrable shadows to maintain the uncertainty of the situation. Several of those were large enough to conceal possible hiding members of the Six.

Spider-Man hopped off the security desk and advanced on him. "And what if I say the hell with waiting? What if I just say I'm not interested in your mind games? What if I just leave you behind and go after the Six now?"

"You won't. I know you too well. You can sense that I have important things to tell you. And you're too consumed with the need to know."

"Right now, after the day I've had, I'm only consumed with the burning need to bounce your head against the wall about thirty or forty times."

The Gentleman seemed amused by that. "I doubt you would ever resort to using such brutal tactics against a powerless old man, however aggravating; were you the sort, you would have utilized them against the publisher of this barely literate American tabloid many years ago."

Gotta hand it to the man; when he had a point, he had a point. "Jameson has a way of growing on you."

"I believe the standard comedic response to that is, like a fungus. Am I correct in that?"

Spider-Man had actually applied that joke to discussions of J. Jonah Jameson more than once, sometimes to his face; the part of him that appreciated his own sense of humor was rankled to find it appropriated now by the Gentleman. He grimaced beneath his mask. "Yeah, I'll give you that one, at least. So if we're really gonna have this kaffeeklatsch now, we might as well get down to it. Who are you, anyway? What is this really about?"

"Two different questions," the Gentleman said, "with, I admit, two completely different answers. If you tell your friend Morgan to check the tape," he indicated a security camera recently unveiled by the retreat of the zone of darkness, "my image alone will be enough to provide you answer to question one. He will have it in his files, I assure you. Of course, I may have aged too poorly to make identification a certainty, or the picture might be as blurry as the owner of that decrepit equipment should be intelligent enough to expect, so you might find it necessary to prod him with the name Croesus. I promise you, a man of his resources should be able to ferret out my identity in short order."

Spider-Man was now nose to nose with the man. "And my other question? The point of all this?"

The Gentleman showed remarkably white teeth. "Profit. Power. Revenge."

"Same things that motivate your employees," Spider-Man pointed out.

"Except that I possess vision on a much grander scale."

"Forgive me for saying this, pop, but I've heard that 'grand scale' crap from a lot of people like you. Ock says it all the time."

The Gentleman nodded to acknowledge Spider-Man's point. "With some justification, I must admit. The man does possess a considerable degree of macchiavellian cunning. Were it not for his over-reliance on those ridiculous robotic arms of his, he might have actually made something of himself. I, however, possess no such handicap."

"So you futz around blowing cigar smoke while making melodramatic pronouncements. I have news for you, bunkie. I'm not impressed."

The Gentleman smiled again. "I promise you, wall-crawler, if you knew the extent of my accomplishments, you would be."

"If you don't give me something more substantial than enigmatic hints, this conversation is over. I have places to go and people to beat up."

"Very well. I suppose that's reasonable enough." The Gentleman sighed, gathered his words, then fixed the web-slinger with a witheringly cold glare. "In essence, I've made my fortunes by investing in, and encouraging, chaos. I'm an expert in breaking things, sometimes on a societal scale, just so I can benefit from knowing in advance precisely the manner in which money will eventually ebb and flow in response. I have made fortunes—more than you can dream—destabilizing democracies, because I can provide the technology of torture used by the dictatorships that rise in their place; discouraging technological breakthroughs, because I have too much riding on the problems they would have solved; fomenting wars, because my arms dealers are in a position to supply both sides; even sowing the seeds of ethnic cleansing, because of all the special financial opportunities that only the most brutally self-cannibalizing societies can provide. Crime, disease, environmental disasters, assassinations—they all provide fine fertile ground for a talented speculator capable of hurrying them along. For what it's worth, I've even been known to invest heavily in the work of certain artists, immediately before arranging for the drug overdoses and tragic accidents that make their work so much more valuable for the collector. I could name some of the best-known tragic deaths of this century, ranging from soulful lady poets to rugged he-man novelists to sex symbol actresses to painfully idealistic singer-songwriters; their deaths weren't all mine, by any means, because there are only so many hours in the day, but I did see many of them coming, and I did contribute enabling circumstances to a significant percentage of the rest. There are endless opportunities in this line of endeavor, Spider-Man. Human heartbreak has always been a growth industry."

Spider-Man, who had remained silent throughout this long speech, needed several seconds to form his response. When he did, his tone was uncharacteristically solemn. "If even half of that ridiculous cock-and-bull story is true, you're a monster."

The Gentleman tossed back his head in a silent laugh. "Ahhh. It is good to see that you're capable of paying attention. No, you're right. Some of that little soliloquy was simply self-aggrandizement, taking credit for tragedies I never even explored. But which parts, Spider-Man? Doesn't your hero's soul ache to know about the precise extent of my own great power and great responsibility?"

This was bad. The Gentleman had just blithely referenced a private credo that Spider-Man had only rarely spoken out loud. The web-slinger tried to remember the last time he'd used those precise words outside the confines of his own skull, and couldn't even come up with a context. He couldn't even remember the last time he'd mentioned them to Mary Jane. If the Gentleman actually knew him that well, so thoroughly that he could practically pluck the secrets from inside his head, then he must have had Peter and his alter ego under close surveillance for years.

Spider-Man's fists were so tightly clenched that his fingers ached. "Who am I to you, mister? I never even spoke to you until yesterday."

"You didn't have to. My concept of revenge is exceedingly . . . persistent. I know we're running out of time—and my employees are probably running out of patience—but I did very much want to cover that ground with you, so I believe we can probably get away with a vivid illustration." He clapped his hands twice. "Pity? Come here."

The darkness retreated from an alcove in the ceiling, and Pity dropped as silently as a cat, landing in a wary crouch by the Gentleman's feet. The web-slinger, who wasn't used to being taken by surprise, hadn't detected her presence at all. He immediately tensed, in light of how formidable she'd proven the day before. But she made no move to attack him. She didn't even stand up. She just remained in that crouch, her expression blank, regarding the wall-crawler with her wide war-orphan eyes.

The Gentleman placed the palm of his right hand on the top of her head, and stroked her hair possessively. "Magnificent, isn't she? Like a finely-tuned machine, designed for one purpose and one purpose only. Serving my will."

Pity said nothing. Of course. But she trembled beneath the Gentleman's touch. Her eyes were as eloquent as any tear-stained hysteria could have been; the old man made her skin crawl. She endured his possessive behavior only because for all her power, for all her strength, for all her youth and vitality, she'd lost whatever inner resources resistance might have demanded of her.

The furious Spider-Man, who operated under no such limitations, fired a web-line at the old man's wrist, whipping the other end upward so it tethered that hand to the ceiling.

The Gentleman grunted, tugged, and found his hand arrested in place six inches above the captive Pity's head.

Pity showed no surprise, no relief, no anger, no grateful appreciation. Her face was as blank as a porcelain mask. But her trembling had stopped.

Spider-Man said: "I can't change anything you've done before today, pops, but I will stop you from touching her that way again."

The Gentleman experimented with tugging his imprisoned wrist. "Oh, dear." He sighed. "I suppose I was being a tad too . . . demonstrative. She's always been especially uncomfortable, accepting my affections in public."

"I don't blame her. What's your problem, anyway? Can't get a date at Century Village?"

"I don't have a problem," the Gentleman said. "She does.

You see, as I really was about to tell you, because it speaks to the point I wanted to make about revenge, I knew her parents quite well. They worked for me, on one of my lesser operations. I trusted them about as well as I trust anybody, which is to say, I honestly believed that they did not possess the wherewithal to betray me. When they did, I was quite crushed."

Spider-Man's lip curled beneath his mask. "I get it. You killed them."

"Not personally, I assure you. I just whispered in the ears of somebody else with sufficient reason to want them dead. But even that wasn't enough. You see, for me, it has never been enough to simply take vengeance on the betrayer. Being as long-lived as I am, I must also take vengeance on subsequent generations. My policy has always been to wait until the children of my enemies grow up and establish themselves in their adult lives, so I can use my influence to utterly destroy any chance they might have of lasting happiness. In this unfortunate young lady's case,"—the Gentleman nodded toward Pity—"having disposed of her mother and father, and learned of her special latent abilities, I devoted two decades to turning her into a creature without hope, and without will, capable of committing any atrocity I choose. Since she has been allowed to keep her conscience, the better to keep her in a constant state of torment, this is a splendidly delicious way to punish her poor dead parents for what they did to me."

Spider-Man couldn't control his revulsion. "You're insane."

"Not at all. Simply evil. Those of you who happen to be players on the other side have so much trouble understanding the difference." The Gentleman checked his pocket watch with his free hand, pursed his lips, and placed it back in his coat. "Time does march on, I'm afraid. In a few short seconds, our grace period will be history, and my ward here will have to turn out the lights again. You will face your old enemies in the dark; I shouldn't have to specify that they, of course, will all be able to see you perfectly well. But I should still have enough time to tell you one thing you and this fine young assassin have in common—you were both targets of mine even before you were born."

Spider-Man couldn't take any more. He leaped . . .

. . . just as Pity stood, and brought back the darkness.

CHAPTER SIXTEEN

2:24 P.M.

Spider-Man knew midway through his leap that he wouldn't get to the Gentleman. He even knew, from the painful tingling at the base of his neck, that Pity was about to take him down hard.

He spun in mid-air, changing his trajectory as much as he could, getting away with nothing more serious than a spine-rattling kick to the side of the face.

Even as he fell, he twisted, turned, swept his own right leg in a blind sweep in the direction of his attacker—and heard a soft feminine gasp as he succeeded in batting her aside. He landed on his hands, flipped away in time to avoid another kick, skittered across the ceiling, and paused beside the elevator bank, searching for the spider-sense impression that would let him know where to strike.

He could sense movement, some nearby, some that must have been coming from the higher floors. He heard scraping metallic sounds, barely audible whispers, the soft scraping of shoes against polished tile. He smelled ozone and—oddly enough—the rich, fragrant stench of an elephant house at the zoo. (Mysterio must have thrown that in). He did not yet have anything concrete enough to act on.

He sprayed four exploratory weblines into the darkness. Three of them impacted distant walls and floors without any other obvious effect; one was rewarded by a distant crash as somebody, getting out of the way in a hurry, crashed into a pane of glass. The noise was too heavy to sound like it could have been Pity. He hoped it was the Gentleman; he was really beginning to hate that guy.

His spider-sense screamed out a warning as every hair on his body reacted to the buildup of a tremendous electrical charge.

It felt too powerful to dodge in the lobby.

Spider-Man hurtled toward the elevator doors, slamming into them with his right shoulder with a force that cratered both layers of flexible metal inward. He disappeared into the shaft just as the lobby behind him exploded with heat and thunder. The light was probably blinding, too, but Pity's darkness had swallowed up all light: probably the last time Spider-Man could count on it helping him.

He heard the beating of massive wings, swooping down from above.

He allowed his spider-sense to pinpoint the danger. In his mind, he saw a razor's edge, plummeting toward him, spinning as it fell, slashing at his throat. Memory alone supplied an image of the Vulture's lean and hungry grin.

Spider-Man leaped past that slashing blade and planted a solid punch on the Vulture's jaw. He was rewarded by a fresh stab of pain as a backslash sliced across his upper arm, drawing blood again. He twisted, grabbed the Vulture by the wrists, and tossed the old man down the shaft. He hoped to hear a thud. But though there were only two elevator levels below the lobby—the upper and lower levels of the basement press room—he heard only a frantic whoosh. The Vulture had recovered and would be after him again in a second.

Spider-Man would have been more than happy to wait for him, but then his spider-sense flared again. He leaped away just in time to avoid a massive explosion that blew what was left of the lobby elevator doors inward in a hail of deadly, supercharged shrapnel. The acrid stench of ozone marked that as another attack by Electro. Electro was serious.

Spider-Man speed-crawled two flights straight up, then leaped back and forth across that section of shaft a half dozen times, trailing weblines. It took him less than two seconds to block that section of shaft with a makeshift net. The barrier would not hold Electro or Doc Ock for long, but did stand a chance of slowing down the others —that is, if he could actually count on them blundering into it. He was pretty sure he could not.

The shaft below grew very hot, very quickly: no doubt Electro, burning his way through the web-barrier. Usually he'd accompany this act with various colorful boasts of how unstoppable he was. Today, he held his tongue. They all were: making the most of Spider-Man's inability to see.

Spider-Man speed-crawled up the shaft, thinking furiously. Interesting, that they could see, when Pity's power swallowed up all light. What were they using to see? Infrared? Ultra-violet? Some form of radar?

His spider-sense spiked, warning of an attack from directly above him.

He leaped to the other side of the shaft and winced as something heavy shattered to pieces on the wall where he had been. Something spun away from the impact and pelted his injured right leg. It felt like a piece of wood. Spider-sense warned him of another hurtling missile, directly above him. He sensed an odd island of safety in the center of whatever it was, launched himself at that island, and realized what this and the previous missile had been only after he passed through the empty space unharmed: a big wooden desk. The empty space was the place where the desk's usual occupant sat.

The desk smashed to pieces on the wall where Spider-Man had been, peppering the shaft below with shrapnel. Somewhere down there, the Vulture cried out in pain and annoyance. Spider-Man would have taken some comfort in that, but he could already sense more office furniture coming his way. It was not merely falling, it was being thrown . . . with the same kind of impossibly enhanced strength that allowed a man to hurl police cruisers.

Ock was up there.

Spider-Man grimaced at the thought of fighting Ock blind, while simultaneously having to watch his back for Electro and the others.

As a computer monitor exploded against the wall beside him, showering his back with glass shrapnel, Spider-Man realized he couldn't do it. His spider-sense might have kept him alive up until now, but it wasn't going to be enough.

He had to turn on the lights.

He didn't have a chance to consider how he was going to do this before he realized he had a more immediate problem: rapidly approaching intense danger signals from both above and below.

He leaped across the shaft again, barely evading the plunge of something that cleaved the air as heavily as a small car. He found the sliding doors to the fourth floor, opening them with a force that drew harsh tearing sounds from the gears, and leaped through. The doors closed shut behind him just in time to protect his back from a rippling blast of heat that must have been Electro, blasting the falling object out of his way.

He had to keep moving.

He was by the elevator bank on a floor dedicated to small administrative offices related to the day-by-day corporate business of the paper. The corridor had the pungent disinfectant scent of a recent thorough cleaning. As Spider-Man ran down that corridor, taking a left at the first intersection, the floor shook from the sound of elevator doors being blasted off their moorings. Up above, the entire structure of the building reverberated from the impact of adamantium tentacles ripping through walls and ceilings as Octavius smashed his way downward through all the floors that separated him from his greatest enemy.

Spider-Man had seconds. If that.

He webbed off the corridor behind him and skittered along the wall until he came to an office door. He kicked his way through that, somersaulted, landed on a desk, and probed the ceiling. It was a false ceiling, composed of plasterboard panels designed to put a presentable face on the water pipes and electrical wiring and air conditioning ducts that formed the true skeleton of any office building. Some of the apparently solid walls that separated adjacent offices at the *Bugle* went only as high as this false ceiling—a good reason why the folks who worked down here sometimes complained that they could hear everything that was going on in the offices on either side. As the ominous sound of wing beats filled the corridor outside, and the sound of tentacles smashing their way through ceilings grew so close Spider-Man could feel it in his teeth, he found himself empathizing. But only briefly.

He pushed up the panel and slipped into the narrow

crawlspace, moving as quickly as he could through the maze of pipes and wiring. Because he was Spider-Man, that was pretty quick . . . but it seemed glacially slow to him. The crawl space was filled with places so narrow that only a man with an extraordinarily flexible spine could have forced his way through; if light had been filtering up from the offices below, he would have been able to move faster, but the artificial absolute darkness had reduced this place to a tactile maze that slowed him down and kept his progress down to a rate only a couple of times faster than the fastest Olympic sprinter can run.

He had to stop and retreat when his spider-sense screamed at full blast at an immediate threat from above.

Plaster dust billowed against this face as the space immediately ahead of him exploded. He heard servo-motors and heavy breathing as Doctor Octopus, still smashing his way through the floors, smashed through the crawlspace on his way down. For a heartbeat, Spider-Man was certain he was about to die. But no; Octopus hadn't found him, he'd merely come very close to finding him accidentally.

The sound of debris clattering into the office below was interrupted by a crackling electric discharge that sent something heavy smashing into the wall. Octopus swore: "Be careful, you cretin! It's me!"

Electro, who commanded enough raw power to reduce the organic percentage of Dr. Octopus to ash and vapor, sounded sheepish. "Sorry, Doc. Coming through the ceiling like that, you startled me."

"Where's the wall-crawler? I thought you were right on top of him."

The Vulture's voice wasn't nearly as respectful of the Doctor as Electro's had been. "We were. But we lost him after he went down this way. He must be in hiding."

"He'll turn up again," Octopus snarled, "even if we have to tear down this entire building to find him. Show me where you saw him last!"

As the three members of the Sinister Six moved out of the office where he'd left them, Spider-Man knew it wouldn't be long before they figured out where he'd gone. He'd gained himself a couple of seconds of breathing space, nothing more.

That and—thanks to Ock's less-than-subtle way of getting from one room to another—a ready-made shortcut to the floors above. Spider-Man scrambled out of the crawl-space and up through the crater left by Ock's passage, leaping another two stories straight up into a room crackling from what Spider-Man supposed were shattered light fixtures. He landed silently, his boots sliding on the pile of disturbed documents now littering what was left of the tile floor.

He would have continued upward after another second or two of getting his bearings, but then his spider-sense warned him of something about to go spectacularly wrong; he didn't realize what that disaster-in-the-making was until something heavy shifted beside him and he realized that a big metal desk, which Ock's violent passage had left precariously dangling on the edge of the abyss, had been sufficiently jarred by Spider-Man's otherwise graceful landing to start sliding it into the crater Ock had left behind.

In the instant before it went, Spider-Man had a heartbeat to consider his options. He considered catching the desk with a webline, but even if he could anchor it to something, the mere act of tethering it would have changed its trajectory enough to send it swinging into some other solid object on the floor below. Octopus, Electro, and the Vulture would hear that and come running. Result: dead Spider. Or he could just let the desk fall and hope that he was lucky enough to have it flatten one or more of them coming back into the office two stories below for another look. That would be convenient, Spider-Man supposed, but his luck was never that good. Besides, he wouldn't have been able to live with himself if just doing nothing led to even the hateful likes of Octopus getting violently killed from his inaction.

That left him trapped with the third option.

The certifiably insane one.

Spider-Man leaped onto the desktop, adhered, and surfed the furniture bomb as it tumbled into the abyss.

"Cowabunnnggaaaa!"

In the less than two seconds it took to fall all the way to the first uncratered floor, the desk tried to flip over from his weight. Spider-Man had to carefully counterbalance it to keep it level. The fall was oddly terrifying; he plunged far greater distances just swinging from building to building on a daily basis, but he usually enjoyed perfect eyesight at the time; now, he had to rely on split-second timing and the guidance of his spider-sense. The part of him that always remained aghast at his crazier stunts insisted all the way down that it could not possibly be enough.

In the half second before the desk hit bottom, he heard crashing and cursing as Octopus and the others rushed back to investigate. He could hear a wall down there shatter as Octavius took his fastest route into the room.

Spider-Man imagined the space below him crisscrossed by questing tentacles.

He leaped off the desk just before it struck. He heard the clang of initial impact, the metallic scrape of the desk sliding down a pair of outstretched adamantium arms, and a pained grunt as the desk slammed into something of mere flesh and blood. There was another, minor, secondary crash—this one metal on metal, evidently the sound of Ock and the desk slamming into an identical desk on the office below. This one was followed almost immediately by a yawning shriek as the floor gave way and sucked Ock and both desks into its great big gaping maw. The final cacophany, as everything landed in a messy heap one floor below that, was so painful just to hear that Spider-Man found himself honestly happy he couldn't see it.

His spider-sense shrieked at him: danger all around him, most intense to his immediate right.

He skittered across what was left of the wall, just one step ahead of an explosion that peppered his back with sheet rock. *Electro.*

He heard a nasal cackle immediately behind him, spun, and kicked in the direction of another spider-sense signal ... hitting nothing but empty air, but crying out in pain as the razor's edge of pain tore along his upper arm. *Vulture.*

He heard a hated, arrogant voice cry out in rage as the cramped office echoed with the servomotors that could only represent adamantium arms snaking up from one flight down. The three of them, moving in deadly synchronization, like the fingers of an inexorably closing fist.

Trapped and blind, choking on the stench of ozone and smoke, pelted by a hailstorm of debris still tumbling down from the upper floors, seared by the heat of a major fire that seemed to be starting somewhere in the vicinity—in short, sensing nothing but immediate, lethal threat on all sides—Spider-Man focused everything he had on his spider-sense and searched for one direction even fractionally less dangerous than all the others.

Nothing.

His foes were laughing.

Nothing.

His foes were about to kill him.

Nothing.

His spider-sense screamed imminent, unavoidable death.

And then, unbelievably, an opportunity: itself so danger-ous that only sheer desperation would have led him to leap head-first in that direction.

Desperately, Spider-Man leaped.

Adamantium tentacles and lightning strikes shattered the wall where he had been.

Unable to see where he was going, Spider-Man passed through a nexus of incredible burning heat that for a moment seemed enough to broil the flesh from his bones. As he passed through, he realized that the lightning-strike Elec-tro had used to blast his own way into his room had left a burning crater in the wall; leaping through that crater was the blind equivalent of jumping through a burning hoop. As he emerged into the cooler air of what was left of the corri-dor, he sensed his upper back smoldering, put it out with a tuck-and-roll, sprayed a glob of web-fluid at Electro's crater to prevent it from becoming a building-wide conflagration, and broke down the locked door into the office across the hall.

He'd hurt Octavius. That was something.

But Octavius was still in the game, and the Sinister Six was rapidly winning its war of attrition. That was something else.

Spider-Man was more sure than ever, now, that he couldn't win this battle blind.

He needed to get his vision back.

He needed to find, and neutralize, Pity.

He leaped through the closed fourth-floor window in a shower of glass, into a world far colder but just as ruled by Pity's zone of darkness. The freezing air felt like a balm on his scalded leg and shoulders, but also illustrated just how badly hurt he was by making it easier to feel the several places where his wounds were still oozing warm liquid heat. He spun, planted his feet on the building's outer wall, adhered, oriented himself, and ran toward the lobby level where he had seen her last.

He could only hope she was still there. He couldn't possibly imagine that she would be—with her providing the Sinister Six their critical advantage, they'd want to keep her on the move—but he didn't have any better ideas. The lobby would be a good place to start.

He was less than halfway to the lobby before he realized that he'd never get there.

Because he was not heading toward the ground.

He was headed up toward the roof.

His sense of gravity had failed him, for once, but he was properly oriented now; he spun on his heels and ran down the wall in the proper direction.

Three seconds later he realized he was running up again.

He froze, completely confused. He was Spider-Man. He never had these problems.

The wind picked up, blasting the heat from his limbs. Somewhere nearby, cloth flapped. A flag, maybe? He tried to remember if there were any flagpoles on the *Bugle* building . . . and then realized that it wasn't a flag. It was a cape.

Mysterio. Using sonics, or gas, or some other kind of gimmickry, to mess with his inner ear somehow: confusing his sense of up and down. The special effects master had already had more than enough time to take advantage of Spider-Man's confusion; but then, Mysterio had never been the type to do things the easy way, was he? No. He had to put on his show, with Spider-Man the appreciative, victimized audience. Putting on a show was what Mysterio was all about.

Spider-Man spun on his heels and speed-crawled in the direction his senses currently identified as "down." He didn't expect to get anywhere; not until this particular annoyance was taken care of. But he did want to hide his knowledge of what was happening.

He heard the cape flap again. Very close now.

He imagined Quentin Beck grinning like a loon behind that idiotic goldfish-bowl helmet of his.

He felt the slightest twinge of spider-sense: enough to indicate that Mysterio was about to start harassing him in some way. That was enough. He leaped out into space, not knowing precisely how high above the street he was, or whether he had his face or his back to the ground. It was enough to know where Mysterio was, and hope that the tricks the old reprobate used to confuse his spider-sense were not being used right now.

They weren't. Spider-Man collided with Mysterio in mid-air. The impact carried them both outside Pity's zone of darkness. The brief return of light was not an amazing improvement; Spider-Man's sense of direction was still wonky, and he was thrown totally off by the sight of the street five stories above his head. There were upside-down crowds at both nearby intersections cheering out loud at the sight of Spider-Man kicking bad guy butt.

Mysterio, riding the air on a pillar of smoke, pummeled the wall-crawler with both fists as he tried to get away. "You won't separate me from my allies, wall-crawler! We have too many surprises waiting for you today!"

"Better villain dialogue would be a start!" Spider-Man snapped back, as he used his superior strength to forcibly steer Mysterio back toward the building.

They re-entered Pity's zone of darkness. Daylight disappeared. Mysterio's punches and kicks gave way to a sudden sharp impact as the two men smashed through another closed window and back into the *Bugle* building. They landed side-by-side on a desktop, shattering a computer monitor and a row of framed photographs. They struggled. A ceramic cup on the desk toppled, releasing a torrent of wayward pens and pencils. Spider-Man rolled over, pinning Mysterio beneath him, taking a knee to the solar plexus but refusing to let himself be knocked off. He seized the boxy wrists of Mysterio's gauntlets and squeezed tightly; the villain cried out as his wrist-mechanisms imploded with a burst of escaping ozone, instantly neutralizing most of the weaponry Mysterio kept inside his costume.

Unfortunately, the right gauntlet flattened out too much; Mysterio had slipped that glove entirely. A second later Spider-Man felt a stabbing pain in the back of his hand as Mysterio jabbed him with one of the spilled pencils. Spider-Man was too much of a professional at this to cry out or fall back, but Mysterio was enough of a professional to take advantage of his momentary surprise; the two men rolled off the side of the desk in a flurry of punches and kicks that suddenly became one-sided as the billowing cape Spider-Man wrestled with abruptly flattened out to nothing.

Even in perfect light, it would have been an impressive magic trick.

In darkness, it was like coming face-to-face to sorcery.

But it was still just the desperate tactic of a bad guy who knew he was defeated and needed to escape. Mysterio, stumbling out the door into the hallway, was already signaling for help. "Octopus! Electro! Somebody! Come in! I'm on the sixth floor, and the web-head's—"

Spider-Man considered another temporary retreat.

But no. If only to keep his own morale up, he really did

need a decisive victory against at least one of these guys, already.

"Guess what, Quentin! This is your lucky day! You get to make me feel a whole lot better about myself!"

He leaped after Mysterio, entering—

—not a *Daily Bugle* hallway—

—but a tropical rainforest. Surrounded by moist muggy heat, he smelled rich loamy soil, heard the cacophony of insects and birds and monkeys, and felt broad leaves part before him—

—but even as he emerged on the far side of the rainforest, it had somehow become a World War Two battlefield, with bursting mortars, deafening machine-gun fire, the sound of screaming men, and the stench of blood and death—

—and then he passed beyond that, and it was no longer a battlefield, but a subway tunnel, informed by the sounds of dripping water, chittering rats, and a full-bore express bearing down on him from dead ahead—

—which somehow became an rock concert, at one of the municipal stadiums, with twenty thousand screaming fans almost but not quite drowning out the lyrics of a dance number that had something to do with killing Spider-Man as painfully as possible—

—which suddenly became a gunfight in the Old West, complete with harmonica music as a soundtrack—

—which suddenly became a crowded Broadway theatre, where a hushed audience sat listening to a soprano sing the hit song "Sonar" from the hit musical *Submarine!*—

—the auditory cues changing every couple of feet, to bombard Spider-Man with perfect stereo reproductions of sounds he could not possibly be hearing in a besieged hallway in the *Daily Bugle* building. They were all perfect, and in the dark, where there was precious little to contradict them, they might have fatally disoriented a man not equipped with spider-sense who hadn't fought this particular illusion-casting bad guy a dozen times before. As it was, they were only delaying actions, and not very effective ones. Spider-Man was still able to sense the fleeing Mysterio stumbling along only a few short steps ahead of him, struggling to get away.

Unfortunately, from the way his spider-sense was acting up, warning of growing danger on all sides, he would soon have more than Mysterio to deal with, here. Octopus and the others were on their way.

Spider-Man leaped over Mysterio's head, simultaneously pounding that stupid goldfish-bowl helmet with both fists. He felt the cracks spread like lightning across its impact-resistant surface. Better yet, he felt Mysterio collapse and sprawl across the hallway like a rag doll. From the moans, the defeated Beck was still moving as Spider-Man raced the rest of the way down the hallway—but he seemed to be out of the fight for now.

One down. No: two, thanks to Mary Jane.

Four left to go.

The two most dangerous, Ock and Electrio, still among them.

The destructive sounds of Octopus, smashing through floors and ceilings in his fervor to reach this floor as quickly as possible, gave Spider-Man even more to worry about. Yes, with his speed, he could probably keep playing hide-and-seek with Ock forever; but how much damage could the *Daily Bugle* building continue to take before the entire structure collapsed in on itself like a flat soufflé? The hostages in the city room wouldn't survive that.

Spider-Man zigzagged down the corridor, sped past the

elevator bank, and turned down another hallway, taking its entire length in three great leaps. He barreled into the door to the fire stairs without even slowing down, rebounding against the opposite wall before the door even time to slam closed.

The *Daily Bugle* had four separate sets of fire stairs, one at each corner of the building. The stairs themselves were fairly standard; steel-reinforced cinderblock, two half-flights for each building floor, turning around at each landing, to form a boxy spiral around a vertiginous central well. There was a narrow foot-and-a-half gap between the stairs on each side, and the half-flights paralleling them from the other side of the well; on the relatively rare occasions when his civilian self had actually needed to use these stairs, Peter had realized that this empty space provided a perfect opportunity for a superhero needing to descend a lot of floors in a hurry. It was the kind of automatic, filed-away-for-future-reference epiphany Peter always had whenever walking around in buildings like a normal person; he didn't always have a chance to use his observations, but keeping them in mind had saved his colorfully-clad butt more than once.

Spider-Man hopped over the railing, flattened himself out as much as he could, and let himself plunge through the center of the stairway.

He fell almost three stories in perfect silence, with only inches of clearance on either side.

He hadn't any particular plans to catch himself until he fell closer to the lobby, which was the last place he'd seen Pity. But then his spider-sense picked up something dangerous racing up the stairs almost as quickly as he was falling past them—and he instinctively seized the next railing, with a grace that instantly transformed terminal velocity to lateral movement in another direction entirely. He swung up and over, vaulted over the railing, and landed without a sound on the third floor landing, just in time to cut off somebody racing up the stairs.

He had a pretty good idea who it was even before he took the first kick to the ribs. The pain of impact was nothing next to the grim satisfaction that came with recognition.

"Why, if it ain't the very girl I'm looking for! Glad I ran into you, sis!"

She said nothing. Of course.

She just pressed the attack, pummeling him with a series of blows that sent him stumbling back, against the reinforced cement wall. The ferocity surprised even him; he was used to enemies who gave no quarter, but the desperation of this particular assault was so extreme it was impossible to avoid the impression that she'd built up a lifetime's worth of rage and only seconds of freedom to expend it all. He reeled, gasped as the breath was knocked out of him, staggered as she off-handedly blocked his own attempt to drive her back, choked from the dust as another kick that missed his head by millimeters cratered the cinderblock wall behind him. At long last, he gathered up all his strength and simply hurled her away—only to do a double-take as his spider-sense pinpointed her landing and adhering to the underside of the landing directly above his head.

He'd learned in their last battle that she was as strong as he was, as agile as he was, and as resilient as he was. Now he knew that she could cling to walls too.

He leaped away a heartbeat before she could tackle him where he stood, spraying web-fluid behind him as he went. She evaded that and went for him again. He threw a punch, got her in the stomach, felt like dying when the breath rushed from her mouth in a wan gasp.

Her next kick slammed him against the railing with a

force that pained even his flexible spine. He tried to dodge beneath her next punch, but she numbed his left leg with a finger-jab to the sensitive nerve junction above his knee, then slammed him again with a roundhouse punch a lot like being walloped in the face with a brick.

She was going to win.

And she was going to win because, despite everything at stake, he did not want to fight her.

He didn't know what it was. Granted, even without what the Gentleman had said, he didn't exactly need telepathy to sense the appalled please-stop-me vibe radiating from this woman in waves. He'd fought other people who seemed more misunderstood than evil, who he had to put down despite overwhelming empathy for their circumstances. He'd even fought other people suffering other heinous forms of mind control, some of whom, like Pity, seemed to possess conscious revulsion of the crimes they were being forced to commit. Always, before, Spider-Man had been able to put aside the misgivings of his heart and do whatever had to be done.

But Pity was different.

He didn't want to fight her at all. Actually knocking her out was going to be like punching himself in the face.

He didn't know why he was having such a powerful, instinctive reaction; he just was.

But as her powerful kicks and punches peppered him across the chest and jaw and upper arms, driving him back, stealing what little was left of his strength, he knew that he faced a choice between what he could stomach and what he could survive.

He let his spider-sense guide him, swallowing another half-dozen excruciatingly painful blows before he sensed that moment of perfect opportunity . . .

... and then he formed a fist ...

... and punched her in the face.

It was a hard blow; harder than he usually permitted himself. Even against the people he was forced to fight, he avoided using excessive force whenever possible. It sickened him to have to do this to her. But he had no choice.

He heard her stumble backward. He heard the soles of her shoes scrape across the landing. He heard her collide against the fire door and slide slowly to the ground.

And then some idiot turned on the lights!

Spider-Man stood, battered, bruised, and exhausted, in a dimly-lit stairwell in one corner of the *Daily Bugle* Building. He was covered with a dust and grime and soaked with his own blood; he favored his right leg as he took a single step forward, to look down at the unconscious form of the mysterious woman named Pity. Oddly enough, he felt none of the eye strain common to people exposed to light after extended periods in absolute darkness; it occurred to him now that he hadn't felt any when fighting Mysterio outside, either. A clue, to how her powers worked?

He didn't know, and right now, it didn't concern him as much as Pity herself, who had curled into a semi-fetal position. Her face was bruised, and her lower lip was swelling. Though unconscious, she still wore a slight frown, as if struggling to reconcile mysteries that had stymied her since birth.

He found himself wondering: *Just who are you, anyway?*

Wish I had the luxury to stand around thinking about it. He leveled his web-shooters, to cocoon her for delivery to SAFE and the NYPD.

But then the stairwell immediately above him shuddered like a locomotive about to come off his rails, and a pair of gleaming, sinuous tentacles curved around the corner of the next flight up. Crazed laughter echoed off the cinderblock walls: "Taking a rest, Spider-Man? Don't mind me—I just want to help!"

Octavius. Of course.

This fight was just beginning.

CHAPTER SEVENTEEN

3:07 P.M.

For SAFE, the NYPD, the Press, and the hundreds of spectators held at bay behind sawhorses, the last hour had been an exercise in helplessness and frustration. For the first twenty minutes or so, the opaque monolith the building had become was just a silent mask, revealing nothing of the events taking place inside; it took the raging demolition sounds that followed to provide any clue that Spider-Man might even still be alive. The explosions, tearing and crashing noises that then filled the rest of the hour hadn't been much help to anybody seriously interested in reconstructing the progress of the battle; and while Spider-Man's brief emergence late in the hour had provided reassurance that he was still in the game, only the sudden disappearance of Pity's zone of darkness provided any indication that it might be going well. The crowds gathered behind the wooden sawhorses at both intersections erupted into wild, spontaneous cheers. A crowd of high school kids—evidently trivia buffs—

even broke into a spirited rendition of the theme song Spidey had used before his super hero days, when he was flirting with show biz instead: the one about Spider-Man, Spider-Man, doing whatever a spider can. Soon, the entire crowd was singing it. Agent Clyde Fury, who had come to genuinely like the webslinger during their brief time working together, sincerely hoped that the sound was loud enough to be heard inside the building—and, perversely enough, that J. Jonah Jameson was one of the listeners.

Morgan didn't take any satisfaction in the moment. "God save me from civilians. Do they think this is some kind of Championship Wrestling match?"

"I don't think so, Colonel. I think they know exactly how serious this is. But they'll take hope wherever they can get it."

Morgan gestured at the building. "Except that this might not be a good sign. Have you noticed it's gotten quiet again? For all we know, they've killed the wall-crawler and this is our first signal that the fight's over! Maybe—"

Another series of concussions, from somewhere inside the building, blew out all the windows on the second floor. Blinding light flared from all the windows on the third.

"Signs of life," Fury said.

Morgan came as close to showing relief as he ever had. "No. Our cue. Come on."

3:10 P.M.

The addition of light may have rendered fighting the likes of Dr. Octopus less than totally-impossible, but it sure didn't make it any more fun. It scarcely mattered that the far-from-good Doctor hadn't been having the best of days himself; he wore his right arm in a makeshift sling, and glowered at Spider-Man through a pair of freshly blackened eyes. He waved his undamaged fist as his adamantium tentacles carried him down the third-story corridor at near-ceiling height. "Do you sense it, Spider-Man? Do you feel the exhaustion sapping your much-vaunted strength? Do you wonder how long you can hold out before you give in to the temptation to lie down and die?"

The main thing Spider-Man sensed was that the lifting of Pity's darkness—and the relaxation of all accompanying pretense at stealth—had freed Octopus to indulge his tendency to rant. This was not an improvement. As Spider-Man narrowly avoided the clutching pincers of a tentacle that had gone for his throat, he gibed, "Do you wonder how long you can keep re-using your old dialogue before you give in to the temptation to get yourself another writer?"

"Keep joking, Spider-Man! It will make killing you so much more satisfying!"

"See what I mean, pudge? The last time you used that one was only a few hours ago!"

Four tentacles slammed into the ceiling above Spider-Man's head. The wall-crawler leaped away from the resulting cascade of falling debris, ricocheted off a wall, then leaped up through the fresh hole in the ceiling. Octopus followed close behind, shouting fresh threats at his old enemy's back.

The fourth floor was smoky and choked with floating plaster dust, courtesy of the last time Spider-Man and his various enemies had passed through here. Moving as quickly as he could, Spider-Man zigzagged from floor to ceiling to wall and back again, staying only one step ahead of the murderous tentacles that kept clutching at him from behind; he might have been able to gain some distance, under normal circumstances, but injury and fatigue had taken its toll on him; he desperately needed time to recover before he could once again count himself in Ock's league. Time that

Ock, who had never been the most generous super-villain in the world, was not about to provide him.

He didn't have the slightest idea what he was going to do when circumstances finally brought him face-to-face with Electro.

He tumbled and rolled and zigzagged around a bend in the corridor, only to have his back pelted with rubble when Ock gained ground by the simple expedient of going through the wall. The tingling of his spider-sense intensified to reflect how much Ock had succeeded in closing the gap. When a pair of pincers snapped shut behind Spider-Man's head now, the web-slinger could actually pick out the sound of the tiny servomotors that powered their joints. He didn't know what to do; he honestly didn't think he could survive another direct assault from those things, but he also knew he'd slowed down far too much to get past them to the vulnerable man at their center.

He put on a burst of speed as the corridor right-angled again, saw a square of bright light at the other end, and realized that the corridor was the problem.

Fighting Ock had always been more a test of agility and endurance than of strength. Merely trading blows was suicide; Ock's strength and his reach were both much greater than his own, and premature assaults always cost the web-slinger more than he gained. Defeating Ock had usually meant spending at least ninety percent of the fight just jumping around, leaping up and over and around and through and sometimes past their slashing arcs until he finally managed to come up with a counterattack the bad doctor didn't expect. The problem with this corridor—any corridor—was that it narrowed the playing field and rendered most of those evasions impossible, limiting the web-slinger's options to simply running away. A fresh Spider-Man might have been able to handle the situation anyway; a tired Spider-Man running on vapor needed some more maneuvering room.

He needed to take this back outside where it belonged.

He aimed toward the square of light at the other end of the corridor and put on a burst of speed, actually gaining a few feet of lead before his spider-sense informed him of a new factor, now directly ahead, that he immediately incorporated into his strategy.

He curled into a cannonball and burst through the closed window in a cascade of broken glass. The dangerous presence his spider-sense had picked up about to break through the window from the other side was the Vulture, who must have completed a couple circuits outside the building just trying to intercept the battle in progress.

The old man's face immediately broke into a hateful snaggle-toothed grin as Spider-Man collided with him in mid-air. Shrugging off the wall-crawler's feeble swats at his face, suffering absolutely no difficulty wrestling the exhausted hero into a headlock, the Vulture even cackled: "Trying to flee, wall-crawler? Or did you simply imagine that this cowardly maneuver of yours might provide you with an opportunity for a little breather?"

Down below, the onlookers were screaming. Spider-Man gasped: "This is . . . New York City . . . Vulchy . . . trust me . . . the air inside's . . . better . . ."

"I should pluck out your limbs and then drop your writhing torso from skyscraper-height."

"Now . . . that's an imaginative image . . . and not a single spleen in it . . ."

Two gleaming tentacles emerged from the broken window, undulating like cobras dancing to an unheard flute. Dr. Octopus appeared at the window, grimacing at the discovery that one of his teammates had caught the web-slinger before he could. "Don't play with him, you old fool! Bring him here so I can finish him off!"

The Vulture responded by putting another fifteen feet between himself and the Doctor's flailing tentacles. "You're not giving this orders this time, Octavius. And you're not taking this moment away from me. I deserve this!"

The Doctor's computer-nerd complexion turned an angry shade of scarlet. "I warn you, Toomes, if you defy me in this, you will—"

3:14 P.M.

The onlookers on the ground perceived what happened next as nothing but a lightning-fast flurry of motion. Even the footage taken at the scene, examined on the nightly news broadcasts, offered nothing but a blur of red and blue, moving too quickly to be captured even by freeze-frame, transforming the arrogance on the faces of both villains to shock and dismay. It was as if the seemingly helpless Spider-Man had erupted, his arms and limbs turning to streaks of explosive energy—not only breaking out of the headlock, but also pelting the Vulture too many times for anybody to count before flinging the oldest member of the Sinister Six at Doctor Octopus like a missile. When Octopus instinctively used one of his tentacles to bat the hurtling form away, the Vulture became less a bird of prey and more an unconscious shuttlecock, about to slam into the building across the street at terminal velocity. The only reason he didn't is that Spider-Man himself plucked him out of the sky with one hand—using the other to fire a webline that transformed their shared trajectory to a perfectly plotted arc that ended with both of them hurtling through another *Daily Bugle* window.

The crowd gasped.

Cosmo the K, watching the battle from his station's paranormal observation copter, blurted: "Holy Cow!"

Mary Jane Watson-Parker, watching from a 12-inch TV mounted on the wall of the Emergency Room where she'd gone to help some of her ESU friends get treatment for their minor injuries, murmured to herself: "Tiger, don't *do* that to me."

Spider-Man's biggest fan, Flash Thompson, who was also watching, jumped up and down on his salvaged convertible sofa, pumping his fist in glee.

The Chameleon, who had slipped away from the wreckage of the ESU stadium in the guise of one of the rescue workers, and laboriously made his way back to the Sinister Six townhouse to nurse his wounds, scowled in disapproval at the instant replay. "Incompetents," he muttered. He did not include himself in the appraisal.

Colonel Sean Morgan, getting the update from the underground utility tunnel which he and a intra-agency squad of ten handpicked SAFE agents and NYPD officers were about to use to access the *Bugle* building now that the Sinister Six had been confirmed busy, grimaced with satisfaction.

Randolph and Mortimer, the hapless would-be Macchiavellians who had been foolish enough to solicit insider information from the Gentleman just last night, and who were now watching the action on a seventy-inch projection TV in their spacious Park Avenue townhouse, relaxed only slightly. The web-slinger wasn't dead. That was good. They didn't particularly care about him, of course, but it wouldn't do for the Sinister Six to succeed in killing him now, at this juncture, when the civilian death count was still zero and they'd followed the Gentleman's advice to wager all their available funds on a casualty rate somewhere in the high four figures. Terrified, now, of being completely wiped out for the second time in one lifetime, they now rested their futures on one forlorn hope: that the *Daily Bugle* building, weakened by the battering it had taken, might topple head-long into the buildings across the street, starting a midtown domino chain that might, if Randolph and Mortimer were lucky enough, take out enough occupied office buildings to make their investment pay off. Every moment the web-slinger succeeded in staying ahead of his enemies brought that much hoped-for eventuality closer to fruition. Or so Randolph and Mortimer hoped, as they watched Dr. Octopus climb across the face of the *Daily Bugle* to pursue the Vul-ture and Spider-Man back through the window they'd just entered. *Please, God,* Randolph and Mortimer prayed. *We deserve this.*

Steve Rogers, aka Captain America, who'd needed less than six hours to complete the urgent business that had brought him to Japan, sat in a darkened hotel room watch-ing an enlarged holo-projection of the battle on his Avengers-issue laptop computer. Despite his faith in Spider-Man's abilities, and the potential international ramifications of the catastrophe he had come here to avert, he hadn't been able to avoid feeling honestly bad about leaving the web-slinger in the lurch during this crisis, and he watched Spider-Man's performance with the analytical eye of a trained super-soldier. He alone saw what most of the observers did not: that Spider-Man's last maneuver, effective as it had been, was the act of an injured man riding the edge of total exhaustion. The web-slinger didn't have enough left to outfight Octopus, let alone any other Sinister Six member who might have been still on the prowl in there—not with sheer physical force, at least. Steve Rogers, who had spent decades defeating enemies stronger, faster, better armed, more numerous, and more ruthless than himself, leaned forward, his chiseled features knitting with concern. *Come on, web-head. Think of something.*

As for the Gentleman, who was already five blocks away, hailing a taxi for a quick hop toward a necessary planned rendezvous in the Diamond District, he didn't pay it any particular attention. He had little real interest in the outcome; it would be nice if Spider-Man fell, of course, but even if the Sinister Six fell instead, with or without that silly cow Pity, his own master plan would be able to continue almost unchanged. If worst came to worst, there were other ways to obtain his next component . . . let alone deliver it where he needed it to be.

3:16 P.M.

With the Vulture out of the fight for now, Dr. Octopus smashed through half a dozen walls pursuing Spider-Man back to the elevator bank. When he found the doors to the last elevator on the right torn off their tracks, he stood at the entrance to the shaft, hesitating just long enough to decide whether it made more sense for Spider-Man to have fled up or down.

Spider-Man, who'd been crouched against the shaft wall two stories up, let go and dropped like a stone. He landed with his full weight on Ock's injured shoulder. The Doctor screamed in agony, and toppled off the edge, his mechanical arms already reaching out for something to hold on to. When he brushed against the central cable, as Spider-Man had intended him to, his tentacles instinctively looped around to grab it. Four sets of pincers closed around the same cable, raising angry sparks as they slid twenty feet down its length without appreciably slowing him. Something gray and sticky, part ordinary cable lubrication and part something else, started to collect around Ock's pincers as they tightened to compensate for the slippery surface. The pincers were completely covered with the stuff by the time he could tighten his grip enough to stop his fall. He bellowed in laughter. "Nice try, arachnid! But you should know by now! I am notoriously hard to kill!"

"Who's trying to kill you, chuckles? I'll settle for just making a fool of you!"

Octopus directed his tentacles to climb the cable and wrap themselves around the web-slinger's throat. But they resisted. They didn't want to let go of the cable. Octopus lifted himself closer to one of the tentacles so he could see what was wrong, and saw the entire grasping mechanism was encased in disgusting, sticky gray glop. Webbing. Spider-Man had covered this entire section of cable. He stammered: "N-but—this can't be! The anti-adhesive coating—"

"—was a problem, all right." Spider-Man's voice was closer, but the web-slinger himself was sheathed in darkness. "Not that my webbing was ever at all effective against those tentacles even when it would stick to them. They're way too strong. Fortunately, your little anti-adhesive trick forced me to rethink the problem."

"B-but . . ."

"Don't you see, Ock? The problem was never getting my webbing to stick to those things. The problem was figuring out a way to get my webbing inside those things!"

Octopus stammered again. And then he fell silent, momentarily stunned by what Spider-Man had just cleverly forced him to do.

By spraying a layer of web-fluid over the lubricated cable, the web-slinger had virtually ensured that Octopus would slide a significant distance down that cable before being able to stop himself. When his pincers tightened, slicing across twenty feet of web-coating like a knife passes through butter, Octopus had unwittingly transformed the nearly-microscopic seams between each pincer and the head of each tentacle into scoops, which virtually force-fed the semi-liquid goo into the mechanism's vulnerable interior. The webbing had completely choked the servo-motors, the ball-joints, and the cybernet-ics . . . jamming each pincer in a closed position.

In short, Spider-Man had figured out a way to stop him with webbing—even after Octopus had contrived a way to render that webbing virtually useless in a fight.

Dr. Octopus, who valued his own intellect above all things, and therefore hated being outsmarted above all things, now found he hated Spider-Man several orders of magnitude greater than he'd ever hated the web-slinger before. "Someday," he snarled, "I will rip your spine from your still-writhing corpse."

"Before or after Venom gets my spleen, and Vulchy drops me armless and legless from a height? Sounds like it's gonna be a messy day." The web-slinger's voice was closer now, but the man himself was still sheathed in darkness. "In any event, I know you well enough to appreciate that you'll fig-ure a way out of this. It won't hold you anywhere near the hour it'll take that webbing to dissolve. I'm sorry, but I'm going to have to knock you out for a little while."

Octopus, once again the unpleasant, universally despised fat kid tormented every day in grammar school, screamed. "Electro! Mysterio! Somebody! *Help m—*"

His voice was cut off in mid-word, courtesy of a web-gag that forced his mouth shut.

But his scream had already summoned help.

The side of the shaft exploded inward, in a shower of brick and plaster, glowing with an unearthly blinding light. A glowing form followed, riding the lightning like a beloved family pet.

The most powerful member of the Six.

Electro.

3:25 P.M.

Pity, who had spent much of the past half hour lying unconscious in the stairwell, may have revived soon anyway; her powers of recuperation were almost as impressive as Spider-Man's own, and a lifetime of training at the hands of the Gentleman had taught her to suppress her own aches and pains in favor of the unpleasant, frequently violent assignments that defined her every working day. She was well on the way back to consciousness when her mind registered the sound of many people racing up a staircase toward her. There was something familiar about the way they were running, too: something about the sounds of boots on concrete, or of metal clinking against metal.

They were almost upon her before her brain put it all together.

She leaped to her feet just in time to see half a dozen heavily-armed paramilitary types, identifiable as a mixed squad of NYPD SWAT and SAFE insertion agents, rounding the landing half a flight down. She even recognized the angry-looking crewcut man leading the charge as Colonel Sean Morgan, just as he locked eyes with her and realized who she was as well.

Half a dozen pulse bolts cratered the concrete wall where she had been. Though one grazed her upper arm, tearing away a furrow of flesh, it was to Pity just another pain to be shunted off into the realm of the totally irrelevant. More to the point was the knowledge that if the authorities had decided to rush the building, this squad would not be alone.

Darkness descended on the stairwell. It was true darkness, Pity's darkness; their flashlights and night-vision goggles would not be able to penetrate it. Almost as soon as it fell, more pulse-bolts erupted out of the darkness—but it was wild fire, the fire of would-be heroes suddenly stricken blind. She heard muttered curses, shouted orders, even a grunt of pain as one of the SWAT officers stumbled and banged her knee on a step.

But there would be others.

The Gentleman had said: *Make sure your teammates know when discretion is the better part of valor. There is too much at stake here, to throw good energy after bad.*

And she always did what the Gentleman said.

She was cursed to do nothing else.

Pity turned her back on her pursuers and raced up the stairs.

3:32 P.M.

The battle against Electro had moved up to the seventh floor—the circulation offices—which were taking as destructive a battering as the four floors immediately below it.

Spider-Man, whose battle plan so far had been a series of desperate evasions and ineffective counterattacks, knew how they felt. Electro hadn't scored any fatal hits yet, but that was more a function of the man's catlike propensity for tormenting his prey before attempting a fatal attack; he had so far chased Spider-Man around the building, up the stairs, and through freshly-blasted craters so many times that the web-slinger had lost count. It wasn't like fighting Electro in the old days, when the guy had just been a charged-up doofus in a starfish mask who could be laid low by a properly-flung bucket of water; this Electro was more like an unstoppable force of nature, who just happened to have the personality and speech patterns of a jumped-up thug. Fighting this Electro, as exhausted as Spider-Man felt, was not only suicidal, but just plain stupid. But Electro was the only one left—and so Spider-Man was forced to play an endless game of outrunning explosions and listening to the man hurl threats while wondering how on Earth to defeat a guy who presented a threat to everybody in this time zone.

Long past wondering just how much of this building was going to be salvageable once the battle was over, Spider-Man leaped over an electric discharge that would have incinerated him and cried: "One thing I need to know, Sparky! Why did Mysterio have to sub for you at the bridge? What were you up to, that the rest of you were so determined to keep secret?"

Electro swooped close, his hands miniature suns. "You'll be dead before you ever find that out, creep!"

"Now, that," Spider-Man noted, evading another powerful series of lightning blasts, "is the kind of rhetorical paradox I keep having to point out to you people! How can I be dead and then find out? Are you assuming I'll pull the standard super-villain trick of being only temporarily dead?"

Electro hurled a sphere of ball lightning wide enough to engulf the entire hallway. Spider-Man kicked down an office door and leaped inside just in time to evade the broiling heat that blackened the entire corridor; he then kicked his way through the sheet rock wall and into an adjacent office just in time to escape the explosion that utterly destroyed the room he had just left.

"That ain't gonna happen, creep! I'm gonna do such a thorough job killing you that the cops are gonna need a vacuum cleaner just to mop up the ashes!"

"Vacuum cleaners don't mop," Spider-Man *tsk*ed. "You really don't think these things out before you say them, do you? And besides, is this gonna be the same day Venom eats my spleen, Ock tears out my spine, and the Vulture drops me armless and legless from a height?"

The next explosion was one of the most powerful yet. Spider-Man half-leaped, half-allowed himself to be carried by the shock wave, which flung him all the way to the right turn at the end of the corridor. He felt something twist in his wounded right leg when he touched ground, and without wanting to, fell to that knee; it was just a cramp, legacy of all the punishment he'd taken today, nothing that wouldn't go away in a couple of seconds if he could only arrange for this maniac to give him half a chance . . . but which would soon kill him if instead he was forced to keep relying on his rapidly-waning reflexes.

Electro stood at the far end of the corridor, his eyes glowing like miniature coals. "Y'know what?" he asked. "You're right. I'm sick of chasin' you around. I'm gonna put a stop to this."

He started walking. Confident. Unhurried.

Backed into the corner of an L-shaped hallway, Spider-Man knew he could probably keep running and jumping, even with only one good leg, even with a pounding borderline concussion, even with exhaustion sapping the strength from his bones, even with blood loss dizzying him in a manner beyond the cumulative effect of all his other wounds. But he also knew he would be fatally slow; Electro would catch him within a minute.

He cast about for something to do. Anything—

And then he heard another collapsing wall, followed by a hideous scraping sound, assault his ears from the end of the branching corridor. He glanced in that direction to see what it was, narrowly resisted a double-take, and thought:

Now that's something you don't see every day.

Having managed to clear the web fluid from only two out of his four adamantium tentacles, Octopus had just emerged from the elevator shaft, dragging not only a section of cable, but also the entire elevator car along with him. The wreckage of the elevator car, only a little smaller than the corridor and significantly worse for wear after being yanked through what had been several solid walls, followed Octopus like a recalcitrant dog being dragged along at the end of its leash; the man himself was reduced to walking on his own two feet, as he needed both of his two remaining tentacles just to keep pulling himself forward. His scowl, as he spotted Spider-Man, was so extreme that it threatened to swallow the rest of his face whole.

"I . . . am . . . Octavius!" Octopus whispered. "And nothing will keep me from your throat!"

Watching, Spider-Man knew at once that Octopus would have needed only a few minutes to free his other tentacles; the man's rage was so completely murderous that he preferred to tear the web-slinger limb from limb first, lest one of his Sinister Six teammates somehow manage that task first.

Under the circumstances, this was actually good news.

Because it gave Spider-Man one of those splendid, blinding epiphanies where he knew exactly what to do.

Oh boy. This is gonna be good.

He took a step forward, and stood at the bend in the corridor, waiting as Octopus approached from one direction and Electro approached from the other. He did not face either one of them directly, instead investing one eye for each, a clumsy but effective method of persuading both men that they had his undivided attention. He gave in to his pain enough to allow himself to waver—an act that prompted both villains to move faster, driven by the expectation of blood.

Then he fell to his knees.

Coming down one branch of the L, Electro swooped toward him, his hands outstretched, his fingers sizzling the air itself.

Racing up the other, Dr. Octopus dragged himself into position and hurled his two free tentacles at the web-slinger's chest.

Both villains shouted as they attacked, both bragged about their own unstoppability and the ugliness of the murder they both imagined they were about to commit, both cackled with the usual mixture of arrogance and hysteria. Neither one, hidden from the other's sight by the bend of the corridor, had any idea that their own actions were being paralleled—almost parodied—by the actions of an equally crazed teammate; fittingly enough, given the kind of people they were, they both spent this moment alone, at the center of a universe that existed only to cater to their respective whims.

Electro took off and swooped toward Spider-Man, his glowing hands clutching at the web-slinger with the potential of lightning about to strike.

At the very last instant, Spider-Man rolled away, allowing Electro to pass through the space where he had been. The two adamantium tentacles that seized Electro at that moment, slamming him against the nearest wall with bone-crushing force, completed a very deadly circuit. The high voltage that passed through those tentacles may have affected them not at all, but that was because they were only machines; the man at their center was only flesh and blood. Octavius jerked, twitched, made incoherent sub-verbal noises, and danced a spastic jig to an angry electric symphony; his Moe haircut standing on end, his eyes wide and terrified, he sank to his knees and then plopped onto his chest, with a thud that reflected the padded adamantium band around his torso much more than the softer sound that would have reflected the man himself. The tentacles retracted only a second or two later, a fortunate mechanical reflex that broke the circuit and probably saved the Doctor's life—but then they lay as still as their master, like marionettes helpless without his domineering will.

"C-cool," Spider-Man said weakly.

He wanted to faint, but there was too much still left to do. He allowed himself a second to examine both Electro and Octopus. Electro looked like he'd suffered a concussion. *But hey* (Spider-Man thought with a wince), *there was a lot of that going around today.* Octopus was breathing only shallowly, and he had developed a little bit of a tan, but he, too, would be all right; he'd had serious electric shocks before and had been all right on those occasions as well. The thin layer of padding that formed an airtight seal between the harness and his flesh may have been an imperfect insulator, but if it kept him from being charbroiled by an accidental zap from his most powerful teammate, then the not-so-good Doctor seemed to be still ahead of the game.

Now Spider-Man had to figure out a way to secure these yeggs, so they wouldn't wake up and start the whole rasslin' match all over again. And he had to hurry, because he didn't have much time before.

. . . before . . .

"Aw, no!"

His spider-sense had just alerted him to the three figures stumbling down the corridor toward him.

Mysterio, Pity, and the Vulture . . .

3:35 P.M.

Colonel Sean Morgan's team was still trapped in the unnaturally-darkened lower floors of the building, unable to quickly find their way past a sea of wreckage that had turned the route into a deadly maze of weakened floors and treacherous rubble.

Morgan couldn't get a handle on the nature of this darkness. It wasn't just an absence of light—his people had been prepared for that, and had come equipped with a variety of special imaging systems, ranging from infrared and ultraviolet to psionic helmets capable of feeding detailed ultrasound mapping directly into the visual cortex. Nothing worked—not sight, and not substitutes for sight. This left open the question of just how Pity managed to exempt her partners from its effects—let alone how Spider-Man had managed to function for any length of time within the affected areas. Morgan couldn't help the feeling that if SAFE ever did manage to figure out just how lady's powers worked, they would also be on the verge of understanding something fundamentally important about her—but that didn't do a darn thing to help him and his people get to where they might do the web-slinger do some good.

Up ahead, somebody cursed as the floor shifted dangerously beneath an experimental prodding from a rifle butt. Clyde Fury grumbled, "I hate to be the insurance man who has to write up this claim! They tore this place to pieces!"

403

"If you can't say something helpful," Sean Morgan snapped, "maintain silence! We need our ears here!"

The only response was another shifting of rubble.

Morgan, oppressed beneath a helplessness that tormented him as few other feelings possibly could, grimaced and thought, *I'm sorry, Spider-Man. We tried. But this one is up to you.*

3:36 P.M.

The three conscious members of the Sinister Six looked almost as rocky as Spider-Man felt. Mysterio, sans helmet, had to support the equally battered form of the Vulture, who could barely keep his eyes open. Pity stumbled along behind them, an ugly blue-black bruise mottling one side of her face. They looked defeated. But they were still dangerous. And they were still coming.

At the thought of having to go through this nightmare yet again, Spider-Man's crest plummeted drastically. "Oh, come on, people! Don't tell me you're still in the mood!"

"Not now," Mysterio managed. "Between you and the authorities . . . who our distaff member, here, has informed us are making their first serious raid on the building—you've won. We just want . . . to gather our wounded—"

"Which is all of you," Spider-Man noted.

". . . and fight another day."

Spider-Man sighed—nothing ever came easy, did it?—and readied himself for another round. "You know there's absolutely no way I'm gonna let you do that, bunkie. Not after all the mischief you've been up to today. Give it up now and I'll see to it you get a VCR in your cell."

"You . . . have better things to do," the Vulture managed . . . and here his face broke into a truly hateful grin.

"True," Mysterio said . . . and now his face twisted into the same grin, a look that bespoke nasty secrets. "Or have you forgotten your friends in the city room? I left a little surprise for you up there."

Hearing the implication behind the words, Spider-Man felt all the strength go out of his knees. Just at the thought of what they might have done, he found himself hating these five people—and their absent colleague, the Chameleon, and their employer, the Gentleman—as much as he'd ever hated anybody in his life. As much as he'd hated the Burglar who'd killed his Uncle Ben. As much as he'd hated Norman Osborn, the night that maniac killed Gwen Stacy. And as much as he'd ever hated himself for not being able to save everybody in danger. He wanted to leap on these people, all his civilized restraint forgotten, and show them once and for all what an angry Spider-Man could do.

But concern for his friends motivated him more.

He turned his back on the monsters and covered the distance between himself and the elevators in two short hops. Entering the shaft through the crater Ock had made yanking the elevator from its mooring, he rebounded off the opposite wall and leaped straight up again, his heart pounding harder than the exertion alone required. On the way, he prayed, *Please. Tell me I interpreted that the wrong way. Don't let them be hurt. Don't let the monsters win.*

By the time he tore open the doors to the tenth-floor city room, he was already steeling himself for the worst.

When he saw what was waiting for them, he knew how banal his mental images had been.

The room was a tableau of corpses.

Most of the people he saw were in pieces, or mangled too badly to be identified. But some were all too recognizable. Betty Brant lay sprawled across her desk, her face blue, her head hanging at an unnatural angle. Ben Urich sat propped up against one wall, his skull crushed, his eyes staring. Arnold Sibert had crumpled across a fallen chair, his shirt a massive rorschach-blot of arterial blood. Glory Grant was a charred and blackened ruin, save for the beautiful, now staring and sightless face that the maniacs had left untouched. Vreni Byrne, Joy Mercado, Ben Ellis, Jake Conover, Auntie Esther, Billy Walters, and a dozen unidentifiable others, formed a mound of bodies, their parts interchangeable, their personalities subsumed by the grim realities of death. Joe Robertson stood upright against one wall, his face swollen, his neck bruised beneath the typewriter power cord that had been used to hang him from a door jamb. And at the center—dyed red by all the carnage—sat the composing desk, dragged out before the elevators to form the pedestal upon which sat the severed, accusing head of J. Jonah Jameson himself, whose mouth, in the Sinister Six's last macabre joke, had been stuffed to bursting with the remnants of his own cigars. Jameson's eyes were wide open, and his mouth seemed to be crying, *See! I told you! I tried to warn them! This is what tolerating a Spider-Man leads to!*

It's all your fault
all your fault
your fault
yours
murderer
Spider-Man, gloryhound
incompetent would-be hero
murderer
we're all dead because of you
YOU

Spider-Man shook his head in mute denial. *No. No. Not all of them. Not everybody.*

I won. I . . . won . . .

And then he stumbled into the slaughterhouse, wailing with the impotence of grief.

EPILOGUE

After midnight.

Spider-Man perched on a wall in a dark room bathed by the nearby hum of engines. He didn't want to be here; that shock of that moment in the *Daily Bugle* city room was still reverberating in his skull—taking even more out of him than his exhaustion and his catalogue of injuries, which a few hours spent at home in the care of his sympathetic and recently heroic wife did little to ameliorate. He'd had first aid, a long bath, and several hours lying down, but he still felt he needed another ten hours of sleep before he'd be able to function: that is, if he was ever able to function. Mary Jane had been furious with him about his insistence on keeping this particular planned rendezvous, in his condition, so soon after the two of them had both fought battles in the same nightmarish war.

But Morgan did demand his postmortems, and Spider-Man had agreed to appear at the Brooklyn Bridge at midnight so a SAFE aircar could pick him up and shuttle him back to the helicarrier.

Why he bothered, he didn't know. Duty, he supposed. Responsibility. (That word again). And maybe a need to keep himself sane.

He could feel his eyes burning from barely-repressed tears.

A door opened, and a SAFE agent Spider-Man had never met before—but who from his cardigan sweater, stooped posture, and thick eyeglasses, did not seem the sort paid for his murderous skill in combat—peered in. His high forehead, topped with a thatch of sandy blonde hair, glinted in the light of the hallway as he said, "Uh, Mister Spider-Man? I've been told to tell you that Colonel Morgan's going to be another couple of minutes yet. Sorry for the delay."

Vaguely annoyed at the man for disturbing him in his misery, Spider-Man nodded. "All right. Thanks."

The agent did not leave. "Want me to get you something while you're waiting? Your file says you're addicted to coffee."

Spider-Man did, but he could think of few things he needed, at this point in his life, less than something to increase the knot of tension at the pit of his stomach. "No, thanks."

The sandy-haired man didn't close the door; instead, he left it open and entered, running his hand along the conference table in the center of the room. "You all right?"

Spider-Man stared fixedly at the floor. "Should I be?"

"I guess not. You have had a rough day." The agent fumfuhed for a couple of seconds, then stepped forward, extending a hand. "Sorry. Troy Saberstein."

All things considered, Spider-Man was not in the mood for a gentle introduction, or for a chat —but he knew this poor guy was not at fault for anything that had happened today, so he shook hands anyway. "Spider-Man."

"I know," Saberstein said, with amusement.

"Yes, I guess you would." The usually glib Spider-Man cast about for something else to say, came up blank for several seconds, and then finally resorted to: "So what's your gig around here, Troy?"

Saberstein hesitated.

"Classified, huh?"

"Not at all. It's just that—well, I suspect that telling you might bring an abrupt halt to this conversation. I'm SAFE's post-traumatic stress counselor."

Spider-Man winced. "Oboy."

"That's right. I'm the guy who has to keep tabs on the mental health of our field agents, to certify them emotionally and psychologically fit for duty after extremely traumatizing situations in the field."

Spider-Man coughed. "So you're SAFE's Counselor Troy, eh?"

It was impossible to tell, the way he was backlit, but something in the way Saberstein cocked his head seemed to indicate a rueful smile. "Yeah, I get that a lot."

"Doesn't sound like the kind of thing Colonel Morgan would go for."

Saberstein's wince testified to a less-than-salutory working relationship. "It isn't."

"Ahhhh. Federal regs, eh?"

"You might say that. Hey, mind if I turn on the lights?"

"Suit yourself."

Saberstein reached out and turned the dimmer knob, increasing the light in the conference room until it was dim and not just blindingly dark. His own features became clearer as he did; a pale, bookish man in his late thirties, whose brown eyes sat unnaturally magnified behind coke-bottle eyeglasses significantly blurred by the tracks of his thumbs. Dressed not in SAFE's ubiquitous battlesuit, but a white button-down shirt, a cardigan, and slacks, he resembled an accountant more than a representative of any paramilitary strike force. He said: "Sorry if you prefer the dark, but I like to see people's faces when I talk to them."

"I don't know if you've noticed this, Doc, but I'm wearing a mask."

"True," Saberstein acknowledged. "But old habits die hard."

"Tell me about it," Spider-Man said.

"Sure I can't get you something?"

"Nothing. Really. In fact, I'm not quite in the mood for a shrink right now—"

"Anybody in the mood for a shrink is really interested in wasting the shrink's time. Besides, I'm not a shrink, and I'm not a doctor, and I'm not offering to be either. And you're not a SAFE agent, so I don't have the power to remove you from duty anyway. But I am wondering if you're okay."

The younger Spider-Man, still formed by the repressed angst of the teenage outcast Peter Parker, might have said something flip or rude; in extreme circumstances, he might have hung the inquisitive Saberstein from the ceiling on a webline. This Spider-Man, who felt infinitely older after what he'd seen in the *Daily Bugle* city room, made allowances for good intentions. "As okay as I ever get, Doc— I mean, Troy. Thanks."

Saberstein nodded, as if accepting that. Three beats later, he blurted: "Do you mind if I bounce something off you, though? Just because it's something I've been wondering about?"

Inwardly, Spider-Man moaned. He'd never be rid of this guy. "What?"

"All those things he's written about you . . . all the ways he's twisted the truth to make your life difficult . . . all the pain he's heaped on your head and all the ways he's stood between you and the people you want to help . . . and despite all the other people there, like Brant and Urich, who should have a bigger claim on your loyalty . . . it was seeing Jameson dead that hit you the hardest, wasn't it?"

Spider-Man was sometimes happy his mask spared him the burden of unwanted eye contact; the SAFE analyst had just nailed the instinctive reaction that Spider-Man would have never volunteered on his own. He considered denying it . . . but after everything else that he'd gone through today, he just didn't have the energy. "Yeah."

"I thought so," Saberstein nodded, betraying no triumph or validation in having guessed right—merely the interest of a man who would have been surprised to hear anything else.

Spider-Man, intrigued by the analyst's apparent certainty, said: "How did you know?"

Saberstein said: "If you promise not to be offended?"

"Hey, that's one promise I never make. Try me anyway."

Saberstein rubbed his chin thoroughly, and said: "Well, long-distance analysis, based on nothing but news coverage and second-hand observation, is never a good idea . . . but after years of following your exploits as best I could, I've always thought you must have one humdinger of a father complex."

Beneath his mask, Spider-Man rolled his eyes. "Jameson? Give me a break."

"You just said that his death hit you the hardest."

"But he wasn't the only one," Spider-Man protested. "That room was filled the bodies of people I respect."

"I know," Saberstein said calmly. "It's not exactly giving up state secrets to admit that your dossier contains analyses on the apparent connections between you and Ben Urich, you and Joe Robertson, you and Betty Brant—even you and Peter Parker, though he was lucky enough to be out of the *Daily Bugle* building when the Six struck. I'm sure you've always seen some of these people as just information sources, but your adventures have centered around the *Bugle* so long that many of them must be friends. Still, Jameson's always at the center of it. He's the one whose approval you've always wanted . . . and the one who's always refused to oblige you."

Spider-Man couldn't believe this guy. "If you even think of using the word 'codependent', I'm out of here."

Saberstein chuckled. "Don't worry. I'm just saying that, for a man who's reportedly saved not only Jameson's life but also the lives of Jameson's son, wife, friends, and employees more often than I can count, the constant denial of affirmation, of approval, must have turned into a greater motivating factor than you realize. Whether or not you actually see Jameson as a father of sorts—and on some level I actually think you do—no sane person in your position would ever be able to avoid deep resentment about his refusal to accept you no matter what you accomplish on his behalf. And you can't help measuring yourself, if only a little bit, by that impossible standard. If that's not a father complex, then I don't know what is."

Spider-Man's ears burned; it seemed that whatever time Saberstein had devoted to perfecting this theory must have been well-spent. He stared fixedly at his hands, wished that he had said yes to Saberstein's offer of a cup of coffee after all, and muttered: "Well . . . maybe you don't."

"As it happens," Saberstein said, "I'm just getting warmed up. It may be that your need to prove yourself to this one man may be one of the factors that's kept you fighting the good fight for so long. If that's the case, then his stupid headlines deserve credit as one of the main factors that have made your continued career as Spider-Man possible."

"Ha! Wish the old goat could hear that one, at least."

"I bet you do. But then there's the reason I've told you all this—namely, that if I'm at all right, and I think I am . . . then there's the other side of the coin. The thorny question of just why he always seemed to hate you with special vehemence every single time you saved his life. Would you like to know why?"

Spider-Man, who knew that Saberstein was far from completely right about his own motivations, but had to admit that the guy was still making too much sense for comfort, sat a little straighter on the wall where he'd propped himself. He'd wondered about the source of Jameson's dedicated antipathy for years, at times attributing it to causes ranging from jealousy to a well-founded distrust of paranormals to just another cynical gimmick for selling newspapers. All of these reasons may have been accurate as far as they went; but as pieces of the greater puzzle they'd always left the big picture too fragmentary to be seen. If Saberstein was as insightful about Jameson as he was about Spider-Man himself . . . . Spider-Man said: "Yeah, Counselor. I think I would like to hear why."

"If I'm right," Saberstein said, "and Jameson's campaign against you is one of the factors that keeps you too stubborn to quit, then maybe some small part of him recognizes that. And maybe, just maybe . . . that small part of him also believes that if he ever did quit hating you ... then you might also quit saving him."

The silence that followed was absolute.

Spider-Man considered the one thing he knew for sure: that entering the City Room, and seeing all the butchered *Bugle* employees laid out in a bloody tableau for his benefit, had been one of the very worst moments of his life. At that instant, he'd felt the bottom drop out of the world. He was still recovering from the shock even now, despite what had happened a moment later, when he'd taken another step ... and found the scene replaced by a vision of his wide-eyed friends and co-workers huddled together in the center of a wrecked room, their arms and legs bound with duct tape. The apparent massacre had been nothing but a Mysterio illusion; just another joke at the expense of Life, left behind by monsters who respected the rules of their own demented game too much to kill any of these people before they'd earned the "right" by first defeating Spider-Man.

Altogether, counting all the battles the web-slinger had fought earlier in the day, the death toll had remained a big fat zero. There had been some minor injuries, some hospital-izations for exposure and hypothermia and stress ... not to mention a barely averted stroke on the part of a certain irascible newspaper publisher when he found out what kind of shambles the web-slinger had "deliberately" made of his building...but so far it seemed that Spider-Man had shut out the bad guys completely. The web-slinger's innate inability to take comfort in that, when there were still so many loose ends still unaccounted for, had prevented him from consid-ering himself the winner. But he couldn't help feeling a lit-tle better now. "You might have something," he admitted. "I just wish you could explain away people like the Six that well."

"Oh, that much is easy," Saberstein said. "They're just greedy, evil, self-absorbed, pigheaded maniacs who care about nothing but themselves."

Spider-Man considered that, then shook his head. "Heh."

"Would you like that coffee now?"

"Yeah, sure. And bring one for yourself. There's something else about this whole mess that I want to discuss with you."

Colonel Morgan showed up seven minutes later, showing enough humanity—(or at least military discipline)—to apologize for his lateness; he said he'd been down in Communications, long-distance crisis-managing another situation involving a deadly supernatural manifestation in New Hampshire. It would have been all-too-easy to deduce from the Colonel's grim expression that things hadn't gone well, but he was Colonel Morgan: he probably wore the same grim expression ordering the chef's special at all-night diners. Even so, he seemed particularly unhappy at the sight of Saberstein. "Didn't expect to see you here, Troy. I didn't direct anybody to inform you we were meeting."

Saberstein took no particular offense. "I have my sources, Colonel. I'd like to sit in on this one, if you don't mind."

"Why?" Morgan asked.

"I invited him," Spider-Man said.

Morgan looked pained. "Why?"

"From what Spider-Man says," Saberstein said, "One member of the Sinister Six—the woman—might be operating under substantial duress. I'd like to get more involved in case there's a chance my input can help find you an opportunity to turn her around."

Morgan grimaced, excused himself, and left the room.

Spider-Man didn't have any trouble figuring out why Morgan felt so uncomfortable around Saberstein—since the Colonel did occasionally participate in combat situations himself, he was probably also subject to the therapist's regular evaluations. The thought of Colonel Sean Morgan being forced to open up to anybody, for anybody reason, was downright funny; Spider-Man, who deeply enjoyed the needling of stuffed-shirts just on general principle, privately blessed the unknown federal regulation that made it possible.

After about a minute, Morgan re-entered with Doug Deeley, Clyde Fury, and an elderly, gray-haired man in bifocals and ill-fitting suit, who dragged one leg as he walked and seemed about as much at home in the helicarrier as Saberstein. Staying as far from Saberstein as possible, Morgan solicitously helped the elderly man to his seat, then took his own place at the head of the conference table. As a sliding panel behind him rose to reveal the usual wall of monitors, Morgan directed Fury and Deeley to sit down. "All right. Thank you for coming out. The content of this briefing will be distributed to all active SAFE personnel first thing tomorrow morning, but I wanted you people to get an early look; it seems that the crisis we experienced today may be only a small preview of the trouble we still have in store. Spider-Man, will you be ready? Your wounds healing?"

Spider-Man, hanging upside down from a webline secured to the ceiling, said, "Not as much as they'd be if I was still home in bed."

"We'd all like to be there, " Morgan said. "But—"

"My bed? Sorry. Too crowded for all of us. But I appreciate the interest."

Though Fury, Deeley, and Saberstein all covered their mouths to avoid laughing, and even the elderly man seemed amused, Morgan seemed ready to chew his cheeks off from the inside; his failure to immediately reprimand the web-slinger for his attempt at humor could only be attributed to lingering memory of all the lives Spider-Man had saved today.

Spider-Man said, "Sorry, Colonel. I'll be okay. I heal fast. I'd prefer to wait a week or two before having to face those guys again, but if I at least get a good night's sleep into me, I'll be able to function."

"They all took pretty bad beatings today," Deeley said. "If we're lucky, maybe they need some recovery time too."

"Which they'll probably take," Spider-Man said, "assuming their plan isn't equipped with any specific deadlines. They may be crazy, but they're not stupid. Well, maybe Electro."

Morgan, who nodded throughout all of this, grumbled once, hesitated, and began again: "In any event, since we don't know how much time we have, I wanted to make sure we all know what we're dealing with. The report the web-slinger provided us about his conversation with the old man who called himself the Gentleman," (which Spider-Man had carefully edited to remove any reference to the Gentleman knowing his secret identity), "clearly indicated a player who needed to be taken seriously. The reference to Croesus was the first clue, but we also examined the videotape from the *Daily Bugle*'s lobby camera, as the man suggested, enhancing the shoddy picture quality as best we could. I also consulted Dr. George Williams here," (Morgan indicated the old man, who acknowledged him with a nod), "who agreed to come out of a well-deserved retirement to be with us today. Williams served an exemplary career with several law-enforcement agencies, including the FBI and the Office of the Treasury; he has also been actively documenting the activities of this particular malefactor for more than half a century."

Spider-Man started. "That long?"

"Indeed," Williams rumbled. "He's been wanted for longer."

"By who?"

"Everybody," Williams said.

As the web-slinger reeled, Morgan said, "With the Doctor's help, we came up with a identification probability of over ninety percent. It's almost impossible for the Gentleman to be anybody other than the man I was afraid he was."

"Who?" Fury asked.

Morgan deferred to Dr. Williams, who leaned forward and spoke in a soft, coherent voice marked by a faint Georgia accent and an almost-imperceptible slurring that testified to substantial recovery from a past stroke. "Well, young man, he's never called himself the Gentleman before, and the man in the video image is a couple of decades older than his last known photograph—but based on his image and some of the information he gave you about himself, we'll all feel very foolish if he's not a very bad boy named Gustav Fiers."

This announcement earned an immediate stunned reaction from Morgan's people, who clearly knew the name.

As a blurry surveillance-camera photo of Spider-Man's *Bugle*-lobby conversation with the Gentleman appeared on the wall of monitors, and as Morgan quietly handed the old man a remote control, Williams continued: "I'm afraid it's not overstating the case to call this man one of the five most wanted international criminals of the twentieth century."

Spider-Man, who had made a career of fighting criminals

both local and international, said, "I've never heard of him."

Williams cocked one of his oversize eyebrows. "I'm not surprised, young man. He's never maintained as high a profile as the kind of maniacs you fight. Indeed, he's gone years at a time without anybody in the international law enforcement community knowing for certain whether he was alive or dead."

Morgan said: "For the last twenty years or so, Dr. Williams has been in retirement and one of the few voices still alleging the Gentleman to be alive."

"Quite so," Williams said—and Spider-Man could detect a note of grim satisfaction of having been proved right after what may have been years of having been written off as just another obsessed old man. "The appalling fellow may have conducted most of his activities anonymously, but he never seemed the type to gently fade away. —But SHIELD, Interpol, the Mossad, the Surete, Scotland Yard, and the FBI all have files on him, thick with the hundreds of dirty deals we've managed to connect with him over the years. Assassination, terrorism, theft, industrial espionage, subversion, sabotage— he's always been willing to help finance it, and sometimes arrange it, so he can make blood money on the outcome."

"An investor in chaos," Spider-Man murmured. "That's what he called himself."

"It's a good description of him," Morgan said. "Among other things, he sold arms to both sides in the Spanish Civil War, ran proscribed technology to both Latveria and the now-shattered Communist Bloc, loaned huge sums of money at ruinous interest to criminal organizations in Europe and Asia, and propped up the Philippine dictator Ferdinand Marcos so that dirtbag could funnel a couple of hundred million dollars into one of his own private enterprises."

"And he's made billions at it, I'm afraid." This from Williams. "His estimated fortunes are not quite as great now as they used to be—since his capture was designated a renewed priority by President Carter in 1979, the UN and associated agencies, working with occasional input from myself, have been having a field day tracking down and seizing his assets. Interpol has a dozen full-time investigators just following his past transactions to buried offshore accounts. Their overall success has long been cited as supporting the theory that the man was dead; I've always maintained that he must have been simply unable to get to the money before we did, without revealing his whereabouts. Even so, he's still believed to still possess direct access to a fortune of several hundred million."

"Which his type would consider a severe comedown," Morgan said.

"Indeed," Williams frowned. "Which I fear will probably render him even more ruthless, and willing to barter lives for profit, than usual. Whatever he has planned for the Sinister Six does not bode well for the City of New York."

Morgan looked at Spider-Man. "I think it must have something to do with the switch Mysterio and Electro pulled at the Brooklyn Bridge."

"Yeah," Spider-Man said. "That one's been bothering me all day long."

Williams coughed slightly, his aged windpipe transforming some of it into an asthmatic wheeze. "I would not be surprised either. In any event, Fiers is a particularly slippery malefactor. One of the reasons he's always been the Holy Grail of law enforcement—mine, at least—is that, in all the years he's been in the top five of the wanted hit parade (and he first starts showing up on the want lists of various international police forces about 1926), he has only come even close to being caught four times."

"Four times?" Spider-Man said. "In seventy-five years?"

"Yes. He's been active since his twenties, and he's pushing his centennial now. This would be our fifth chance to get him. If we get that far."

"I'm beginning to get the picture," Spider-Man boggled. "We're talking about the mugbook of Dorian Gray."

Only Williams and Saberstein broke smiles at that. Williams said, "What we're talking about is a very dangerous and ruthless man, who does not mind escaping over the bodies of others. If you don't mind—"

"Go ahead," Morgan said. "They need to hear this."

Williams clicked the remote, revealing a sepia-toned family photograph of a well-to-do family of five: a regal father, a phenomenally beautiful but distracted-looking mother, a serious-faced young girl of four, and two robust pre-adolescent boys. They were all dressed formally, One of the boys was circled. "This is the Fiers family, circa 1911—a handsome group, I suppose, and one that absolutely shows a life of ease and prosperity. They were what was then called old money; previous generations had amassed a tidy fortune in the slave trade prior to the American Civil War, moving into railroads, shipping, and construction by the turn of the century. There is some evidence that the father, August, pre-figured his son's despicable business practices, arranging catastrophes and profiting from the fallout. Although then American by citizenship, they were European royalty by pre-tension; the father had even used some of his disposable income to purchase noble titles for himself and his bride, Elizabeth. The daughter, here, is Isadora; the younger boy is Karl and the elder is our man, Gustav.

"Seen in this shot, the family seems blessed with good fortune. And, indeed, their aristocratic background served them well when they crossed on the *Titanic* in 1912; the family got into one of the first lifeboats and survived without a single casualty. Alas, Isadora was a casualty of the encephalitis epidemic who died, having slept most of her life away, in 1967; Karl rejected his family's wealth and became a committed (if reportedly still stuffy) anarchist, active in many violent terrorist groups over the years; Gustav inherited the family yen for money—as well as the lion's share of the family's pre-existing fortune—and spent the twenty years after this photograph quadrupling the Fiers coffers with investments in blackmail, bootlegging, and—using Karl, who by then had developed the knack—contract murder. He became a respected advisor, and occasional money-lender, to organized crime during the twenties and thirties, though he never deliberately socialized with the type; they were far too low-class for a refined gentleman of breeding like himself. Still, he is known to have participated in several notable murders himself, and is rumored to have been an invited participant in one of Al Capone's notorious baseball bat parties. By the mid-thirties, he was already a wanted figure in several countries.

"On May 6th, 1937, when I was a young treasury agent working as part of an intra-agency task force dedicated to another investigation entirely, we learned almost by accident that Fiers was about to arrive in this country under an assumed name. Even then, his capture would have been a substantial coup. We rushed to an airfield in Lakehurst, New Jersey, to meet his zeppelin as it disembarked." The monitors on the wall behind Morgan and Williams blinked to old newsreel footage of the zeppelin *Hindenberg* as it erupted into flames, crashed, and burned. "Unfortunately, he expected us, and vanished in the panic."

"Holy Cow," Fury exclaimed. "He survived the *Titanic* and the *Hindenberg*? Both?"

"Nothing holy about it, I'm afraid. He was just a young boy during the *Titanic* disaster—too young to be guilty of contributing, though his father, a heavy investor in rival shipping, cannot be written off as a planner. Gustav was, however, at the prime of his life during the much later *Hindenberg* incident. Although we cannot prove he caused the explosion, I have long suspected his deliberate involvement . . . and I believe that it had less to do with his concerns about capture than with his then-substantial investments in airplane technology. That catastrophe, which spelled the end of an entire mode of air travel, enhanced the value of his holdings considerably."

The picture on the monitors changed again, this time to a photograph of the fortyish Gustav Fiers, dapper in an exquisitely tailored white suit, sharing drinks with a group of similarly-clad men at a table in a smoky nightclub. Fiers, visible only in profile, and partially obscured by the blurred leaf of a potted fern in the foreground, was circled. "In 1942," Williams said, "Fiers was operating in Vichy Casablanca and earning a tidy living playing the Allies against the Axis. He ran arms, forged letters of transit, and financed phony airlines that collected inflated sums for travel to safe havens and then turned wanted refugees back to the very people who were hunting them. His biggest operation during this period was secretly working with the American auto manufacturer and—you may or may not know this—fascist sympathizer Henry Ford to set up the string of international subsidiaries that permitted Ford to continue doing business with the enemy even at the height of the war."

"Ford did that?" Spider-Man gasped. "You're kidding me!"

"Not at all. Look it up; it's history. Ford sold the Axis automotives and military vehicles throughout the war, while continuing to do business in America. Fiers was one of the conduits he used to facilitate that operation. Please note that Fiers cooperated not because he shared Ford's contemptible politics—from all evidence, he has no politics—but because his profiteering gave him a strong financial interest in keeping the war going as long as possible. Late in 1942, the War Department sent me along to advise the early super hero team known as the Invaders—then composed of Captain America and Bucky, the original Human Torch and Toro, the Submariner, Spitfire (a simply charming woman, by the way) and Union Jack—as they flew to Casablanca to apprehend Fiers; we almost got him, but he blew up this very nightclub seen in this photograph and slipped away while the local authorities were still sifting through the bodies. That was the second incident."

"I didn't know about that one," Deeley said. "Captain America couldn't get him?"

"Neither the good Captain or his colleagues, myself included, who," Williams said wryly, "I do recall also mentioning."

Deeley shook his head in amazement.

"The third incident," Williams said, clicking the remote again. This time the image changed to a significantly older Fiers, still clad in white suit, captured in profile as he crossed a busy street in what looked like a semi-tropical Asian city. "The City of Hue, Republic of South Vietnam. This photograph of him was taken by accident by a business traveler in the early days of the War. He is believed to have been there to set up a drug distribution network with the cooperation of certain unscrupulous elements in our own government. Incidentally, his brother, Karl, may or may not have been involved in this operation; they may have been politically night-and-day, at least in their attitudes toward money—Gustav being motivated by the acquisition of wealth for its own sake, and Karl being motivated by the wholesale destruction of societal institutions—but there's every reason to believe that they remained close until Karl's eventual death in a limousine explosion, a few years ago.

"In any event, Gustav was not in Hue when it was turned to rubble by the Tet Offensive; by then, his network was running on its own. When intelligence sources at the time placed him over the border in Cambodia, the army sent one of its most reliable agents up the river to apprehend him if possible and terminate him with extreme prejudice if necessary. That man was later returned alive but blinded, with his tongue cut out, and in the throes of a hopeless, forcibly induced addiction to heroin."

"I'm beginning to really hate this guy," Spider-Man said.

"He does tend to fuel obsessions. Believe me, I know. Where was I? Ah, yes. Fiers himself was not located again for several years, though he continued to associate himself with various dubious enterprises. He is known to have associated himself, distantly, with A.I.M, Hydra, the Red Brigade, and several other well-known terrorist groups. He was next, and last, located during his fourth close call, which was about twenty years ago. The *Croesus* incident." Williams clicked his remote and changed the image on the monitors to a colorful, sunny, tourist-brochure photograph of a gleaming cruise liner festooned with bright lights as it sailed into a glorious sunset. "The *Croesus* was a Mediterranean casino cruise so exclusive that even the rich and famous needed written invitations just to board. The price of a ticket was somewhere in the upper obscene. This made it a natural gold mine to start with, but Fiers being Fiers, that was not nearly enough for him; he supplemented his income by using hidden tightly-focused microwave beams to give selected members of his clientele cancer and radiation sickness, so he could later make a mint predicting the inevitable effect on their respective currencies."

"Nice," Spider-Man muttered.

"Isn't it? What he didn't know at the time was that representatives of British, Israeli, American, and Canadian intelligence had infiltrated his organization. I was far too old for field operations by this point, alas, but I did function in an advisory capacity. We got the goods on him, and came close to shutting him down—but he found out what we were doing at the last minute, blew up his ship, and got away again, this time in a submarine. That didn't stop him from later financing or otherwise arranging the assassination of several of the agents involved."

"He got the Americans," Morgan said, conversationally.

"Yes. He did. And he covered his tracks so well that we didn't even know it was his doing until a couple of years ago."

Spider-Man, already boggled by the sheer length of the Gentleman's resumé of corruptions, suddenly went very tense. He spoke in a whisper: "How's that?"

"Well, that's not really relevant—" Williams began.

"It might be," Spider-Man said, with absolute urgency. "Tell me anyway."

"Well, it involves the villain known as Red Skull, who was also actively wreaking havoc at the time—"

"Only it wasn't the real Red Skull," Morgan corrected him.

Williams sighed—and for a moment he looked like the weight of all his years had just descended upon his shoulders all at once. "I knew this was going to be a lengthy digression. All right. For the benefit of those of you who might not know, the original Red Skull, the infamous Nazi spymaster personally appointed by Hitler, disappeared immediately after World War Two and didn' t show his face, such as it is, for decades. At the time of the *Croesus* incident, he was presumed long dead. But soon after that he reappeared to take up his old habits . . . which him a major capture priority."

Morgan took over. "What we didn't know back then was that this wasn't the same guy who gave Captain America and the Invaders so much trouble during the war. The Nazi Skull was one Johann Schmidt; this fellow was a completely unrelated communist copycat by the name of Alfred Malik, using the Skull's reputation to form a new terrorist organization under his own banner."

"Schmidt's taken over the role again, hasn't he?" Fury asked.

"Yes. Having been artificially rejuvenated a couple of times, he's done just that—and he's responsible for almost all of the nastiness you probably think of when you hear the Skull name. Malik, who was a relatively small-timer, went into hiding when the original Skull returned, on the theory that the first guy wouldn't take kindly to the plagiarism. Didn't help him much, since he was still assassinated by one of the original boy's agents a couple of years back."

"It is a complicated pattern of associations," Williams admitted tiredly, "and it isn't rendered any better by getting ahead of ourselves. Let's leave the Nazi Skull out of this; he's not involved."

Morgan cut to the chase. "The point Dr. Williams is trying to make here is that, when the Commie Skull, Malik, first made his appearance, nobody in law enforcement had any inkling that he wasn't the same guy."

"Exactly," Williams said. "And the same Americans who had spearheaded the operation against Fiers were eventually given the assignment to get the Skull next. They infiltrated his organization, gained his trust—"

". . . only to be recognized, killed and framed for espionage against America," Spider-Man broke in, his voice oddly strained.

Every head at the table swiveled to look at Spider-Man.

"You've heard this before?" Williams asked.

"Didn't know all of it. Go ahead."

Williams coughed. "The agents were a married couple, Richard and Mary Parker."

Saberstien, who had previously mentioned the web-slinger's suspected connection to their son Peter Parker, started at this; he glanced at Spider-Man, but otherwise remained silent; everybody else at the table, intent on Williams, failed to notice the moment.

"The Skull set them up to die in a plane crash and doctored up evidence that made them look like traitors to their country. Their names were eventually cleared, many years later, but the one thing nobody ever knew—at least until a postmortem investigation into Malik's dealings turned up information about his organization—was just how Malik identified them as double agents in the first place."

Spider-Man was afraid he already knew the answer. He didn't want to hear it. He desperately needed to. His voice sounded strangled as he said: "How?"

"Gustav Fiers told him."

The blood pounded in Spider-Man's ears. He thought of the things the Gentleman had said, about having been Peter Parker's enemy since before Peter Parker was born, and about having taken more from Spider-Man than all of his other enemies put together. He now knew what the sociopath had meant, and the knowledge was so shattering that he wished he could flee from this room, screaming his parents' names. Instead, he just cocked his head, grateful for the mask that permitted him to maintain a facade of only professional interest.

Williams said, "Fiers, who was professionally affiliated with the Commie Skull at the time, probably because Karl may have also worked for the organization, recognized the Parkers and betrayed them to Malik. Malik's financial records clearly indicate a cash disbursement to Fiers specifically in exchange for this information. It was not a hard sell; Fiers only took a token payment of one dollar American, which was apparently his ironic way of devaluing their lives."

"When this connection was discovered," Colonel Morgan said, "it tremendously increased Intelligence interest in bringing this lifelong ratbag to justice. People in our business take it personally when somebody goes the way the Parkers went. Not that anybody, other than you, Dr. Williams, ever genuinely expected we'd have another shot."

"Yes," Williams nodded, sadly, "given his age, which is not all that much greater than mine, the man's been believed dead or too decrepit to cause trouble for years." He turned away from Morgan, and addressed Spider-Man in a voice as cold as the terrible knowledge it conveyed: "But one thing's for certain, Spider-Man. If Fiers is financing this incarnation of the Sinister Six, then he's not just doing it for fun. The man plays only for tremendous stakes. He's planning something big . . . and profitable . . . designed to renew his depleted fortunes while leaving a whole lot of people dead."

There was more, with Morgan, Williams, and the SAFE agents spending the better part of the next hour discussing their preliminary plans for interfacing with the FBI, the NYPD, and other agencies in what was probably a doomed effort to track down the Gentleman by conventional investigation.

Spider-Man barely heard any of it. Because another, even more terrible, aspect of all this had just begun to occur to him.

He thought about the parents who had been stolen from him.

He thought about the smile on the Gentleman's face as he bragged about what he had stolen.

He thought about the Gentleman's claim that he always pursued his vendettas into further generations.

He thought about the baby girl in the photographs Mary Jane had found. The one who might have been Peter Parker's previously unsuspected older sister.

He thought about Pity, who had been taken from her murdered parents, enslaved, and conditioned into a murderous thing tormented by a very intact conscience. He thought about how her parents had, like Peter Parker's, been executed for their betrayal.

Pity was the right age.

And if the Gentleman was telling the truth, she had the right background.

Spider-Man didn't want it to be true. It was too big to be true.

But in this small room, high above a city that knew any

number of monsters and any number of secrets, the question could not denied.

Was Pity really Carla May Mendelsohn?

Was she . . . Peter Parker's sister?